C000120024

For
King and
Country

The daughter of a Durham miner, Annie Wilkinson now lives in Hull where she divides her time between supporting her father and helping her grandchildren.

Also by Annie Wilkinson

A Sovereign for a Song
Winning a Wife
No Price Too High
Sing Me Home
Angel of the North
The Land Girls

ANNIE WILKINSON

For King and Country

**SIMON &
SCHUSTER**

London · New York · Sydney · Toronto · New Delhi

A CBS COMPANY

First published in Great Britain by Simon & Schuster UK Ltd, 2007
This paperback edition published by Simon & Schuster UK Ltd, 2015
A CBS COMPANY

1 3 5 7 9 10 8 6 4 2

Simon & Schuster UK Ltd
1st Floor
222 Gray's Inn Road
London WC1X 8HB

www.simonandschuster.co.uk

Simon & Schuster Australia, Sydney
Simon & Schuster India, New Delhi

A CIP catalogue record for this book
is available from the British Library

PB ISBN: 978-1-47111-542-4
EBOOK ISBN: 978-1-47111-544-8

Printed and bound by CPI Group (UK) Ltd, Croydon, CR0 4YY

The makers of war sacrifice their pawns,
but what do the pawns sacrifice? This book
is dedicated to them, on all sides and in
all wars. God help them.

Acknowledgements

My thanks to the many people who have given me
help and encouragement, especially:

Rene Collier, Librarian, for a great idea.
Dr Luffingham, Archivist, for medical background.
Richard Barsby, Northumberland Branch of *the
    Western Front Association.*
John Eaton, Sheffield poet and wit, for an incident.
Rilba Jones, for help with research and the loan of
    books.
All at *Hornsea Writers* for constructive criticism.
Peter Walgate at the Mitchell Centre for help with
    my wayward computer.
Carl Bridge and Roger Beckett, of the *Menzies
    Centre for Australian Studies*, for information on
    the Australian Imperial Army and for
    recommendations for reading.
The staff at Newcastle Central Library, Durham
    Clayport Library, Hull Central Library, and

Greenwood Avenue Library, the Women's
Library, London Metropolitan University, and
Tyne and Wear Archives.

I am also indebted to all who have published
material on the Great War on the internet, including *www.spartacus.schoolnet.co.uk.*, *www.1914-1918.net*,
www.firstworldwar.com and *www.bbc.co.uk/history/war/
wwone*, to name a few. The British Journal of Nursing
Archives, held by the Royal College of Nursing
online, were extremely helpful, as were innumerable
authors, some of whom are listed below:

W.D. Lowe, *18th Durham Light Infantry*, Oxford
    University Press, 1920

G. Grey Turner, *Rutherford Morison and his Achievement*,
    Newcastle Medical Journal, Volume XXIII, June 1948

Richard Holmes, *Tommy: The British Soldier on the Western
    Front 1914–1918*, Harper Collins, 2004

John Laffin, *The Western Front Illustrated, 1914–1918*, Alan
    Sutton Publishing Ltd, 1991

Max Arthur, *Forgotten Voices of the Great War*, Random
    House Audio, 2003

Michael McKernan, *The Australian People and the Great
    War*, Thomas Nelson, 1980

Eric Andrews, *The Anzac Illusion*, Cambridge University
    Press, 1993

E. Scott, *Official History of Australia in the War*, Angus &
    Robertson, 12 volumes: 1934–42

Chapter One

'Kath's sister got married last week,' her mother said.

'Lucky Kath's sister,' said Sally, wrapped in an old apron and concentrating on the job of applying Zebo blacklead to the bars of the grate.

With a despairing sigh her mother lifted the half-bucket of soot Sally had raked out of the flues, and went outside to spread it on the garden. The clatter of the bucket being replaced and then the bang of the outhouse door heralded her mother's return to the kitchen.

'Pity you can't find a man.'

Sally put the blackleading cloth aside to apply plenty of Brasso to another rag. 'Do you not read the papers, Mam? Do you not realize there's nearly two million surplus women, and most of them young ones? And there'll probably be a lot more before this war's finished, so somebody has to go without a man.'

'Pity it's got to be you, then. Pity you've been left on the scrap heap.'

'Well, what choice have I got, like? I'm not a raving beauty, am I?'

'Neither's Kath's sister, but she's got a bit of go in her.'

Meaning I haven't, Sally thought. She paused in her task to stare into the steel door of the oven and saw Sarah Wilde reflected there; unprepossessing spinster of the parish of Annsdale who, compared with her sisters, was untalented and depressingly ordinary. If not – with eyes too small, and nose too large – downright plain. She smeared on the Brasso to obliterate the image, and covered all the steel trimmings of the range in similar fashion before lifting the fender onto a kitchen table covered with newspapers, to set to the task of cleaning it there and save her knees.

She thought she'd done well to land the job at the hospital, for 'many are called, but few are chosen', as Matron had told her at the interview. She'd stuck it for the best part of a year already, and it was a job that would last her the rest of her life if she stuck it out to the finish. It might even provide her with a bit of a pension if she lived to be old. Nursing was a job she could take a pride in, but no good expecting any congratulations here. For Sally's mother, every woman who wasn't a wife was a failure, although why she should still think that after some of the beatings

2

she'd taken while her husband was alive was more than Sally could fathom.

Her mother didn't seem to grasp it; there were a million men dead, any one of whom might have made Sally a husband. Might have. In her mind's eye she saw them, lying helpless on the battlefields of France with the life oozing out of them, and slowed at her work. 'I could have me pick, I suppose, if I could go and bring one of 'em back to life,' she sighed.

'What? What did you say?'

Sally shook her head to dispel the gloomy vision. 'I said you don't seem to realize how lucky our family's been, Mam. You've got two sons and a son-in-law, and they've all come through unscathed so far, touch wood. But when I was in the Post Office, about a week ago, the postmistress told me Mrs Burdett had a letter saying Will was missing.' Sally's lip trembled and she turned her face away, sniffing and swallowing her tears before she added, 'And today she got all his poor bits of things sent back to her, everything except his watch; that's gone missing.'

Her mother failed to notice her distress. 'That woman, she knows everybody's business, and she doesn't mind broadcasting it, either. "Oh, Mrs Wilde, I saw you had another letter from your John the other day," and she looked at me as if she expected me to tell her what was in it! I wonder the Post Office don't get rid of her, and get somebody that knows how to keep her nose out.'

'She does no harm. A lot of people like getting the news about what their neighbours are doing. Poor Mrs Burdett, though, she must be breaking her heart. You've got four daughters Mam, and only the youngest not married. If you think that's a tragedy you ought to go and talk to her. All her lads are gone, now.'

Her mother lifted the kettle from the gas ring, poured boiling water onto the tea leaves, and gave it a thoughtful stir. 'I know. Once had four strapping sons, and now she's got none. All the hard work and pinching and scraping she had bringing them up, all gone for nothing. She'll have a lonely old age, if she lives that long. I'd go into a decline if I were in her shoes. But I won't tempt Providence by saying I've a lot to be thankful for. The war's not over yet.'

Her mother poured two cups and handed her one, looking at her with an expression that said, and if you can't get a husband, you'll end up just the same as Mrs Burdett. Lonely.

Sally put the rag down. She might as well have a rest for five minutes, while the polish dried. Her hands were filthy, the nails blackened, but not much use in washing them yet. She lifted the tea to her lips. Her mother was right, but the men who were left could have their pick of much prettier women than

4

Sally – or women who had more 'go' in them. They both understood it only too well, and sat in silence, avoiding the topic.

Her cup empty, Sally picked up the brush. She'd give the range a good rub, every bit of it, then go over the lot again with the velvet polishing cloths. Get a right good shine on it, then go and see her sisters, and maybe her brother John's wife if she had the time. 'I think I'll have a walk down to the Cock Inn and pass half an hour with our Ginny once I've finished this, Mam,' she said, 'and then I'll get the lend of her bike and ride into Annsdale Colliery and call on our Emma, and then maybes go round to Elsie's.'

'If you're going to see them, you'd better go and see Arthur, as well, while he's on leave. He'll want to know why if you don't. Lift your feet up. I want to take the mat out and give it a good shake. I don't think I'll light a fire today; it'll save a bit of coal. It's the sort of weather that turns the milk sour.'

'Our poor Sal. Only one day off a month – it's not much, lass. And living in the nurses' home, it must be like being in a bloody convent.' Ginny finished pouring a glass of whisky for a burly pit overman, and handed it over the bar to him with a wink.

'You always give a generous measure, Ginny, war or no war,' the man commented.

Ginny rattled his money into the till, and gave him his change. 'Keep the workers happy, that's my motto. Especially the ones who're our best customers.'

'I sometimes wonder where you get it from, though.'

Ginny laughed. 'Ask no questions, and you'll be told no lies. Shout if you want me, Ben. I'm not expecting a pub full, so I'm going to have five minutes with our Sal, before she goes back to the hospital.'

Sally followed her sister upstairs, to her living quarters. 'Aren't you worried about leaving them in the bar on their own?'

'Not with Ben keeping an eye on things. I'd trust him with my life'

'I hope he doesn't realize where the cheap whisky comes from. I wouldn't trust him far enough to tell him that, if I were you. You'd get wrong off the bobbies if he let on. You might get locked up.'

Her sister grinned, and chucked her under the chin. 'Don't be daft, my little Methodist-Miss. I've already said; I could trust him with my life. But don't worry; he's got no idea.'

Sally breathed a sigh of relief. 'By, you're a warm 'un, our Ginny. I don't know how you dare. Have you heard from Martin?'

'Aye. I get a letter or a field postcard nearly every day, unless he's somewhere he can't send one, or the post's delayed. They've taken plenty of punishment

For King and Country

from the Germans these past few months, and a lot of the officers are out of the war, one way or another. They've made Martin a Second Lieutenant – promoted in the field, he told me the last time he wrote. An officer and a gentleman doesn't sound much like my husband, does it? An officer's lady doesn't sound much like me either, come to that. By, but they must be getting desperate over there, if they're turning socialists into officers!'

Will Burdett, dead! She could hardly take it in. Sally passed his house on her way to her sister Emma's in Annsdale Colliery, the mining village a couple of miles distant from her mother's cottage in rural Old Annsdale. The curtains were drawn and there was no sign of life inside. Sally hesitated, wondering whether to knock, and give her condolences. Better not. Mrs Burdett might be asleep, and it would be a shame to disturb her. She'd call and see Emma first, and then call on John's wife, and then better go and see her brother Arthur. She'd leave enough time to call on Mrs Burdett on the way home.

After an hour with Emma and her family, and another a few streets away with John's Elsie, Sally reluctantly pointed her wheels in the direction of Arthur's house.

'He's out. Gone to the Club.' Arthur's wife Kath flung open the door, to reveal a kitchen in chaos.

'Why, what's been going on here, like?' Taken unawares, Sally wasn't quick enough to disguise a look of horror.

'Come in, if you can get in.' Kath's fists descended to her hips, her elbows splayed in the attitude of a woman who would stand no nonsense. The tone of her voice confirmed Sally's suspicions; she was glorying in the devastation. What a homecoming for her brother, Sally thought, as she did as she was told and got in, picking her way towards an empty kitchen chair over spilt sugar and basin, broken crockery, and a scorched and screwed up tablecloth.

'He started a row because our Robson wouldn't go to him. What does he expect? He's been away in France that long the bairn doesn't know him. So he lost his bloody temper and chucked his breakfast on the fire. All that good food, wasted.'

Kath looked at her, an expectant gleam in her dark eyes. Although Sally had long experience of Arthur's moods she wouldn't be dragged into any criticism of her hot-tempered brother. After an uncomfortable pause, she said: 'So what did you do?'

'What did I do? I soon fettled him! "Oh, that's the game we're playing, is it?" I said, "Well, I'll help you, then!" and I ripped everything off the table and chucked it all into the hearth after his breakfast, and I pulled all the cups down, and they went onto the fireback, an' all, and the bloody tablecloth went on top of the lot!' Her words came out in a torrent, and Kath's eyes were flashing now as she relived the episode. 'And it nearly went up in flames, so he had to pull it off the fire and stamp them out. You can have a cup of tea if you want. I've been to me mam's to get a couple of jam jars to drink out of, and I've made a pot.'

'Where are the bairns?'

'Oh, they're at me mam's.'

'I'll give you a hand to clean it all up.'

Kath sloshed tea into a couple of clean jam jars. 'No bloody fear. It's staying where it is 'til he gets back. He can clean the bugger up. He started it.' The milk jug seemed to have escaped the devastation, and was still whole. Kath lifted it and sniffed suspiciously at the contents. 'It's gone off a bit. Do you want any, or would you rather go without?'

'I'll go without.'

But the jam jar was too hot to hold, and she would be a captive until the tea was cool enough to drink. She took off her straw hat and sat down. 'I don't know how you dare, Kath. Aren't you frightened he'll belt you?'

'No. He'll have my brothers to reckon with if he tries that on.'

'Hm,' Sally said, without conviction. She wouldn't rely on that to stop Arthur. She'd never known him back down from a fight with anybody. 'It can't be good for the bairns, though,' she said, 'all this rowing.'

Kath stopped and raised her eyebrows, giving her a look that made her feel every inch the hopeless spinster she was, a look that seemed to ask: and how do you know what's good for bairns? *You've* got none.

Sally flushed slightly, and Kath grinned.

'Oh, a good row clears the air sometimes.' Her grin broadened as she added, 'And we always enjoy making it up afterwards. I'll probably end up pregnant again. Oops, sorry, maybes I shouldn't have said that, with you not being married, and being a bit prim and proper, like.'

Sally fanned herself with her straw hat, her flush deepening. Arthur had met his match with his wife, no doubt about it, and she might manage to tame him, if he didn't kill her first. But she couldn't say she really liked Kath, and she'd far rather she kept their private business to herself, especially *that* sort of business. She changed the subject. 'I heard Mrs Burdett got another letter.'

'Aye, their Will. A bit of bad luck that, like. And he fancied you an' all, or he looked as if he did when I was watching him dancing with you at your Lizzie's wedding.'

Something inside her shrivelled at Kath's words, and Sally shook her head. 'No, he didn't. No more than the rest of the lasses in the village. I think Will fancied every lass he saw.' And he fancied himself, an' all, she thought, but kept that to herself. It wouldn't be right to speak ill of the dead, especially a lad who'd laid his life down for his country.

'And every lass he saw fancied him, an' all. All bar you. You're such a head–in–the–clouds dreamer I don't think you even noticed him giving you the glad eye. I think that must have been the attraction. Do you remember him lending you that book, after your Lizzie's weddin', and then a week later he went all the way to Darlington on the train, to get it back again? I never heard of him going to so much trouble to see any other lass before.' She grimaced and gave a shrug. 'Too late to bother about it either way now, I suppose; his courting days are over, like a lot more. My sister's just married a cousin of his. Did your mam not tell you?'

'Why, she told us your sister was married, but she didn't say it was to Will's cousin. I hope they'll be very happy.'

'Aye, so do I, like.'

Sally took a couple of sips of scalding tea, her fingers burning. 'I start on a new ward tomorrow.' She wasn't going to tell Kath it was a men's ward, the first one she'd been on, and give her room for any bawdy comments.

'Oh, aye? Why, that'll be a change for you. Rather

you than me, though. Me dad was in hospital once; he said he'd never want me to be a nurse. They have some right dirty jobs to do, and they work all the hours God sends.'

'He's right about that an' all, the hard work, I mean. I would never have believed how much a pair of legs can ache. They used to keep me awake at night. But they're not so bad now.'

Her legs were the one feature she could be proud of, that she could show off with the new hemlines, and she'd feared nursing would ruin them, that all the constant running up and down would make her lovely calves bulbous, and they'd look just awful. She smiled, and stretched them out in front of her. Her ankles and calves were as shapely as ever.

If Will had fancied her at that wedding reception as much as Kath appeared to think, Sally hadn't noticed. No, that wasn't it. She'd determinedly failed to notice, because there was hardly a lass in the village who hadn't fallen at his feet. He'd loved and left nearly every one of them at one time or other, and her pride couldn't stand the thought of being just another one of the crowd. If he thought he was going to add her to the list he could think again. Will Burdett had far too big an opinion of himself and she wasn't going to give him any room to boast about her. So she'd danced all night with him, but refusing to succumb to his attempt to charm her, she'd hardly given his handsome face a glance.

But trust Kath to notice Will's interest in her. That lass had a one-track mind, always leading up to ... something. Something disgusting. But Arthur was just the same. They suited each other very well, when you came to think about it.

Or maybe not. Sally couldn't see any woman wearing the trousers for long in her brother's house. Kath might think she could get the best of him, but there would be some sparks flying at Arthur's if and when he came back from France for good, and she wouldn't want to be in Kath's shoes when they did.

She was coming up to Mrs Burdett's door. She really ought to go in and see her. It would be a long time before she got another day off, so if she didn't do it now, the condolences would come a bit too late. But maybe now was too soon, and what on earth could she say? 'I'm sorry?' What good would that do? 'It's terrible?' Well, the poor woman already knew that, and far better than anybody else. 'I know how you feel,' maybe? But she didn't, and she never would know how it feels to lose a son. She would never have any children to lose. She slowed and stopped the bike, and let one trim little foot in its polished black shoe come to rest on the road while she stared at the house, its curtains closing it off from the world, turning it in on itself. After a moment or two's hesitation she lifted herself back onto the saddle, and pedalled home.

Her life was not going to go as she'd thought a few years ago, when, like all the other young lasses, she'd peered into the future, trying to glimpse the faceless husband and children who might be hers. After this murderous war had culled the best part of a generation of young men, it wasn't likely that that longing would ever be satisfied. In all probability she would never be the woman she'd always imagined she would be, happy in her family, loved by husband and children. She might as well face the fact. She would be forever a spinster, just one among hundreds of thousands of surplus women who would never learn the secrets of the marriage bed, never feel a husband's kiss nor hold his baby in their arms.

None of Mrs Burdett's sort of grief would ever touch her; she would be alone. She straightened her back a little, and lifted her chin. She'd have to muster all her courage and soldier on, like the poor lads who were still fighting. Her biggest problem would be keeping herself out of poverty, and saving enough for her old age, but she would do it, somehow. She didn't intend to be a burden on anybody.

What a shame, though, that she'd been out when Will had called at the Doctor's for that book he'd lent her. They hadn't asked him in to wait for her; she wouldn't have expected them to, she was only the housemaid, after all. But now she'd never see him again to return it. And although theirs had only been the fragile beginnings of a courtship that had fizzled out when he went to France, she felt tears pricking her eyes at the pity of it all.

The well-polished range, the focal point of the kitchen and the housewife's pride and joy, was gleaming bright when she got back home, but the fire was still not lit. It was silly, on a day like this, but she would have liked to see it burning in the grate before she went back to the hospital, to see warmth and comfort and good cheer reflected in all those polished surfaces, rewarding her for her work.

On the train to Newcastle Sally eyed the other passengers, especially some of the servicemen returning on leave to the wives and families they were fighting for. They were bonny lads, most of them . . .

She turned her head to stare out of the window at a field full of ripening corn. It would be a good harvest, as long as the weather held. The weather had to hold, and she had to stop weaving fantasies about other women's men. But that's what you do, when you haven't got one of your own. Stop it, Sally, she thought, and think about something you *can* get – a good career for yourself. Some women would love to be in your shoes, the ones who're married to gamblers, or drinkers, or wife beaters, or pulled down with dozens of bairns, and never a minute's peace or rest from constant drudgery. There's far worse things than being on your own.

Her eyes were drawn back to the soldiers, and chanced to meet the bright, blue eyes of a corporal, who smiled at her. But he was probably married, with half a dozen kids. She'd bet her life on it, somebody as good-looking as that. She quickly lowered her eyes and looked out of the window, and after a while lapsed into a daydream.

'Your brothers are in the army, did you say? Well, they're doing hard and dangerous work for their country, and if they're unlucky enough to be injured, they'll need good nurses to pull them through. We need girls who are willing to put the good of the patients before everything else, and that means self-sacrifice,' Matron had impressed on her at her interview. 'The question is, are you ready to make that sacrifice? I don't want any dabblers, or dreamers. I want serious, practical, patriotic girls who're willing to dedicate themselves to work that really counts.'

'Huh!' She gave a little grunt at the memory. Never a truer word was spoken, and she'd certainly needed every ounce of dedication and self-sacrifice she possessed to support her through the months of backbreaking work that followed Matron's warning. But she'd never intended to be a dabbler or a dreamer, and she'd thrown herself into nursing, heart and soul, on the women's wards. But tomorrow was going to be different. She was to start on her first men's ward, and the thought gave her a twinge of . . . what was it? Apprehension – or excitement?

Her glance stole back to the corporal. By, but he was a bonny lad. She dropped her gaze to examine the clean hands folded in her lap. There would be plenty of men who needed her, probably for years to come, judging by the numbers of soldier patients they were getting lately. The hospital was bursting at the seams, with fifty-odd men crammed into wards designed for half that number. Except the officers' ward, of course. They didn't cram officers in like sardines.

Still, officers or men, they were all heroes and they were all hurt, and the hands that would minister to them were scrubbed immaculate, the nail-tips white. She looked at those hands, pictured them ministering to a grateful blue-eyed corporal, imagined his expression of admiration, and smiled to herself until the wheels rattled her over the points of the largest railway crossing in the world and carried her into Newcastle Central Station.

Off the train then, to hurry along the platform under its domed glass roof, to stream out through the exit with the crush of people and hasten towards the hospital, and the patients who awaited her.

★

Annie Wilkinson

As soon as the maid called her, Sally was out of bed and brushing and pinning up an abundance of brown hair. A good wash came next, and then she began to dress, fastening the corset that pulled in her already trim waist, pulling up the black stockings and hooking them carefully to the suspenders. Now for the beautifully laundered long-sleeved dress that she would wear for half a week before it was washed again, and then the collar and cuffs, rigid with starch, and then the apron. It was pressed into a long, hard board, and Sally carefully pulled out the folds and put it on, adjusting the starch-stiff bib at the front. How on earth did the laundry manage to get the things so beautifully stiff, and white? They were generous with the starch at home, but they could never get things done as well as the hospital laundresses managed. Her cap was the same. She pulled the strings at the back to gather it to fit, and carefully pinned it on. It flattered her features like a lace-edged halo. She gave her image a smile of approval and then tightened the stiff white belt around her waist. And lastly the shoes with their smart, two-inch heels, black and gleaming with polish. Standing before the mirror she smiled, for once liking the look of herself: trim, and shining clean, her hazel eyes clear, her pale face as bright as the morning.

They had done no real nursing at all yet, she and the other new probationers, but had got through plenty of work that any housemaid could have done: dishing out bedpans and stripping beds and making them up again, and interminable rounds of cleaning, and careful damp-dusting, making sure no bacterial-laden dust particles were scattered into the air – as if any bacteria would dare show their faces in those wards, with their enamel painted walls and tiled dadoes, and polished parquet floors. There wasn't a corner for a microbe to hide in. Much of the sheer drudgery that maintained that gleaming, sterile splendour fell to the lot of the first year probationer; hard, unremitting work that made Sally's legs and back ache so much they kept her awake at night, and all done for nothing but bed and board, as part of the famous 'trial period'. It seemed to her that the trial period was nothing but a way of getting a lot of unpaid labour for the hospital.

Sacrifice? It was that all right. It was a system of slavery, really, but at least the uniform was provided, and she'd managed to get a watch and a pair of scissors *and* a nursing dictionary second hand and hardly used, from a girl who'd just failed the trial and been sacked for being 'not interested in her work, and too free with the soldier patients'.

With a fluttering apprehension in her stomach, she made her way to 7b. A faint smell of sepsis greeted her as she entered a full ward of thirty-odd men lying in the cast iron beds ranged along the walls.

'This ward's only meant to take twenty-four, but

when we're "on take" we end up with beds squashed down the middle, as well,' Staff Nurse told her, pushing a strand of brown hair back under her starched cap. 'We've sometimes had to find space for fifty, and ended up with beds in the corridor as well. Amputees, gunshot wounds, shrapnel wounds, bullet wounds, fractures, we get the lot, wounds everywhere they can get a wound, from head to foot. The lucky ones have got clean wounds, the unlucky ones septic. Depends whether the missile bounced into the mud or not before it hit them. Some chaps are in for their hernias doing, massive ones, some of them – they've taken some punishment with that incessant trench digging, and heaving stuff about – constant heavy labour. I've no time to take you round them all now, but tag along when Matron comes to do her round, and you'll get an idea. Here, Nurse Armstrong!' she called to a third year Sally had seen often in the Nurses' Home, 'take her and show her the ropes, will you?'

The routine was similar to the women's wards Sally had been on, and she and Armstrong sped down the ward making beds, easy when the patients could sit out, a bit more difficult when they couldn't. A corporal of about fifty, who was lying flat on his front, put a foot to the floor and gingerly eased himself onto his feet. The pillows were on the chair placed at the bottom of the bed, and the bed stripped almost as soon as he was upright.

For King and Country

'What happened to you?' Sally asked, tightening his clean bottom sheet, working like an automaton in perfect rhythm with her partner.

'Me? I got a lump of shell-casing in my backside, and it ploughed right down my thigh. Plenty a lot worse, though, lass.'

'Half of his buttock shorn away,' Armstrong told her, when they were out of earshot. 'He'll be limping the rest of his life. We had to knock him out before we first did the dressing. Why, man, the stink! We were glad to get down into that sluice for a smoke when we'd finished, to get the stench out of our nostrils. Sister always turns a blind eye to that. I reckon she thinks we need a few puffs, at times!'

She nodded towards the couple of sufferers they were approaching, both just skin and bone, and both attached to saline drips. 'That one broke both legs, and had to drag himself yards into a shell-hole. Says it must have been about five days before anybody found him. The one next to him got it through the chest, and while he was down the bloody Germans gave him the bayonet in the stomach, and then they walked over him, and he was on the battlefield two days before they got him to the field ambulance. It's a miracle he got here alive.'

When the beds were done, Sally went round with a bowl of disinfectant and a cloth, taking the dust off locker tops, windowsills and bedsteads. Many of the men said very little, but a few wanted to talk, and one man of about twenty-five became so familiar she blushed with embarrassment, and turned the conversation by asking about his wound.

'Bullet in the shoulder, bonny lass,' he told her, with a hunted look in his eyes. 'A clean wound, and healing well, worse luck. It's odds on I'll be back in France before long'

She stopped her wiping and stared at him. 'Why, you wouldn't want it septic, would you?' she asked. 'You might end up with septicaemia. People die of that.'

'I'd risk it. It would be a sight better than having to go back over there.'

She shook her head wonderingly and hesitated, then moved briskly off, unwilling to risk any accusations of fraternizing, or slackness.

'The lucky ones have got clean wounds,' Staff Nurse had told her, but as she was beginning to learn, a lot of the patients saw it differently. For some, the truly lucky ones were those whose filthy wounds or massive hernias would keep them in Blighty for good.

Clean or dirty, there was little chance of Sally being allowed to dress any of the wounds. Sister was a middle-aged martinet, who made herself clear. 'I'll have no untrained juniors poking their fingers into wounds on my ward. There's too much of that in the auxiliary hospitals, society women with their pearls and their nursing outfits from London fashion houses meddling with matters they don't understand.'

'Why, I suppose they're only trying to do their bit, Sister,' Sally said.

'They're trying to get their photos in the papers, you mean. Usually before they've even worked a week – wearing caps as big as bed-sheets that would be flopping in septic wounds and then in the soup, if they had to do any *real* work! No, they're out to take all the credit for the work *we're* doing, the *real* nurses. It's an absolute scandal! But I'll have no amateurs let loose on my ward. You'll need a bit more experience before I'll let you touch any of the patients here.'

Half the patients and staff on the ward had over-heard her, and most were grinning from ear to ear.

'Crikey,' said Sally after she'd shot off up the ward, knowing instinctively that it would be useless to say that she'd helped with many a sterile dressing while working in Dr Lowery's house, and had helped him set more than one broken limb. That would cut no ice with this sister.

'She hates the society clique,' Armstrong said. 'If there's anything in the papers about the wonderful VADs, or the honourable Lady So-and-So and her convalescent home, it's like a red rag to a bull. We see eye-to-eye on that one, though. I was a VAD for a year in a Red Cross hospital, and I saw some very rough-and-ready methods, and not much discipline either. Still, I don't suppose they thought it mattered much, as we were dealing with the "typical products of the slums", to quote one lady. Anyway, I decided I'd get a decent training, and then go back and work in a military hospital. Only *now* I won't get in.'

'Why not?'

'The Army Council's decided that only VADs of two years' standing will get their names on the roll of military nurses, and that's a piece of work that's been managed by the Red Cross as well, I've *no* doubt. Sister thinks so, too.'

'Why do you want to be an army nurse, anyway?' Sally asked.

'I come from an army family. My father's a regimental sergeant major'

'Ah.'

'Still, we live in hope. A lot of things are going to change after the war, once soldiers and women get the vote. Even the War Office will have to move with the times then! Have you joined the Nursing Association yet?'

'No,' said Sally. She hadn't even thought of it.

'Well, you should. "*L'union fait la force*", as our allies say. If workers want their rights, they've got to make themselves felt, and we can only do that together. You will join, won't you?'

'Oh, yes,' Sally said, but wondered why she should,

while she was being kept strictly to routine menial work, interminable cleaning and bedpan rounds. Worse was washing out the sputum mugs used by men who had been gassed. That was a job that made her stomach heave, and worse still was having to clean the filthy, blood-stained, slimy stuff off the ward floor if a container was accidentally knocked off a locker. That made her gag until the tears filled her eyes, and none of that sort of work seemed to have much to do with real nursing as far as she could see, other than ensuring the essential cleanliness.

Still, real nursing might be even more horrible in this place. She occasionally caught the sight and the scent of some of the wounds during the dressing round: wounds to make you sick, wounds to make you weep, wounds that were far and away worse than anything she'd ever seen at Dr Lowery's. A mere glimpse of Sister or Staff Nurse pulling yards and yards of pus-drenched gauze out of holes big enough to put your fist in was enough to make her feel woozy. All in all, she didn't envy Armstrong who, as a third year probationer, had the dubious honour of helping with such dressings and even doing some of the more minor ones on her own.

'It makes you sick at first, but in the end you seem to cut yourself off from it and treat it as just another job,' she assured Sally. 'They get them down to theatre and pack their wounds with antiseptic paste as soon as they can, so you're not usually doing the really bad ones for long.'

Sally was far from convinced, and secretly she began to wonder if she'd made a mistake; if this was a job she was really cut out for after all. She often sat with the other nurses at the long ward table during visiting hours, when everything was done and the ward was quiet, cutting dressings or rolling bandages, watching the visitors troop in and occasionally jumping to her feet to take a bouquet of flowers to the sluice to put it in a jug of water then triumphantly bear it back and place it on the patient's locker, a sweet-scented testimony to loveliness. She couldn't help but hear the visitors' enquiries and the usual responses from the men: 'I'm all right . . .'; 'I'm all right, hinny . . .'; 'I'm all right, pet.' She sometimes glanced up for a minute or two to watch them all, bathed in the golden light of the afternoon sun, and wondered what the visitors would say if they could be on the ward in the middle of a dressing round, to inhale the smell of sepsis and see just what it was that lay beneath the neat bandages, the clean sheets, and the smiles.

There was a less long-suffering, less dutiful, revolutionary little cabal, though, who often gathered together on the verandah or in the day room to smoke and conspire against the state. Whenever she over-heard them Sally felt as if she were back in the Cock Inn, listening to her brothers and brothers-in-law.

For King and Country

A private with a shattered ankle and a dirty chest wound who looked about twelve years old often had an ominous glint in his feverish eyes. 'Do you know what field punishment number one is?' he once demanded. Sally didn't, but was soon enlightened. 'It's having your pay stopped for up to three weeks, being worked to death shovelling shit or something just as nasty, and then being tied to a gun wheel for hours every day with your arms stretched up above your head. The buggers did that to me last spring.' He paused for breath for a moment or two and gazed into the middle distance, in spirit probably back on that gun wheel. 'Oh aye,' he added, 'I hope I may run into the officer that did that to me again once the war's over, supposing I'm still fit to stand. We take orders from one-pip wonders who cannot tell their arses from their elbows . . .'

'What *is* a one-pip wonder?' Sally interrupted.

'Usually a public schoolboy on his first outing without his nanny, who stands idle while other men work and waits for the sergeant to tell him what orders to give,' one of the older men told her, echoing her brother Arthur's words: 'A lot of the officers are nothing but kids and the men have to play nursemaid to 'em, half the time.'

'There were one-pippers, two-pippers, three-pippers too, just standing about with f—.' another private piped up.

27

'Nothing to do,' a corporal cut in, with a glance towards Sally and a warning look at the private.

'But what does it mean?' Sally insisted.

'A one-pip wonder is a second lieutenant,' the corporal said, 'the lowliest of the commissioned officers. Not a lot of use, most of 'em. A good sergeant's worth ten of them in a scrap.'

'And what good will any scrap do us?' an older man wanted to know. 'We've got two supposedly Christian nations slaughtering each other, and for what? Who gains anything except war profiteers and politicians and kings and kaisers – people who start wars from their nice safe places in the rear and then wear themselves out going to shows and races, and visiting hospitals, and pinning medals on people, and shoving other mothers' sons to the Front to be slaughtered. And what's the use of a medal anyway, when you've lost your life, or your limbs? You can't eat a bloody medal.'

'It'll never happen again in Russia,' the lad with the shattered ankle gasped, through a bout of coughing. 'They've had enough of serfdom there. They've swept their tyrant away. Oh, yes!'

Oh, yes. The arguments were so familiar they made her smile. It all felt so comfortable, being with them. Apart from the overcrowding, and the smell of sepsis, sickness and carbolic, it was almost like being at home.

★

For King and Country

'You're being transferred, Nurse. You take your day off tomorrow, and the day after you report to 7a.'

'That's the officers' ward, isn't it?'

Sister gave her a brief but friendly nod. 'Yes. Don't look so worried; you're a good worker, and you'll do all right. If we'd been keeping you, I'd have given you a chance as dirty nurse on the dressing round next week.'

Praise indeed. Sally's jaw dropped at it, but before she could close her mouth and collect herself enough to say thank you, Sister had already picked up the telephone, signalling her dismissal.

Oh, dear. She'd far rather look after the tommies, if she had the choice. Oh, why did it have to be her? She'd only been on the ward a month, and she'd stayed on her other wards for three, at least. And only half a day's notice of her day off – no time to write and warn her mother. But she had no choice other than to do as she was told, and so she got the train home and caught her mother distempering the kitchen ceiling in the failing light, with the whole house upside down and nothing in it that would make a decent meal.

Chapter Two

Sister Davies scowled and, raising her arm, pointed in the direction she intended Sally to go. 'Get on that ward, Nurse. That's where the patients are. You're no use to them dithering about in the kitchen.'

'One of the patients asked me to fill his water jug, Sister,' Sally protested.

'Why, get a move on then; don't take all day. I'll have no slackers on my ward. I want everything done to time. You can go and start the round.'

'Yes, Sister.' The cutting tone deterred her from asking which round. She picked up the jug and left the refuge of the kitchen for the officers' ward. It was a far cry from 7b where, before she left, they had had fifty patients crammed like sardines into the same-sized space that in the officers' ward was reckoned to be bursting at the seams with twenty. There was an acre of space between the beds, and getting to the other end of the ward wasn't like running an obstacle race; there were no beds down the middle here, and you could go the full length without bumping into something. And also, she thought with regret, without some of the men calling jocular little compliments to you as you passed, teasing you and making you laugh. It looked as if nursing the officers was going to be a more subdued business altogether.

She glanced back to see Sister Davies following, her flat feet splayed out so far they almost justified the probationers' nickname for her – 'Quarter-to-three-feet'. Another old dragon, she well deserved the complaints and criticism about her that resounded round the four safe walls of the probationers' sitting room.

'What round comes next?' Sally whispered, as she passed a kindly-looking ward maid.

'The medicine round, I think, Nurse.'

The medicine round? Surely Sister couldn't have meant a first year probationer to start that? Dreading having to ask again, Sally gave the patient his water jug and turned to approach Sister, but she was busy with the patient in the top bed, and a couple of others were calling to Sally for things the men on 7b would have got for themselves, or for each other.

'May I have a bedpan, Nurse?'

They evidently got bedpans whenever they asked here, not like downstairs where they usually had to wait for the bedpan round, Sally thought. She sped to the top of the ward for the screens, then into the sluice for the bedpan.

'Nurse! Nurse! Over here! No, take that to the patient, and then go and wash your hands.' Staff Nurse Dunkley's voice was sharp and peremptory.

Sally jumped to obey, and then presented herself to Dunkley, who indicated the bandages obscuring the patient's face. 'Take them off. I've just admitted him. He's got shrapnel wounds to his face and left arm. His notes say they're dirty wounds, and he hasn't spoken a word since they brought him off the battlefield; probably shell shock.'

Sally nodded. She'd seen plenty of nerve-shattered men on 7b. After they arrived most of them seemed completely dazed and lay in bed hardly moving for the first week or two. The ones whose wounds had healed were as jumpy as cats, waiting to be sent back to France. She'd seen one or two of them physically sick at the thought of it, but the doctors saw very little of that, that shock to the men's nerves. They came and looked at them for about five minutes, decided what needed to be done about their wounds, and were gone.

'Christopher Maxfield's his name. He's a second lieutenant with an Australian regiment,' Dunkley continued, 'and that's about all we know about him.

He looks done for, anyway. I hope somebody in France has informed his family, because we can get nothing out of him.'

Carefully unwinding the bandage, Sally said: 'Why, he's a long way from home, then.'

Staff Nurse's blue eyes appraised her. 'The house surgeon's coming up to see him, and he'll want these dressings off. Do exactly as you're told, and see if you can learn anything.'

As she gradually uncovered a hollow-cheeked, grey face adorned with the stubble of a few unshaven days and a thick, untidy moustache, Sally felt a fluttering in her stomach. She'd never been so near to a wound almost fresh from the battlefield before, but she managed to keep calm.

The bandage was off. Stained with blood and discharge, the dressing pad obscured the whole of the left side of the patient's face. He tensed, and the bloodshot hollow eye that looked into Sally's eyes was full of terror.

'Get the dressing off, Nurse.'

Sally gingerly took hold of one corner of the pus-contaminated pad and tried to lift one corner, to loosen it. The patient gasped, and reached up to grasp her wrist and stop her pulling.

'Come on, now, take a few deep breaths. Relax, and it won't be so bad,' said Dunkley. 'It's got to come off. Both dressings have got to come off before the doctor gets here. He'll want to have a good look so he can decide what needs to be done.'

Can't we soak it with something and wait a bit, until it'll come away easier and not hurt him so much, thought Sally, but a doctor couldn't be kept waiting, and a lowly probationer just coming to the end of her first year couldn't very well breach hospital etiquette so far as to question a staff nurse's judgement.

She steeled herself to the task, and the quick, darting eye that kept glancing into hers reminded her of a wild animal at bay. The patient released his grasp on her and held tight to the side of the bed. His breathing became faster and faster still as bit by bit she eased the dressing from his flesh, and then his panting became a moan and, sick to her stomach, she stopped pulling.

'Ready, Nurse Dunkley?'

The voice was soft, and Staff Nurse turned to flash a welcoming smile at the house surgeon who appeared at her side. 'In a tick, Dr Campbell.'

'Hello, Lieutenant, let's see what the damage is,' the doctor said, extending a hand to shake the patient's uninjured right one, 'and what we can do to mend matters. You realize we're dealing with a hero, nurses? Lieutenant Maxfield's got the Distinguished Conduct Medal *and* Bar which tells you he's won the award twice! Perhaps you'll tell us how you came by it when you're feeling a bit better.'

The patient shook his head slightly and groaned. He'd looked feverish at the start, and was sweating now. The dressing was still stuck, and Sally could no more have tugged at it again than shoot him. No matter, Staff Nurse Dunkley ripped the last of it off with the forceps, and the Lieutenant let out a sound that cut Sally like a knife.

'There, now,' Dunkley said, quite unperturbed.

What a sight! The eye was gashed out and blackening blood congealed in the broken crater, with fresh blood oozing from points around the margin where the dressing had been torn off – and such a stench from it, of blood and putrefaction.

Sally suddenly felt light-headed. Her mouth filled with water and she swallowed frantically, but it was no use. She was going to be sick.

'Quick, Nurse! Over there, into the sluice!' Staff Nurse Dunkley rasped. Sally clamped a hand over her mouth and bolted.

She reached the sluice just in time. Ugh, how foul it was, that taste of vomit. Safe from the sight of staff and patients, she retched until she could retch no more, then thought of that wound, and retched again. The image of the sluice receded and she held onto the sink as her knees buckled under her and the world went black.

She found herself lying on the cool sluice floor and after a minute or two raised a hand to her face. Her skin felt cold and clammy and her throat felt burned with the acid from her stomach.

'Ugh.' With hazy, disjointed thoughts of the wrong she would get if Staff Nurse came in and caught her, she dragged herself to her feet and turned on the tap to run cold, clean water into her cupped hands to swill her mouth, and rinse her clammy face.

Oh, God. What on earth had possessed her to come here? She'd no more idea of nursing than the man in the moon. Kath's dad was right. It was worse than any housemaid's job. She found a clean huck-aback towel and dried herself, then pulled her apron straight and went back to face them all: the staff nurse with her faint smile of contempt, the doctor whose handsome young face held nothing but amusement at a little probationer's weakness, and the patient, whose mutilated face would have made her sick again had that been possible, and whose eye, filled with anguish, stared straight into hers.

Down in the probationers' dining room, Sally sank into a chair beside Curran, an Irish girl who'd started at about the same time, glad to take the weight off her feet. Conversation stopped until the waitress had served them supper.

'I'm starving,' said Sally. 'I was sick this morning, and I didn't get enough to eat at dinner time to make up for it.'

'Oh, morning sickness!' One of a family of fourteen, Mary Curran gave her a knowing look. 'We all know what that means.'

'Don't be daft. I saw the most horrible wound I've ever laid eyes on, that's all. It made me heave.'

'Aren't you the lucky one? Sure, an' all I've seen is bedpans and buckets of soapy water, and all I've done is bedpan rounds and cleaning and tidying, and the same slaving I've done since I started. The nearest I've got to the patients is rubbing their backsides with methylated spirits on the back round. That sister's got a hatred for the Irish, so she has.'

Armstrong, who was sitting at an adjacent table, put down her fork. 'How many of your set will stick it until you qualify, I wonder? Beale and Batty have gone already.'

'Well, you know what Matron says,' said Sally.

'Nurses must be subjected to discipline and severe training if they are to develop character and competence,' Curran groaned.

Armstrong shrugged and picked up her fork. 'Some people just don't want to be disciplined, I suppose.'

'At least Beale and Batty went of their own accord,' Sally said. 'Poor Keeble got thrown out.'

'Poor nothing. It might be the luckiest thing that ever happens to her in her life,' said Curran. 'I'm sick of being disciplined and kept out of all the interesting jobs, so I am.'

Armstrong snorted. 'It's good for you. You'll end up with a much higher character than the rest of us.'

Curran gave her a look, and detecting a trace of hostility, Sally hastened to smooth it away.

'Why, man, if you'd had to watch that dressing you wouldn't have called me lucky. When you realize men are doing things like that to each other, you know the devil's out of his chains all right. But Staff Nurse Dunkley didn't turn a hair. She cleaned it up and then put a dressing on. The night nurse'll have to change it every four hours. What with everything else there is to do, she'll probably be half dead before she gets off duty tomorrow morning.'

'She'll have to do it, though. Until they get him to theatre, it's the only way to stop it going septic, or gangrenous,' said Armstrong. 'If he gets that, he's had it.'

'He's already got it, if the smell's anything to go by,' Sally said, then stopped talking and ate ravenously, reflecting on the dispassionate way Staff Nurse had done that dressing, as if it were the most normal thing in the world to clean congealed blood and discharge from around a man's eye pit and pack the holes in his face with gauze wrung out in antiseptic solution. That was what was needed to stop fatal sepsis in its tracks, what it was to be a trained nurse, and how much more use she was to the patients than someone who had to dash to the sluice to be sick.

Funny she could think of it now and not have her appetite ruined. She stopped chewing, and took a sip of water. 'Poor feller though, she gave him some gyp. It's the first time I've ever heard a man scream, and she didn't show him much sympathy. He's a decorated officer but by, she made his eye water.'

It was an understatement. By the time Staff had finished with his face, sweat and tears were running off the Lieutenant's unshaven cheeks until Sally had seen his ear fill with them. She had pitied him to her soul, but pity wasn't a scrap of good to anybody; she could see that now. She was in nursing for better, for worse, and she'd have to get over her squeamishness.

'I'm going to be just like her,' she announced. 'I'm going to dedicate my life to looking after the patients, and I shall think it a privilege.'

'I hope you won't be like her,' said Armstrong, picking up her plate to join them at their table. 'Dunkley's as hard as the hobs of hell. When I was on women's surgical she came to relieve once when we were short-handed, and I was with her when she did a dressing on a sixteen-year-old who'd had a breast abscess lanced. She jabbed that ribbon gauze into the cavity with the sinus forceps until we nearly had to scrape the poor little thing off the ceiling. It made my toes curl, and I asked her afterwards what she thought she was doing. "Serves her right," she said. "Unmarried mothers!" – and I thought, you bloody

For King and Country

bitch. She reported me for insubordination into the bargain.'

'Armstrong!' Sally exclaimed, 'I've never heard you swear before.'

'I don't, usually. Dunkley might be an efficient nurse, but she's not a very humane one. She's here to find a husband, and not much else, so I've heard,' said Armstrong. 'She's got her hooks into Dr Campbell, by all accounts. They've been seen out together, anyway.'

'Ah, so that's it,' Sally murmured. She'd had a feeling Dunkley hadn't liked him joking with her about her sprint to the sluice.

'I'll tell you something funny about him, though,' Armstrong grinned, lowering her voice and leaning confidentially towards them. 'We had this old body on the ward at about the same time. A notorious old . . . well, she'd made her living down on the Quayside, and she must have been sixty if she was a day, and in the last stages of syphilis. Well past being infectious.'

'Ugh!' said Sally, with a shudder.

'But you know from the lectures what havoc it wreaks with the body; we've all been well warned about that since the start of the war. Anyway, she had general paralysis of the insane as well as everything else — mad as a hatter, like they are when they get to that stage, all sense of decency gone. I used to hate bathing her, she'd ask us to do all sorts of filthy things

41

with her, and she loved it if she could embarrass us. Oh my word, a repulsive old woman! She tried to drag every man that came into the ward into bed with her, acting as if she was still seventeen and a raving beauty. Anyway, you know what Dr Campbell's like, fancies himself no end, and he was always giving the good-looking nurses the glad eye. Never gave me a second glance, of course, and you can see why . . .'

'Sure, and I can't see anything of the sort. There's nothing wrong with you!' protested Curran.

'Let's face it, Curran, I'm plain and poor, and not up to Dr Campbell's exacting standards by a long stretch. Still, I am human, and he was always so off-hand with me, I began to feel a bit annoyed. So when Sister was at supper one evening and he was taking the chance to show off to a couple of lovely young probationers in the office along with another houseman, and just me and my ugly mug left on the ward to do all the work while they had their cosy little gathering, I don't know what got into me, but I thought, "I'll take him down a peg." So I walked into the office, with my face absolutely straight, and I looked him in the eye, and quite serious, I said: "Oh, Dr Campbell, you've got a big admirer on the ward, and she says she'll die if you don't go and give her a kiss before you leave!" You ought to have seen him,' Armstrong laughed. 'Swelling with conceit, absolutely thrilled to bits with himself! So they're all looking at me, and he bats his

eyes and simpers a bit and he says: "Well! Who is it?"
"Rosie Ramsden!" I said, and I couldn't help it, I burst
out laughing. I wish you could have seen his face!
If looks could kill I'd be stone dead, but the rest of
them were like me – howling!'

'You've made an enemy there, then, Armstrong,'
Sally said, when the laugh was over.

Armstrong was thoughtful for a moment. 'No,'
she said. 'He's not that bad. He's vain, and he likes
women, but he's not vindictive. In fact, he's treated
me with a bit more respect since then. I don't envy
Dunkley, though. She'll have her work cut out trying
to make *him* forsake all others. She'd better keep him
on a very short lead.'

'I pity her if Matron finds out, as well,' said Curran.
'Sure, and she'll be down the drive with her suitcases.
I don't blame her, though. What woman wouldn't
get her hooks into him, given half a chance, and who
wants a man nobody else wants?' She looked at Sally.
'You're wasted on the officers' ward, so you are;
you've got no enterprise at all. I only came to nursing
to get a good catch, and what do they do but keep
me skivvying on women's wards. They must have
read my mind.'

'Aye, I suppose they did,' Sally said. 'They probably had an idea that if they put you on the officers'
ward you'd flirt with them all, and then they'd have
to kick you out for being *morally doubtful'*

'Nature takes no notice of morality,' said Armstrong. 'I read that in a book somewhere, so that means it's true.'

'Ach, there's not much Nature here; sure and we're nothing but a lot of old nuns. Come on,' Curran jogged her elbow. 'Let's get back to the cloister; see if we can get a cup of tea before it's time for the lecture.'

Oh, for pity's sake, the twice-weekly lecture. Another hour taken up. They'd have no time to relax at all before it was time for bed. Sally stuffed another forkful of food into her mouth, imagining what her mother would say to see a daughter of hers eating like a wolf. Never mind, she just had time to finish the meal, grab a cup of tea and fling herself into the deep feather cushions of one of the settees in the probationers' sitting room, and tuck her aching legs under her for a few blessed minutes until Home Sister came to usher them all into the lecture.

'It was in the last years of the last century that pathologists began co-operating with clinicians to detect microbes of diphtheria and tubercle bacillus in the throats and sputum of living patients,' the pathologist began, 'rather than waiting until they were dead to carry out our investigations, as we had before, ha, ha, ha!'

Ha, ha, ha. He really was hilarious. Sally stifled a

yawn, and was rewarded with a sharp jab in the ribs from Curran's elbow.

'. . . and that's how departments of clinical pathology came into being. Then the war came, and laboratory work proved itself of some use in the treatment of wounds and the prevention of sickness . . .'

It was all very fascinating, and Sally heard enough of what he said to get much of the lecture down in the sort of automatic writing that the mediums were good at. Details of bacteriology, the sowing of culture media with discharges from wounds, the cutting and staining of sections of tumours and tissue – all slid across the surface of her numb brain, ran down her arm and through her pencil almost of their own accord.

Why do they always give us these lectures when we're half asleep, she wondered, heaving herself up what seemed endless flights of stairs to her room. Roused a little by the exertion, she scanned her notes before putting away her notebook and undressing for bed. What bliss it was to lie down and close her eyes. She tried to go over the lecture in her mind, to fix it in her memory. It was no use. Her thoughts would wander off the subject.

They wandered to the conversation in the dining room, when she'd told the others that Dunkley hadn't shown the lieutenant much sympathy. Truth was, she'd shown him none. She'd seen the task, and had been oblivious to the man and his distress. At the memory of that distress, that awful panting and moaning, and the eye that in its agony kept darting into hers, Sally's heart contracted. A DCM and Bar might be proof of a man's courage, but courage didn't make anyone immune to torture.

That Dunkley, though. The only man she'd been aware of was Dr Campbell, and the patient might as well have been a block of wood for all the notice she took. Still, she'd got the job done, and that was what mattered, after all.

But was it *all* that mattered? High moral standards were all well and good, but judging other people like she judged the girl with the breast abscess wasn't right, and neither was taking it out on her. Sally went through Florence Nightingale's demands in her mind. A nurse must be sober, honest, truthful, trustworthy, punctual, quiet and orderly, clean and neat. That was all. But surely, something was lacking from the list. Nurses should be kind. And it would be so much the better, she thought, with a wry smile, if they had no sense of smell.

The image of that soldier's wound was the last thing in her mind before her thoughts became disjointed, her eyelids drooped, and she fell asleep, with the festering stench of that putrefying face pervading her dreams.

★

For King and Country

The night nurse disappeared into the office to give Sister Davies the report, leaving Lieutenant Maxfield's washing bowl on his table. There was a flush on his cheek, and he seemed to be asleep. Sally put a gentle hand on his good shoulder to awaken him. In an instant he roused, wide-eyed, like someone surfacing from a nightmare.

Still voiceless, he mouthed: 'Who am I?' and his uncovered eye held all the fear she'd seen the day before.

'Why, you're Lieutenant Maxfield.'

He looked unconvinced, so she took down his chart, to check the name and make certain she had it right. He nodded slightly when she showed it him, and winced as he relaxed against the pillows. Sally pulled open his locker drawer, found soap and flannel, retrieved his hospital towel from the back of the locker, placed it across the bed, then wet and soaped the flannel. 'I just have to help you to get washed. Did you sleep all right?'

He replied with a little one-sided shrug, then pointed to his throat and mouthed the word 'Gone.'

'Gone? Do you mean your voice? Do you mean you've lost your voice?'

He nodded. Sally wiped the uninjured side of his face with the flannel, and towelled it dry. 'You've got a bit of bristle. Shall I ask the barber to come and shave you?'

He put a protective hand to his moustache, and

gave a little shake of his head. She washed and dried his good hand, and put his things away in his locker. 'I suppose you remember you're going to theatre this morning? It means you won't get any breakfast. Still, you won't have to starve for long. You're first on the list.'

He answered with another shrug. Afraid that the horror she'd shown yesterday at the sight of his wound had upset him, Sally hesitated for a moment before lifting the bowl, wondering whether she should say a few words to try to make amends, but his eye was closed again, shutting her off.

Who knew what these men had lived through, she wondered as she carried the dirty water to the sluice. Her brothers said the papers didn't tell a tenth of it. Most of the men coming back from the Front were a bit peculiar, and some of them out of their minds altogether, fit for nothing but mental asylums. It was best to take no notice and just carry on as normal.

Night nurse was leaving the ward, looking dead tired, and Sister Davies was standing at the office door, beckoning impatiently to her. Sally sped up the ward and was last to sidle into the office, to stand beside another, more junior probationer.

'Nurse Wilde's here, finally, so with her permission, I can give the report.' Sister looked sternly round them all, then began the night nurse's summary. 'The young captain in the side ward next to my office has died. Kidney failure. The doctor's signed the death certificate and the night nurse has performed the last offices . . .'

'What are the "last offices"?' whispered the girl next to Sally.

'She's laid him out,' Sally murmured.

'Oh.'

Sister Davies paused and gave Sally a hard stare. 'When you've finished, Nurse.'

Sally flushed, and Sister continued. 'We're waiting for the porter to take his remains to the mortuary, then you can strip the bed and swab the mattress and the bedstead with carbolic. There are six patients for theatre. The list starts at ten o'clock, and Lieutenant Maxfield's going first. He's had a bad night, his temperature's still up and his pulse is quite rapid, so he'll be on four-hourly observations when he gets back . . .'

Sister gave the report on all the other patients, and then fixed the probationers with an unsmiling stare. 'We're going to be busy with the theatre patients, but I expect all the routine work to be done to time. As soon as you finish one job, you go into the treatment room and look at the book and do the next thing that hasn't got a tick in today's column. You tick things off as you do them. If you get stuck, you ask me, or Staff Nurse. So no need to stand idle in the kitchen or the sluice, or gossiping with the patients. Off you go, then. Get a move on.'

They filed out of the office double quick.

Sally took the junior probationer assigned to help her make the beds to the laundry room to stack the trolley with clean linen. 'What's your name?' she asked

'Crump, Nurse. Margery Crump.'

Sally carefully initiated Crump into the mysteries of hospital bedmaking as they went along. No flapping of the sheets to raise bacteria-carrying dust, all corners properly mitred, and all pillows turned with their openings away from the ward doors to give the beds a neat appearance when viewed from Matron's vantage point, when she arrived to do her round. The probationer was a good pupil and after the first empty bed the next couple were done quickly and efficiently. Then came Sally's chance to show her how to make a bed with the patient still in it.

'All right, Nurse, this is Captain Smith. He's had his appendix out. People usually feel very sick after the anaesthetic, so that's the reason for the Rhyle's tube, passed down their noses, you know. And if they're not vomiting, they can have half an ounce of water down it, and if they keep that down, they can have a bit more later on, and then more the next time, if they're still keeping it down. Captain Smith's only just had his Rhyle's tube taken out. He might get a slice of toast soon, if he's lucky.' She smiled at the Captain, amazed to discover how much she herself had learned.

For King and Country

They were moving on to the next patient when the porter, a taciturn Belgian refugee of about forty, came rattling down the ward with the theatre trolley for Lieutenant Maxfield. Dunkley helped to stretcher him onto it and picked up his notes, ready to accompany him. 'You know how to make the bed, Nurse Wilde. Bedding turned up and into the middle so that we can lift it easily when we bring him back on the stretcher.'

Sally nodded, and looked towards the trolley. She would have wished Maxfield good luck, but he'd turned his face away.

First into the sitting room that lunchtime, Sally heard a frantic fluttering. A tiny bird had flown in under the sash, and was battering itself against the windowpane. She went to catch it but it fluttered away and found refuge behind a pile of books. Drat it; the cat had got in as well and was creeping towards the shelf, stalking the poor wild thing. The cat leaped up to the shelf, and began to claw at the space behind the books.

'No!' Sally was beside her in half a dozen strides. She swiftly put the cat down, then drew out the books until she could see the bird sitting with eyes wild and beak wide open, gasping with terror. She felt its bony legs and claws, felt its palpitating fear as she took it quickly and gently in her cupped hands and carried it to the open window, with the thwarted cat mewing and complaining at her ankles. A pretty, tiny bird, some sort of finch, it flew upwards in its haste to get away and hit the wall opposite, where it clung with wings outstretched, flattened against the bricks, for a full minute. She marvelled at the way it kept its grip on the brickwork for so long before gliding to the ground and, hoping the poor thing wouldn't die of its ordeal, she watched it, sitting motionless on the paving stones. It stirred, and a minute later she saw it soaring skyward.

She felt very satisfied with herself. That was her good deed for the day, and now her friends were thronging into the room, chattering and laughing and making a beeline for the tea trolley.

'Wilde! What are you doing, woolgathering? Sure, and I thought you'd have poured us a cup of tea!'

'Sorry! Just coming.'

Curran was already pouring. 'Will you look at this girl, with a ward full of handsome fellows making eyes at her – she even forgets the tea. It's turned her head entirely!'

Sally laughed at the expression on Curran's face. She was cheerful company, as were most of the probationers, and Sally was never so happy than when joking and clowning with them. Whatever disasters might have happened on the wards, once shared they always shrank in size until they could be laughed away. None of the officers had made eyes at her, and the theatre cases had been too wrapped up in their own concerns to bother making eyes at anybody, but she didn't mind playing up to Curran.

'It couldn't make up for the row I got from Sister, though, when Dunkley told her I'd forgotten to clean the sputum mugs. But she didn't tell me to, so it must have been her that forgot.'

'That bitch of hell! Sure and could she not have given you a row herself, without running with tales?' said Curran. Armstrong and the others chorused sympathy, and the conversation moved on to other topics.

But Curran's face remained a mixture of outrage and glee. She was bursting with something, and when Sally got up early to get back to a busy ward, she followed her.

'So now I'll tell you something about that young madam, that'll make you laugh,' she said, as they raced along the corridor. 'But don't let on who it was, because I wasn't supposed to hear!' Curran looked swiftly round, and dropped her voice. 'Nobody's supposed to know – but she's been seen coming out of the doctor's residence! And *very* late at night! The hypocrite! The shameless young ...! Now what do you think she's getting up to, and what might happen if Matron gets to know? You could have a fine revenge there.'

Sally's eyes widened and she let out a long, low whistle. This was a crime of such magnitude it took her breath away. A sacking offence. A never-live-it-down, unforgettable, irredeemable error that would ruin Dunkley's career and reputation for ever and ever. She hoped, for Dunkley's sake, that Matron would never hear of it.

Chapter Three

Nurse Dunkley had just come back from theatre when the summons came. She was wanted in Matron's office. She left the ward, white but with her shoulders back and her head up, braced for what was to come. Sally never expected to see her again.

A couple of hours later Sally helped the porter lift a lieutenant with a belly wound back into bed. They removed the poles from the stretcher and, careful of his wound, Sally gently eased him onto one side, and then the other, to push and pull the canvass out from under him. 'All right, Lieutenant? You're back in the ward, safe and sound,' she told him. He opened a groggy, bloodshot eye and lifted his hand to his nose, to finger the Rhyle's tube. There would be no food for this fellow for a long while.

One patient back and the trolley stood ready for David Jones, the twenty-four-year-old with the fractured femur who was next to go down. Sister called her. 'You can go with him, Wilde. Stay with him until they've wheeled him into theatre, and come straight back.'

'Yes, Sister.'

The porter was already dragging Jones feet first out of the ward, and Sally ran to catch the end of the trolley, meeting as she did, a pair of big, brown, fearful eyes that put her in mind of a calf being led off to slaughter. She put a reassuring hand on Lieutenant Jones' arm.

'Will you hold my hand, Nurse?'

She laughed, thinking he was joking, but he wasn't. Well, there'd be no harm in it, she supposed, and gave him her hand. The porter was doing all the pulling, and it wasn't difficult to keep the trolley steady with her other one.

'I'm an awful coward, aren't I? But I'm dreading it, and dreading waking up after it. I'd rather die than lose my leg. God gave me two legs, and I want to take two to my grave.'

She gave his hand a squeeze. 'You're not a coward, but there's no infection, so I wouldn't worry about losing your leg.'

'My name's David. I'm not a proper officer, you know. I joined as a private and worked my way up from the ranks. I've only been a second lieutenant a week.'

She watched them wheel him into theatre then

raced back to the ward, hoping she'd been some use to him. Everybody said you always remember the patients you admit yourself. Sally hadn't admitted David Jones, but she wouldn't forget him if she lived to be a hundred.

His bed had been rigged up with a confusing array of beam and bars and pulleys and weights resembling some medieval instrument of torture. Three hours later they lifted Lieutenant Jones back into it complete with Rhyle's tube in his nostril, and splint on his leg. With a worried frown Sister set about the task of attaching his leg to the weights. 'Watch me. You might have to do the next one,' she told Sally. 'His leg's in a Thomas' splint, and the weights keep the bone pulled straight so it'll set properly. He'll be able to pull himself up with that monkey bar above him – when he comes round, that is.'

Staff Nurse Dunkley returned just as they were finishing the task, and not exactly as might have been expected. Not the slightest bit abashed, she fairly waltzed into the ward and her chin was even further up than when she'd left. Sister's face was a study, a mixture of deep disapproval, and absolute relief.

'Staff Nurse Dunkley reporting back on duty, Sister,' she trilled, and although she kept her face straight, Sally knew that on the inside, she was laughing.

★

Half a dozen probationers squeezed into Sally's room that night, all privy to the secret of Dunkley's disgrace, all striking poses of outraged virtue while eager for every salacious detail.

'And her professing to be such a *lady*! I've seen ladies like her walking the streets.'

'She's got no shame, that is a certainty.'

'What I want to know is, how did she get away with it?'

Curran gave a delighted chuckle. 'Sure, and you never will know, because *you're* not girls for listening behind doors.'

'And you are! Curran, you know something! Come on, spill the beans.'

'Ach, you're worse than I am; you're nothing but a lot of old scandalmongers, so you are. You ought to be ashamed of yourselves, but I'll tell you anyway. Matron gave Dunkley her marching orders, and sent her to pack . . .'

'How can she have?' Sally protested. 'She came back to the ward, and worked the rest of the shift.'

'She did so. And if I hadn't had to go back to the nurses' home to change my apron because I had it covered in sick, we'd never have known why.'

'Why, then? Come on, Curran, spit it out!' Armstrong urged.

'Jesus, Mary and Joseph, and isn't that what I keep trying to do, only you keep interrupting! And hadn't

For King and Country

I just got inside my room when poor old Matron came puffing and panting along, chasing down the corridor after Dunkley? "Wait a moment Nurse Dunkley," says she, "Come back to my office and we'll discuss the matter further." And Dunkley stopped and full of impudence, the young divill says: "But Matron, what can there be to discuss? You've believed a lot of malicious gossip, and you've dismissed me." Then Matron says: "I'm willing to reconsider," and Dunkley says: "Reconsider? This wouldn't be anything to do with a *certain substantial subscriber*, would it?" and Matron said they wouldn't go into that, but she could stay. But that wasn't enough for Dunkley, insolent young pup that she is! She said she wasn't going to stay anywhere where she was believed to be an immoral person, and she'd tell her grandfather how she'd been treated and see what he thought about it, and in the end, I felt sorry for Matron. She had to *beg* the bitch to stay.'

'The cheek!'

'So it turns out that because her grandfather's rolling in it and he gives a bit to the hospital, she's got away with it!'

'Aye, the powers that be can turn a blind eye when they want, when money's involved, like. It makes you sick.'

'One law for the haves, and another for the have-nots.'

'As it was and ever shall be, world without end, amen. Oh, my word, if it had been any of us, we'd have been thrown out quicker than you can say knife. That's Matron's idea of justice, I suppose. It's disgusting,'

'That's a lot of people's idea of justice. Money talks.'

'But what else could she have done?' Sally asked. 'If he took all his money away from the hospital, there might not be enough to pay all the wages, and there'd be a lot of patients couldn't get treatment, and that wouldn't be justice, either.' And remembering Sister's relief when Dunkley returned, she added, 'And she's still an efficient nurse.'

'She's a slut.'

'And a hypocrite. It's an outrage.'

'There's another outrage, an' all. One none of you lot seem to have thought about,' said Sally.

All eyes were upon her. 'What's that?'

'It's this. We're all crying for her blood, but she could never have gone there if Dr Campbell hadn't asked her, could she now? So he's just as much to blame as she is, but there's nobody screaming for a pound of his flesh, or talking about sacking him!'

'But he's a man!'

'He's a *doctor*!'

Sally's eyes widened and she gave an emphatic nod. 'Aye, he is! That's where the outrage comes in. The difference we make between them. She's a slut, but nobody says a wrong word about him. And I bet he'll be back on the wards tomorrow, twinkling his blue eyes at us all after nearly getting her the sack, and everybody'll still think he's wonderful.'

There was a pause, then Armstrong said, 'My word, she's right. You're absolutely right, Wilde.'

'Aye. Tell me the old, old story.'

'Men have always got away with it, so they have,' said Curran, her expression suddenly gloomy, 'and I suppose they'll get away with a lot more, now they're all dead.'

'Even so,' someone muttered, 'she's still a slut. And a hypocrite.'

A week after his operation Maxfield was still sleeping badly, according to the night report. News from home might buck him up, put him on the road to recovery, Sally thought, as she handed him his letter. 'I think that's the first one you've had since you've been here, isn't it, Lieutenant Maxfield?' But instead of the pleasure she'd anticipated, she saw pure shock on his face and his hand shook a little as he took it from her.

She passed on, to dish out the rest of the post, and was at the bed opposite when she chanced to glance up at him. He was looking at his letter and laughing, silent laughter, with shoulders shaking, and tears running from his exposed eye. The sight was so strange and so irresistible that the patients and ward staff watching him began to grin. Sally was smiling with the rest when he put a hand to his brow, and the merriment on the ward petered out into silence and eyes were averted at the appalling, embarrassing sight of a grown man, a *Lieutenant*, crying like a baby.

Sally was going to get the screens to shield him from the gaze of the ward, when from the corner of her eye she saw David Jones, struggling for breath, just as she'd seen an asthma patient on her first ward. Maxfield was forgotten.

'David!' She dashed towards him, calling to Crump, urging her to fetch Sister.

'Oh,' he gasped and clutched at his chest, and she was in turmoil, wondering whether she should leave him as he was, or lay him flat, or whether propping him up with more pillows might help him breathe better. She was thankful to see Sister Davies' splayed feet striding determinedly down the ward with the probationer trotting behind. Lieutenant Jones began to cough.

'Screens, Nurse.'

The probationer ran and set screens across the bed, but too late to prevent the other patients from watching Jones' face turn livid, or from seeing the blood stained phlegm he coughed into the receptacle Sally had snatched off his locker. Sister went to telephone the houseman, but not before Sally had felt the edge of her tongue. In future, she was to address the patients by their titles, and *never* their Christian names.

Maxfield was out of bed when she went to take his four-hourly temperature. She found him sitting on the verandah absorbed in watching a spider, trembling like an aspen leaf on a thread of its own spinning between the bars of the balustrade. He attempted a smile, and pointed to it.

She watched it for a moment. Its jerky movements reminded her of a patient she'd seen in the clonic stage of epilepsy. 'Maybe's it's having a fit,' she smiled.

He shook his head and frowning, mouthed: 'Shell-shocked!' and before she had time to protest he reached out and, looking straight at her, crushed it between his finger and thumb.

'What for did you do that?' she protested. 'It wasn't hurting you.'

'Coward!' His lips shaped the word.

She stiffened. Horrible man. For two pins she could have told him that he might have the DCM, but it didn't entitle him to destroy God's creatures for nothing. 'You're not supposed to be out of bed at this time. Come and I'll take your temperature inside, before we both get wrong from Sister,' Nanny-like, she shooed him back towards his bed and shook the thermometer down as he eased himself onto it. Before she placed it under his arm he snatched a pencil from the top of his locker and slowly and painstakingly wrote on the edge of his newspaper: 'How is he?'

For an officer, his writing was poor, no better than a five-year-old's, and she could hardly decipher it. 'Lieutenant Jones? As well as can be expected.'

He took up his pencil for another effort. 'Hopeless,' he wrote and, after a moment's hesitation, he handed her his letter and nodded, his expression telling her to read it.

Dear Max,
   I'm sorry, but I've given the house up . . . I'm living with someone I met at work . . . Fed up of wasting my youth on my own . . . at least we've no children . . . clean break . . . I shouldn't think this letter is a complete surprise . . .
   Edna.

Sally skimmed it over, and blushed slightly as she replaced it in its envelope and handed it back, without comment. But his eye was on her as she read his thermometer, seeming to want a reaction.

She marked his temperature chart, and joined the dots. It was coming down nicely, and he was still looking at her.

For King and Country

'It's terrible.' She could think of nothing better to say, but no matter. She had no time for idle chatter with the patients, and was bound to cop it from Sister if she didn't get a move on. She raced away, to do as all the others did and save a bit of time by putting half a dozen thermometers to cook in their four-hourly armpits, before coming back to the first one to start reading and recording them all.

'Why, what do *you* think?' she demanded, after supper that evening, as she sat with her stockinged feet tucked under her in the sitting room and sipped her tea. 'He never should have shown me something as private as that. I didn't know where to put myself.'

'Maybe he wants you to know he's footloose and fancy-free. Maybe he's on the lookout for a new wife and he thinks you'll fit the bill,' Armstrong said.

'Well, I don't. For one thing, I don't think he even remembered he had a wife before he got that letter. For another, he's Australian, and if he's not sent back to France, he'll be going back there, if he can remember where he lives. Dunkley said he didn't seem to remember anything when she booked him in, but she hadn't time to get to the bottom of it, because he's lost his voice and had to write everything down. And he's *thirty years old.*'

'That's only ten years older than you.'

It was, but then, and she didn't like to say it, then

65

there was his *face*. It was cruel, when men had fought battles to protect them that women should recoil at the wounds they'd received; but it was so, and she couldn't help it. If you'd loved a man before his looks were destroyed it would be different; if you'd sworn for better, for worse and till death do you part, you'd do it, if you'd ever had any real feelings for him at all. But to feel any attraction for somebody with a face like Maxfield's if you hadn't known him before, well! It would be impossible. And the way he'd crushed that poor, harmless spider – it showed there was an ugly side to his nature as well as to his face. Even so, far away from the ward, among her friends in the comfort of the probationers' sitting room, it was as much as she could do to prevent herself from shuddering at the thought of him.

Had Edna known about her husband's broken face before she wrote that letter? Terrible if she had. Either way, Edna would never have to look at it now. She'd certainly had some 'go' in her, and she'd gone. But Maxfield should never have embarrassed her by making her a party to his private business. Why had he done it? Perhaps it was all part of the injury to his head, like his memory. Perhaps it wasn't fair to expect anything from a man who couldn't remember his own wife, couldn't even remember who he was

What a horrible predicament to be in, and the one

person who should have been there to help him gone off with somebody else. She felt a sudden pang of pity, and of fear.

The chief was ready to make his entrance into the ward, flanked by Dr Campbell, a couple of respectful junior doctors, Sister Davies and Staff Nurse Dunkley. Sally tacked on behind them, to pick up the patients' notes and X-rays as they were finished with, and to speak only when she was spoken to, which was not at all. Dr Campbell's blue eyes twinkled in her direction as she jumped forward to open the ward door for the entourage, and Dunkley stared at her with compressed lips as she sailed past. Sally closed the door and trailed in her wake.

They went in a clockwise direction, stopping at every bed to discuss the fractures, amputations, gunshot and shrapnel wounds and facial injuries inflicted on their 'cases', along with the treatment planned or already given, and the patients' progress. Nurse Dunkley carefully avoided Dr Campbell's eyes, Sally noticed. The chief was polite to all the patients, listening to their comments and giving serious answers to their questions.

Maxfield still looked pale and gaunt, but apart from his moustache, he was now clean-shaven. The chief inspected the dressing on his face, and returned to the end of the bed to talk to his students. 'Abundant discharge, I see, and a rather oppressive odour. But his temperature's down, which tells us there's no more septic absorption. What can we expect him to tell us now that's ceased?' The chief addressed his question to the junior housemen.

'That his pain's relieved, and he feels generally much better, sir,' said the braver of the two.

'Quite right. How are you, Lieutenant?'

'All right, sir,' was Maxfield's soundless reply.

'Of course, the eye's gone, old fellow, as I expect you realize.' The consultant's tone was kindly, and Maxfield nodded, keeping his moustachioed upper lip very stiff.

'But there's every hope you'll keep the arm. We'll take the dressing off once more and have a good look at it and if everything's satisfactory the next one can stay on for a couple of weeks, so you won't be troubled with any more painful changes.'

Maxfield nodded.

'How's your appetite?'

Sister answered for him. 'Not very good, sir. He hardly eats anything.'

'That won't do. Give him some of the mixture, Sister, to take whenever he likes.'

'Yes, sir.'

The entourage passed onto the next bed. 'Very difficult trying to converse with a patient who's lost the power of speech,' the chief remarked, and addressed himself to the shyest of the housemen. 'What's your opinion, Doctor?'

'I can find no damage to the larynx, sir. It may be connected to his head injury, or it may be purely functional. Perhaps brought on by shock.'

The chief gave a grim smile. 'Well, lucky for him he's an officer, and safe from the electric shock cure for mutism. That gets men back to the Front in short order.'

With David Jones, the chief's tone was almost paternal. 'Let's see, a week after your operation, isn't it? And how are you getting on, young man?'

David gave the great man a shy smile. 'Tired. But a bit better, thank you Doctor.'

'How is he, Sister?'

'A slight fever still, sir, but he's improving. He's eating a bit better.'

'Good, good. Well, you're bound to be tired. And how's that pain you had in your chest? Any better?'

'Yes, thank you,' said David, 'And Doctor, thank you for saving my leg.'

A kindly nod and a 'plenty of rest, young man', and then the chief led his followers towards the fireplace in the middle of the ward, which served for both heating and ventilation. Sister went to answer the telephone, and Nurse Dunkley answered a call from a patient further up the ward.

'Are you really better, Lieutenant Jones?' Sally whispered.

'All the better for seeing you, my angel.'

'Shush,' she laughed, 'if Sister heard you . . .'

He nodded towards the group round the fire, intent on listening to the professor's teaching session. 'She won't. She's gone, so I'll tell you. Do you know, Nurse, we all look forward to seeing you come on duty every day, because you're the nicest of the lot. You *are* an angel, but I've told them all hands off, you're mine.'

Sally laughed, and brushed off the compliment. 'What's the Welsh for blarney? A lot of Celtic flannel?'

Eyes wide, David insisted, 'No, it's right, Nurse. They all call you "Smiler".'

'Get away,' she said, and scooped up his notes with the rest to take them into the office, a glow of pleasure burning inside her. He was such a bonny lad, with his dark wavy hair and his big dark eyes with their thick lashes – eyes that could have you mesmerized – and his smile, and his lovely, deep, sing-song Welsh voice . . . He was nice, not stuck-up like some of the other officers. But then, he came from the same sort of home that she did, she was sure of it. She hoped he'd really meant it, what he said.

'Nurse Wilde!' She turned at the sound of Dr Campbell's voice and seeing him coming towards her, went to meet him. 'The chief wants the notes and

For King and Country

X-rays. We're to have one of his famous fireside tutorials on the interesting cases, including the fellow who made you dash to the sluice to be sick. If you find something to do nearby and listen hard, you might learn something.'

Lieutenant Raynor had lost his left arm and his right one was immobilized in a splint. Sally sat by his bed giving him his late morning cocoa through a feeder cup and trying not to make him feel like the helpless cripple he was, when the chief led his acolytes over to the long sash window on the other side of the bed. He held an X-ray up to the light, so that Sally had a perfect view.

'This was taken at the base hospital in France, before they put our patient on the ambulance train. What do you see?' the chief asked one of the housemen.

'Comminuted fracture of the radius, sir.'

'Obviously, and caused by a shell fragment that picked up a quantity of battlefield mud before tearing through his clothing and embedding itself in his arm. What else?'

'Lighter streaks, sir, and the arm looks swollen.'

The chief laughed aloud. 'Well spotted. Very faint and very few, but "lighter streaks" indeed. And what might they be, bearing in mind the condition of the soil on the Western Front?'

Sally's patient turned his head away from the cup and leaned forward to try and glimpse the X-ray.

The other houseman couldn't contain himself. 'Gas, sir!'

'Yes, gas, sir! Those lighter streaks are gas. Caused by?'

'Clostridium . . .'

'Clostridium perfringens, more often than not. Symptoms?'

'Pain, swelling, fever, rapid pulse, sweating, sir, and anxiety,' one of the housemen volunteered.

'Vesicle formation, foul-smelling discharge, progressing to a drop in blood pressure, renal failure, coma and death, if not treated,' Dr Campbell chimed in.

'Excellent. Now describe the onset.'

'Sudden and dramatic . . .'

'Not you, Dr Campbell. Let one of the juniors speak.'

The keenest young houseman volunteered. 'Inflammation begins at the site of infection, sir, and painful tissue swelling, brownish red discolouration . . .'

'Yes. And you, your turn now. What do you find on palpation?'

The shyer of the two answered. 'Crepitus – on palpating the swollen area, sir.'

'Excellent. And the affected area expands so quickly one can see the increase within a very few minutes, and the tissue is rapidly destroyed.' He paused for a dramatic moment, and then rounded on his eager student, with an eye like a hawk. 'So why do you suppose it wasn't?'

Taken aback, the houseman stuttered, 'I . . . I don't know, sir.'

The chief smiled. 'I'll enlighten you. The radiographer at the base hospital spotted it on this X-ray; the bacteriologist saw the bacilli microscopically on a wound smear – Gram-positive, of course – and so our man was one of the lucky few to get the new French gas gangrene antitoxin, along with his tetanus antiserum. Had it been his leg, they might simply have amputated, but to lose an arm is more disabling. So the surgeon did a thorough debridement of the wounds and immobilized the arm and then the nurses started four-hourly irrigations that were continued throughout his journey by hospital ship and hospital train to us. Quite a feat of organization.'

Debridement? What was that? She'd have to look it up in her nurse's dictionary. But the chief was still in full spate. 'Motor function appears to be intact, as are the radial and ulnar pulses, and they're equal to the contralateral side. We have also excised the wounds to remove decaying muscle and sequestrum and we've bipped them, which is to say we've irrigated them thoroughly with 1 in 40 carbolic acid, dried them with methylated spirit, smeared them with bismuth and iodoform paraffin paste, and packed them. The arm you've seen on X-ray is now resting comfortably in a sling. Luckily for our patient it's his right one, and we can be fairly confident he'll keep it. As I never tire of impressing on you gentlemen, dirty wounds must be thoroughly explored and cleaned, or they *will not heal.*' He looked at Sally. 'Did you hear that, Nurse?'

She rose to her feet. 'Yes, sir.'

'Yes, sir. Although this wound is perfectly capable of healing, if the patient had sustained it before the days of antisepsis and asepsis, he'd certainly have died of septicaemia. That's blood-poisoning to you, Nurse. Do you know why we don't change dressings every day here, or even every week?

'No, sir.'

'Explain to her, Dr Campbell.'

'Because the job's done properly in the first place,' said Dr Campbell. 'All infected matter is removed, then the wounds are covered with antiseptic paste. And as nurses tend to be less careful about aseptic technique once a wound starts to heal, especially a dirty wound, they sometimes introduce more infection.'

The chief gave her a stern look. 'So be very careful how you do your dressings, Nurse. Everything sterile, and a strict no touch technique. Always, always always!'

'Yes, sir.'

Debridement. Sequestrum. Debridement. Sequestrum. She liked the words, savoured them, and as soon as she got the chance she'd look them up and know what they meant. Little by little she'd make this closed, mysterious world of medicine open up some of its secrets to her. The chief led his party back to the middle of the ward to expand on his views on the management of wounds, but too far away for her to hear properly.

'I wish I'd asked him about the pain I'm getting in my jaw, and my back and legs,' her patient murmured. 'And I wonder if I got gas gangrene antitoxin? I can't remember.'

'You should have asked him,' said Sally.

He gave her a disparaging look. 'Now that would be frightfully bad form, wouldn't it, Nurse? One doesn't want to make a nuisance of oneself.'

'Well? Did you learn anything?' Dr Campbell stood leaning against the door of the linen room the following day, while Sally was pulling clean sheets and pillowslips off the shelves.

'Yes.' Her arms full of linen, she turned to go back to the ward, but he blocked her way.

'What, then?'

'The pale streaks on the X-ray were gas, caused by bacilli that multiply in dirty wounds and destroy muscle and cause blood poisoning as well. Sequestrum is dead bone, and debridement means cutting all the dead stuff away. Oh, and crepitus is a sort of crackling. I remembered that as well. I'll have to get back with these, Dr Campbell. Staff Nurse is waiting.'

'Well, you seem to have the initiative to find things out. Very well done, Nurse.'

She gave him a brief smile as she edged past him.

'And after enduring all that, all our patient seemed to care about was his bally moustache! Incredible, isn't it? He wouldn't let Nurse Dunkley shave it off before his operation, and he was still hanging onto it when we wheeled him into theatre. Isn't that right, Staff Nurse?'

Nurse Dunkley had materialized beside them, with a reproachful look for Dr Campbell and a frosty frown for Sally. 'Isn't what right?'

'Second Lieutenant Maxfield. He's very attached to his moustache. Of course, we indulged him in his little eccentricity, and let him keep it. What else could we do? He's a hero.'

'I'm sorry, Dr Campbell, but Nurse Wilde has too much to do to waste time talking about moustaches. Go and start making that empty bed, Nurse Wilde. I'll be with you in a moment.'

It sounded like a threat. Sally turned to go, but Dr Campbell caught her eye. 'He was right, you will make an excellent nurse.'

'Who was right?' Sally and Dunkley chorused, but

their only answer was a smile. A smile with a hint of mockery in it – though whether for her or for Nurse Dunkley, Sally couldn't tell.

She left them, resolving to put Dr Campbell and his comments out of her mind and concentrate on what she was supposed to be doing – re-making that empty bed. If only she'd remembered to tell Dr Campbell that Lieutenant Raynor had been complaining of pains in his neck and back. She hesitated, and almost turned back, but the thought of Dunkley's face deterred her. Never mind, Raynor's pains were probably from being stuck in bed a lot of the time, and having to support that sling. She'd tell him to mention it himself during the next doctor's round.

She was at the far end of the ward when Dunkley caught up with her and loomed so close and with such violence in her eyes that Sally recoiled. 'Don't you know there's a rule against familiarity with the doctors, Nurse Wilde?' she almost spat. 'See that it doesn't happen again, or Matron will get to know, and you'll be down the drive, with your suitcase.'

She flounced towards the stripped bed, and after a stunned moment Sally followed with the bedding.

Chapter Four

The ward was understaffed as usual, and as usual there was no shortage of work to be done. Sally went to the sluice and quickly set up a bathing trolley. She'd been a bit apprehensive about bed baths, and had been relieved on finding them a thoroughly decent business. Let a man wash his own face, neck and arms, then wash chest, back and legs for him, and then cheerily hand the flannel back to him and hold the sheet up like a tent over him, concealing him from your view while he did 'round the Middle East' himself. Everything neatly accomplished, and both parties spared any embarrassment, but then, she hadn't yet had to bath anyone with injuries like Lieutenant Raynor's.

With the other probationer to help, she should have at least a couple of patients bathed before the theatre list started at ten o'clock. They set to with a will and got further than they anticipated, abandoning

79

the bathing trolley by David Jones' bed after the first patient had been taken to theatre and the orderly had wheeled in the mid-morning drinks. Sally went to get a cup of cocoa for Jones.

'Wake up, Lieutenant Jones.'

He drowsily reached up a hand for the monkey bar and pulled, but to no purpose. 'I've no strength today, angel,' he sighed.

'Nurse, not angel,' Sally whispered, and caught Crump's eye. 'Come and help me, Nurse.' Second Lieutenant Jones gave a feeble laugh as they joined hands under his thighs and hoisted him into a sitting position, and then he broke out into a cold sweat. The colour drained from his cheeks, and he began to gasp for air.

'All right? All right, David?' Whether he heard her Sally couldn't tell, but he didn't answer. 'Fetch Sister. Quick,' she ordered, and Nurse Crump bolted for the office. Sally curled her fingers round David's wrist and pressed in the tips in the hollow above his thumb. His pulse was rapid, and she tried to count it while watching his struggles for breath.

Sister arrived, took one look at him, and went to telephone the houseman. Sally pulled the screens across the bed space, and she and the probationer stood helplessly by as their patient lost all awareness of his surroundings.

'I've sent for the porter, as well,' Sister told them,

on her return. 'We'll get him moved into the room next to my office.'

As soon as they'd transferred him Sally helped Sister Davies to prop him with pillows to sit him up, as far as could be managed with his leg attached to the weights. All afternoon, whenever she was in his room or near it, Sally listened with dread to a strange alteration in the rhythm of his breathing: noisy, deep and rapid for a minute or two, then slower and more shallow, until it stopped altogether for what seemed an age. Then he seemed to suck all the air in the room into his lungs in a deep and noisy draught, and the cycle repeated itself – as if he kept forgetting to breathe until death almost claimed him, and then he suddenly remembered, and evaded it.

She was in David's room with Sister when Dr Campbell walked wearily onto the ward after the list was finished, and stood in the doorway. 'He's Cheyne-Stoking; you can hear it halfway down the corridor. Ten days after a three-hour operation! Ye gods, he might have had enough consideration to last a bit longer, after all that bally work! Don't look so shocked, Nurse Wilde. Dying's a poor return for all the work we did on him, and it looks very much as if that's what he's going to do.' He turned to Sister Davies. 'Very little to be done, I'm afraid, except keep him sitting up. Send for me when you want the death certificate signed. It can't be long.'

The words were barely out of his mouth when David's breathing stopped. Sally stood hardly breathing herself, waiting for it to begin again, but in vain. Dr Campbell applied a stethoscope to his chest, and gave Sister Davies a brief nod. She pulled out the pillows to lay him flat and closed his eyes, then covered his face with the sheet.

Sally dried the young face that Dunkley had just washed as gently and carefully as a mother might have. His eyelids had lifted, and his mop of black hair, black brows and dark, empty eyes stood out against the yellowing flesh. Now Dunkley handed her an arm, wet, limp and lifeless. The sheet they'd folded back across his hips preserved his dignity until they'd washed his trunk and, as if he'd been alive, they moved it just enough to expose and wash each leg in turn. The break in his thigh distorted the shape of one leg, made his knee and his foot lie at odd angles. Dunkley picked up lumps of tow with forceps and packed them into his throat to prevent any leakage from his stomach and then pulled him onto his side, to wash his back, and take more lumps of tow to pack his rear before allowing him gently to fall onto his back.

Now the sheet was off, and for the first time in her life Sally saw a fully-grown man entirely naked. Dunkley washed the last part of him that awaited washing, and while Sally dried him she cut off a length of narrow bandage, for the tying of that member whose virility was gone forever. She tied it tight, and finished the knot with a neat bow.

Hard to preserve any dignity now. His body looked faintly ridiculous, and unutterably pathetic. They slipped on the white shroud, combed his hair, and closed his staring eyes, and he reminded Sally of nothing so much as a big, broken doll. Dunkley put pennies on his lids to keep them closed, crossed his hands on his chest, and then put a pillow under his chin to prevent his jaw from dropping.

Sally took one last, lingering look at him as she wheeled the trolley away from the darkened room. His poor parents, to lose such a lovely son. And he would have made a loving husband, and a father. Such a waste. All that promise of future generations, all that youth and love and laughter, that vibrant life, all were stilled, soon to be as cold as the clay that would swallow him. How pathetic, how helpless, how vulnerable he seemed. As are we all at the last, she thought, feeling that she, too, stank of death.

Ah! There came the porter, rumbling along the corridor with the mortuary trolley.

Odd that it should come as a shock, the following morning, to go on duty and see his bed empty and made up with clean linen ready for the next patient.

It bore testimony to an enormous void, the lack of Lieutenant David Jones on the ward, and the sight of that emptiness cut her in a way that laying out his body had failed to do. Her hand pressed against the ache in her chest and met the crisp stiffness of a starched apron bib.

No time to mourn him. Better get a move on and get the washing bowls out for those men who were confined to bed, and get the junior to help the ones who couldn't manage to wash themselves. Then breakfasts, and the bedmaking and ward cleaning to be done, and then temperatures. Dunkley would do the blood pressures and the medicine round and it would be time for the mid-morning drinks. By that time the dust would have settled, Sister would start on the dressing round, and with a bit of luck she'd choose Sally to help her. There was no theatre list today, but some patients were moving on, and they were expecting a couple of new admissions.

'You're going to the convalescent hospital today, aren't you, Lieutenant Hogan?' she asked, for nothing more than to make a little polite conversation whilst she stripped the bed he'd occupied.

'The military convalescent hospital, yes,' he said, in that broad Australian accent she found a little hard to follow. 'Run along the lines of a prison, I'm told. Make sure none of us escape.'

Sally heard a snort, and turned to see Major Knox's

mouth turned down in an expression of derision. 'Vewy necessawy, when they're dealing with Aust-walians. I don't say it of the officers, but the lower wanks have a nasty habit of wunning off.'

'What did you say?'

Knox's sneer became more pronounced. 'I said the Austwalians have a nasty habit of wunning off,' he barked. 'They're the most undisciplined wabble in Fwance, and they've no weason to be otherwise, wet nursed by their government as they are.'

'My bloody oath, mate, you're lucky you're lying in that bed, or I'd . . .'

Knox gave him a look of contempt. 'Start a bar-woom bwawl? Another thing our antipodeans are good at. But before you do, wemember that stwiking a senior officer cawies a severe penalty, even for an Austwalian.

Sally looked from one to the other, despairing of them. Did they never, never learn? Hadn't they seen enough of death? Were they so fond of war that they had to start another one, in the middle of the ward?

Hogan leaned over Knox, and raised his fist, then changed his mind. 'Ah, you're not worth it. Just let me get out of here; I'll be glad to get back to Australia. Australians treat their men like men, and not like tin soldiers who've got nothing better to do than stand around waiting to be sent to the slaughter by some idiot Englishman. The Australian troops began to see the light about the British officer class with Gallipoli, and what happened at Fromelles – and Pozieres and Bullecourt and Poelcapelle – destroyed any illusions they had left. It's not the Hun that the Anzacs are sick of, *mate*, it's British staff, British methods, and British bungling.'

'*Gallipoli!*' Knox exploded. 'Gallipoli was a minor sideshow! And we lost four times as many men as you. And at Pozieres the Austwalians were weckless enough to diswegard German firepower and they paid the pwice. At Bullecourt they were incompetent. We're at war, and in war orders have to be given, and obedience *enforced*, and the death penalty concentwates men's minds on the task in hand. An offence that gets our men shot wins an Austwalian a fwee passage home to Mother, and that's bad for mowale among our twoops. A few exemplawy executions among your men would be a *jolly good thing*.'

Sally stared hard at Dunkley, silently willing her to do something to stop this nasty scene going any further. Dunkley met her gaze, and did nothing.

'You're the people who're bad for *mowale* among your *twoops*, mate, and the Australians came to fight the Kaiser's army, not to be killed by the bloody English – and they came as volunteers in a war that hasn't got much to do with Australia, when you think about it!' said Lieutenant Hogan, the volume of his voice increasing with his wrath. 'The Australian people will never stomach conscription, and you'll be whistling for volunteers if you try shooting any of the diggers. It's clinging to your bloody feudal, obsolete ideas of discipline that's made the English Army so rotten it's never achieved one successful offensive in the whole bloody war! Your idea of discipline is to teach men to salute and then get them to kick a bloody football while they walk into enemy fire, you idiots! And the poor bastards have a straight choice between obeying your damned fool orders or being shot by a firing squad. The Australian Army's proved that letting men use their own initiative is the *best* foundation for discipline, not the worst! If any more proof were needed.'

At last, Dunkley intervened. 'Gentlemen, please! Behave like the officers you are, please.' She was doing her best to appear horrified, but Sally had a feeling she'd been enjoying the argument, until it started going in favour of the Australian.

The porter appeared. 'Zey are all walking wounded, *n'est-ce pas?*'

Sally nodded. 'Yes. The other two are in the day room, with all the luggage.'

Hogan went to Maxfield, and gave his right shoulder a friendly squeeze. 'So long, mate. I wish I were leaving you in better company than these English idiots. When you get home, show that DCM you won to your Ma, and then throw it on the fire, for what it's worth.' He turned to Sally. 'No offence to you, Nurse. You're all right, and if your army'd had better officers, a lot more of your men would be coming home. '

'None taken, Lieutenant Hogan. Good luck.' She offered her hand. He gave it a hearty shake, and marched off singing under his breath, but just loud enough to be heard:

Goodbye, English generals, Farewell Douglas Haig,
Since we've joined the Army, we've been your
   bloody slaves.
Gallipoli was a failure, France a bloody farce.
You can take your whole Imperial Army
And shove it up your. . .

'Evewy sort of indiscipline, that's what the Aust-walians are good at,' Knox reiterated, as strains of the song died away. 'Set of wuffians. I awarded a man field punishment before I got this,' he indicated his wound, 'and no sooner had the sergeant tied him up, than he was thweatened by a wabble of "diggers", until he'd no alternative but to let the fellow loose. But deserting's their weal speciality. They take off by the score. By the hundwed, in fact, on the Somme, and it would only have taken a couple of exemplawy executions to stop that wot.' He heaved himself up in bed, and looked in Maxfield's direction. 'And they're the only fighters in Fwance, to hear them talk. Well, they're not.'

In Sally's limited experience of the one or two she'd met on the men's ward, the Australians were like the pitmen she knew, not the kind to lie quiet under an insult. She looked towards Maxfield, expecting to see anger on his face at the very least, but there was nothing.

'Can you imagine what Austwalia must be like?' Knox went on, to nobody in particular, for nobody answered him. 'One enormous bloody sergeants' mess. Fwightful.'

Sally put the soiled bedding in the skip and, glancing up at Knox's face found it easy to imagine him dishing out punishment. She wondered whether he'd ever sentenced anybody to death, and had little doubt that he had.

Another officer, a quiet, bespectacled captain who had lost a foot and was in no danger of being returned to active duty said: 'Of course, we must have discipline, but I must say I think that stringing men up on gun wheels for hours at a stretch in the sight of their fellows is a very degrading sort of punishment.'

Knox's face turned puce. 'It keeps them in the line,' he barked, 'and if it's done pwoperly, they don't come back twice. The only alternative's imprisonment, which gets the culpwit out of the line and burdens other men with an unfair share of his duty.'

'Perhaps so, but with all the wayside crosses that they have in France and Flanders, I think that tying men up in the attitude of crucifixion gives a very bad impression altogether. It causes a good deal of resentment.'

'Wesentment?' barked Knox, evidently feeling a good deal of resentment himself at that moment. 'We're fighting a *war*, and if we have to discipline certain elements in our own side to win, so be it. It's a gwim duty, but it's a necessity.'

'I daresay it's a duty some of us have more relish for than others,' said the bespectacled one, resting his book on the bed. 'I've heard you use the phrase "exemplary executions" twice, and I can't help thinking that the sentences meted out often *do* have more to do with deterring others than with strict justice to the offender, and in my opinion, it's a very bad thing.'

Knox looked at him as if he were a peculiarly noxious worm that ought to be trodden on. 'You're mistaken in your opinion. They serve a vewy useful purpose, and you deserve to be shot yourself for making such an allegation,' he blasted.

The bespectacled one shrugged in the mildest manner possible, and returned to his book.

'Humph!' Knox snapped his newspaper open, and conversation ceased.

The day room was empty now, and as quiet as the grave. Sally went inside and looked for a record, then

For King and Country

lifted the polished mahogany lid of the new Columbia Grafonola, a gift to the officers from some ladies' committee or other. She put 'Suvla Bay' on the turntable, a record that she'd often heard Hogan play, and listened for a moment or two to the lament, thinking how queer it was that men with such rough exteriors were often so sentimental underneath.

> In an old Australian homestead
> With the roses round the door
> Stood a lady with a letter
> That had just come from the war.
> With her mother's arms around her,
> She gave way to sobs and sighs,
> And as she read that letter,
> The tears fell from her eyes.

> Why do I weep?
> Why do I pray?
> My love's asleep, so far away.
> He gave his life that August day,
> And now my heart lies there in Suvla Bay . . .

Too many deaths on August days, she thought, as she walked back into the ward. Poor lads, poor ladies, poor mothers. Poor David, and now her heart would lie in this hospital, where he had lain.

But Sally's mood of gentle sorrow was soon

dispelled. Major Knox was out of bed with his newspaper folded under his arm and the minute he reached
the day room there was a scraping of the gramophone
needle and the lady's lamentations came to an abrupt
halt.

Dunkley had gone to supper and Sister was in the
office when Sally stood guard by the ward door to
collect the visitors' tickets and let them into the ward.
After that she sat at the table by the fire to join another
probationer who was cutting strips from sheets that
people had donated and which had subsequently been
well boiled in the laundry. Sally sat down beside her,
to start rolling the strips into bandages.

Most of the officers were too far away from their
families to have many visitors, Maxfield among them.
His bed looked untidy, the worst on the ward, and
he'd made the top sheet grubby with his newspaper.
What if Matron walked onto the ward and saw it
now? No one would put it past her to appear during
visiting hours, and there was no substantial subscriber
waiting to shield Sally from her wrath.

She jumped to her feet and went to tidy him up.
'You know, Lieutenant Maxfield, you're supposed to
sit in your chair to read the newspaper. You've got
printers' ink all over the sheet.'

'Sorry,' he mouthed.

'And you haven't had any of your mixture the

chief ordered for you.' It was still standing on his locker hardly touched, the chief's pet tonic of raw eggs beaten in rum. She held it out to him.

He pulled a face, and scribbled on his newspaper in his shaky handwriting, 'Signed the pledge.'

She smiled, warming to him. Maybe he was a Methodist, like her. But even if he was, he had to take it, to get better. 'You can't have signed the pledge,' she joked. 'You're an Australian! Besides, it's medicine. The consultant says you've got to have it. Come on, drink up.'

'Cruel,' he wrote, but took the glass from her. She folded her arms and began to tap her foot, watching him gulp the stuff down. He handed her the empty glass, and she watched as the words: 'Lovely eyes' fell from his pen.

A day ago she would have shrunk from a compliment from him, but there was an odd vulnerability about him, and her pity for David seemed to have expanded into pity for the whole world, and so she smiled.

He pointed in the direction of David's bed, and mouthed, 'Dead?'

She nodded, and tears filled her eyes.

'Shame.'

She nodded again, not trusting herself to speak.

He scribbled again. 'Clean bed. Looked after. A lot worse.'

She nodded, 'Aye, I suppose so.'

'How many from your village killed?' he wrote.

Enough of this, or she really would be in tears. She shook her head, and fled with the empty glass towards the kitchen, to compose herself. Five minutes later she was back at her post, busily rolling bandages, conscious of that eye with its peculiar mixture of wariness and pleading, which seemed always to dart towards her, and none of the others.

'You get your dressing changed today, Lieutenant Maxfield. Will you come and get into bed, please?' Sally asked him. 'Sister will be along in half a minute.'

He nodded, but instead of following her to his own bed, he went over to Knox, dropped the newspaper under his nose and stood glaring at him, as if demanding a reaction.

Knox glanced down at the paper, and then thrust it back at Maxfield. 'All wight, all wight. Jolly good show, I admit it. I wasn't talking about you, or men like these. It's the sort of filthy animal who leaves his chums in the lurch I've no time for.'

Maxfield shrugged.

Sally put down her dressing tray on his bed-table and waited for him. 'Does Major Knox know you got the DCM and Bar?' she asked, when he was finally sitting on the bed, and she was unrolling the bandage securing his dressing. He grimaced and gave another careless shrug.

Gently, gently she began to loosen the dressing, and it lifted much more easily this time. 'There,' she said at last. 'It's off, but I'll just leave it in place until Sister . . .' but no, here was Sister, almost beside them. Sally picked up the dressing with the forceps and turned her back on Maxfield to put it into the receiver and in that instant he was out of bed and making for the bathroom.

Forceps in hand, she stared after him. 'What are you doing?'

'Get back into bed this instant,' Sister Davies demanded.

Too late. He was already in the bathroom. Sally hesitated, looking at Sister.

'If he's gone to look in the mirror, he's in for a shock,' she said. A wave of her arm sent Sally after him. 'Go on, Nurse. You'll get there quicker than me.'

She heard a cracked and broken cry, and was just in time to see Maxfield raise his right hand to his wound. She dashed forward and gripped his wrist. 'Don't touch it! Don't touch, or you'll get infection in!'

He wrenched himself free and backed away from her, but fearful for his wound she pressed forward, trying to take his hand again, until, backed into a corner he slid to the floor and crouched there with his thighs pressed to his chest, shielding his mutilated face from her with his right hand, his broken limb hanging in its sling. She dropped one knee to the floor and squeezed his hunched shoulders. 'Don't touch it, or you'll undo all the good work the surgeon's done,' she insisted.

'Oh, God,' he croaked. He was shaking, and his breath came in gasps. That, and the warmth of him, and the bony feel of his shoulder made her stomach lurch, touching some protective instinct in her. He tried to shake her off, prickly, as if he were angry with her, as if his disfigured face were somehow her fault. She removed her hands but stayed beside him, not knowing what to do or say, until Sister Davies came in and read him the riot act. He got up after that and followed her, this Australian Lieutenant of thirty years with DCM and Bar, as quiet as a lamb, and dashing tears off his cheek with the back of his hand.

'Do you think it'll be all right?' Sally asked, when Sister Davies took her into the office after she'd finished the dressing.

'The wound? Probably. I'm not so sure about him though. I think he got a bigger shock than he'd prepared himself for. Still, now he knows. And he had to see it sometime.'

'It's horrible, isn't it?' Sally shuddered.

Sister Davies gave a disapproving frown. 'None of

that, Nurse. He'll have enough of that to contend with when he gets out of here, with his mutilated face that might say to an employer: "Well then, this is the sacrifice *I* made for my king and country. What about *you*?" People won't want to be reminded, especially people who've stayed at home and done little or nothing. That's if he can get anybody to employ him at all. I don't think many of the young flappers will be flapping round him, either, asking what he did in the war. It's plain to see. He had half his face blasted off.'

Sally's fingers curled round the note he'd thrust into her hand before she'd left him.

'Me too. Gone.'

Are you from Dixie? I said from Dixie!
Where the fields of cotton beckon to me.
I'm glad to see you, tell me how be you
And the friends I'm longing to see?
If you're from Alabama, Tennessee or Caroline,
Any place below the Mason Dixon line,
Then you're from Dixie, hooray for Dixie,
'Cos I'm from Dixie too!

'I used to play the banjo myself, when I had two arms,' Raynor said, tapping his feet in time to the music. 'I fancied myself another Ollie Oakley at one time, and I gave them many a tune in the mess, classical banjo, you know. I've got a J.E. Dallas five string, a really high quality instrument, just about the best you can get.' He tilted his chin in the direction of the gramophone, and said, 'But then I got a passion for ragtime, and I wished I'd got a four string instead. Or rather, I should say I *had* a banjo. It was supposed to have been sent back from France with the rest of my stuff, but it's never arrived. Everything seems to go west there, one way or another. I suppose it hardly matters now.'

The strains of ragtime music usually drifted into the ward during visiting time, when those ambulant officers who had no visitors wandered off into the day room to lounge about and converse with each other, or play a hand of cards. Raynor always joined them, but Maxfield, never; and Sally thought it an awful pity. The laughter and camaraderie might have taken him out of himself a bit and done him the world of good, but he held himself aloof. Why was that, she wondered? Maybe because he couldn't talk, or maybe it was because he was the only Australian on the ward, and didn't feel at home among the British. Maybe he just couldn't be bothered, or the others couldn't be bothered to try to make conversation with him.

She took her seat at the table near the coal fire with Nurse Crump, and sat listening to the low hum of the visitors' conversation whilst folding squares of gauze into dressings, counting them into piles of ten, then putting them into bags and packing them into a steel drum to be sterilized.

'Have you noticed,' Crump said, nudging Sally and glancing towards Maxfield, 'how he's on the qui vive all the time? And he always seems to be watching you. That eye seems to follow you everywhere you go. It reminds me of a bloodshot gooseberry. Maybe he fancies you.'

Inwardly Sally shuddered, and Sister's words flashed into her mind. None of that, Nurse. 'Rubbish. But he got a horrible shock this morning, when he saw the mess his face is in,' she said. 'And just look, he's making the sheets dirty with his newspaper again. I'll go and have a word.'

He watched her approach, and when she stood beside him pointed to the margin of his newspaper. Beside a column rejoicing in the capture of Mont Saint Quentin by Australian troops he'd written, 'I'm hideous'. She read the words out loud, and after a moment or two looked him in the eye. 'You mean your wound's hideous.'

He took the paper from her and underscored the words, then wrote beneath 'same thing'.

'No it's not,' Sally protested. 'Are people only their faces, then? Are we nothing more than what's on the outside, what people can see?'

He shook his head, then nodded it, then shrugged his shoulders and lay back against his pillows, staring at the ceiling, shutting himself off from her. Sally folded the newspaper and put it in his locker, replaced the chair and went back to her task of making gauze dressings, forgetting to say anything about the newsprint on the sheet, but thinking suddenly of her own image in the brasso-smeared door of the oven.

'. . . and he'd written "I'm hideous",' Sally concluded. 'Not "my wound looks hideous – *I'm* hideous".'

Curran and Armstrong were both sitting on her bed, and she on the bedroom chair facing them, all in their nightgowns and sipping a last, steaming cup of cocoa before bed.

'Well he is hideous,' said Curran. 'Sure, you said so yourself.'

'No, I didn't. I said his face was a mess. I didn't say anything about him, himself.'

Armstrong looked thoughtful. 'I catch your drift,' she said, 'but he's right, isn't he? I mean, as far as the world's concerned, "I'm hideous" and "I have a hideous face" come to the selfsame thing.'

'As far as the *world*'s concerned,' Sally conceded, 'I suppose they do. But it's a bad job if the *person* concerned thinks that. The face is something different to the person underneath, surely?'

'Not for long,' Armstrong said, 'and certainly not for women. Whatever people see in your face is what they see in you, and it affects how you see yourself.

For King and Country

My sister, just for one example. My word, people are a lot softer on her than they are on me, and I'm certain it's because she's better looking. I've had to learn to be more of a fighter. Pretty girl, plain girl, ugly girl. Your face decides whether any man'll ever want you for a wife, for a start. Nobody picks an ugly girl.'

'But you're not ugly, Armstrong.'

'I'm not beautiful, either. I'm twenty-two years old, and if I were a beauty, I'd be married by this time. Your face, well, it fixes your life's path. It's your destiny.'

'My face is my fortune, sir, she said,' Sally mused. 'But is it me? If I've got an ugly face, am I ugly all through, like a stick of Blackpool Rock has "Blackpool" all through? But that idea only applies to women, surely? Men aren't despised if they're not handsome, are they?'

'You should know the answer to that one yourself,' said Curran. 'You never stopped going on about David Jones, and his beautiful eyes, and his bonny hair . . . Sorry. I shouldn't have mentioned him, but it's true. You've an eye for a handsome face yourself.'

'Oh,' Sally sighed, remembering her last sight of David. Except it hadn't been David. David was fled, gone to some mysterious place where she couldn't reach him, beyond help, and beyond suffering.

Not Maxfield, though, he wasn't beyond pain. The image of him shrinking from her in the bathroom, shielding his face from her hit her then. And of the two of them, he was the more to be pitied. After a moment she asked: 'Do you ever feel so much a part of them that you are them, that it's all happening to you too?'

'Sure, and what's the girl going on about now?' asked Curran.

'Sympathize with them so much, I mean,' said Sally. 'Do you ever feel what's happening to them as if it's happening to you? You know, sweating when they're having their dressings done, being as scared as they are when they go down to theatre, and glad when they're back, and all right? Things like that?'

'I do not,' said Curran, heaving herself up and moving towards the door. 'How could I carry on with it, if I did? Come on, Armstrong, it's nearly half-past ten. Let's get to bed before Home Sister plunges the corridor into darkness, and we have to grope our way back.'

Armstrong followed her, and, hesitating in the doorway turned to Sally, beaker in hand. 'I know what you mean, and I do feel for them to a degree, but certainly not as if it's happening to me.'

'I do,' said Sally, and watched them shuffle along the corridor for a little way before she closed the door and turned to the mirror to put curling pins into the front of her hair. An ordinary pale little face with its nose a little too large, its two hazel eyes looked out at her, and she suddenly wondered how it would feel to see one of those eyes gone, and half of her face mashed to a bloody pulp. She shuddered, wishing she could stop such imaginings, could stop feeling for some of the men as she did. But their wounds wounded her, she was helpless to prevent it, and her deepest desire was to deliver them from that seventh hell of suffering that held them.

But it was beyond her power, and now Home Sister was calling them to put the lights out. 'Oh, God!' Sally tutted in irritation and took a last look in the mirror, suddenly grateful for her unremarkable features. She turned the light out, and then it struck her. Oh, God. Had Maxfield really said 'Oh, God,' or had she imagined it? She mused on it as she groped to put the last of the pins in and then got into bed, but before she could decide, she was asleep.

Chapter Five

Thank God for a day's respite, though, to get away from that chamber of horrors and be reminded that there was another world, Sally thought, as the train carried her homeward. The wheat harvest had been a good one, the best for sixty years some said and stooks of corn stood in the fields, bathed in the golden light of the late afternoon. In Sally's eyes they bore proud testimony to England's durability, and her heart swelled with pride. It was beautiful, and she would have liked to enjoy the panorama in peace, left to her own thoughts.

It was not to be. A girl whose family had once lived in Annsdale Colliery and was going back there to visit a relative had plonked herself down in the next seat. 'Why, aye, we've done all right since we moved to Newcastle,' she said, in answer to Sally's polite enquiries. 'Me dad's got an overman's job, and now, what with the army taking the hospitals over, me mam can get a bit extra with taking lodgers in. The patients' visitors, you know. They come from miles away, a lot of them.'

'Why, that's all right for your mam, then,' said Sally.

'Oh, aye, they're good company an' all, the visitors, most of 'em. We had an Australian, a month or two ago. I asked him what had happened to his "mate", they call 'em "mate" you know, and he laughed, and said he was on one of the dermatology wards.'

'Oh.' Not wanting to encourage her, Sally said nothing more. But Elinor didn't know when to shut up. Innoculated with a gramophone needle, that lass, and she'd been the same since they were at school together.

'Oh, aye. It sounds as if you know what that means, an' all! I had no idea, until I heard him telling me dad his mate had got one of the filth diseases, and he'd done it on purpose, because he was fed up with the war. He said: "He paid a woman in France five francs to give him it, so he could get away from the firing line." My dad said he was a mad bugger; he'd got something he'd never get rid of, and then the Australian said: "If you'd had a taste of the trenches, mate, you wouldn't be so sure about that. Quite a few blokes took her on. Some of them thought it was a joke!" He said there was a whole workhouse down south had been converted to a VD hospital for Australians, and they'd christened it the "First

Australian Dermatological Hospital". Later on, me dad comes up to me, and he says: "Did you hear that? They'll be laughing on the other side of their faces before they've finished, when they're blind and paralyzed." I said: "Why, no, Dad, I didn't hear anything," and he said: 'Never mind, Elinor, but I'm warning you. You keep away from them soldiers in the workhouse infirmary, because if I find out you've had anything to do with 'em I'll bloody kill you. In fact keep away from the bloody lot. Have nothing to do with any of 'em. They're not clean."'

'Poor things,' Sally murmured.

'You're not going to tell me you feel sorry for them, are you? Why, they've brought it on theirsels, man!'

Sally shrugged. 'I suppose they have, in a way, and in another way, they haven't. They've got no homes to go back to when they get leave, have they, so they're more open to temptation, like.'

'They've got more money than the English lads, an' all,' Elinor said, her eyes hungry. 'They get four times as much. My dad says they've always got money to go out and get beer, and go out and get women an' all, I suppose.'

'There you are then. More money, and miles of ocean away from home. So it's the war that brought it on them, isn't it? It's the war that drove them to it. And we really don't know what it's like over there in

France, Elinor, so we shouldn't judge, should we?'

'Ee, you are a funny one, Sally. And are you going to have to nurse them, like?'

'I expect they'll have the orderlies looking after them.'

'Well, I feel sorry for you if you have to, the dirty things. You should have come to work in the laundry, like me. Then you'd be working under Board of Trade regulations and you'd never have to work on Saturday afternoons or Sundays, and you'd have two evenings a week off as well, instead of working all the hours God sends.'

The table was set, and a small fire was glowing in the range when she got home. 'It's not that cold yet, and what with the coal shortage, I don't use any more than I have to,' her mother said, lifting the stew pot from the oven with a thick cloth and setting it on the table, where its brown glaze gleamed in the light of the fire and gas mantle. 'I managed to get a ham shank from the butcher, though, and I've had it simmering in the oven all day with some split peas. I threw a few carrots in after I'd stripped the meat from the bone, near the end.' She lifted the lid, releasing both steam and a mouthwatering aroma, and began to ladle the broth into bowls. 'Come and get it down you, it'll soon warm you up. I've got some potatoes baking as well, and there's a dab of butter to go on them.'

For King and Country

Sally took off her coat, and sat down. 'By, it smells lovely, Mam. I hadn't realized how hungry I am.'

She ate gratefully, and in silence. After several attempts at conversation, her mother gave up, and when the meal was finished, asked, 'What's the matter, Sally? I've been looking forward to seeing you and hearing your news for days, and you haven't got a word for the cat.'

Sally pushed her plate away. 'Sorry, Mam. Only I've seen some things lately . . .'

'I know,' her mother jumped in. 'I've heard about some of them. Horrible things. I know I've got two lads in France, but you can talk to me about them, you know, if you want to. I'll understand.'

'That's just it, I don't. I don't want to talk about it,' she said. 'I want to get away from it.'

'What did I tell you? I said nursing would never be any good to you. You've never been strong . . .'

'It's not nursing that's supposed to be any good to me, Mam,' Sally cut in, 'it's me that's supposed to be some good to nursing.'

The kitchen was chilly in spite of the fire. She rose abruptly from the table and went upstairs to find her old cardigan – the warm, comforting grey one, darned at the elbows and fraying at the cuffs, that she only ever wore in the house because, although she couldn't bear to part with it, really it was only fit for the rag bag. Her room was dark and smelled of polish when she went in to fumble in the drawer for it. She found it at last and hugged it tightly to her for a moment as if it were an old friend, then slipped it on and went downstairs to help her mother with the washing up.

Poor mother. Restless, snappy and unable to settle to anything, Sally had spoiled her evening for her, and had wanted nothing but to be out, and alone.

The Leazes next to the hospital in Newcastle was a good place for a stroll, and Jesmond Dene was even lovelier, and worth the half hour walk it took to get there from the hospital, but for Sally, neither could hold a candle to Old Annsdale. The nights were drawing in, and although it was only eight o'clock, the light was fading. With no idea in her mind other than to get away from the house and her mother's probing and to breathe clean country air, Sally found herself wandering along the lane to Annsdale Colliery, glad to be away from the stink of pus and carbolic, the sight of wounds that took months to heal, and the constant demands for Nurse to do this, and that, and something else, and the knowledge that however hard Nurse worked she would never, could never, get through all the tasks allotted to her. But somehow, she did.

Here, in this lonely, darkening place she was free, with nothing but the rustling of the wind in the trees and the occasional hoot of an owl for company, such sounds as must have been heard in the world from the beginning of time. She abandoned herself to them and to the sweet scent of the good earth, the mother and end of us all. The winding gear of the colliery village stood black and silent against a red sky, and by the time she reached its terraced rows of tiny cottages her restlessness was gone, replaced by a deep calm.

There was a light on in Mrs Burdett's house, and someone was just drawing the curtains. In one fluid movement and without a second thought Sally walked through the gate and closed it behind her. The door was opened by a grey, gnarled old man she'd never seen before.

A little surprised, Sally asked, 'Is Mrs Burdett in?'

In unfamiliar accents, he bade her: 'Coom in, mi duck. You'm here at the right time. Kettle's nearly boiled,' and led her into the kitchen, where sat another stranger. A gaunt lady with hollow eyes and an old, sagging face smiled and got up to greet her, the ample folds of her too large dress held close with a belt. Sally gave them a brief smile. 'I came to have five minutes with Mrs Burdett. I didn't realize she had visitors.'

The woman's hand flew to the white roots of her brown hair and her eyes darted to the oval, mahogany framed mirror that hung over the mantelpiece. 'Don't you recognize me, Sally?'

Sally sank slowly down onto the sofa. 'Oh, Mrs

Burdett, I wouldn't have known you. You've lost so much weight!'

'It's not good for your appetite, hinny, losing all your sons.'

'Oh. Oh, dear,' was all Sally could say.

'I'll make the tea,' the old man volunteered, and shuffled towards the kettle. Sally gave Mrs Burdett a questioning look.

'My father,' she said, with the ghost of a smile. 'He's a widower. Poor old codger, he's come all the way from Staffordshire. He thinks I need looking after.'

'Oh, Mrs Burdett!'

'She'm been dwine since the first one went west, and now they'm all gone, she'm pining away,' her father said. 'You'm doing no good here, Bess. With the men gone, they'll throw you out of the house for sure, once the war's over.'

'And when's that going to be, Dad?'

'Sooner than you think. We've got the Germans properly on the run now. They'll be bellocking for mercy afore long.'

Mrs Burdett gave a mirthless smile. 'I've heard that one before,' she murmured, and Sally, who had hardly understood a word her father had said, looked at her for an explanation.

'He wants to take me back to Staffordshire to live with him. He's on his own, as well.'

'Ah,' said Sally.

For King and Country

'You talk some sense into her,' came the father's voice. 'She'll do better among her own people where she grew up, instead of biding among strangers, worriting herself away on her own.'

'I've lived here over twenty-five year, and he still talks about me being among strangers,' Mrs Burdett murmured. 'And I'm not moving.'

Her father brought in the tea. 'And I'm not such an old fool I can't guess why,' he said. 'You'm all alike, you women; clinging on, when there isn't a hope in hell.'

Mrs Burdett's nostrils reddened and her face fell as she looked towards the dresser where a group of photographs stood, all of sturdy, handsome young men. 'Oh, my poor lads, my bonny, bonny lads. There must have been a mistake. There must be one of them left! There must be one.'

She whispered it, and in her lustreless eyes was something near, Sally thought, to the edge. Not quite sane. Her father glanced at her and saw it too, and a shadow passed over his face. With no words of comfort for either of them, Sally could only repeat: 'Oh, Mrs Burdett!'

She stayed over an hour, listening intently to the old man's tales of the family and trying to understand him. Mrs Burdett hardly spoke and Sally said little enough herself, but being there seemed to be enough to show sympathy, to the father at least.

The wind had freshened and there was a thin crescent moon when they opened the door.

'Yow'll never find your way. It's nearly pitch black,' the father said, with an anxious glance at his daughter. 'I'll get the hurricane lamp and walk with you.'

'No,' Sally said. 'I know the road like the back of my hand. I could walk it blindfold.'

But he insisted on lending her the lamp, at least. To save argument she took it, and rather than give him the chance to change his mind again and come with her she walked quickly away, into the darkness and the cool air that caressed her cheeks like a lover.

What a strange turn her life might have taken on the night of Lizzie's wedding. If she'd actually believed he was serious she might have given Will a lot more encouragement. If he'd really liked her as much as everybody seemed to think she might even have ended up married to him. Then she'd have been another Mrs Burdett, in widow's weeds and probably living in the same house as his mother, related to the old man who'd given her the lamp, maybe even with a bairn clinging to her skirts.

If, if, if. But fate takes strange twists and turns, and had decreed otherwise. It seemed to be part of the divine plan that she should nurse, and for all its trials she was beginning to be happy in nursing, and would no doubt be nursing for the rest of her life, or until she was too old.

She looked up to the vastness of the sky and watched a cloud drift over the moon, obscuring its faint glow, and was glad of the lamp to light her three miles of mystical solitude. Odd that she should feel such transcendent calm after poor David's death and after visiting a mother almost driven to madness by the loss of her sons. But no matter how deep they are or how much they consume us, what are our human troubles after all, measured against the ageless earth, the boundless sky, the stars, the eternal, immortal, imperishable universe? What do they signify, compared to that?

Her mother was frantic when she got in, but Sally cut through her protests. 'Mother, I've just understood something,' she said. 'We can't be beaten. I can't tell you how I know it, but I do. In the end, we'll win through.'

Back on duty early the following morning, she went straight into the sluice to read the Esbach's albumino-meters. There were six of them. It was the night nurse's job to set them up, to fill up each glass tube with the patient's urine to the first mark, top up with reagent to the second mark, mix the two by inverting the tube twelve times, seal it with a bung and set it aside for twenty-four hours. Now the albumin, the protein that had leaked from the patients' kidneys had settled in the bottom of the tubes as a white sediment, very plain to see. Her mind entirely on the task, Sally carefully took readings from the scales on the sides of the tubes and recorded them just as carefully in the book. The young captain with the belly wound who'd had his operation on her day off had a high reading, and Lieutenant Raynor's was still quite high as well. Dr Campbell would be coming directly after breakfast to see them, and he'd want to know.

She went straight to the captain's bedside, and Maxfield was at her elbow, thrusting his notepad under her nose.

'Where've you been?' the uneven handwriting read like an accusation, and the look he gave her was the same.

'I had a day off,' she shrugged, picking up the captain's chart to record his result.

His hand shaking, Maxfield scribbled, 'You didn't tell me.'

She laughed, and after replacing the chart turned to face him. 'I didn't realize I had to get your permission.'

It sounded more mocking than she'd intended, but there was no time to bother about it now. She ignored his frown and passed on to fill in the rest of the charts. Crump had gone off duty with the 'flu, so although they had another probationer, Sally had too much to do to smooth Maxfield's ruffled feathers, or wait for him to compose his dispatches. She had to get a move on; Sister would soon be giving the report, and she'd want the results before the doctor's round. And there were breakfasts to give out, and beds to make, and temperatures and medicines to do, patients to be discharged and new ones admitted, and somebody, probably her, would have to go down to the porter's lodge to get the new admissions' notes. Always too much to do, and never enough time. She was making progress, though – she was doing less ward cleaning and Sister was trusting her with more and more real nursing.

Maxfield shuffled off back to his bed, looking very disgruntled. Oh, dear, she really had offended him. Never mind, she'd be as pleasant as she could next time she saw him, and he'd get over it.

Before he left the ward that morning, Dr Campbell took a moment to hold his own tutorial, in imitation of the chief. 'Very well, Sister,' he challenged. 'Let's see whether your probationers bring their critical faculties to work with them. How serious is it, this albuminurea?' He nodded towards the man with the belly wound, and then rounded on Sally.

She answered him shyly. 'I don't know, doctor.'

He looked at Sister, and grimaced. 'I told you so. They leave their brains in the nurses' home.'

Sally spoke up. 'I only know that if it's due to fever, it nearly always disappears when the fever subsides, and if that's the case, it's not serious.'

'Then why did you say you didn't know?'

'Because I don't know what's causing the captain's albuminurea, doctor. It might be fever, or it might be something I don't know about. So I don't know enough to say how serious it is.'

Dr Campbell raised his eyebrows. 'Good! A nurse with a capacity for rational thought!'

Sister gave him a sour look. 'She wouldn't last long on my ward if she hadn't.'

'That's not all she has,' Dunkley cut in, smiling sweetly. 'She seems to have found an admirer in our Australian hero. He's forever following her about, writing her little *billets doux*, isn't he, Nurse Wilde?'

'Really?' Dr Campbell said, but Dunkley's face fell when interest sparked in his eyes. 'Really?' he repeated, his eyebrows moving up another notch and his mouth turning up at the corners.

Sister Davies' expression soured further. 'We won't keep Dr Campbell any longer,' she said, as the trolley came rattling onto the ward with the morning beverages. 'He's got plenty to do, and so have we. Dunkley, you can do the medicine round, and then admit the new patients.' To another probationer: 'You, nurse, give the drinks out, and help the patients who can't manage. Nurse Wilde, we're late with the

118

temperatures Get them done before the patients get their drinks, and when you've finished, I want a private word with you in my office.'

That sounded ominous. Better not give Sister any more reason for vexation than she already had, thought Sally, moving smartly off in obedience to the command. But really, she herself was the one who ought to be vexed, what with Dr Campbell's mischief making, and Dunkley's spite. And she suspected he knew exactly what he was doing, deliberately using her to make Dunkley jealous. And then there was Maxfield, always at her elbow, getting under her feet, wanting to know things about her that were really none of his business. It was his fault she was being hauled into the office, and she'd be lucky if she didn't get sent to Matron.

She got to Maxfield's bed and shook down his thermometer, but before she could put it under his arm there he was again, with his shifty, penetrating green eye and another one of his 'little *billets doux*' – 'Did you have a nice day off? What did you do?'

'Nothing. I stayed in and talked to my mother,' she answered him.

The whole ward seemed to be watching them when up popped, 'When are you having another day off?'

She lowered her voice. 'Not for a month. But why don't you speak? I know you can.'

'I can't,' he mouthed, and shook his head.

She shrugged. No point in arguing; she might as well let him have it his own way.

Was it really only the day before yesterday when she'd walked to Annsdale Colliery and back, and felt so tranquil? It felt like a million years ago – a million bloody years ago.

But she'd defy anybody to try feeling tranquil on Ward 7a.

'Holy Mother o' God! And falling over himself to talk to you, and him an officer, an' all!' Curran said with feeling, as they sat together in the dining room, waiting for the maids to serve them lunch.

'Hardly that,' said Sally. 'He can't talk, remember, or he says he can't. His voice went, something to do with his nerves, they think. And I wouldn't mind, but it's always me he gives his notes to, and the whole ward's beginning to make comments. I wish he'd pick on somebody else.'

This brought a fresh spurt of sympathy from Curran. 'Sure, and the poor man must feel awful lonely, and him not able to utter a word.'

Armstrong gave a sardonic smile. 'Probably Curran's worst nightmare, that. Not being able to utter a word.'

'Sure, and could anything be worse for cutting you off from other people entirely than not being able to utter a word!' Curran exclaimed. 'The poor soul never gets any visitors, and none of the other officers talk to him.'

'Not surprising, if he can't talk back,' said Sally. 'And I've got my doubts about that. He's not very sociable anyway; even if he can't talk, he could join them for a drink in the day room. They've asked him plenty of times, but he won't. And he's . . .'

'What?'

So horribly mutilated was what she'd been going to say, but it seemed so awful to give that as a reason for not wanting to befriend a man that she stopped herself just in time. And anyway, none of the officers had seen his face. All they ever saw was bandages.

'He's the one with the bad facial injury, isn't he? The one that made you sick?' said Armstrong, looking very thoughtful.

Sally nodded.

'My mother's cousin's boy had his jaw taken off by a lump of shrapnel, well before the Somme. They got him healed all right, and sent him to a convalescent hospital. He hadn't been there a week before he drowned himself. It's awful the way it takes people, disfigurement.'

They stared at her, appalled. 'You never told us that,' said Sally.

'I try not to think about it. They live miles away, in Manchester. We hardly ever see them. But I should think your Lieutenant Maxfield's probably feeling pretty low. He's probably picked on you because you've got that sort of sympathetic face, Wilde – "like patience on a monument".' Armstrong seemed to be only half in jest, and after a pause, added, 'When you get a minute, why don't you talk to him properly? Ask him what he wants to know, and tell him. Get to the bottom of whatever it is that's bothering him, let him get it all out of his system and then tell him straight, well, maybe not that he's getting on your nerves, but that he'll end up getting you the sack if he carries on. If he's got a shred of decency, he'll leave you alone after that.'

Sally had just changed the saline drip of the captain with the belly wound and was hanging the fresh bottle on the stand when, out of the corner of her eye, she saw Maxfield padding across towards Raynor with the feeding cup.

Sister Davies nodded approval. 'Well done, Wilde. We'll make a nurse of you yet.'

'Thanks, Sister.' Sally put the empty saline bottle on her tray and picked it up to follow Sister to the treatment room. Maxfield was playing nursemaid now, holding the spout to Raynor's lips, helping him to drink his afternoon tea, and Raynor was making no objection. It made quite a touching scene.

She wasn't quite so touched on her return to the

ward though, when after all the patients had finished their drinks and she was collecting the cups, Maxfield started following her again.

'What do you call your village?' his note read.

Conscious of Dunkley's eyes on her, she said: 'What makes you think I live in a village?'

Knox exploded. 'Confound the fellow, it's painful to watch! Can't he see she doesn't want him bothewing her?' He got out of bed, tapped Maxfield on the shoulder, and took him aside.

Sally burned with embarrassment. As sorry as she felt for Maxfield she didn't want him hounding her, and especially not so obviously that everybody noticed. She couldn't help feeling grateful to Knox, much as she disliked him.

A couple of days later, as Maxfield was holding the feeding cup to his lips, Raynor suddenly started coughing, spluttering cocoa everywhere, on himself and his newly changed sheets. Eyes watering and face red he pushed Maxfield's hand away, spilling more of it.

What a mess. Maxfield looked at Sally in alarm, and she hastened to reassure him. 'Never mind, you were only trying to help. I'll go and get some clean sheets.'

Judging by that odd smile on his face, Raynor must have thought the incident amusing, she thought, as she hurried up the ward to get clean linen. Maxfield strode alongside her and tried to grip her arm. She evaded him, and almost ran to the linen room.

He was waiting by Raynor's bed when she got back with the linen, complete with his notebook.

'For the love of God,' she muttered under her breath, borrowing a phrase of Curran's as she tried to sidestep him, 'you really will end up getting me the sack, won't you?' But he stood determinedly in front of her, holding it right in front of her eyes.

'TETANUS!' she read.

As they moved him into the remaining empty single room, Sally saw all too clearly that there was no mirth in Raynor's smile; his helpless grinning was caused by a stiffness of his facial muscles beyond his control. Trismus, they called it, and she raked her memory to recall the lecture they'd had on tetanus. Ah, yes, that was it, 'the involuntary spasm of the masseter muscles', and 'risus sardonicus' was the name of that awful grin it caused. They heaved the bed back against the wall as gently as they could, and pulled the blinds. Maxfield had followed them, pushing Raynor's locker with his good arm, and now stood in the doorway with it. Sally took it from him, and placed it against the bed.

A move from the ward to a single room was always a bad omen for a patient, and poor David Jones had drawn his last breath in this one. Sally remembered how they'd waited and waited for him to take another, and gave an involuntary shudder.

Sister nodded brief thanks to Maxfield and closed the door, then murmured to Sally: 'No bright light, and keep him as quiet as you can. This would happen just now, wouldn't it, when we're a nurse short, and not a spare pair of hands in the hospital. But he can't be left alone. I'm sorry, but that's your afternoon off gone west, Nurse. You'll be spending it in here with the first case of tetanus we've had for months. Anyway, well done for spotting it.'

Oh dear, oh dear, and after hearing all the chief's exhortations about the importance of observation, after hearing them repeated by every sister and senior nurse on every ward she'd worked on, had she now to admit the truth – that she had seen nothing beyond a grin, and the credit for 'spotting' anything more sinister belonged to a patient? It was tempting not to; Maxfield couldn't tell, after all. But she couldn't help it; the truth would out.

'It wasn't me, Sister. It was Lieutenant Maxfield.'

Even in the gloom Sally could see the glow of approval die in Sister's eyes. 'Oh, well,' she said, and left the room, closing the door quietly behind her.

So much for honesty, Sally thought, curling her fingers around Raynor's wrist and gently pressing their tips along his radial artery. His pulse was rapid, and he had broken out into a sweat. She found his flannel and wrung it out in cool water at the sink, to mop his fevered brow. She had just put the cloth away when the junior houseman arrived, the cocksure one who knew everything. He took a wooden spatula from the pocket of his white coat.

'Hello, old fellow, just open wide,' he said in jocular tones to Raynor, who was in no position to do anything of the sort. No matter, the houseman bent over him and inserted the spatula right to the back of his throat. His teeth promptly clamped down on it, much to the delight of the houseman. 'There you are, Nurse! The bite reflex, instead of the gag reflex – it confirms the diagnosis, of course. No samples to the lab needed here. I'll just give him a sedative, and then a test dose of horse serum, and we'll see how he reacts to that, what?'

Chapter Six

'I could swear on a stack of bibles it was him,' said the night nurse, a few days later. She was standing by Maxfield's empty bed, having collected almost all the washing bowls in by the time Sally stepped onto the ward. 'In the middle of the night, and he shouted it: "Muddy!" Hasn't spoken a word since he woke up, though.'

Sally felt a pang of sympathy. 'Muddy? Why, France is famous for mud, I suppose. I've heard tell of men drowning in it.' Maxfield, poor man, was probably engulfed in it in his nightmares. If only he could have some visitors, people from his own regiment, or even his own country to take an interest in and write his notes to, it might stop him brooding and getting wound up, take his mind off things for a bit and help him get over his nerves. It might even stop this obsession he seemed to have with her. Maybe she should act on Armstrong's advice.

'Go in and see Lieutenant Raynor, will you?' the

night nurse said. 'I've been with him as much as I could, but he's been on his own for nearly an hour now.'

But Lieutenant Raynor was not on his own. Maxfield was at the door of his room, beckoning to her, and her sympathy was transformed into irritation at the sight of him. But when she entered the room she saw Raynor's lips drawn back in a bizarre grimace, his eyes wild and wide. He struggled to speak through clenched teeth, to tell her what was obvious. He was in pain. He couldn't swallow and his mouth, his throat, and his arms were going into terrifying spasms. Sally fled, to fetch Sister.

Her alarms made little impression. 'I've seen him. The chief will be here in a few minutes to do his round. You go and stay with him, and send Lieutenant Maxfield back into the ward. Breakfasts will be up soon. Fetch me if he gets any worse,' Sister said.

Deflated and more than a little apprehensive, Sally returned to Raynor's room. 'Sister says you have to go back onto the ward,' she said, and suddenly had a bright idea. Why on earth hadn't she thought of it before? 'You know, Lieutenant Maxfield, I've heard there are a few Australians in the other infirmary,' she said. 'Maybe there are one or two officers who could get permission to come and visit you, or you could go to see them. Shall I ask about it?'

Maxfield's reaction was the opposite of what she

expected. He tensed. His lips turned down in a grimace of disdain and repulsion and he shook his head.

'All right,' Sally shrugged, a mite offended. 'I won't mention it, then.'

He must have heard what they were really suffering from, those patients in the so-called dermatology wards, and thought himself too good for them. He was probably particular about what sort of person he mixed with. She wondered why that should surprise her in an Australian, but it did.

'What will give this patient the best chance of recovery?' the chief demanded, turning to the shyest houseman. 'To perform a tracheostomy now, or to delay it until his breathing becomes *really* difficult?'

'To do it now, sir.'

Doctor Know-All was craning forward, his every feature screaming: 'Me, sir!'

The chief ignored him, his eyes fixed on his more reticent pupil. 'Will you elaborate?'

'Because delay makes complications more likely, mostly because of aspiration of secretions.'

His voice was so low that the chief had to lean towards him to hear. 'Leading to?' he prompted.

'Bronchopneumonia, sir?'

'Quite. It's affecting his larynx,' the chief said. 'You'd better do it, Campbell. Then he'll need careful nursing, for two weeks at least. I'm sorry to put such a burden on you when you're so short-staffed, Sister, but we really have no alternative.' He turned to Campbell. 'Better do it here – and disturb him as little as possible.'

'Get everything ready, Nurse Dunkley,' Sister said. 'You can assist.'

Lieutenant Raynor was stretched out with a sandbag under his shoulders and neck, fully conscious after the local anaesthetic, and struggling to breathe.

'Odd he never made any complaint,' said Dr Campbell, fingering the portion of his neck not covered by sterile cotton drapes. 'He must have had some inkling, some stiffness around the site of his injury, possibly, or his arms, or his jaw, some aching. Something.'

Sally had been sent into Raynor's room, to stand by Nurse Dunkley and watch the procedure. 'But he . . .' she began, and then broke off, not daring to continue, not daring to admit, guilty, guilty nurse, that he had complained, of his jaw, his back and his legs, and he'd had a bit of a temperature, and she should have reported it, because she ought to have known he wouldn't do it himself.

Dr Campbell was muttering to himself, too absorbed in his task to take any notice. 'Well, at least we have one nurse on the ward capable of making an intelligent observation,' he murmured. 'Sister sounded very impressed when she telephoned me – as was I, when you turned out to be right. Well done, Nurse Wilde.'

Dunkley gave a saccharine smile. 'Pity we haven't got a doctor to match her,' she murmured.

'Hmm,' Campbell said, and conversation ceased.

Sister obviously hadn't set him straight, but now was certainly not the time, Sally thought, not while he had a scalpel at the lieutenant's throat. She wasn't going to say anything to Dunkley, either, or that madam would take pleasure in shattering everybody's illusions about her, and make her look even more of an imbecile than she really was.

The scalpel was laid aside, and Dr Campbell inserted a dilator, and then pushed the silver tracheostomy tube into the carefully made incision. They heard an inrush of air, and saw their patient relax, no longer having to fight for every breath.

Dr Campbell secured the tube with tapes. 'Ten minutes, start to finish,' he told Raynor. 'Now,' he picked up a Rhyle's tube, lubricated the end with liquid paraffin, and eased it as gently as possible into Raynor's left nostril, 'swallow if you can, and keep swallowing. We don't want to cure you of tetanus, to kill you of starvation. You nurses had better tube feed him with egg and milk mixture, two hourly to start with, until he can eat. That should give him something to fight with.'

But wasn't there a ninety per cent mortality with tetanus, Sally wondered, as she watched Dr Campbell finish the task. He left Dunkley to tape the tube to Lieutenant Raynor's nose and cheek.

'He will be all right, won't he?' Sally pleaded for reassurance.

Dr Campbell shrugged, raised his voice for Raynor to hear, and stressing the words, said: 'The longer the incubation period, the better the outlook, all other things being equal. He'll certainly recover with good nursing, and that seems to be in abundance on Ward 7a. Wouldn't you agree, Staff Nurse?'

But Dunkley missed this oblique invitation to instil a healing confidence into Raynor. 'Hardly,' she said, 'since so many nurses have gone off to France and the military hospitals. And now, just to put the tin hat on it, we've got one of our probationers off.'

'Ah, but not your best one! Nurse Wilde must be worth two of any other nurses. Nurse Wilde came to us highly recommended by her last employer, did you know that?'

'Yes. Too good to be true, isn't she?' said Dunkley.

'Did you know that, Lieutenant Raynor?' Dr Campbell continued. ' No, don't talk yet, but after a while, when you're up to it, just put your finger over that hole I made above your collar bone, and try it. You might manage all right.'

'Thank you,' Raynor attempted to say, and

promptly went into convulsions, painful to watch.

Sally glanced anxiously towards Dr Campbell. 'We won't start worrying yet,' he assured her. 'There's no involvement below the waist. In bad cases the whole body bends right back like a bow, until the heels almost hit the back of the head. That really is a spasm.'

Raynor's convulsions subsided, and Dunkley picked up the instrument tray. Dr Campbell gazed at Sally for a moment or two with a quizzical expression in his eyes, and then with voice lowered asked Dunkley: 'Did I mention that Nurse Wilde's last employer happens to be a relative of mine, in Darlington? See how intently she's listening to us, Staff, and with such a demure tilt of her head, one might almost believe butter wouldn't melt in her mouth. Charming, isn't it?'

'Oh, charming,' Dunkley agreed, through gritted teeth.

What was he getting at, Sally wondered? If Dr Lowery was his relative, he must know her employment there had ended in disaster. And whatever the recommendation had been as to her nursing skills, her most recent performance showed it was hardly deserved. Except for her belated realization that whatever suited his wife didn't suit Dr Lowery, she hadn't developed much skill in observation in Darlington, and she could have kicked herself to Darlington and back for her lack of observation in

Raynor's case. Still, she wasn't going to announce her failure to these two. If Sister had wanted them to know, she'd have told them.

The thought occurred: perhaps she had told them, and now they were merely amusing themselves at her expense. 'One might *almost* believe butter wouldn't melt . . .' She'd have given anything to know exactly what Dr Campbell had been told about her to give rise to a remark like that. Whatever it was, he was certainly enjoying himself with it – and was he baiting Dunkley, or was she in on the joke as well?

He opened the door and stood aside for Dunkley to pass, giving Sally a lingering glance before he followed her. A plague and downfall of susceptible women, that man. Sally would certainly be on her guard against him, and would have been even without the warning Sister had given her during that private interview in the office.

'You're a better nurse than I am, Lieutenant Maxfield,' Sally joked a week later when she went into Raynor's room and found him there. And in Lieutenant Raynor's case, it was true. Maxfield's devotion to the cause of his recovery was unflagging. Whenever he was left unattended for a moment Maxfield was in his room, silently ministering to him or simply being there. He had stopped following Sally about, stopped writing her notes, and the wariness in that eye which had always seemed to be darting in her direction was gone. In its place was a closed off look which had begun to disturb her, because it seemed to her that it was accompanied by a strange sort of flatness in him. She was haunted by the idea of him ending like Armstrong's relation, and thought, thank God for Raynor. Raynor's illness seemed to take his mind off himself. Without Raynor to tend he might have sunk into despair.

She placed her tray carefully on the bed table, draped a clean cover around Raynor's throat, and announced, 'I've come to clean your tube, Lieutenant.' Let loose on it for the very first time without either Sister or Nurse Dunkley looking over her shoulder, she crossed to the sink to wash her hands until they were surgically clean and dry them on the freshly laundered towel. Maxfield went to the door, and as he put his hand on the knob she had a sudden impulse to do as Armstrong had suggested, and try to get to the bottom of his queer obsession with her. 'You don't have to go, Lieutenant Maxfield,' she said, glancing at Raynor, 'as long as Lieutenant Raynor doesn't mind you staying.'

Raynor indicated that he didn't mind. Conscious of Maxfield's eye on her, Sally slid the smaller, inner tracheostomy tube out of the larger one and carefully cleaned off the secretions encrusting it. 'You once showed an interest in the village I'm from, Lieutenant

Maxfield,' she said. 'Well, I'll tell you. It's nothing out of the ordinary, but I love it. It's an ordinary village with a bonny church and a market square with houses around it and a few little streets behind, a blacksmith's, and a few shops, a pub, and an old coaching inn not far off that's kept by my sister and her husband. The houses are all made of stone, and it's all beautiful and clean, and there are quite a few farms nearby. It's called Old Annsdale. You might have heard of the Annsdale Hunt? But I don't suppose it's very likely, you being from Australia. Maybe Lieutenant Raynor has, though. It's quite famous.'

Lieutenant Raynor put a finger over his tra-cheostomy, to force air through his larynx and enable him to gasp a 'Yes!'

'Aye, well,' Sally went on, 'there's a pit village not far off called Annsdale Colliery, and that's not so clean and not so beautiful either, but I love that place an' all, because that's where I was brought up until me dad got killed. He was a pitman. My brothers are both pitmen, but they're in France now. Me sisters are all married, the eldest to the landlord of the inn I told you about, the middle one's husband works in the pit, and the youngest but me got married to a captain in the Army a couple of year ago. I'm the youngest of the family, plain and ordinary, and that's all there is to know about me. It's not much.'

Maxfield listened intently, tugging at his moustache,

not interrupting her once and at the end of it looking at her as if willing her to tell him more. But there was no more. She replaced the clean tube, overjoyed that she'd managed the job without triggering any spasms. She looked at Raynor with her bright, nursey smile, her eyes shining in triumph. 'There, that wasn't so bad, was it?' she said, removing the cloth and dropping it on the tray with the rest of her equipment.

Maxfield was using Raynor's notepaper to scribble her another message. Well, she'd asked for it; she'd set the thing in motion, and now she'd have to see it through to the end. She took it from him, and read:

'You look, but you don't see!'

What did he mean? He must be talking about Raynor's tetanus. She looked him straight in the eye, her pleasure in a job well done dashed to the floor. 'Do you think I don't know that?' she said.

'Wait, wait,' his lips formed, but she wouldn't wait. Instead, she collected her tray and her dignity, opened the door and quietly left the room.

Maxfield had made himself so useful in the ward whilst nursing time was being devoured by Lieutenant Raynor that it would have been hard to bear any grudges, even if Sally had wanted to. With hardly a week passing without discharges or a death, and then more admissions and operations, the ward was rarely still, and they were only too glad of his help. Whilst

Sally flew about doing the more exalted tasks Sister now entrusted her with, she often saw Maxfield helping the orderly and the junior probationer giving out food and drinks, collecting crockery and cutlery after meals, and generally fetching and carrying for the other patients, ignoring Knox's baleful eye and his barbed comments about 'TGs behaving like charwomen'. To the mild disapproval of a couple of the officers and the great amusement of the rest, Maxfield occasionally indulged in Chaplinesque mimicry of him behind his back, and though Knox suspected he was being made fun of, he never managed to catch him at it. Sally sometimes watched Maxfield, thinking he wasn't like an officer at all, he so put her in mind of some of the lads she'd gone to school with, but if he caught her watching he ceased his antics and looked away, never allowing his gaze to rest on her for long, these days.

'Matron's halfway round the next ward. Get a move on,' Sister barked, 'And you'll have to manage without me. There's work in the office got to be done.'

Nearly here already! It wouldn't be long until she was on top of them. At least Crump was back on duty, the beds were made, and the observations and the medicine round done, but what a disgrace the ward looked, with the bathing trolley in the middle of it and men and their belongings all lying about any old how. They worked feverishly, tidying patients and sitting them up straight, making the half dead look hale and hearty, plumping pillows and making sure they were placed with the openings away from the ward door, smoothing and straightening top sheets, throwing books and magazines and newspapers and slippers into lockers, hanging up dressing gowns, lining screens and trolleys up like soldiers on parade, and ruthlessly removing from its vase any flower that had dared to wilt since they came on duty. Maxfield rushed about among them, half in mockery, half in earnest.

'Get back into bed, Lieutenant Maxfield!' Dunkley ordered. 'Matron will be here any minute!'

He turned a deaf ear and carried on with his tidying, snatching a vomit bowl off a locker top and displaying it's contents to Sally as he passed her on his way to the sluice – not enough spit to cover a six-pence. She stared after him anxiously. Sister might choose to turn a blind eye to Maxfield's appointing himself VAD nurse cum ward maid, but Matron would certainly have something to say about it. 'For goodness' sake!' she hissed, when he emerged from the sluice.

They heard Matron's voice in the corridor, and as Sally hurried with the others to greet that all-powerful figure appearing at the top of the ward she saw him hop into bed.

'Sister asked me . . .' Dunkley said.

Matron looked her straight in the eye. 'You're both excused, Nurse. I want to see how the probationers are progressing.'

Oh, dear, thought Sally, please, not me!

But she had no choice. Matron was already walking into Lieutenant Raynor's room, bidding him good afternoon, and looking inquiringly at Sally, waiting for the report.

'Lieutenant Raynor, Matron. He had an amputation of his right arm. His left is fractured, but healing slowly. He was diagnosed with tetanus, and had a tracheostomy because of breathing problems. It's twelve days since his first spasm. They were quite severe, but he's had none at all for the past twenty-four hours. He's lost a lot of weight, but he'll be getting his tubes out today, and Doctor says he'll be able to take a light diet.'

Matron gave her an approving smile, and had a few words with Raynor before passing on to the other patients. Sally walked deferentially behind, desperately trying to recall each patient's diagnosis and treatment, and usually succeeding. Nurse Crump was not much help, not having progressed much beyond cleaning and basic work.

Major Knox was an easy one to remember. 'Gunshot wounds to the chest, Matron, and a badly fractured shoulder. The wounds are clean and he was for discharge, but he had blood stained sputum again yesterday, so he's being kept in.'

She excelled with Maxfield. 'His facial wound's healing, but his arm seems to be inflamed; Doctor thinks there may be more sequestrum. He might have to go to theatre again for another exploration and debridement.'

There, that should show she wasn't a complete dunce. Matron seemed impressed, and by the time they got back to the top of the ward Sally had forgotten her nervousness and had begun to enjoy herself. She was almost sorry when the round ended.

'Very satisfactory, Nurse Wilde,' Matron said. 'You demonstrate something many nurses seem to lack, a keen interest in the progress of your cases. Well done.'

Sally was elated. Matron was every inch a lady, so nice to all the patients, so polite, so fair and so encouraging, she thought, her smile stretching from ear to ear as she watched her cut Dunkley dead on her way out of the ward.

September slid into October, and the shutters closed out the darkness beyond the long sash windows. The few visitors were gone, and apart from the crackling of the fire the ward had lapsed into a peaceful, cosy silence.

'These are the jobs you want when your legs and

back ache, and you can hardly keep your eyes open,' Sally said as she and Nurse Crump sat at the table in the middle of the ward, tearing the blue paper off rolls of gauze. Her legs felt heavy and every bit of energy was drained out of her, so that she was glad to settle to the easy task of making swabs until it was time to go off duty.

'It'll not last long, you watch,' said Crump. 'As soon as we get settled, some awkward bugger'll want a bedpan or something.'

Crump's was a voice that carried, and Sally's eyes widened in warning. 'Shush,' she hissed, casting anxious glances at the patients, hoping they hadn't heard. One or two evidently had and were grinning from ear to ear, including Raynor, who'd been evicted from his private room after having his tracheostomy tube removed. Major Knox wouldn't find it so amusing though, thought Sally, turning round to check on him. He was snoozing on his bed with his newspaper on his chest, and thank the good Lord for that, or there would have been trouble.

'Be careful,' she murmured unrolling the gauze along the table and then taking the scissors to cut it into squares. 'Somebody might report you for swearing.'

Crump took one of the squares. 'I know,' she whispered, 'it came out before I had time to think.'

She folded the gauze, raw edges to the middle, and then in half. 'Is that all right?'

'Aye, it is. Try to speed up a bit though. Let's get as many done as we can, before we go off.' She gave the ghost of a smile, 'And remember to be a bit more polite. You're on the officers' ward now.'

'Nurse, nurse,' came Raynor's voice, which might have been plaintive had he been able to wipe the grin off his face, 'My water jug's empty, I've dropped my magazine on the floor, and it's time I had my glass of port. Chief's orders.'

Crump rolled her eyes in a way that asked, 'What did I tell you?'

Sally chuckled, pleased to see that Raynor was well enough to enjoy making a nuisance of himself. He was painfully thin, though. 'Away and get them for him then,' she urged.

Crump scraped her chair back and stood up, but she was too late. Maxfield was out of bed, retrieving the magazine. He lifted the water jug and walked towards them with it, not stopping to give it to Crump as Sally had anticipated, but going on up the ward.

'Lieutenant Maxfield, you're not supposed to go into the kitchen. You'll get wrong from Sister!' she called, but couldn't drag herself up to chase after him.

Crump shrugged, and sat down again. 'She probably won't see him. Let him fetch it if he wants. Save my legs.'

'He still needs his port,' Sally said, but Crump appeared not to have heard. So, neither willing to move, they cut and folded their squares until Maxfield came down the ward with the full water jug. He placed it on top of Raynor's locker, and then found the bottle of port inside, and began to pour it into Raynor's feeding cup. Raynor drank it, and then Maxfield lit a cigarette, and held it to his lips. Nursing duties finished, he joined them at the table and began to throw the swabs into the autoclave drum.

'You shouldn't be doing that, Lieutenant Maxfield,' Sally protested. His only reply to that was to pull up a chair, and sit down to the task.

'Tch!' Crump's eyes rotated in their sockets again, by which Sally understood that she could have done without the intrusion.

But the lieutenant showed no inclination to move and, bone tired, Sally took the line of least resistance. 'Well, if you're going to join the production line, Lieutenant, you'll have to do the job properly. You count the swabs into piles of ten, and you put them in one of the cotton bags, and it's important you count them right. Then you put the bag in the drum,' she said, 'but it'll not be easy, with just one hand.' She felt Crump's eyes on her, and dropped her voice. 'Don't worry. If Sister sees him, we'll call it therapy.'

Maxfield put a hand in his dressing gown pocket,

and out came the notebook. 'Bossy. Officer material,' he wrote, with a nod in Sally's direction.

They worked in silence for a while, their conversation inhibited somewhat by this overwhelming masculine presence. Maxfield sat clamping the bags to the table with the elbow of his broken arm while stuffing swabs inside and then pulling the drawstrings, before tossing the bags into the drum.

As he concentrated on the task, Sally saw the uninjured side of his face in perfect profile, and caught her breath. 'He's got a . . . a look of a family that come from my village. You'd take him for one of their brothers! Ooh, and they were a bonny set of lads. Funny, him an Australian, from all that way off.'

'There must be plenty of Australians look the same as people in England, seeing as they all came from England in the first place,' Crump said, increasing the pace of her folding to keep up with Maxfield, who was now waiting for supplies. He looked up, and nodding his agreement took up his pencil.

'My cousin went to Australia when he was on the merchant ships,' Crump continued, 'and he wrote to me Aunt Clara to say he was never coming back.'

'Did he join up?' Sally asked.

'Oh, aye, he joined up in Australia after the war started, like, and he went to Gosforth to see them all when he was on leave. But he says he's going back when the war's over. He'll never live in England again.'

Maxfield pushed the notebook under Sally's nose. 'My uncle said you couldn't take a bad photograph of me if you tried. I was a looker, handsome enough to be in the films.'

What's that got to do with anything? Sally wondered, glancing at his face. There wasn't much trace of the 'looker' there now. He was a fraction less tense around the jaw, a little less hollow around his eye, not as haggard as before – but still gaunt, with skin of an unhealthy cast, and all that ugliness lurking under the dressing. Get that off, and you could certainly take a bad picture. Was he trying to court her? The idea of it caused a fluttering in her stomach, and she left off her cutting to turn from him, and remove the guard from the fire. Better change the subject.

'I've got two brothers in France,' she said, slowly picking up the tongs to put a few lumps of coal on the blaze. 'Poor lads, when I get comfortable beside a nice fire like this, it makes me wonder where they are, and what they're doing. I sometimes slip into the chapel after supper, and say a prayer for them.'

'Fancy,' said Crump, 'I'm not one for chapels and churches myself, but I suppose I don't need to be. Our family's all girls.'

'Either wounded?' Maxfield wrote to Sally. His writing was a lot clearer, and accomplished with rather less effort, and it was on the tip of her tongue to comment on it; but he'd probably take offence at the suggestion that it had been bad before. She kept her observation to herself.

'No, we've been lucky, although some think it lucky if they get a blighty wound to get out of it,' Sally replied, lifting her chin. 'Neither of my brothers have. They've never been wounded, and they've never shirked.' Her voice held a touch of pride.

After a long hesitation Maxfield wrote, 'Has anybody been killed in your village?'

'Why, yes,' Sally said. 'There's the manager at the Co-op, his lad's gone, and the drayman that used to take the beer to our Ginny's pub, and some of the lads that used to work at the pit. Between the two of them, our little villages sent more than a hundred men to help the country, and there's over thirty will never come home again. Last time I went back I heard one poor lad had his leg off just below the hip, and another had an artificial foot. One's lost an arm and four of them had wounds in the leg and another was shell-shocked. And they're not the only ones; you see a lot of men with wound stripes.'

Maxfield nodded, staring intently at her, waiting for more.

'They're not downhearted, most of them though. You can see them laughing together sometimes; they manage to keep cheerful. Aye, the men in our two villages have done their level best for their country, all told. There's one poor woman in Annsdale Colliery lost all her sons. It doesn't seem fair, does it – although I hope and pray my brothers get through the war all right – it doesn't seem fair that she should lose all hers, and other people none of theirs.' She leaned back in her chair, and met his gaze. 'I've wondered now and then who you put me in mind of, and it's them. Just a look round the eyes, you know, and the way you lift your chin a bit when you're listening. Have you any relations called Burdett?'

The lieutenant shook his head, fingers playing on his moustache.

'Hibbs, then?' she asked, remembering the grand-father's name.

Another shake, and after a long silence, 'Migrated from Staffordshire,' he wrote.

Sally nodded, and glanced at the ward clock. Five past nine already. 'Time we were off duty, Nurse Crump,' she said, 'and I'm not sorry, either. I'm worn out today.' She re-rolled the gauze and went to put it back in the cupboard with the scissors, while Crump and the lieutenant put all the remaining bags in the drum. After wishing him a good night Sally took the drum into the treatment room and opened it.

'What for are you doing that?' asked Crump, watching her pull all the bags out.

'Because that man's had a bad head injury, and

For King and Country

I think it's affected his brain, so I'm not letting this lot go for sterilizing before I make sure there really is ten swabs in every bag. It'll be a bad job if they're taken out for somebody's operation and there's not. They might get the count wrong. No need for you to stop, though. Just report to Sister, and she'll let you go.'

Crump was off like a shot, and Sally systematically counted the all the swabs in every bag before replacing them in the drum. She needn't have; the count was right. She closed the drum, and almost jumped out of her skin at Maxfield's sudden appearance behind her.

'Oh, oh,' she pressed a hand to her starched bib. 'I nearly had heart failure.'

The melancholy expression on his face, and the sadness she saw in his hazel eye calmed her fright. He shrugged and spread his hands apologetically, then showed her another note: 'How is the woman whose sons were killed?'

She felt a rush of sympathy for him. Not many men would show such concern about a poor soul they'd never even seen. 'Why, just like anybody would be,' she said. 'She was such a canny soul but she's gone as thin as a rail, the weight she's lost. It's just dropped off her. She'll go home herself before long I think, or end up in the asylum, poor woman. But Lieutenant Maxfield, you'll have to stop wandering about in places you're not supposed to go. I'll get wrong off Sister if you carry on.'

She switched the light off and following him out of the treatment room almost bumped into Sister and Dr Campbell. He hailed Maxfield. 'Here's the man I want!'

Sister's eyes narrowed and she drew her greying brows together in a frown. 'Time you were off duty, Nurse Wilde,' she said, 'instead of fraternizing with the officers. Come along, Lieutenant Maxfield.' She waved her arm in the direction of the ward, ordering him in.

With a reluctant look at Sally, he obeyed. Before he followed, Campbell raised his eyebrows at her, and winked. 'Oh, you're in trouble, Nurse Wilde,' he whispered. 'Wilde by name and wild by nature, eh?'

Chapter Seven

Maxfield lay unconscious on the trolley, his left arm freshly dressed and splinted. The dressing on his face had also been changed; it was smaller, and fastened with strapping rather than bandages.

'They've done his facial wound an' all,' Sally commented to a theatre nurse she recognized from the nurses' home.

'Thought they might as well, while they had him on the table, I suppose.'

'What's it look like?' Sally asked, surveying the lustrous sweep of rich brown lashes that lay against the gaunt cheek of Maxfield's uninjured side, and the dark moustache hiding his upper lip.

'Why, it's no oil painting, but it might not be too bad, after it's healed properly.'

'How's his arm?'

The theatre nurse pulled a face. 'They pulled a few splinters of dead bone out and bipped it. They might be picking them out for a year if he's unlucky, but it'll never heal while there's any left.'

'Sequestrum,' said Sally.

'Fancy word,' said the theatre nurse. 'Dead bone to the ignorant. That'll do for me.'

Sally laughed. 'Me an' all, but I like to know what the doctors are talking about. Do you like working in theatre?'

'Aye, I do,' she said, glancing down at Maxfield, who lay without stirring. 'They never complain, never want bedpans, and they're in no position to give us any trouble, are they?'

Still in his white theatre gown Dr Campbell appeared, and taking hold of the lobe of Maxfield's ear gave it a ferocious nip. Maxfield groaned, and Campbell nodded. 'He'll come round soon. Where's that bally porter? Go and find him, will you?'

The theatre nurse went, and glancing again at his patient, Dr Campbell said, 'You can take your friend back to the ward as soon as he gets here.'

'He's not my friend, he's a patient,' Sally contradicted, and glancing up flushed slightly at Dr Campbell's sly smile.

'Your would-be friend, then. Still following you all over the ward, I've no doubt. And do you know, I think I begin to see the fascination. It's that virginal butter-wouldn't-melt-in-my-mouth look that's so irresistible.' So close that she felt his breath on her ear, he whispered: 'I wonder if you do it deliberately? I wonder what fires smoulder under that starched bib you wear?'

She moved away, too uncomfortable and taken aback to reply.

He gave a mocking little smile, and continued his appraisal through half-closed eyes. 'It's nothing to be ashamed of, the desire to attract a mate. It's a primitive instinct, after all. And everybody knows that the sexual impulse is heightened in wartime, in both men *and* women.'

She took another step back, her eyes widening and her narrow brows rising. How dare he say a thing like that to her?

He looked at her steadily, still smiling. 'Yes,' he emphasized, 'the sexual impulse is heightened, even in sheltered girls from good families.'

'Good families like Nurse Dunkley's, do you mean?' It was out before she could stop it.

'Naturally like Nurse Dunkley's. She's a widow, after all, and still young; but I mean girls like you as well. All girls feel that longing, and feel it all the more at times like these. It's logical, isn't it – all this death; we're driven to compensate.'

'Yes, you've done your share of compensating, Dr Campbell,' she said, her voice tense and high. 'You got one young nurse the sack, by all accounts.' Really, what was she thinking of? Talking to a doctor like that, with such disrespect, was likely to get her the sack. But he'd started it.

'What makes you think that?'

More guarded now, she muttered, 'Same thing that makes you think Lieutenant Maxfield follows me about. Common gossip.'

'Whose gossip? A certain sister, for example?'

'Common gossip,' Sally said, and thought: good old quart'-to-three feet. She put me wise to you, at any rate.

'Never mind,' Dr Campbell said, quite undeterred. 'I can guess, and in return give you another example of gossip, and tell you that Maxfield's not the first admirer you've had. There were some questionable goings-on in the Lowery household, while you were there.'

Her shock turned to confusion, and her cheeks flamed.

Dr Campbell glanced again at Maxfield and then gave her a speculative look, seeming to enjoy her discomfiture. 'I imagine he must have been quite a good-looking chap before his injury. He might have had more success if you'd known him then.'

She clamped her mouth tight shut, and turned away from him. Sexual impulses and primitive instincts, indeed. What decent man would talk like that to an unmarried girl?

But it was true. She'd felt those strange urges when

with Will Burdett, and in the Lowery house. She felt them sometimes still, at night, lying in her narrow little bed. She felt them now, staring down at her patient's face, and also a growing dislike of Campbell, because however true it might be, such things should never be spoken of – *were* never spoken of by decent people. For a girl in her shoes there was only one thing to do with the sexual impulse, as he called it, and that was squash it down, right down, until she squashed it out of existence. *Entirely,* as Curran would have said. And really, when you were exhausted after a day on the wards, you hardly thought about such things at all – and if you did, your aching feet and your breaking back took your mind off them, more often than not. She gave a sardonic little smile. Primitive instincts and sexual impulses might as well go hang themselves for all the good they were ever likely to be to Sally Wilde.

He eased himself up a little, and took the tiny medicine glass from her.

'Sip it slowly, or you'll be sick.'

He nodded, and sipped.

'They're transferring me to the children's ward after I get my day off,' she told him, wondering whether he'd have the wit to realize it was all because of his following her into the treatment room.

A cloud seemed to darken that hazel eye, and his

lips turned down a fraction. At least he had the grace to look sorry. He took another sip, and then signalled towards the locker, where his blasted notebook and pencil lay. She handed them to him, suppressing a sigh.

'I'll miss you, Sally,' he wrote.

Sally? She gave him a quizzical look, and demanded, 'Who told you my name?' She'd never been called 'Sally' on the ward, and she'd never given her Christian name to any of the patients; it was strictly forbidden. All the nursing staff were called Nurse or Sister by everybody, from the consultant to the ward maids and orderlies. There were nurses whose Christian names she didn't know herself, Sister's and Dunkley's and that theatre nurse's, to name only three.

He shrugged, seeming not to understand the question, and scribbled, 'When will you see Mrs Hibbs?'

'It's not Hibbs; it's Burdett,' she corrected him.

'He's unhinged, Sister,' she said; it sounded so much more polite than just plain barmy. 'He wants me to take a letter to a woman in our village who's lost all her sons in the war, somebody he's never even laid eyes on, because he reckons she needs a son, and he needs a mother! Why, how can I do that, Sister? Mrs Burdett wants her own lads, not a stray Australian who's half out of his mind.'

For King and Country

'I've never seen any signs of madness in him — other than that peculiar attachment to you,' Sister said, with a rare laugh. 'And when you think about it, the idea doesn't lack logic. Tell him to post his letter, if you don't want to take it.'

Logic! As if logic had anything to do with a woman who was half demented with grief after losing all her four sons. Sister Davies had no children of her own, and she obviously hadn't much imagination, either. 'I haven't given him her address,' Sally said, 'and I won't. She's no more likely to want to take him on than a ewe would want a lamb that wasn't her own.'

'And what do the shepherds do? Wrap the orphan lamb in the skin of the mother's dead one.' But the smile was gone when Sister Davies' leaned back in her chair to look Sally in the face. 'I suppose you're right, Nurse. Well, avoid him as far as you can; leave the other nurses to attend to him. One more day on duty, and then you take your day off. After that, you'll go onto your next ward and this will all die a natural death.'

Sally remembered Maxfield's distraught face when she refused to take his letter, and the way he'd pressed it on her, time and again. She steeled herself to breach the bounds of etiquette and contradict. 'I don't think it will, Sister. I think there's something badly wrong with him. He's shell-shocked, or something.'

Sister frowned disapproval. 'That's not something for a qualified nurse to say, much less a probationer. Diagnosis is outside our province. Still, I'll ask Dr Campbell to see him, if you're so concerned.'

'What some people will do to get a man!' Armstrong exclaimed, peering at them over her newspaper as they sat together in the probationers' sitting room.

'What? Who?' Curran demanded, craning her neck to see the paper. Sally, sinking into the deep feather cushions of the armchair opposite with her shoes off and her legs tucked under her, was half asleep and not much interested. Her mind was still on Maxfield and his letter.

'Here's an advert in the paper, from a woman whose fiancé's been killed. She's offering herself as a nursemaid to any officer *however badly wounded* who'll marry her. Honestly, what some people will do to be Mrs somebody or other.'

'Sure, the poor woman. She's lost her man, and she's probably half out of her mind with the shock of it. And why shouldn't she take a wounded soldier on?'

Sally woke up and leaned forward. 'Let me have a look.'

Armstrong tossed the paper across to her. 'What happens when she gets over the shock of losing her fiancé and wants to live again, that's what I'd want to know, if I were in the wounded officer's shoes. Will she have any use for him then?'

But Sally was deep in the letter. Here was a tragic woman advertising for a soldier to care for, and on Ward 7a was Maxfield, who seemed to be offering himself for adoption. They were made for each other.

Dr Campbell was just leaving the ward as she returned from tea. 'You're better at diagnosing tetanus than war neurosis, Nurse Wilde,' he told her, after they'd almost collided in the corridor. 'There's nothing of that sort wrong with him at all.'

'Apart from the fact he won't speak.'

'*Can't* speak. That may be a result of the head injury, and for the moment it's of very little consequence. His wounds are likely to keep him here for a few months at least, so he's got ample time to get over his mutism. His only other sickness seems to be his unrequited passion for you.'

Sally gave a little snort of derision.

'Too cruel,' he grinned. 'Poor fellow.'

'Well nurses are forbidden to fraternize with the soldier patients, aren't they, Dr Campbell?' she muttered. Raising her eyebrows for a fraction of a second she walked past him, giving another gentle snort at the thought that that nurses were forbidden to fraternize with doctors as well. And why would she want to? Neither were worth ending up on the carpet in Matron's office for, she thought, as she pushed the kitchen door open.

Ah, there was the paper she'd left on one of the shelves that morning. Sister would be letting her go to catch her train in an hour or so, and she'd give it to Maxfield just before she left the ward for good.

She'd avoided him all day and now, looking pleased at her approach, he took the paper from her and read the headline, 'Allied Forces Capture the Hindenberg Line,' and then turned his face up to hers and smiled, reaching for his notebook.

'The tide has turned, at last!' he wrote.

'They'll be bellocking for mercy, afore long!' she said, remembering Mr Hibbs' words, and Maxfield's Staffordshire connections.

He looked at her in pure astonishment. She gave a satisfied smile, and taking his pencil from him ringed the advertisement she wanted him to read. He studied it with close attention, and then tossed the paper away with such a look of disgust as she'd never seen on any man's face in her life before. She'd acted for the best and now, with his one-eyed glare, he was really letting her know she'd put her foot in it.

'Well, why not?' she demanded. 'She *wants* somebody to look after, and I don't think Mrs Burdett will. So what's the difference?'

For King and Country

He picked up his letter to Mrs Burdett and thrust it into her hand.

A halo of mist surrounded the moon, and there was a nip of frost in the air. Sally pulled her coat around her, drew in her breath with a shiver and hurried along, the metal tips on her boot heels tip-tapping rapidly along the cobbled back alley until she lifted the catch on the garden gate. A cheerful, if small, fire welcomed her when she opened the back door, and a delicious aroma pervaded the kitchen.

'Thank the Lord for that,' she said, closing the door behind her. 'What's in the oven? I'm starving.'

'A hare our Ginny gave me. It should be all right. I've had it hanging a week, and it's been in a low oven all day. Hang your things up, and come and sit down.'

Sally flung coat, scarf and hat onto the peg on the back door, then holding her icy knuckles briefly against her mother's warm cheek she gave an appreciative sniff. 'Smells out of this world!'

Her mother really had pulled out all the stops. The table was covered with a lace-edged white cloth and set for two. A few chrysanthemums sat in a squat blue vase in the middle, with a dish of redcurrant jelly beside it. Watching her lift the old brown stewpot out of the oven, Sally felt a flood of affection for her mother. The pot was soon on the table, followed by a jug of rich brown gravy, forcemeat balls, mashed potato and mashed turnips.

'Ohhh,' she said, busily filling her plate, 'This is my idea of a homecoming. We get enough to eat in the hospital, but they can't touch your cooking, Mam.'

'There's a blackberry and apple pie to finish,' her mother said.

'Hot winter food. I love it.'

'We've a lot to be thankful for,' said her mother.

It was hard to believe a month had passed since her last day at home, but summer's fields of golden corn were now wastelands of burned and blackened stubble, and autumn rushed to meet her as she set out for Annsdale Colliery. It was a jewel of a day, cold and brilliant, the trees full of leaves of russet and gold. High in the sky she spotted the flap, flap, flap, gl-i-i-de of a sparrow-hawk on the lookout for prey, and a few minutes later a flock of fieldfares with one or two redwings among them flew across her sight. She walked on, listening to the leaves rustling underfoot, drinking in the beauty of the natural world, and hugging that book of poetry lent to her so long ago by Will Burdett.

'You're on your own, again,' Sally said, looking round the still, silent cottage that had once been so full of life. The ashes were cold in the grate, all trace of the old fellow and his belongings were gone, and Mrs Burdett was sitting in the armchair staring at a pile of photographs.

'Aye, I'm on my own again. He didn't want to leave me, but he had to go in the end, to see to his own place. Poor old Dad. But he'll be all right, my sisters will look after him.'

'What about you?'

'It hardly matters now, does it?' she said, her eyes on the photographs, all of her boys. 'My brother was a keen photographer, you know, spent every penny he earned on it. He finished up going to work for a newspaper, and after that he got his own little business. He took no end of photos of the boys when we went to visit; developed them all himself. I'm glad. I wouldn't have had all these otherwise. Everybody I loved is gone, and these are all I've got left. It's a good job I never realized that when they were being taken. My happy days are gone, lass, all in the past. I live in the past.'

'Oh, Mrs Burdett! Don't you love your dad, and your brothers and sisters?'

'You're young, you can't understand. It's not like the boys you've given birth to, the ones you've lived for.'

'Mrs Burdett, it's freezing. Have you no coal?'

'Aye, I've enough coal.'

'Anything to eat?'

Annie Wilkinson

'I can't be bothered with it. No appetite. It's weary work, this living just for the sake of being alive.'

Sally opened the pantry door. There was nothing inside but an old shopping bag, a pansion and a few empty stone jars. She picked up the bag. 'How long is it since your father went?'

'A week. Two weeks. About that.'

'You'll have to eat. Have you got any money? I'll bring you something back from the Co-op. I'm going for me mam's messages.'

Mrs Burdett put her photos down with a sigh, and went to the dresser to find her purse, but was distracted by the framed portrait photos of her grown sons in their khaki uniforms. 'Here, look at these. These were the last ones they had taken, before they went to join the bloody army. He was the last one to die, Will, my youngest.' She turned to Sally with a fearful jealousy in her eyes. 'He was a bit sweet on you, did you know that? You might have got a bonny lad for your husband, if he'd lived. My brother used to say: "He looks just as handsome from any angle, Bessie. He ought to be in the films. You couldn't take a bad photo of Will if you tried."'

Her knees turned to water, and how she got out of that house Sally never knew. How she stood at the counter in the Co-op and kept the tremor out of her voice, and then went back to Mrs Burdett's and talked

164

to her as if there was nothing amiss was beyond her. And all with Sister Davies' ridiculous words ringing in her ears – the idea doesn't lack logic. The idea doesn't lack logic! No, no more it did, once you realized. She had a hollow feeling in her stomach, and a tightness in her chest as she directed her steps towards home, and she thought: what's the matter with me?

Fright. That was it. Fear. Enough to make your hair stand on end. Who would ever believe she'd nursed him, bed bathed him, stood by him while he was unconscious, and failed to recognize Will Burdett, when she'd known him all her life? How could she explain it? And why hadn't she? But who expects to see a dead man from her own village in a stranger from another continent, to see a coal hewer transformed into an officer, years and years older than the lad she knew? Transformed into a wreck of a man, stinking of sepsis, with an ugly, mutilated face, who she'd avoided looking at as much as she could? Perhaps if she'd heard his voice she'd have known, but he'd never spoken . . .

Well, now she knew why. He'd deserted, he must have. Why else would he be writing letters to his mother, while still pretending to be an Australian? What did they do to people who knowingly sheltered deserters, she wondered? Was it the same as treason? She ought to go and turn him in. What would the police do if they found out she'd been sheltering him?

They'd never believe she hadn't known who he was, a lad from her own village. She shivered. She wouldn't think about it. This was her day off, and she wouldn't get another one for a month, and why should she let him ruin it? She was going to a new ward, and she'd probably never see him again – and what was he going to do, poor lad? She wished she'd brought that letter to Mrs Burdett now, instead of leaving it in the nurses' home.

No! Good job she hadn't. If he'd been honest, he'd have asked her, straight – 'Take this letter to my mother.' He'd deserted and carrying messages, now that *would* implicate her, up to her neck. There'd be no denying that. She would not think about it. It was a brilliant, cold day, speeding into autumn, the time of year she loved best, with the trees full of russet, and red and gold, and the rustle of fallen leaves underfoot, and listen! Listen to the cry of the geese, those brave winter visitors, how many miles must they have flown, all the way from the Arctic? She looked up to watch them, flying arrow-like, and at any other time the sight and sound of them would have delighted her. And look, over there on that bank, there was a jay's feather, striped blue and black, and beautiful, and the bird would be hiding its acorns now . . . But however many times she dragged her thoughts away, tried to distract herself with the wonder of nature and the day and fix her mind on cheerful things, it

returned the next instant to *him*. Lieutenant Maxfield.
Will Burdett. Oh, my good Lord, what's going to
happen to me, she wondered, – and her heart nearly
stopped at the thought – if I don't turn him in, I
might end up in gaol, be given years of penal servi-
tude, and then I'll have lost my good name and my
livelihood. What will my mother do then? It'll kill
her. I'll have to do it. I'll have to turn him in.'

She'd have to do it. But how could she do it? It
was hopeless; she couldn't get rid of the thought of
him. It swelled like a dam inside her, waiting to burst.
She'd have to talk to somebody, and there was only
one person she'd dare to talk to about this: Ginny.
She turned in the direction of the Cock.

Her mother had invited Emma and her children to
have tea with them. All boys, their ages ranging
from seven to twelve, they were bonny, bonny lads.
Sally looked at Jem, the eldest, with his dark mop
of curls and his smooth, beautiful skin and his clear
eyes, sitting cross-legged by the fire reading while the
others chased around him, and the tears started to her
eyes. Another few years, and he might be running off
to join up, might come back like some of those poor
lads in the hospital, might come back with a face like
Maxfield's. Like Will's. The thought was more than
she could bear.

'Cat's got your tongue tonight, Sally,' her mother

said, after the visitors were gone. 'Emma must think it was hardly worth her while coming down, for all the conversation you had.'

'I've been to see Mrs Burdett. It's upset me, that's all. Really upset me.'

Her mother had a guilty look. 'I'd go myself, but . . .'

'But you've still got your lads, and it might be like rubbing it in. I know. Go anyway, will you, Mam? And take her some of that jugged hare. There's a bit left, isn't there? Try and get her to eat. She'll have to keep her strength up.'

Her mother wavered, and then met Sally's eyes. 'All right, then,' she said. 'I will.'

'Away, then, bonny lad,' Sally urged. 'Take your clothes off, and we'll give you a nice hot bath.'

A pair of wide dark eyes stared out at her from an emaciated face with dirt ground into every pore, but the boy made no attempt to move. She gave him an encouraging smile. 'Away, then, Alfred, take 'em off and come to me.'

Behind him, Curran suddenly raised a hand to remove her cuffs. Quick as a flash, the boy flinched, and ducked.

'Holy Mother of God!' Curran exclaimed, 'and what did the young divill think I was going to do, lynch him? Come here, you young . . . and let's have those rags off you. I don't know why the police brought him here. Sure, and there's nothing wrong with him.'

Sally caught Curran's eye, and shook her head slightly. 'Come on, Alfred,' she appeased him, 'the water's lovely and warm. Just get undressed, and have a nice bath. Then you can sit at the fireside in some nice clean pyjamas, and we'll get you a nice cup of cocoa and a biscuit, won't we, Nurse Curran?'

'Sure, and that's what we'll do,' said Curran, pointing at the boy's sparse hair, 'when we've been through this with the bug rake.'

At the mention of food, the boy's enormous, wary eyes had become hopeful. Sally nodded, looking directly into them. 'A biscuit as soon as you've had your bath, and a cup of cocoa and another biscuit after you get your hair done,' she emphasized.

He gave her a doubtful look, and then made up his mind. He moved slowly, but in the end the rags fell to the floor. The boy's knees and elbows looked huge in his wasted limbs, every rib and notch on his backbone was plain to see and his hip bones protruded sharply.

'Will you look at that,' Curran breathed, her face stricken. 'It's the Irish Famine, in front of me eyes! I'll go and make the cocoa.' She fled the bathroom.

Sally lifted the boy into the bath, not too arduous a task. 'All right, pet.'

'Where's me mam?'

His teeth were black and rotten, and the lice were thick in his wispy hair. She wet it, and dipped her fingers into a jar of soft green soap. Gently working the soap into a scalp studded with scabs, Sally said: 'I'll try to find out for you.'

After spending the best part of an hour cutting Alfie's hair and going through what remained with a fine tooth comb Sally went to report to the office.

'He's asking where his mother is, Sister. I said she was probably in the workhouse.'

'She's not in the workhouse,' Sister replied. 'She's in the asylum.'

'There's something else. He is covered in bruises, Sister. I thought it was dirt at first, and I only realized when no amount of soap and water would fetch it off.'

Bristling with indignation, Sister burst out: 'Well, whoever's done that to him, it won't be his father. He got his name and number in the *Police Gazette* for deserting the army over a year ago and they've been calling round to the house looking for him ever since, but he's never gone back there as far as they know. When they went yesterday the door was locked, so they broke in and found the three-year-old dead and the mother out of her mind. They said there wasn't as much as a crust of bread in the place, but they found a half empty bottle of gin. She'd managed to find money for that, all right; we can guess where from.

That child they brought here is eight, and he hasn't been to school for a month. Have you weighed him?'

Sally nodded. 'He's one stone twelve pounds; I've written it on his chart. But how do they know his father deserted? A lot of men are blown to bits, and there's nothing left to find, my brother says. They're just missing presumed dead.'

Sister's voice was heavy with sarcasm. 'They don't get blown to bits when they're home on leave. They go missing, but you don't presume them dead when they were last seen on a troop train in the middle of England, do you now? No, Nurse. He deserted, and judging by what the police said about the state of the house, his wife's probably had nothing off him for months, so it looks as if he's left his family in the lurch as well. Despicable coward.'

'What about the separation allow—'

Sister gave an impatient snort. 'There's no money from the Government paid to deserters' families, and why should there be? The taxpayers have got enough to do looking after people who do their duty. There's nothing medically wrong with that child, either; he's here under false pretences. The doctor should have sent him straight to the cottage homes at Ponteland.'

Here was a nurse who didn't mind diagnosing, Sally thought. She inhaled slowly. 'I suppose they'll stand his father in front of a firing squad, if they ever find him.'

'No worse than he deserves, is it? You're late for your break, Nurse. You'd better go now.'

'Yes, Sister.' Halfway out of the office door she turned and said: 'What shall I tell Alfred about his mother, Sister?'

'Tell him she's being looked after in another hospital. It's the truth.'

Daylight was just beginning to fade when Sally returned. Only half the size of an adult ward, the children's ward looked cosy with its Lilliputian beds and chairs and a bright fire in the little stove surrounded by its nursery fireguard. Engulfed in a hospital dressing gown, Alfred was sitting in a miniature rocking chair beside it, toasting his toes and drinking his cocoa with Curran dancing attendance on him.

'I put a pillow under his behind, and one at his back,' she said, 'or the bones might rub through his skin entirely. He likes the pictures, don't you, Alfie? The Lady Mayoress did a good day's work when she had them put up, so she did.'

'Alfie, is it?' said Sally, looking at the tiled pictures of nursery rhymes adorning the walls. 'Why, I like the pictures an' all. Which is your favourite, Alfie?'

He looked towards a picture of Little Jack Horner with his pie, its glaze gleaming in the flickering firelight. 'That one,' he said.

★

'It's grand we're on the same ward again, Wilde,' said Curran, when they were seated at the table that evening waiting for the maid to bring supper.

'Why, yes, it is,' Sally agreed, suspecting this was just an opener.

'Sure, and I had a surprise when I saw you this morning. And you were only on the officers' ward a month!'

'Aye, I was.'

'And I thought you were there for three.'

'So did I.'

'You'll miss the officers.'

'One or two of them. But I'm just as happy nursing the kids.'

'You've changed your tune. Sure, you used to say we couldn't do enough for the soldiers, after what they'd sacrificed for us.'

'I did.'

'You've changed your mind then?'

'What about?'

Curran looked at her in exasperation, and leaned back in her chair. 'You're not going to tell me, are you – why they kicked you off the officers' ward? Was it Dunkley?'

Sally caught sight of Crump, sitting with her own set at a table at the other end of the room, and gave her a tiny wave. There had been no recriminations about the incident of the treatment room from anybody; she hadn't had to explain that she couldn't help Will – no, Maxfield – following her about, everybody seemed to know it. She'd simply been told that she was being transferred to the children's ward. She'd been relieved, and now she was more relieved than ever. She could never have carried on the deception if she were on the same ward as him, knowing it all. It was lucky for both their sakes she'd been moved, and if he had any sense, he'd keep away from her.

'Was it Dunkley?' Curran repeated.

'The powers-that-be work in mysterious ways,' Sally replied, 'their wonders to perform. The soldiers aren't the only ones damaged by the war, and I am still doing something for them, anyway. I'm looking after their bairns.'

'Deserters' bairns, do you mean?'

Sally nodded. 'Them an' all. They can't help what their fathers have done, but they take the brunt of it. They're the worst off of the lot, when you come to think.'

Armstrong appeared, and gave them a nod as she sat down.

'Funny, though,' Curran mused. 'You only lasted a month on 7b as well.'

'I hope to do better on the children's ward. Maybe they'll shift you to one of the men's wards, Curran, but not until I've got my bearings, I hope. What's Sister Harding like?'

'Sister Harding?' said Armstrong. 'An out and out snob. "He's a very intelligent child, Nurse, a very intelligent child,"' she mimicked. 'Intelligent means middle class with Harding, and the further up the pecking order the parents are, the better she rates the kids. Raggy-arsed starvelings with lice and impetigo are never intelligent as far as she's concerned, even if they're as bright as buttons.'

Sally believed it. She pictured Edith, the child in the single room near Sister Harding's office, a beautiful, dark-haired ten-year-old girl with blue lips and bruises everywhere, and such anxious eyes. Her father was a solicitor, and her mother the daughter of some prominent local family, and the pair of them were in despair because their darling had been given a death sentence, a diagnosis of leukaemia. Sister Harding had praised Edith's intelligence and let it be known that she thought it a scandal that a C3 child like Alfie was likely to survive while this worthier child of more worthy parents would not.

They ate and chattered on, and Curran seemed to forget Sally's quick despatch from the officers' ward. Then as they stood up to leave, Crump signalled them to wait, and came bounding over.

'Lieutenant Maxfield's been like a cat on hot bricks since you left, Nurse Wilde!' she announced. 'He asked me which ward you're on. Shall I tell him?'

'No.' Sally offered no explanation with her flat

refusal, despite Crump's downcast expression. Why should she want to see him, an unworthy man who'd deserted his country? A traitor who had made her love him, and then deserted *her*?

Chapter Eight

Five minutes peace, that was all she wanted. She hadn't had a minute to herself all day, and now she wanted the noise to stop. She had to escape from these chattering, laughing, good-hearted girls, and have five minutes of blessed stillness, to herself. She excused herself from tea in the sitting room and slipped away, along the main corridor towards her little raft of peace in an ocean of storms, the hospital chapel. It was always empty at this time.

She opened the door, and quickly closed it again, her heart pounding. *He* was there. Alone, and like a spider waiting to trap her in his web of deceit, there sat the deserter in the stillness of her sanctuary, his maimed side towards her covered by its dressing, shielding her from his sight. Appalled, she fled down the long corridor, hardly seeing its warm teak parquet tiles flashing beneath her flying feet. Through the winter garden and into the nurses' home and up the staircase two steps at a time, until she reached her own room, where she threw herself on the bed with a breathless, strangled sob of fear.

Why should she risk her neck because of his cowardice? He'd dropped her like a hot brick as soon he'd joined up, had never even told her he was going. She'd never had as much as a postcard from him since, and now he was trying to make her his accomplice. She, Sally Wilde, who'd never put a foot wrong in her whole life, who'd never even ridden the tram without a ticket, never done anything remotely against the law, why should she let him drag her into something like this? She had her good name, and a responsible job and a mother to think about. How could he expect her to risk all that and maybe even end up in prison because of *him*? She remembered a woman her brother used to bring home, a suffragette who'd spent months in gaol for breaking a car window, and sat up with a shock. The sight of her after her discharge wasn't something she would easily forget, so dark had been the circles under her sunken eyes, so thin and pinched she'd looked – hardly strong enough to walk. Sally shuddered at the memory.

She ought to have stayed in the chapel. She should have had it out with him, told him once and for all that his shameful game was up and he needn't write her any more blasted notes. She wanted nothing more to do with him. That's what she'd do, and she'd do it now, or she'd be as much of a coward as he was, and he'd be after her till kingdom come, wanting her to be his go-between. She sprang to her feet and ransacked the shelves until she found the book he'd lent her, the book she hadn't left at his mother's, after all. If she hurried, he might still be there, and she could give it back to him and have it all over with.

He showed no surprise at the sight of her, and his hand went to his pocket for that blasted notebook, but she held up the book he'd lent her, right up to his face. He froze, and the heavy chapel door swung to behind them. They were alone.

Her voice was icy. 'You can forget that panto-mime. This belongs to you, I think.'

'You think right. When did you realize?'

That voice! The lilt of her own accent, so deep and so masculine, so thrilling to her ear, she would have known him from a million if only she'd heard him speak. She hesitated, and then thrust the book into his hands. 'You *can* talk, then.'

'Aye, I can talk. I couldn't at first, and lucky for me, an' all. Lucky for me my brains came back before my voice did, or it might have been a bad job for me. So, as far as everybody else is concerned, I've lost the power of speech and I've lost my memory. I know *nothing*. When did the penny drop, finally?'

'When I went to see your mother. That's when I realized.'

The green eye widened and lit up under its rich brown arch, and there was hope in his voice. 'You've given her the letter, then?'

'You must have had a bit of a struggle to write that, being left handed,' said Sally. 'But no, I haven't.'

'Why not?'

'Because I didn't take it with me. I left the hospital still thinking you were Lieutenant Maxfield, who'd gone wrong in his mind because of a fracture to his skull and because his wife in Australia had gone off with another man, and I thought Mrs Burdett had enough trouble without being saddled with somebody like that.'

'So how did you . . .?'

'Because she showed me your photo, and do you know what?' Sally could hear her voice becoming shrill, and rapid. She took a deep breath to calm herself, and lowered it. 'She used the selfsame words you used yourself: "You couldn't take a bad photo of Will if you tried." That's when the penny dropped.'

'Nobody'll ever say that again. Will they?'

They wouldn't, but she turned away rather than confirm it.

'No,' he said. 'I saw you when you took the dressing off, when I was terrified you'd recognize me and open your mouth, but there wasn't much chance of that, was there? I made you sick. No, nobody'll ever call me "bonny lad" again. This is a face only a mother could love, and she will, an' all. So did you tell her I'm alive?'

'No. I ought to give you up to the authorities by rights, you know that, don't you?'

'Do I?'

'Do you know what the penalty is for shielding deserters?'

'No, Sally, I don't. I know what the penalty is for deserters, though. They get shot.'

Seeing him before her, hearing her own name on his lips and hearing him speak the fate that awaited him without a qualm in those deep, familiar accents was too much. Tears glistened in her eyes. 'Why did you do it, Will? To let your own king and country down – how could you do such a cowardly thing?'

A deep, angry flush rose to his cheeks, and a frown darkened his brow. 'Cowardly thing? It took more guts than anything I've ever done in my life. You mind one of those poems we used to recite last thing on a Friday afternoon at school, when we were bairns? Well, it must have had a message for me, because I couldn't get it out of my head:

> Beyond this place of wrath and tears
> Looms but the horror of the shade,
> And yet the passing of the years
> Finds, and shall find me, unafraid.

Annie Wilkinson

It matters not how straight the gate,
How charged with punishments the scroll,
I am the master of my fate:
I am the captain of my soul.

'You mind the one? Well, in the end I made my mind up I *would* be the captain of my soul, and nobody else. So I took my life back from my king and country and into my own hands, and I'm not sorry. And I'd be far enough away now, if I hadn't got a lump of shell casing in my face.'

'Oh, God,' she breathed, 'this is terrible.'

'King and country?' he repeated. 'They've no loyalty to us, we're nothing but pawns in a bloody game, Sally man, and I wouldn't care so much if it was a game they were any good at playing, but they're not; they waste men's lives, as if they were cattle. "Backs to the wall?" Whose bloody backs? Not theirs! "Every position must be held to the last man; there must be no retirement?" But they retire and bloody sharp about it, twenty miles behind the lines to some chateau where they can get sodden with whisky, and leave us to the slaughter. They'll keep their bloody upper lips stiff until they've done for every one of us.'

Sally was silent.

'Nothing to say, then? No? Not that I've any quarrel with a lot of the junior officers, I haven't, apart from they get far better rations and billets than us. But when it comes to the fighting they're as badly used as we are, if not worse. I've seen too many good men's lives thrown away, all sorts of men, rich and poor, my own brother among 'em.' He gave her a long hard stare, and then tilted his chin upwards in a gesture part challenge, part derision. 'Anyway, you're the last person on earth to sit in judgement on me, Sally Wilde. You're like all the rest, prattling and romanticizing something you know nothing about, thinking yourself such a little saint for ministering to the poor, suffering soldiers. All you bloody civilians are heroes, every last one of you. Well, turn on me, turn me in if you want to, but don't you dare call me a coward. You're the reason I went to France in the first place, you and your bloody white feather.'

Her cheeks turned to whey. 'White feather? What are you talking about? I never gave a white feather to any man.'

He turned to face her, his green eye glittering, his face flushed. 'No, you left it with the doctor's wife,' he said, and though low, his voice was full of fury against her. 'Do you know what Knox said the other day? "Of course, the people who are weally to be pitied are all these poor gels who'll have to go thwough life without husbands to look after them." The lunatic! He can't have been in the same bloody war as me. The people who are *really* to be pitied are the lads who lie out on the battlefields dying in agony, and the poor bloody stretcher-bearers who end up the same way, trying to bring them in. They're the people I'll save my sympathy for. Lucky I daren't open my mouth, or I'd have told him the women of England have got what they deserved. They sent their hopes of marriage and bairns away in droves with their white feathers, and now they deserve to be barren and alone for the rest of their miserable lives. Lay white feathers on their shrivelled old spinsters' graves, I say.'

Shocked to the core she looked at him and wondered if this hateful torrent was really coming from Will Burdett, the lad she'd grown up with, the laughing idol of all the school. No. This was a man, much older, much harsher, disillusioned and ugly, and sitting in judgement on her and the rest of womankind.

'It might not be the ones who deserve it who end up barren and alone, though, Will,' she protested. 'Did you not hear what I said? I had nothing to do with any white feather.'

He seemed not to have heard her. His mouth quivered, but his voice was low and steady as he went on, 'I'm not going the right way about this, am I? I hate having to beg you for anything, but just keep your mouth shut a bit longer, will you, Nurse Wilde? For my mother's sake, if not for mine. You're in no danger, really you're not. I've been here two months without being found out, and I'm not likely to be, in

an Australian uniform. Thank God Maxfield's wife
ditched him. There was never a man more relieved
than me when I got that letter, because it means
there's not likely to be any more, and I've blackened
the faithless Australian bitch enough to convince
everybody in the hospital, I think.'

'Who is Lieutenant Maxfield?' Sally asked. 'Where
is he?'

'Dead and buried, or dead at any rate, or I wouldn't
have his uniform. And I've a good chance of getting
away with it now – unless you give me away. Just let
me get this bloody arm right and I'll be off. You'll
never have to be bothered with me again.'

'Be off? Be off where? Where can you go,
with . . .?'

She startled at the sound of the door. It opened, to
reveal Home Sister. 'It's time you were in bed,
Nurse.'

'Yes, Sister. I was just coming, Sister,' and with
as natural an air as she could muster, Sally turned to
Will and said: 'Good night, Lieutenant Maxfield. I'm
sure your prayers will be answered.'

Home Sister followed her out, and walked with
her in silence to the nurses' home until they reached
the foot of the stairs. Then very quietly, she said, 'You
know we must act *in loco parentis*, don't you, Nurse?
That means we have to protect you as carefully as
your parents would, and it's a grave responsibility. I'm

sorry to say it, but the Australians have got a very bad reputation. Would your mother like to think of you being alone with one at ten o'clock at night?'

'But I was in the chapel, Sister!'

In tones that would brook no opposition, Home Sister warned her: 'Even in the chapel, Nurse, if you find yourself unchaperoned, you must leave – at once.'

'You and your bloody white feather . . .' Again and again the words came back to mind, and he'd seemed so convinced of the truth of them he wouldn't even hear her denials. In a state of shock Sally sat on her bed, staring at the wall. Was that why she'd heard no more from him after he'd called for the book, why he'd joined up, why he'd never written to her? And if he thought she was responsible for giving him that white feather, he probably blamed her for everything that had happened to him in France as well: blamed her for his arm with infection so deep in the bone he might face amputation in the end; blamed her for his shattered face – and was blaming her even now; and it had made him cruel and bitter, ugly in his heart.

'You left it with that doctor's wife . . .' What had Mrs Lowery said to him? She must have told him that that feather came from her, Sally. What a filthy thing to do, but what a wonderful revenge for her. Hell hath no fury . . .

But maybe she'd been deluding herself, thought Sally. Maybe she'd never meant any more to Will than any of the other girls he'd walked out with, just a bit of fun and nothing more. Maybe, but he'd written to her every day for a week; he'd travelled all the way to Darlington to see her; he'd told her she'd stolen his heart, and he'd seemed so genuine.

'Oh, Will,' she sniffed, and wiped the tears from her cheeks with her hands. Really, she'd better find a handkerchief, and she'd better stop calling him Will, even to herself. From now on he had to be Lieutenant Maxfield, even when she was in her own room, in her own head, in her own dreams, otherwise she might end up making the mistake that would send him to a firing squad. All she had to do was keep her mouth shut and say nothing, and know nothing, and he'd find his own solution, that's what Ginny had said, and he'd said much the same. Nothing else was asked of her. She opened a drawer, began to rifle through it, and then there was the call for lights out. Damn.

She dried her face on the corner of her apron, then undressed in the dark and got into bed. He must have deserted just before the start of the Battle of Amiens, or just after. 'Don't call me a coward,' he'd said, but what else did you call a man who deserted his country and his comrades during a battle, if not a coward?

Annie Wilkinson

The image of that letter he'd given her loomed into her mind. It was lying in her drawer in this very room, at this very moment, waiting to jump out and proclaim to the world that she was aiding and abetting a deserter. If only she were rid of it! She thought for a moment of sticking a stamp on it and dropping it into the post box, but if she did that the postmistress might look at the postmark, and recognize her handwriting, and start asking why she was writing to Mrs Burdett. What a mess! What a tangle! But she'd have that incriminating envelope out of her hands as fast as she could. She'd be first into the nurses' sitting room after the next meal, or the last to leave, and she'd throw it in the grate, and watch it shrivel in the flames.

She shivered. The bed was icy, and she'd been too late to fill her hot-water bottle. She drew her knees up to her chin, wrapped her feet in her nightie and closed her eyes, willing sleep to come and knowing it would not. After what seemed an age she fell into an uneasy doze, to be chased all night by phantoms of policemen and magistrates and irate majors, laughed at by Mata Hari, that beautiful spy who'd been shot by the French, and sneered at by the Lowerys who were blaming her for everything – and how she rued the day she ever set foot in their house. But worst of all were Will Burdett and his mother: she with her eyes dark-circled and full of reproach, he with his murdered face, taut and angry, and fearful despite his brave words.

Funny, though. That ruined face had made her shudder while it belonged to a stranger. Now it was Will's it seemed less to fear and more to cry for, in some mysterious way.

'He's obsessed with food,' Sister Harding said. 'He eats all his own, and he's got to be watched, because I've seen him stealing off the other children's plates as well.' She stared intently at Sally and Curran, as if challenging them to say they hadn't noticed.

Little Louise, in agony with Still's disease; Joshua, strapped to his sloping bed and blue-tinged because of his heart defect; Mary, swollen with Bright's disease; Ernest, ill with Hodgkin's disease, none had any appetite to speak of, and neither had the other children on the ward the probationers called 'kids' medical'. They would all be a lot harder to cure than Alfie, who needed only nourishment – and that seemed to be Sister Harding's principal objection to him.

'He doesn't really steal it, Sister. He just eats what they leave,' Sally ventured.

'Steals. He's not given the food, he takes it. What's more, it's not hygienic for one patient to eat food that's been put in front of another. It's not to be encouraged, Nurse. That child's got no business to be here at all. The sooner the doctor comes to discharge him the better. See that he doesn't take any more of the other children's food.'

'Yes, Sister.'

'This is a sin,' Sally said, scraping an uneaten potted meat sandwich from Louise's plate into the pig bin in the kitchen. 'There's nothing the matter with this; none of the kids are infectious, and to let good food go for pigswill when another child could eat it, it's a sin. In fact, I'm not going to do it.' She put the plate in the sink, then gathered onto one plate all the untouched food from the other children, covered it with a bowl, and put it in the cupboard.

'Sure, and you'll get kicked off another ward if she comes in here and sees that. You might get kicked out of the hospital entirely.'

For a fraction of a second Sally hesitated, then said: 'She's not likely to see it, is she? I'll give it to Alfie when she's gone over to the other kids' ward for one of her confabs with Sister Fawcett.'

'And what if he tells her?'

Sally paused for thought, then said: 'He's not likely to, is he, if he thinks he's stolen it. If I just leave it where he can see it he'll help himself, and then he'll keep his mouth shut about it.'

Curran's eyebrows shot up. 'Tch, tch! Leading a

child into the ways of unrighteousness. And I always thought you were such a good-living girl!'

Sally rounded on her. 'Do you blame me? Do you think we ought to be feeding pigs, before children?'

Curran backed away, and put her hands up in mock surrender. 'Sure, and I do not, but he does get his own food, Wilde, and much more might not be good for him yet. And another thing – he's got enough to battle against just being a deserter's child, without anybody setting him on the road to being a thief into the bargain. Have you thought about that?'

Deflated, Sally thought for a moment. 'No, and you're right. But I can't stand the thought of him being hungry, man. I'll just leave one sandwich out for him.'

'Sure, and that'll be enough to put temptation in his way.'

'What do *you* think about deserters, Curran?' Sally burst out. 'Do you think they deserve to be shot?'

'It depends why they've deserted, entirely. You'd think Alfie's daddy certainly deserved to be shot, but the ones you hear of who've been shell-shocked, I'm sure they don't. But you'd get everybody pretending to be shell-shocked, if they could get out of the war that way. The Irish lads, now, I don't think they'd desert. Where would they go to? They've no homes in England, and they daren't go back to Ireland when they're on leave – not since the Easter Rising. Sure, and they'd get strung up for fighting alongside the English.'

'Would you report a deserter, if you knew of one?'

'I would not, indeed! Not if he was Irish.'

'What if he was English? Wouldn't you think he'd let the rest of the lads down, left them in the lurch, like?

'How would I know that, unless he told me, and he wouldn't do that, would he? "Judge not, that ye be not judged." That's a good motto.'

'Would you help him to get away, though?'

'Jesus, Mary and Joseph, that's something else, I'd have to think about that one. I wouldn't want to get meself locked up. But I wouldn't stop him from getting away himself.'

'Not even Alfie's dad?'

'Not even Alfie's dad. Sure, and you're asking some peculiar questions, Wilde. Do you know where the man's to?'

'Why no,' Sally said. 'How could I?'

When Sister Harding departed for the ward on the other side of the long corridor, a potted meat sandwich mysteriously made its way to Alfie's locker and, making a great show of seeing it there, Sally frowned and said: 'Why didn't you eat your sandwiches, Alfie?'

At the word 'sandwich', he sat bolt upright with his

fists gripping the arms of the rocking chair by the fire, and turned towards her, eyes wide and ears cocked. 'I did, Nurse. I ate them all.'

'Now don't tell fibs. You've left one on your locker, and if you don't eat it, I'll have to throw it away.'

He was out of the chair like a shot and at his locker, greatly puzzled. 'Why, I thought I'd had them all, like.'

'You must have forgotten. Hurry up and finish it, pet. We want to wash the plates.'

It's a sin to steal a pin. Rather die than tell a lie. They were precepts she'd grown up with and had wholeheartedly believed, but now, watching Alfie eat, Sally began to think there must be exceptions, circumstances where stealing or lying might be justified.

Alfie's eating a tiny sandwich was not a long process, and Sally was taking the plate back to the kitchen when she heard the telephone ring. Although still a little nervous of it, she went into Sister's office and picked up the receiver.

'Have you got the bulletin, Sister?' a disembodied voice demanded.

She looked at the instrument, as if for an explanation, and then carefully spoke into the mouthpiece. 'The what?'

'The bulletin. This is the *Evening Chronicle*, ringing for the bulletin.'

'Oh, yes, I'm sorry. Sister's not here, but I think this is it, on the desk. Shall I read it over the telephone?'

'That's the usual way, pet. We stopped using carrier pigeons a while ago.'

Sally blushed at her own stupidity. At admission, every patient's relatives were given a number to check in the paper every night, to find out how the patient was progressing. Sally picked up the bulletin and read it out. Three of the numbers had 'dangerously ill' written beside them, and Sally guessed they must be Edith, Joshua and Ernest, and the number with 'improving' must be Alfie. The rest were 'very ill', 'slight improvement', or 'much the same'.

When she put the receiver down, Sally's glance fell on the paper rack on the desk, full of printed forms, letter paper and envelopes. An envelope would be very useful, and she had just run out. She separated one, just one, then stung by conscience took fright and pushed it back. If she carried on like this, she'd find herself on the slippery slope to perdition. Honest and trustworthy, that's what a nurse was expected to be, and that's what Matron and the sisters believed she was. Bad to let them down, and not only that, she thought, a good reputation's like virginity – when it's lost, there's no amount of tears and sighs will get it back.

★

'You write a lot of letters, Armstrong,' Sally said, when they were sitting cosily round the fire in the probationers' sitting room. 'I don't suppose you've got an envelope and a stamp you could give us the lend of? I want to drop my sister a line.'

'I've got envelopes. Do you want one now?'

'Aye, if you don't mind.'

'Oh.' Armstrong looked reluctant, obviously un-willing to sacrifice her comfortable chair right beside the fire to one of a dozen or so other probationers who were milling about with envious eyes on the best seats.

'Meet you upstairs before lights out, then,' Sally said. 'There's something else I want to do, anyway.'

He was alone again in that peaceful place, facing the altar to the right of the door, kneeling with head bowed and chin supported in his palms with every appearance of being deep in prayer, but waiting, in any event, for her. She knelt in the pew behind and to the right of him, and from that angle he looked the perfect young officer with the perfect profile. He turned slightly, giving her a glimpse of the gauze and strapping covering the other side of his face. 'I thought you'd come,' he said.

'I can't stay more than a minute. I got a warning yesterday for being here on my own with you, and I daren't let her catch me again.'

'Meet me on the Leazes, then, by the bandstand. In about ten minutes.'

'I daren't, Will. I daren't, for my soul. I'll lose my job if I get caught fraternizing with the soldiers.'

'*I daren't, Will,*' he mimicked. 'Who's the coward now?'

'Look, I'll send your letter to our Ginny. Your mother should have it before the week's out. I can't do any more,' she said, and stood up.

'That's right,' he said. 'No fraternizing with the soldiers. You might find out what it is to be a woman, and you don't want to risk that. Away and jump into your good little nun's bed, then.'

She blushed, and left without another word.

Chapter Nine

While Curran was at supper the following day the telephone rang in Sister's office. Sally was surprised to hear Dr Campbell on the line. 'You've an empty cubicle on your ward, haven't you?' he demanded, very abrupt, and with an urgency in his voice she'd never heard before.

'Yes, Doctor.'

'Have you had diphtheria, Nurse?'

Strange question. 'Yes, Doctor, when I was eleven. I think they gave me antitoxin after it, as well.'

He sounded much relieved. 'Good. Get the cubicle ready and prepare for an emergency tracheostomy at once. We've got a case coming in, and it'll be better done on the ward so that we won't have to disturb him afterwards. We'll be with you in five minutes.'

Diphtheria? What was he asking about diphtheria for? Diphtheria cases shouldn't come into this ward, or even this hospital; they had to go to the City Hospital for Infectious Diseases. 'But, Dr Campbell . . .'

she protested, and heard the click of the receiver being replaced at the other end.

But Dr Campbell, Sister Harding's been called home because her father's had a stroke, and I'm here on my own. The only other probationer has gone off to supper, and so has Sister Fawcett, and she's sharing herself between both the children's wards, and it'll take longer than five minutes to go and fetch her, and I've never set up for a tracheostomy on my own before! She'd have told him it all if he'd given her the chance, and the way her heart was pattering in her chest, she might have added – and I'm absolutely petrified. She stared at the wall above Sister's desk for a moment or two, trying to collect her scattered wits.

Five minutes, he'd said. It didn't really leave her enough time to have a seizure, so she'd have to calm down and do the best she could. Get Curran and Sister Fawcett back, for a start, and no need to go running after them with a telephone staring her in the face – just do what Sister would have done. She picked it up, and with trembling fingers dialled, for the first time in her life.

Message given, she breathed a sigh of relief. Next, find 'tracheostomy' in the reference book on the desk. She skimmed through it, and oh, mercy, what were they going to use for instruments? She'd seen none on this ward. She took a deep breath and straightened her apron, and at the office door she almost collided with an orderly, who was holding a glass tray covered with a chromium-plated lid similar to the one she'd seen during Raynor's operation. Thank goodness for that. Just hope Dr Campbell had sent everything he needed, and all nicely sterilized in strong carbolic.

She took the tray into the cubicle that had once been Edith's. 'If there's nothing can be done for her, she might as well be at home,' her parents had said, and they'd taken her. It was a mercy they had or all these kids might end up with diphtheria, Sally thought.

Whatever was Dr Campbell thinking of, admitting a case like that here?

Still alone on the ward, Sally had just set the trolley and boiled the kettle to rig up a steam tent when the child was carried into the cubicle by Dr Campbell himself. Mrs Lowery, of all people, was close on his heels and in a state of near hysteria.

One glance at the child that Dr Campbell laid gently on the bed convinced Sally that he was almost at death's door, near suffocated, with beads of perspiration standing on his pale skin, and such anxiety on his little face.

'He's in shock,' Dr Campbell said, and time seemed to slow as Sally moved towards their patient, feeling nothing now but an icy calm, noting the sucking in of the spaces between and under his ribs as the blanket fell away from him, the swelling of the glands of his neck and the strain of his neck muscles as he gasped for air. Little Christopher Lowery's face was blue, and he looked at her with unseeing eyes as she cast the blanket away and wrapped a drawsheet tightly round him with firm, calculated movements, pinning his arms to his sides and making it impossible for him to struggle.

'All right, Kitten, all right. We're going to make it easier for you to breathe now.' She made soothing noises while picking up the sandbag and placing it carefully under his shoulders to raise and extend his neck. *Spine and neck must be straight,* she remembered; *keep the windpipe in the midline.* Without a second thought she commanded his mother, 'You stand at the top of the bed and keep his head absolutely steady, Mrs Lowery. I'll control his body.'

The patient was in the perfect position. Dr Campbell took his scalpel from the tray of antiseptic solution and rinsed it.

'Ooh,' Mrs Lowery winced, and turned her head away.

Swift and competent, he made the incision. There was an inrush of air and a splutter of mucus, and relief was instantaneous; the strained little face began to relax, even to its eyelids. Christopher's breathing quietened and the blueness faded from his lips.

The job was done. 'There you are, Beatrice, crisis

over for the moment,' Dr Campbell said, inserting the inner tube.

Mrs Lowery looked at her boy, her eyes filling with tears. 'Oh, thank God, thank God! And thank you Iain,' she choked between her sobs. 'Thank you.'

The task finished, Dr Campbell straightened up and gave her a nod and a smile, then turning to Sally, who was removing the drawsheet and sandbag, he boasted: 'Under ten minutes this time, I think, Nurse. Not long to save the life of a seriously ill child, is it?'

'No, Doctor,' Sally said, anxious for the other children on the ward now that the threat to Christopher's life was past. 'But, you see, we're very understaffed at the moment, and unless Curran and Sister Fawcett are back, I'm the only nurse here, and we have a lot of seriously ill children. How can I go onto the ward and nurse them after dealing with a case of diphtheria?'

He frowned. 'You can't. Of course not.'

'Then somebody will have to be found to nurse the others, Doctor. Would you mind speaking to Matron about it, and explaining things to Sister Fawcett?' Underlying the sweet but determined smile she gave him was the message – and if you won't, I'll have to.

'Certainly I will,' he said, and to Mrs Lowery, 'You see what a fix we're in, Beatrice. He won't be able to stay here. We'll transfer him to the City

Hospital for Infectious Diseases tomorrow morning. In the meantime, Nurse, I'll have a private word with you.'

Sally followed him outside the cubicle, and met his disapproving gaze. 'You ought not to have said that in front of his mother, Nurse Wilde. The other children aren't her concern.'

'But they are mine, Doctor, and how else was I going to say it?'

'As I've done now. You should have asked to speak to me privately.'

Wholly unrepentant, she said, 'I'm sorry, Doctor. But it's my duty to see that the other children are properly cared for.'

With an air of frosty professionalism, he said, 'The night staff will be coming on duty shortly, which will solve the problem of the other children. You must apply yourself to nursing the child you have charge of, and his condition is critical. Keep him under careful observation, Nurse, colour, respirations, pulse, keep the tube clean, and keep a sharp eye out for any bleeding from the wound. He mustn't move at all, not even to sit up.'

'I know that, Doctor,' she said, well remembering her own sojourn in the City Hospital, though her infection had never been so bad she'd needed a tracheostomy

'His pulse is irregular. Diphtheria toxins can

affect the heart, and we mustn't put any strain on it. I'm sorry, but you'll have to special him until a replacement can be found. Let me know at once if he deteriorates.'

He opened the door, and this time stood back to let her enter before him. Sally stood by while he approached the bed. 'I'm going now, old chap,' he told Christopher. 'You'll be all right. Nurse Wilde will look after you, and I'll see you in the morning.'

Mrs Lowery sprang to her feet at his farewell nod to her. 'And now I'll just have a private word with you, if you don't mind, Iain,' she said, and followed him out.

Sally watched the cubicle door close behind them, and could well imagine what hoity-toity Mrs Lowery's private word would be. 'Do you realize, Iain, that that girl is the housemaid who . . .? Surely you can find someone else to nurse Christopher?' Or something of the sort, but it seemed they were out of luck – Mrs Lowery and Sally both. It would be a miracle if anyone else could be found to nurse Christopher. Sally caught his eye and smiled.

'Sally!' he mouthed.

'Hello, Kitten. You won't be able to talk just yet, but never bother. If you want anything, just wiggle your fingers at me, like this,' she said, giving him a demonstration. 'I'll be watching.'

With drooping eyelids he gave her a feeble smile,

copied her wave and, as his mother stepped back into the cubicle, fell asleep.

Of all the women in the world, we must be the two who'd least have chosen to spend a minute together, and here we are, stuck with each other's company for the whole night, Sally thought, sitting upright on a straight backed chair whilst Mrs Lowery sat furiously crocheting a doily in the armchair on the other side of the bed, carefully avoiding her eyes.

There was a tap on the door, and Sally opened it. Curran had pulled the screens round the door of the cubicle, and was standing just beyond them. 'Night Sister says it's got to be done,' she said, 'and she says you've both got to stay in there now. Neither of you must go onto the ward, or near any of the children. She'll come and have a word with you as soon as she can. God knows when you'll get off duty, Wilde, but I've put some tea and a sandwich down there for you, just outside the door.'

As Curran retreated down the corridor, Sally picked up the tray and took it into the cubicle. 'Mrs Lowery? Mrs Lowery – I've got you some tea.'

'Huh?' Mrs Lowery lifted her head, gave a brief nod, and returned her attention to her crochet work. Sally handed her a cup, but it was ignored, so she put it on the bed table and lifted the corner of one of the sandwiches. Shipham's Paste, by the look of it.

She sat down to eat, and to drink her tea while keeping one eye on Christopher. Mrs Lowery gave her a mildly disapproving glance.

'I've had no supper,' Sally told her, wondering why she felt it necessary to explain, and annoyed at herself for doing so. Not that Mrs Lowery was taking much notice of her. By the time Sally had finished eating, she'd dropped the doily onto the bed, and lapsed into a doze. Sally put the tray of crockery outside the cubicle, and sat down again to continue her watch on Christopher. Out of the corner of her eye she could see his mother who, with head back and mouth open, was slumbering, the worst of her woes behind her.

Sally could hardly bear the sight, and turned her chair to get her out of her line of vision. It was impossible. She couldn't escape the sight of her or the sound of that gentle snoring, and even if she had been able to avoid seeing her, the thought of Mrs Lowery had taken possession of her mind. She turned to look full at her for an instant thinking: *you're* the reason Will went to France. It's because of your spite I never heard another word from him after he'd been to your house in Darlington. To this day he believes I gave him that white feather, and that's your doing. It's because of *you* that his face is ruined and his mother's gone into a decline. If he gets court-martialled and shot, if she dies of her broken heart, it will all be *your fault*. Everything that led up to this horrible, horrible mess was started by *you*, and your malicious feather.

A wave of hatred engulfed her as she watched Mrs Lowery slumber on, oblivious. Overtired and overwrought, she became more and more wakeful, wanting to slap this self-satisfied, self-centred madam awake, wanting to scream, 'Do you realize what you've done, Mrs Lowery? Do you remember the lad you gave the white feather to? Do you remember destroying my chance of a husband, by telling him it was from me? Do you know he's the fourth son his mother's sacrificed to her country, and she'll be dead herself before long, the way she's going? Do you think you deserve to keep your own son, Mrs Lowery, after playing a trick like that?

Was it the fifth or the sixth hour of her watch? Sally hardly knew, but she came to with a jump. 'Kit!'

His swollen neck was tense, his fists clenched, his face contorted in the struggle for air, and he was thrashing out helplessly with his legs. Sally sprang to her feet in alarm and stood over him. His eyes as big as saucers and full of terror, were upturned to hers, making her heart beat wildly. The tube must be blocked.

'What? What?' Mrs Lowery awoke. 'What's the matter?'

Sally peered down the tube, but no, it was clear; it would be useless to remove it. Perhaps it was badly positioned, obstructed somehow by something that had got below it. Sally pulled at it gently, in the hope that that would improve matters, but the child's breathing was becoming more and more distressed, with a wheezing stridor when he inhaled.

'What's the matter with him?' his mother shrieked. 'He can't breathe! How can that be, with a tube in?'

Sally heard Night Sister's footsteps in the corridor. 'Stand in the doorway and call Sister,' she said. 'Tell her to fetch Dr Campbell, this minute.'

Mrs Lowery stood in the doorway and shrieked again. At a loss for what else to do, Sally tried artificial respiration, raising the child's arms over his head, and pressing hard against his ribs in bringing them down again to the sides, listening to Mrs Lowery's appeal to Night Sister and then to Night Sister's rapidly receding footsteps, and praying for Dr Campbell to get there.

'Cough, Kitten, cough!' she urged. He did, and after what seemed an age, Sally caught sight of something appearing at the mouth of the tube. Mrs Lowery came to stand on the other side of his bed.

'Pass me that, please,' Sally said.

'What?'

'That crochet hook. Quick.'

With her heart in her mouth Sally gently inserted the hook into the tube, but she was too late. Kit breathed in, and the thing disappeared down the tube again.

'What are you doing?' Mrs Lowery cried, but Sally ignored her, watching the hole in Kit's throat like a cat watching a mouse. He coughed, and there it was again. Quickly, gently, Sally inserted the point of the crochet hook into the hole and deftly scooped the thing out. Relieved of it, Kit breathed easily and closed his eyes, his face relaxed.

Dr Campbell swept into the cubicle and seeing his cousin, stopped short. 'I thought there was an emergency!'

'Oh, Iain, there was,' said Mrs Lowery, pointing to the object on the sheet, 'until Nurse got something out of his throat! He seems to be all right now.' She collapsed into her chair and hunted in her bag to find a lace handkerchief to dab her brimming eyes and blow her nose.

'Let me see.' Dr Campbell took a swab from the tray and used it to pick up the piece of glutinous, grey matter. 'A typical piece of diphtheria membrane. It must have broken loose and blocked his airway below the level of the tube. It's a fine bacteriological specimen, Nurse, but how on earth did you manage to capture it?'

Sally had moistened a swab with surgical spirit, and was cleaning the crochet hook. She held it up for him to see, before returning it to Mrs Lowery.

'I see. Forceps would have been better.'

'There were none to hand, Doctor.'

'Well, no harm done, I suppose.'

'He looked as if he was going to choke to death,' Mrs Lowery said, looking at Sally with tears spilling onto her cheeks. 'Oh, I'm so glad she was here. So thankful Dr Lowery got her into nursing. It must have been Divine Providence . . .'

The voice trailed off under Sally's dispassionate gaze and her wry and thoughtful smile. She'd got herself into nursing, so no need for him to take any credit for it – and as for Mrs Lowery's thanks, she could keep them. Sally would have liked nothing better than to make her pick up a pen and admit her evil lie about that white feather on paper, in a letter to Will. But she daren't; she daren't so much as mention his name for fear anybody might guess he was still alive. No, as far as the world was concerned, Will Burdett was dead and gone, and she'd be wise to think of him as dead as well, and dead to her.

At six o'clock, Matron came bustling onto the ward like a woman who means business, announcing that she herself would take over the nursing of the diphtheria case until he was sent to the City Hospital for Infectious Diseases. She stood outside Kit's room, holding out a theatre gown. 'This is to protect the rest of the hospital from you,' she said.

Sally put her arms in the sleeves, and then turned for Matron to tie the back.

'Now you go straight to the bathroom in the

nurses' home, and run a hot bath. Then strip to the skin and bundle all your clothes up in the gown. What can't be sterilized will have to be burned. Then you have a good scrub and wash your hair before you touch another thing.'

As Matron rolled her sleeves up, Sally did exactly as she'd been told. Dead tired, she walked straight back to the nurses' home along an empty corridor, touching nothing, remembering the glad day her mother had arrived at the City Hospital to bring her home. Her joy had been mixed with sorrow at waving goodbye to nurses she'd never see again, but the worst thing was parting from her rag doll, knowing it would be burned.

She shook her head. Those women had saved her life, and she'd hardly thought of them for years. What a thankless job nursing was at times, but nobody could deny that it was useful and necessary – and never monotonous.

Heavens above, four o' clock in the afternoon! She must have slept over seven hours, and she'd meant to be back on the ward for three. They must have been run off their feet, covering Sister Harding's absence and hers as well. Sally dressed hurriedly in a freshly laundered uniform and rushed to the ward. She was halfway down the long, main corridor when the sight of Crump coming out of theatre reminded her of the officers' ward and Will, and she still hadn't had time to get a stamp and post that letter for him.

'All right, Nurse Crump?' Sally greeted her.

'Aye, all right where I am. But you've had a time of it on the children's ward, by all accounts. There was a death just before dinner time, so I heard.'

Sally went pale. 'Not the diphtheria case?'

'I don't know. I only heard half the story, but Curran was there when it happened. Awful when it's a child that . . .'

'Yes,' Sally nodded, and hurried off, suddenly feeling a dead weight of shame for fantasizing about Kit's death in her deep desire to punish Mrs Lowery. And had the poor kid really died? Poor little Kitten, who'd really loved her when she'd worked for his parents, and who'd looked at her last night with such trusting eyes. Much as she detested his mother, she'd never meant any harm to him; never could, never would hurt a hair of his head. She moved swiftly towards the ward, her dread increasing with every step that drew her nearer.

'Sure, and it wasn't Christopher Lowery. Your diphtheria case was stretchered out with his mammy beside him to the fever hospital not long after we came on duty; Matron saw to that. Alfie's gone as well, to the Ponteland Homes.'

Relieved, Sally asked, 'Who was it, then?'

'It was Ernest.' The tears stood bright in Curran's eyes when she added, 'The poor little feller was sitting on my knee just before dinner, and he turned his face up to mine, and he said, "Oh, Nurse, I am poorly," and the next minute, he died in my arms.'

Sally clasped Curran in her arms. 'Oh,' she said, 'oh, I am sorry.' She felt relieved too, that sorrow was the only thing, pure and clean, unalloyed by guilt.

Dr Campbell was just coming down the stairs leading to the residents' quarters as Sally was walking along the main corridor that evening. He stopped at the bottom of the stairs and waited for her. 'You might like to know how your patient's getting on since his transfer to the City Hospital, Nurse Wilde.'

'Yes, Doctor. I would.'

'Holding his own, so far. His number is 18, if you'd care to watch his progress in the *Evening Chronicle*.' He handed her the paper.

'Yes, I will. What puzzles me though, is why his mother brought him all the way to Newcastle. Why did she not let her husband look after him in Darlington? Why did he not go to the fever hospital there?'

'She didn't bring him all the way to Newcastle; she was here already, spending a few days with my mother. They're sisters.'

'Ah. I see.'

'When he became unwell they sent for the dodder-
ing old quack they've had since childhood, whose
opinion they set great store by – or did, before this.
The old fool told them it was nothing more than
pharyngitis and it would clear up within a week.
They believed him, until they could see the boy was
slowly suffocating, and then they telephoned me and
came haring up here in a taxi. You have to admit,
I justified their confidence,' he smiled, preening
himself.

You kept me up all night, an' all, and put the fear
of God in me for the other kids, Sally thought, and
didn't return the smile.

He must have read her mind. 'I incurred Matron's
displeasure too.'

'Not surprising, since Matron had to help with the
nursing.'

'Oh, I don't know. I think the old trout rather
enjoyed getting stuck in. She likes the occasional
drama.'

Disrespectful young so-and-so! Sally gave him a
disapproving look, but said nothing.

He persisted. 'Of course, she told the chief, and it's
put me in bad odour with him as well. But I could
hardly see my own cousin in extremis, and refuse to
treat him, could I?'

'No, you couldn't. But it would have been a bad
job if he'd passed it on to any of the others.'

'He didn't. Between us, we made sure of it. You wouldn't have refused to help him, would you?'

'No,' she admitted. 'I wouldn't.'

'I believe he's got rather a soft spot for you.'

'I'm fond of him, as well.'

'Not the only member of that family you were fond of, I believe, or who was fond of you,' he probed.

Oh, and judging by that expression on your face, you'll soon be talking about primitive impulses, she thought. Well, she'd nip that in the bud, and quick about it. 'I'm sorry, Doctor, but this is where we part company,' she said, stopping at the chapel door with a little shrug and a close-lipped smile. We're not all like Dunkley, she thought, or that silly lass who got her marching orders. We're not all intent on turning ourselves into concubines for doctors. 'I'm just popping in here to say a little prayer for Kit.'

'Oh well, say one for me while you're about it.'

'I will. I'll pray you mend your ways.'

He gave an incredulous laugh. 'The impudence!'

But she was already gone, leaving the chapel door to swing shut behind her and his *Evening Chronicle*.

Chapter Ten

Maxfield was sitting alone in the pew nearest the door, and turned to face her. 'What's in that?' he demanded, as soon as the door had closed. 'Another candidate for martyrdom?'

'What?'

He tilted his head towards the *Evening Chronicle* 'What's in the paper?' he repeated. 'Some Lady Bountiful looking for a poor soldier to exercise her charity on? As long as he's an officer, of course.'

Sally pulled herself up to her full, dignified five foot three inches. 'I don't know what's in the paper, Lieutenant Maxfield, except the hospital bulletins,' she said.

'Good. Because I don't want anything to do with any bloody society woman who wants a pitiful cripple to parade round so that she can show her friends how patriotic she is, doing her bit for the country. I'm a *man*, and I want a woman who wants a man, not some bloody self-appointed saint who wants a good work.'

Pitiful, he said! Why, what could be more pitiful than this exhibition? What could ring more hollow than shouting about his manhood, when he'd – how had Major Knox put it? Left his comrades in the lurch. She could hardly keep the contempt out of her voice. 'I doubt you'll ever get one, then.'

'What do you mean by that?'

'I mean I doubt any woman would go to all that trouble.'

'I doubt it, an' all, for somebody with a face like this.' His hand went up to the dressing on his face and she regretted her words when, despite the broad shoulders and the thick moustache, his lip trembled. She remembered with a shock that he was six months younger than her, and barely twenty.

Now subdued, she said: 'I didn't mean that, and neither did the lady who wrote the letter. I mean somebody as rude.'

He grimaced. 'My mother would, though, she'd go to some trouble. Have you posted my letter?'

'No, I hadn't a stamp, and I haven't had time to go and get one,' she said.

'No? Well then, there's no danger of you putting yourself out for any smashed-up soldier, is there?'

She suddenly felt it beneath her dignity to explain to this peevish child why she hadn't had time to get a stamp. He wouldn't have wanted to listen, anyway.

'Not much. I think I'll go now, Will.'

'You're a hard-hearted little . . .'

She wouldn't listen to any more of it, but as soon as she turned to go, Will's voice changed.

'I've got some stamps, Sally,' he urged her. 'Meet me outside, where the pillar box is, in ten minutes, and we'll post it.'

'I can't. We have to be in bed, and it's lights out at half-past ten.'

'They treat you like kids, and you let them. I wouldn't put up with it. It's as bad as the bloody army. You can't make the simplest decision, because they don't believe in that. Don't show any sign you've got any brains; the officers don't like to see them. Just say, "Yes, sir, no sir, three bags full sir! Permission to scratch my arse, sir?" All right, just bring the bloody letter here then, and I'll post it myself.'

She was about to refuse when the chapel door opened, and Dr Campbell walked in. 'I say, I got halfway down the corridor before I realized I hadn't got my paper. I didn't mean you to keep . . .'

Sally held the paper out for him and he took it, his eyes resting for a second on her flushed cheeks, and then on Maxfield, who turned away.

'Am I interrupting something?'

'No, Doctor,' Sally said. 'I only came in for a minute, and now I'm going.'

★

She hadn't even put pen to paper yet but she'd do it this minute, and have done with it all before she closed her eyes that night. She found some notepaper and picked up her pen.

Dear Ginny,
Will you take this and push it through Mrs Burdett's door, without letting anybody see you?
Love,
Sally.

Nothing more needed saying, did it? She read it over, and decided not, and then she remembered what Elinor had said when she'd come with a pail and a pair of tongs to collect that disease-contaminated uniform. 'Sally, man, I don't know what for you want to be taking chances with things like diphtheria,' she'd said. 'There's a couple of jobs going in the laundry. Why don't you come and work with us? You'll get a right laugh with some of the lasses.'

But laundry work would be a poor swap for nursing, Sally had told her. No matter how exhausting or even dangerous it might be, nursing was the only job for her and she wanted no other. Elinor had gone away holding the pail at arm's length, shaking her head.

Mrs Burdett, though, she might well want any job

in the Infirmary once she knew her son was alive and a patient there. Sally picked her pen up again and scrawled 'P.S., Can you let it drop that there's a couple of jobs going at the laundry here, so that Mrs Burdett gets to know? It might give her the chance to see him, if she can get a one.'

Yes, if Mrs Burdett got a job in the laundry, it would be dark by the time she finished work. Then Will could meet his mother on the Leazes, and nobody would be any the wiser.

She addressed the envelope to Ginny, and then folded her letter and tucked it inside. The one Will had written to his mother wouldn't go in, so she folded his envelope tight round its contents along the top, and down the side, to make it fit inside hers. Her envelope was stuffed so full she could only just manage to seal the contents inside, and when she looked at it she thought she'd never seen such a suspicious-looking package in all her life. It seemed to want to call attention to itself. A host of hideous possibilities sprang into Sally's mind. What if she fell downstairs on her way to the post, and the envelope burst open? Somebody might read it, and then she'd end up in the hands of the police. What if she lost it, or the postmistress saw something sinister about it, and reported it?

Silly, silly lass. She knew how silly she was being, but she couldn't dispel the fear. She'd get rid of that letter as soon as she could, and then try to stop thinking about it.

There was a fog coming down, and she could barely make out the figure standing in the shadows by the pillar box.

'You came. I didn't expect it, but I'm glad,' he said as she approached. They stood together in the darkness, their voices muffled by the mist, their faces turned away from the few passers-by.

'An' I hope you're in a better temper, an' all. Have you brought your stamp?' Sally whispered. 'I couldn't get a one.'

'Aye.' He took the letter from her, stuck the stamp firmly in the corner and dropped the letter in the box. 'Look,' he said, turning towards her, 'I'm sorry for some of the things I've said, but I'm stuck here like a rat in a trap because of these bloody wounds not healing right and I'm wound up to top doh all the time. If I could be off, get lost in some fairground or something I'd be all right, but there's no chance of that now, with a face like this. And I wouldn't dare anyway, for fear of my arm going wrong. Who'd dare risk losing his arm? So I'm stuck, helpless, and it's driving me up the wall. I'm like a cat on hot bricks all the time, thinking somebody'll come looking for a dead officer before long and find a fraud, or somebody sharper than you might recognize me, or you might let something slip. Then I'll be for a bloody firing squad.'

'Somebody sharper than me. Well, thanks very much, I don't think,' Sally said as they turned, and began to walk back in the direction of the nurses' home.

'Well, you weren't very sharp about tumbling to me, were you, thank God? Or about seeing anything wrong with Raynor.'

'He had the chance to tell the doctors what was wrong, and he said he was all right.'

'Of course he said he was all right. People say they're all right if they're dying, because they know that's what you expect them to say, and you don't want them to say anything else. And half the time you haven't got time for them to say anything else, so it would be bloody pointless anyway. So they say what you want them to say; they say: "I'm all right," but inside they're screaming, "Look at me! Can't you see I'm in agony? Can't you see I'm dying? Can't you see it's torture, wondering whether this thing's healing, wondering what the hell I'm going to do if I have to have it amputated, wondering how any lass is ever going to want to look at me again, with a face like mine! Make me right again, for pity's sake! *Cure* me!"'

'Well, then,' said Sally, 'we can't be expected to read minds, can we?'

'You can't be expected to have any imagination either, by the look of it. And now you're in a huff.'

'Hm,' said Sally, and after a pause added, 'we've got too much to do to have any time to spare for mind-reading, and we're not supposed to fraternize with the soldiers, either. Anyway, to get back to getting caught – I thought you said there was no chance, because they take you for an Australian?'

'There's less chance, but that doesn't mean I don't have nightmares about it,' he said. 'You wouldn't give me away, would you, Sally?'

'I haven't so far, have I?'

'How do I know? The way you look at me sometimes, I wonder if you might.'

'Well, I haven't, and anyway, you might just as easily give yourself away, shouting things like "muddy" in the middle of the night.'

'Muddy? Why would I say that?'

'How do I know? But the night nurse said you did, but then she let it pass because she had better things to do than bother about it, just like I once heard you say 'Oh God,' and I let it pass.'

'I won't dare to go to sleep now.'

'People don't seem to take all that much notice. Like you said, they haven't got the time, and Dr Campbell thinks it hardly matters that you don't talk, because you've got enough to keep you in the hospital anyway.' Impulsively, she reached out to squeeze his hand. 'Whatever happens, Will, it won't be me that gives you away. And I'll have to stop calling you Will,' she added, letting go.

He sighed, and shook his head. 'Aye. You remember when Jones died and you were crying? I thought, Sally man, you might just as well cry for me, an' all. To all intents and purposes, Will Burdett's as dead as David Jones.'

Remembering David Jones' lifeless corpse, Sally said: 'I don't see how you make that out, though.'

'Don't you? Why, what is a man's life, when you come to reckon up? Whatever it is, mine's gone. I'll never be able to be Will Burdett again. I'll never dare go back to live in Annsdale, or anywhere near. I envied you every time you were going back home on your days off, because there's nothing I'd like better, but I'll never be able to. Name gone, home gone, brothers gone, friends gone. Even my face gone. It's terrible. It's terrible to want your life back, and know you never can have it. I sometimes think that of the two of us, that Welsh lad was the lucky one.'

'That's a wicked thing to say.'

He stared at her, his face like stone. 'The man who fired the shell that destroyed my face took my life from me as surely as if he'd killed me. He made me dread anybody looking at me, dread having to go out, dread looking in the mirror. I doubt if any woman will ever want to look at me again, either.

You won't. I couldn't believe it when I saw you didn't recognize me. And then the dressing came off and I saw what was in store for me on your face, before you ran away to be sick.'

'Only because yours was the first wound I'd ever had to help dress,' she protested. 'A lot of nurses are like that at the start, but they soon get over it; they have to. Armstrong says she fainted so often the sister on her ward had to teach her to sit down and put her head between her knees whenever she felt like that, and she did for a while, but she got over it, and she can tackle anything now. Anyhow, I wouldn't have thought you'd care one way or the other what I think about your face. I wrote to you three times after you came to Darlington, and you never answered.'

'I got the first one, and after that I went to the training camp.'

'You never answered it, and I sent you two more.'

'I know that.'

She watched him in silence for a moment, near enough to see the movement of his jaw as he gently ground his teeth. 'Well then,' she said, 'after the third letter I thought I'd demeaned myself enough, writing to somebody who never wrote back, but I suppose it's because of that white feather. You thought it was from me, and you still think it.'

They were coming to the end of the avenue of

trees lining the approach to the nurses' home, and without a word he took hold of her hand to stop her going any further.

'Well, it's all too late to mend now,' she said, 'but just get it through your head, Will. I never left you any white feather.'

'So you keep saying.'

'I keep saying it because it's true,' she said. 'Anyway, what shall I call you, supposing we ever meet again?'

'Call me Lieutenant Maxfield, or Max if you want to get familiar. That's the name Maxfield's wife put on her letter. That's who I seem to be now, if anybody.'

'All right,' she said. A wave of weariness engulfed her, making her almost too stunned to think, but a queer idea took shape from that fog of fatigue: two Christophers lives were hanging in the balance, and if the child survived, so would the man. She would say a prayer when she got back to her room, for both of them. She turned towards the nurses' home.

'Don't go in yet. Come for a walk with me in the park.'

'What, in this lot? We'd never find our way back again if it came down any thicker. Anyway, I can't go another step. I'll have to go in. For one thing I'm dead tired, and for another, it's the rules.'

'Oh, aye. The Rules. Let's not forget them,' he said.

★

Annie Wilkinson

Thursday, 24th October, 1918

Dear Sally,
   The bairns got three days extra off school
this month for tatie picking. They pulled the last
of them up in the freezing cold yesterday, poor
kids. Their school's had over six hundredweight,
so that wasn't a bad effort from the pupils, was
it? Our Emma's lads got a good share for helping
with the planting in spring. So they'll be all right
for the winter, and they've given some to me
mam, and a few to a neighbour who's lads have
all gone west. They told her they'd heard there
was a job going at your place and all, so you
might see her up there before long . . .'

Sally clutched the letter to her chest, crumpling
it in her hands. Thank God. Oh, good. Good, good,
good, good, good.

'You're wanted in Matron's office immediately,
Nurse. There's somebody waiting to see you,' Sister
Harding told her when she reported on duty.
   Nobody was ever wanted in Matron's office, unless
it was something dire. 'What's wrong, Sister?'
   'I'm no wiser than you. You'd better go and find
out.'
   Sally walked swiftly along to the administrative

226

block, her guilty mind racing ahead of her. She shivered, and her teeth almost started to chatter at the thought of discovery. No, that was no good. She took a couple of deep breaths and pulling herself up to her full height, swept through the teak- and leather-panelled hall and along the corridor to Matron's office, hoping for the best. Hoping it would be a complaint from a patient, or a relative.

She tapped on the door. 'Come in!' The voice didn't sound at all ominous. Sally opened the door, to see Matron sitting beaming behind her desk, with Mrs Lowery sitting opposite her, nearest the door.

'Mrs Lowery's called to tell us about our patient's progress, Nurse,' she said.

Mrs Lowery rose to greet Sally. 'More than that,' she said. 'To give my thanks to both of you.'

An unwelcome sight, Mrs Lowery, but Sally's face registered nothing but relief that it was she and not the police, either civil or military. 'Christopher must be doing all right, then?' she said.

'Yes. Yes, he is, although he'll be in hospital for at least another two weeks, the doctors say. The danger to his heart, you know. But how kind of you to show such concern ...' Mrs Lowery's eyes widened and met Sally's for a fraction of a second before she turned to Matron. 'I hope you'll accept my apologies for bringing Christopher here, but a mother's feelings, you know, and I was in such a panic. And you, Nurse Wilde, I'd like to give you a small token of my thanks for what you did.'

She held out a small, beautifully wrapped box, with a smile that crinkled the skin round her soft blue eyes and curved her lips until they just showed the tips of her even teeth. And had she offered her envelope and its feather to Will Burdett with just such a smile, Sally wondered, as he stood all unsuspecting on her doorstep?

She shot a glance towards Matron, and kept her hands firmly by her sides. 'I'm very sorry, Mrs Lowery, but we're not allowed to accept anything from the patients, it's the Rule.'

Mrs Lowery's pretty face suddenly looked as if it had been slapped as she stood there with her hand still foolishly outstretched. She appealed to Matron. 'But he isn't a patient now. Not here, anyway.'

And Sally knew by Matron's approving smile that she was going to open her mouth and say something like, 'You may accept it, Nurse Wilde, on this occasion.' But Sally was too quick for her, 'I'm very sorry, Mrs Lowery, it makes no difference. I did no more than my duty, and I don't want any more than the wages I'm paid.'

That familiar frown passed over Mrs Lowery's face, and disappeared. 'But if you hadn't . . . Please, take it.'

With a smile that did not reach her eyes, Sally stood

firm. 'Christopher's getting better, and that's enough reward for me.'

Mrs Lowery put the package on Matron's desk. 'I'll leave it for you.'

Patient or no, rule or no, Matron's approval or no, Sally was determined she would take nothing. With eyes like flint she looked full into Mrs Lowery's face. 'No. You mustn't. I cannot accept it. Really.'

Matron looked more satisfied than ever, and Mrs Lowery looked humiliated. Sally left the office.

'Do you remember that young lad who came to your house looking for me, Mrs Lowery?' she would have liked to have said. 'Why, he'll never come home again. The only small token his mother got was the buff envelope telling her he was missing. She sent four bonny lads to France, and there's not one of them left. Do you not think that's a shame?' Her conscience would have done the rest, if she had a conscience. But that wasn't very likely. Overwhelmed by the force her own vindictive feelings, and glad of that small chance she'd been given to vent them, Sally walked back to the ward, grinding her teeth and wondering how she could call herself a Christian.

That evening in the chapel, she showed Will Ginny's letter. When he handed it back she folded it carefully and put it back in her pocket. 'I shan't be coming here again,' she said, 'and maybe you'd better not, either. We've been caught twice and I'm not going to risk it again.'

'No, you carry on coming, and I'll stop. It would look even more fishy if neither of us came.'

She nodded. 'I might. I'm not sure. Good luck, Will.'

'Same to you. And, Sally – thanks.'

'Indeed, I will not!' Curran exclaimed.

'Are you sure?' Sally said, secretly glad that she would be the one to go, but putting up an argument for appearances' sake. 'You can borrow my cloak if you want to change your mind. It would be a breath of fresh air, and grand to get away from the ward for half an hour.'

'It would be a breath of smoke, and where would I be away to? To a fine old anti-popery party! No, Wilde, you go and burn the poor old papist yourself. I'll stay here with the kids who can't go.'

'Don't be daft, Curran, I doubt if anybody really knows what the Guy's supposed to be. It's just a good bonfire and a few burned spuds for the bairns.'

Curran was adamant. 'You go.'

So Sally threw on her cloak, and took hold of Mary's wheelchair 'All right, then. Ready, Mary?'

'Aye, I am.' Mary returned the smile, from her wrappings of dressing gown and blankets.

Louise was similarly bundled up, her upturned

little face eager for the fun. 'Isn't it exciting, Nurse?'

'Aye, it is,' Sally said.

Her face fell when the Belgian porter arrived and took hold of her chair. 'But I wanted you to push me, Nurse Wilde!' she protested.

Sally looked at the porter's rather forbidding face, as he steered Louise's chair away regardless of her protests. Sally followed with Mary, and two other ambulant little patients in train, out of the ward and into the throng of other children and their attendants, all making their way along the main corridor towards the bonfire.

'We'll swap chairs on the way back, shall we, Monsieur Dubois?' she suggested, when they reached the conservatory and together began to lift Louise's chair out of the door and onto the field.

Taciturn as ever, Monsieur Dubois shrugged assent.

'Do you know whose idea it was, the bonfire?' Sally persisted, as they parked Louise just near enough to feel the warmth of the bonfire piled high and already blazing.

Another shrug, and then, 'Some of ze officaires, I zink. I was 'ere when ze Zeppelins bomb ze shipyards. Zay would not 'ave 'ad a bonfire zen.'

'Aye, well, the air force has put paid to the Zep raids for good now, haven't they?' said Sally, following him back into the conservatory. 'Now they've flattened the Zeppelin sheds at Tondern. And we're

well out of range of the Gotha bombers, thank the
Lord. Your English is getting a lot better, Monsieur
Dubois.'

'Wait. I carry ze 'eavy end,' he said, as they prepared
to lift Mary's chair.

'Thank you.'

'*Ça ne fait rien.*'

'San fairy Ann,' she laughed. 'Well, I suppose that's
English now, in a way.'

'That's what some of the soldiers say, san fairy
Ann,' one of the children piped. 'What does it mean?'

'Eet doesen't matair.'

The little boy looked puzzled. 'He means that's
what san fairy Ann means, Jack,' Sally explained. 'It's
the same as saying it doesn't matter.'

Sally sat with her other patients on a log beside the
wheelchairs, to watch Lieutenant Raynor, and Will,
no, *Maxfield,* and a couple of other officers tending
the fire.

Maxfield stood well away, but Raynor eventually broke away from the group, and walked across
to her.

'They look as if they're enjoying it.' He nodded
towards the children, their smiling faces illuminated
in the glow.

'Loving every minute,' she assured him, rising to
her feet. 'Whose idea was it?'

'Mine and Major Knox's.'

For King and Country

'Really?' Sally tried to mask her surprise at the thought of crusty old Knox wanting to do something for the children, but Raynor saw through her.

'His bark's a lot worse than his bite, you know, and the children were just an excuse. Really, most of us are nothing but a lot of overgrown kids ourselves. Have you seen our Guy? We've even got one or two potatoes burning in there as well, just for the spirit of the thing. Of course, they'll be black on the outside and raw in the middle, so the kitchen staff have promised to bring some decently cooked ones out soon, with a few sausages as well.'

'I see everybody's been doing their bit,' she said, her eyes on Maxfield, now a black silhouette against the flames.

'He'd have liked to come across to have a word, but he was afraid he might frighten the children. Or that's his excuse,' Raynor said, and there was something reproachful in his voice. She flushed, as he went on, 'Oh, here's Dr Campbell, come to join the party. Excuse me, I want to have a word with him.'

Sally pulled her cloak around her and dragged her eyes away from Maxfield to resume her seat beside her charges who, round-eyed and smiling, were watching a couple of soldiers with a little group of other children round them preparing to toss the Guy on the flames.

'One, two, three,' they shouted and up he went,

with a resounding cheer from both men and children, and laughter from her charges.

'You can have the potato, but not the sausage, Mary,' she warned shortly afterwards, when the kitchen staff brought split baked potatoes and bits of well-cooked sausage round on trays. Mary took only potato.

'I can have everything, can't I Nurse,' Louise grinned, devouring food she'd have refused to eat on the ward, and with every appearance of relish. Sally was shaking her head in wonder at the sight when Dr Campbell materialized from the shadows.

'It doesn't take much to make them happy, does it?' he said, offering her a hand to help her to her feet.

She took his hand, struck by its strength and coldness. 'Why, no, it doesn't. How's your cousin?'

'I thought you were watching his progress in the paper.'

'I am, but "improving" doesn't tell us a lot, does it?'

'It's all anybody *can* tell us, according to his mother. I heard she tried to give you a little token of her gratitude, and you wouldn't take it.'

'We're not allowed, are we?'

'Exceptions can sometimes be justified, Nurse Wilde. I'm sure Matron would have let you have it, if it had been put to her in the right way. Mrs Lowery was frightfully disappointed.'

Sally was obdurate. 'Yes, but the rules are there for

a purpose, aren't they; to stop people buying preferential treatment, and if they apply to one they should
apply to all, I would have thought.'

He shrugged. 'It couldn't have bought preferential
treatment after he'd been discharged. I think Mrs
Lowery had the impression you had some objection
to her, personally.'

'Well, I don't know why she should think that,'
Sally lied. 'How could I have?' And then she remembered what a nurse should be − sober, honest,
truthful, and all the rest of it. But you couldn't always
be that and be tactful as well, and which mattered
most? Really, what was she turning into? The sort
of person who could never live up to Florence
Nightingale's standards, and that was a fact.

'Do I detect a tinge of sarcasm, Nurse?'

'I hope not, Doctor,' she said. 'I hope you don't
detect any sarcasm.' Which neatly avoided the lie of
saying there was none.

'What really happened when you were in that
house in Darlington?'

After a long silence Sally said: 'When I was in
that house in Darlington two of us decided I'd be a lot
better out of it, and now I see I didn't get far enough,
coming to Newcastle. It's time I took these bairns in,
Dr Campbell. Mary's shivering.'

'No, I'm not, Nurse,' Mary said. 'I'm warm, at
the front.'

'And freezing at the back, like I am. Sister Harding didn't want you out longer than half an hour, Mary. Look, here's Monsieur Dubois.'

The porter gave Mary a rare smile, and nodded to Sally. 'Ready?'

Dr Campbell stepped forward to restrain her, and take her end of the chair himself. 'You intrigue me, Nurse Wilde. There's something about you I can't quite put my finger on. Quite a little enigma, aren't you?'

'I don't like to show my ignorance, but what's an enigma, when it's at home?' Sally asked, casting a last glance round for Maxfield. There he was, standing just beyond the fire, the unwounded side of his face illuminated in its glow, and except for that horrible moustache looking exactly like the old Will, reminding her just what a 'looker' he once was. A wave of panic swept over her. If she could recognize him, others might too. He should have more sense than to stand about among hordes of people. She stooped to hide her face, and usher her ambulant charges inside.

Dr Campbell sent the porter on ahead, and returned with Sally for Louise.

'Thank you, Dr Campbell,' Sally murmured.

'*Ça ne fait rien*, as the porter would say,' he said, with a smile at Louise. 'I'm not such a bad fellow, after all.'

For King and Country

But Sally's eyes were on Maxfield, who turned his head and waved at her. She surreptitiously waved back before helping Dr Campbell with the chair. 'Thank you, Doctor,' Louise piped with something of an edge to her little voice, as they carefully put her inside.

'Thank you, Doctor,' Sally echoed, taking sole charge of it, and with the other children in train heading back towards the ward.

Halfway along the main corridor, and well out of earshot, Louise said: 'San fairy Ann to him, an' all. I don't like that doctor.'

'Why, Louise, why ever not?' Sally asked. 'He was kind to you.'

'He's too nosey. And he was telling you off.'

Chapter Eleven

The bonfire was still burning when they went off duty, and as she and Curran passed through the conservatory they saw Armstrong among a group of others, watching it through the window. Sally threw her cloak over her shoulders and edged between them to the conservatory door.

'Wilde, you absolutely stink of smoke!'

'Aye, I know that. And seeing as I already stink, I'm going out again. I can see one or two of the patients I've nursed, and I want to know how they're getting on,' she said, stepping out into the cold night air.

'Fraternizing? You'll get wrong, Wilde!' one of the girls called, but Sally continued down the steps and onto the field. There was a new moon, and away from the fire, the night was pitch black. If Will were still there, she might find out whether his mother had managed to contact him.

Curran and Armstrong followed her, both without

cloaks. 'I see they've finished burning the poor old Guy,' Curran said. 'Holy Mother of God, it's freezing. Let's get to the fire.'

'There's something so primitive about gathering round a fire, isn't there?' said Armstrong. 'Something tribal, somehow. We used to have some grand Guy Fawkes nights at home . . .'

There was no Will to be seen, but several soldier patients were still standing about or sitting in wheel-chairs drinking their beer ration and smoking. Sally separated from her friends and went to exchange a few words with the young revolutionary with the shattered ankle she'd nursed before she went to the officers' ward.

He hoisted himself up on his crutches at her approach. 'It was bloody freezing this time last year in the trenches. We couldn't have a nice warm fire like this,' he said. 'Daren't let a light show.'

'I suppose not.'

'They're about finished now, though.'

'Who? The Germans?'

'Aye. It won't be long now.'

'How do you know?'

'I read the papers. Their allies have had it. Turkey's surrendered. The Austrian army's destroyed. And their civilians are starving, thanks to the blockade. Vienna's in a bad way, and a lot of women and kids who were rioting for food in Essen have been cut down by their own army! Umpteen wounded and some of 'em killed, an' all. We'd be in the same state, if it hadn't been for our merchant seamen.'

'I know,' said Sally. 'We're lucky to have them. We've got some brave men in all the services.'

'Aye. It looks as if we'll pull through. They've stopped going for our shipping with the U-boats now; they wouldn't have done that if they thought they could win. Scared of what's going to happen after the Armistice. There'll be a price to pay, but I think the Germans blame their Kaiser more than they blame us; they want shot of him altogether, and they hate Prince Willi even more.'

'None of you will ever have to go back to France, then.'

'Not me, anyway, I've had it for any more soldiering.' He jerked his head towards his fellow patients and snorted. 'Look at us, the 3C classes of the Empire. There's some were never fit to go in the first place, and we're buggered altogether now, the best part of us. Fit for nothing but selling matches and begging on street corners, and I shouldn't be surprised if that's what a lot of us will be doing, before long.'

'I've heard the government's going to have a Ministry of Health, to start looking after the bairns, make sure all the women can have a midwife, and that. So things will be a bit better for the young ones coming up.'

'Aye, they'll want to start breeding plenty of cannon fodder for the next showdown.'

'I hope not. How's your ankle?'

'All right. I thought they'd end up lopping it off, but it's healing better than I thought.'

'And your chest?'

'Not good. I reckon I'll have had it if I get this Spanish 'flu. There's a couple of lads got brought onto our ward, and shifted off straight after when it turned out they'd got it. We heard one of them's got septic pneumonia. That'll be the finish of him, and after coming through everything in France, an' all. There's people dropping like flies. Still, the parsons keep telling us God's in his Heaven, and all's right with the world. All I can say to that is He ought to be court-martialled for sleeping on his watch.'

'The Lord works in mysterious ways his wonders to perform,' Sally said. 'I've still got a bit of faith, so I'll say a prayer for you.' She spotted Raynor. 'Oh, there's somebody else I want to see.'

'That'll do us a lot of good, *praying*,' he called after her. 'It's not prayers we want, it's a bloody revolution.'

Raynor was swaying slightly as she caught up with him. 'Kiddie-winkies safely tucked up in bed, are they?' he asked.

'For the past hour, at least. Have you been at the port again, Lieutenant Raynor?'

'Port and cigs. It's the chief's sovereign cure for tetanus.'

'I know, but I think you've gone overboard a bit tonight, haven't you?'

'Aided and abetted by Maxfield, yes. Thank God we've got one good arm between us.'

'So Lieutenant Maxfield's still looking after you?'

He nodded. 'Regular nursemaid. He's a good chap, although I know you don't think so. He's about somewhere, which will be your cue to disappear, I suppose.'

'I suppose. Goodbyeee,' she said, matching her actions to his words. She'd gone no more than a dozen steps when she felt a hand on her arm. Dr Campbell again.

'I say, those poor little things on children's medical, they make you feel humble, don't they?'

She moved out of reach. 'Yes, Doctor, they do.'

'They do, indeed,' he repeated, leaning back the better to look at her. 'Do you know what I realized, after you took that poor little thing back to the ward?'

'No, Doctor.'

'I realized you hadn't told me a bally thing about what really happened in Darlington.'

'Did you?'

'Yes, I did.' He moved towards her and the hand was back on her arm.

She cast a last glance round the field. There were

one or two black silhouettes in the shadows, but nobody she could distinguish as Maxfield, and in any case she saw no prospect of shaking Dr Campbell off as long as she stayed outside. Better give it up as a bad job. 'Nothing happened,' she murmured, and caught sight of Armstrong just going up the conservatory steps. 'Excuse me, Dr Campbell. It's getting on for bedtime, and my friends have gone in. Home Sister will be out looking for us before long.'

'Shame. I should have liked a nice long conversation with you,' he said, giving her arm a squeeze. 'Get to know you better. A little enigma, our Nurse Wilde, a riddle I have to work out. An en-ig-ma.'

'Good night, Dr Campbell.' She smiled and before she broke loose from him it was on the tip of her tongue to ask if the chief had prescribed him a ration of port as well. He'd certainly had a glass or two of something.

'My word, you seem very friendly with Dr Campbell,' said Armstrong, when they were back in the kitchen of the nurses' home, standing over the kettle to make sure they had first claim on the boiling water.

Sally spooned cocoa into three beakers and added a drop of milk to each, then handed one of them to Armstrong. 'Not really. I once worked for some relations of his as a housemaid, and I left,' she said.

'That was just before I started nursing. I don't know what they've told him about it, but not enough to satisfy him. He wants to know the far end.'

Armstrong began stirring the cocoa to a paste. 'What's there to know?' she asked.

A group of fellow probationers stuck their noses in the door, and conversation ceased. 'Put the kettle on again, when you've finished, will you?' they asked, and disappeared.

'Go on, then,' Armstrong prompted.

'Go on what?'

'With your tale.'

Her spoon scraping vigorously round the beaker, Sally said: 'There was a bit of trouble, that's all.'

'What about?'

She paused in her stirring. 'Why, them two and me, I suppose. I hadn't been there much longer than a month when he – he was a doctor, an' all, I think I told you that – he asks me to go into his evening surgery and help him with a feller who'd had one too many, and then fallen and nearly bitten his tongue off. You know, hold the man's head still and get him to keep his mouth open while he put the stitches in.'

'Couldn't she have done it?'

'His wife? She wouldn't. She couldn't stand the sight of blood, but I was quite happy to be doing something a bit different. Anyway, it got to be a regular thing, and then she starts to think I'm not getting

Annie Wilkinson

enough of the housework done, and I'm in the middle of it all, trying to please them both. I couldn't please either, at the finish. He comes and asks me to help, and I'm looking at her, and she's looking at me, and I don't know what she's thinking, but I'm thinking: "Why, I cannot help it, can I? I'm just the skivvy; I have to do what I'm told."'

'Oh, my word. So what happened in the end?'

'In the end, I finished up working for him and then working twice as long again for her, making sure she got her pound of flesh, so I was on my feet all the hours God sent. The bairn sometimes had nightmares an' all, but she never got up with him; that was always me. In the end, I was just about on my knees, pulled all ways between the lot of them. So I decided I liked his sort of work a lot better than hers, and I applied for nurse training, and I think I would rather starve now, than take another job in service. And that's all there is to that.'

'Is it?' Armstrong put her beaker down, and began to stir the mixture in Curran's. 'Maybe Dr Campbell's getting bored with Dunkley. Fancies a change, and his relations are just an excuse to get you into conversation,' she said.

'I hope not,' said Sally. 'I wouldn't like to get on the wrong side of Dunkley, either.'

'No,' said Armstrong, thoughtfully. 'But he's the one to watch, really.'

For King and Country

The kettle shrieked, and Sally lifted it off the gas, to top the beakers up with scalding water.

'Anything a bit – you know,' Armstrong continued, 'about a girl, and he can sense it a mile off. You'll have heard about that young probationer he got into trouble?'

'Why, who hasn't?' Sally refilled the kettle, and set it on the gas ring again.

Armstrong spooned sugar into the cups. 'Anna Sugden,' she said. 'She started at the same time as me, and we got on pretty well. Poor little thing, I knew she had a passion for him, most of us had, but she had it bad. It stuck out like a sore thumb. She used to sneak into the doctors' quarters as well; Dunkley wasn't the first at that game, and she won't be the last. And he's not the only doctor to smuggle a girl in, either. Sugden said the housemen keep a book of all the nurses they get up there. Needless to say, my name isn't in it. Don't mind me saying this, Wilde, but I hope yours won't be, either, because he wouldn't cop the worst of it – you would.'

Sally grinned. 'I don't mind you saying it. But I'm not as green as you seem to think. I couldn't be, not with a brother like our Arthur!'

Armstrong picked up two of the beakers. 'Brothers have their uses, at times.'

Sally lifted the other one. 'Away then. Curran must be out of the bath by now, and we'll get ten minutes before lights out. That's another reason I'd never entertain service again – having a laugh with the rest of the lasses. It might be like a nunnery here, but we're good company for one another. It's a sight better than spending hours on your own scrubbing and rubbing for somebody like Mrs Lowery.'

After lights out she closed her eyes, and was transported back to the tiny room where she used to stand among shelves of gleaming amber jars of medicines and pills, and lotions and potions, each with its enchanting label in Gothic lettering bordered in gold. She'd never minded being on her own in there, at the back of the surgery, counting out pills and putting them in tiny bottles, making out labels and gluing them on. What pride she'd taken in scooping lanolin or zinc and castor oil cream out of a massive jar with a palette knife and squashing it down into a little pot, and then levelling the top and screwing on the lid, with the happy thought that it would soon cure little Johnny's nappy rash. How carefully she'd poured the gentian violet through that tiny, chipped enamel funnel, knowing what a hideous stain it would make if it got spilled on the teak counter. Instead, her steady hand would guide it safely into an even tinier bottle, to be taken home and painted onto the inside of a baby's mouth to cure its thrush, or onto a patient's skin to get rid of ringworm. She'd loved being the doctor's little helper and was never happier than in that tiny dispensary. Yes, happy hours they'd been, when she would jump to attention as soon as the doctor called her, to help with fractures or stitches or some such thing, and then listen entranced as he explained what was wrong, and what had to be done. And all the time she'd been learning, learning, learning, and hero-worshiping the man who treated her, a lowly little miner's daughter, as though she had some intelligence, as though she had a brain.

But then Mrs Lowery had begun to resent the time the housemaid spent helping the doctor, and whenever he called for her she would find something – some trifling task in the house or the kitchen that had to be done by the housemaid, that minute. Then the housemaid began to resent Mrs Lowery, although she was certain she'd never shown it. Things were coming to a head, but it was when the doctor started wanting to take her out on his calls with him, Sally knew there was going to be trouble.

She'd only told Armstrong half the tale. The rest didn't bear thinking about. She turned on her side and pulled the pillow down to support her neck, then drew her knees up and tucked her feet into her nightie, determined that she wouldn't think about it, because if she let her mind start running on that track, she'd never get to sleep. But determination availed nothing; the more she dragged her thoughts away from the Lowerys, the more they were drawn back.

She'd lain there for five minutes or so, becoming more and more wakeful, when her ears pricked up at the sound of something spattering on her window. Nothing but a gust of rain. It would soon put the last of the bonfire out. But no, there it was again, not rain, something else – gravel. Thanking her lucky stars that Curran and Armstrong were back in their own rooms she crept out of bed and carefully raised the sash, to peer out into a night that was as black as pitch, with only a thin sliver of a moon hanging in the sky, giving no light at all. She could make nothing out, and then she heard it, a muted hiss:

'Sally! Sally!'

What was he thinking of, doing such a stupid thing? If anybody heard him ... She slipped her slate blue serge skirt on over her nightie, put on her good coat and her hat and, stealthy as a cat, groped her way out of her room, along the corridor, and down the back-stairs, to find the back door was locked.

Oh, heavens, she ought to have known. She racked her brains for the nearest escape route, but there was nowhere nearby. The conservatory doors would be locked by now as well. She would have to go the full length of the bottom corridor, and see if she could get out of the window in the probationers' sitting room. As silent as a serpent she slid along, gained the sitting room, crossed to the window and raised the sash.

With nerves as taut as a bowstring, she slipped out of the window. He must have been listening for the slightest sound because he was there beside her in a moment. 'Have you gone wrong in your mind?' she whispered.

'I wanted to talk, that's all. To hear my own voice, talking to somebody who knows who I am, before I do go "wrong in my mind". Come on, there's still a bit of light from the bonfire.'

'But throwing gravel at my bedroom window, man!' she protested, trying to keep up with him. 'What if somebody heard you? And how did you know which one?'

'Reconnaisance. They teach you that in the army. And nobody did see me. Anyway, I'm beginning not to care.'

'What? Well then, what about me? I care. I don't want to spend years of my life sitting in a cell, sewing mailbags.'

'That's not very likely.

'Of course it's likely!' She gave an exasperated sigh. 'What's brought this on, anyway? It's not so long since you were begging me to carry letters to your mother, and keep my mouth shut about it, and now I have, you're going to end up getting us both caught. Just have a bit of patience. She'll find a way to get to you.'

'She already has. I saw her yesterday, sitting on the platform in Central Station.'

They'd reached the corner of the building, just within sight of the bonfire's dying embers. Sally stopped, and after walking on for a few paces, he returned, to stand beside her. 'Central Station! What a stupid place to choose!' she hissed. 'The amount of people who go through there! Anybody might have seen you.'

'Anybody might, but they wouldn't take any notice. Not when it's dark and they're all intent on getting home. A soldier in an Australian uniform, hiding behind his newspaper? People wouldn't be looking for Will Burdett under that lot. They wouldn't be looking for me at all. I'm dead, remember?'

'You soon will be, if you carry on the way you are.'

'You should have seen the way she looked when she first saw me; she didn't know whether to laugh or cry, and she hasn't even seen what's under the dressing yet. She looks about fifty years older an' all. She's gone as thin as a rake. It bucked me up no end, I can tell you.'

'Well, at least she knows you're alive now. She must be glad she's got one of you back.'

'You wouldn't have known it. After a bit she just sat there beside me with the tears dripping off her nose end, and I'm behind the paper, cracking on

I don't know her. And then she got on the train, and I'd have sold my soul to get on with her and go home but I just had to sit there, and watch it go, and think: it's finished. It's all changed – we're not even the same people. I can't be your son; I can't be Will Burdett any more, and you'd be better off if you'd never had me, or any of us. It was the same when I saw you at the bonfire, and you were talking to some of the lads and then Dr Campbell shoved his way in. If Will Burdett had been alive they wouldn't have stood a chance, I'd have been in the thick of the fun and games, but instead of that I kept out of the way. That's where I seem to belong now, out of sight.'

'It was you I was watching for when Dr Campbell got a hold of me, and if he hadn't, I'd have been able to wait a bit longer. I'd have wandered about until you saw me, and we might have had five minutes out of everybody's way.'

'That's just it, Sally, man. I'm sick of it, sick of trying to keep out of everybody's way, and fed up of pretending to be somebody I'm not. Can you understand what it's like, living like that? You can't. It's a bloody nightmare.'

The meeting with his mother should have cheered him up, and instead it had cast him down further than ever, Sally thought. But brooding and feeling sorry for himself were no good. She'd have to snap him out of it.

'Stop it, man, or where's it going to lead? What did your mother say, anyway?'

'She's got the idea I'm going back to Stafford with her, to live with her father. One of her brother's lads is dead, and the other reckons he's going to Canada after the war, so there's an opening in the photography shop.'

'Well you could do that, surely? You could have a rosy future there,' she encouraged, 'A sight better than working down Annsdale pit.'

After a long silence came a long sigh. 'Aye, it might be all right, if it were all straightforward and above board. It might be Hibbs and Nephew, at the finish, but the police never stop looking for deserters, Sally, and the first place they look is among their relations. There's talk about an Amnesty now, you hear it all the time. But there'll be no amnesty for lads like me, I'll tell you that for nothing.'

'But they won't be looking if they think you're dead, and they won't go all the way to Stafford, surely.'

'Somebody'll put two and two together before long.'

'They will if you go parading round Central Station with your mother very often,' she said, 'but nobody in Stafford knows you from Adam. Your grandfather and your uncles will vouch for you, and you'd be out of the way at the back of the shop most of the time.'

For King and Country

'Kept out of sight in the darkroom, you mean? You haven't been listening, Sally, man. I'm fed up with it. I'm sick of keeping out of sight and creeping about like a thief. And I love my mother, but I don't want to spend the rest of my life hidden away with her and my uncle, I want to be making a life of my own among people my own age. I want a normal carry-on, with a wife and family like everybody else. I wish to God I'd never deserted.'

'Why did you, then?'

'Not because I'm a coward, although I know that's what you think.'

'Keep your voice down!' she warned. 'Why, then? Why did you desert?'

'It's time you went in, Sally. You've a day's work to do tomorrow, and I shouldn't have got you out of bed. I should never have got you involved in this. I never intended to.'

But he wasn't going to get out of it as easily as that. 'Well, you did get me out of bed, and you did get me involved, and I'm here now, so you might as well tell me.'

But he was off down another track, with the same expression of disgust on his face that she'd seen when she showed him the newspaper advertisement. 'Do you mind that time the teacher had us reading *The Tempest,* and she made me read the part of Caliban, that "deformed monster of the island"? I dreamed about that the other night. She must have had the gift of prophesy, that old witch.'

'She wasn't an old witch, but she had the gift of taking you down a peg or two, for baiting one of the poor lasses, as I remember – calling her monkey-face and telling her she had a big nose and sticking your fingers down your throat pretending to be sick when somebody said they'd seen you kissing her, until you had all the other kids rolling about laughing,' she snapped, engulfed in a flood of anger and shame as a memory that had been buried for years resurfaced and hit her with the force of a sledgehammer.

'I don't remember that,' he said, but it was obvious from the look on his face that he did.

'Well, I mind it very well. I had a habit of putting my hand over my nose for years after that,' said Sally, overcome with pity for her soft, shy twelve-year-old self whose heart had been lacerated by the conceited idol of all the girls.

'Why, I never said it, anyway.'

'You did, though.'

'Can't have.'

'Oh, yes, you did.'

'Oh, no I didn't! Anyway, Nurse Wilde, the pantomime's over, and it's time you went to bed, like the good little infant you are. You're out of bed when you should be asleep, and you're fraternizing with the soldiers. You're breaking the rules twice over.'

'You're a fine one to tell me that, when it's you got me out of bed.'

'Well, seeing you're going to sacrifice your life to nursing, you'd better not take any notice of me, you'd better go and do what the home sister tells you, even supposing she tells you to jump in the Tyne. I'm glad you can stand being told who you can talk to and what time to go to bed, just as if you were a kid, by a lot of old maids who never had any bairns of their own. It's lucky you love being so bloody subservient. It'll make your vocation easy, and when you're an old maid yourself you'll get your turn, nailing all the young ones down. That's something to look forward to, is it not?'

A lot of old maids! The insult to herself she could have swallowed, but she was stung to fury at this assault on the dignity of women she respected by a man who owed them nothing but gratitude! And that was his opinion of nurses whose years of hard training and devotion had gone a long way to saving his arm, and what was left of his miserable face. 'Yes, it is,' she said, 'and I'll tell you something else. If Will Burdett's dead, he's nobody to cry for. He was a rotten little beggar when he was a kid, and I don't think he'd ever have got any better.'

'He got better enough to go all the way to Darlington, chasing after you. He thought he was chasing a lass who had a heart, but she turned out to be a sour old maid in the making, with vinegar running through her veins instead of blood. I can see it all as clear as crystal now. Pity I couldn't then – I'd never have gone to collect my white feather.'

Chapter Twelve

'Never mind the Champagne, my pets,' Armstrong declared. 'I'll stand you all a celebration cup of tea!'

The results of the final exams had been posted on the noticeboard, and she stood by the trolley in the probationers' sitting room dispensing a strong brew from the massive brown enamelled teapot into the cups ranged on its surface. One of her own set picked up a cup, and nodded towards another third year sitting nearest the fire.

'Academic Armstrong, you're bound to get the gold medal for our year, if Pauline Richmond doesn't pip you to the post.'

Sally looked at Richmond, a very stately person who, like most of the seniors, lacked Armstrong's egalitarian attitudes and usually kept herself aloof from first years. Sally had hardly exchanged two words with her since she started nursing, and imagined that her ideas about what was good and bad for discipline would be very similar to Major Knox's.

The rivals' expressions became more guarded. 'I don't know,' Richmond said. 'The rest of you have passed as well. We've got some strong competition.'

'Not from me, you haven't, and not from the rest of our set, either,' said the third year.

'I'm glad we're all safely through, though,' another said. 'Wouldn't it have been horrible if any of us had failed? They'll be keeping you on as a staff nurse, I suppose?'

Evidently embarrassed by her good fortune Armstrong turned pink, and admitted, 'Yes, if I want to stay. But don't worry, they're too short-staffed to get rid of anybody just yet.'

Not all the finalists would get taken on, Sally surmised. They were such a small group it might have been possible, but only the medal-winners would have any hope of a staffing job. The hospital wouldn't want to pay a lot of qualified nurses while it could get a supply of probationers on the cheap. How awful for the women the hospital hadn't chosen to keep, Sally thought, taking her tea. 'There's really no chance of you doing Army Nursing, then, Armstrong?' she asked. 'Is there still a bar on women who haven't done two years as a VAD?'

'No, there's no chance, and if there were I wouldn't take it now. If the army wants its men looked after by untrained volunteers for a pittance, I can't stop it. I pity the men, but I've got no well-to-do family supporting me, and I want a decent salary in exchange for my years of hard training. I started doing a bit of serious thinking when I was nearing my finals, and when I got my little holiday I did a bit of finding out.'

'Finding what out?'

'Finding money out, my pets,' she said, lifting her own cup and going to stand with her back to the fire. 'Since I'm taking myself to market, I want the best price on offer. So I went to a British Nurses Association meeting and talked to a few of our colonial colleagues. My word, I got my eyes well and truly opened, I can tell you. As soon as the war's over I'm hanging up my halo and I'm going to work in the colonies for an eight-hour day and decent pay.'

The questions came thick and fast. 'What!' 'Where?' 'Armstong, how can you?'

'Who with?' Sally asked. 'And what about your family?'

Armstrong shrugged, and took a sip of her tea, then said, 'So many questions! I'll try to explain, and maybe that'll answer them all. The most a sister can earn here is about forty pounds a year, fifty at the absolute maximum, right?'

Right, some nodded, but other girls were shaking their heads, Sally among them.

'I don't know,' she said. 'I've never asked. I've never thought about what anybody gets, except me.'

'Well, take my word for it, you'll never get more than fifty, and you'll be lucky to get that – in England. Hardly the pathway to affluence, is it? So you can look forward to a lifetime of twelve-hour days looking after other people, and a bleak old age with nobody looking after you.'

'That's true,' Richmond grimaced, the first time Sally had known her to join in a discussion with junior probationers. 'Remember poor old Sister Harrison with the whiskers on her chin and the cap that tied underneath with strings? I used to see her coming on duty when I first started. She did night duty until her legs were so swollen she could hardly stand, and she's in the workhouse now.'

'Sure, and the people she nursed will have forgotten her entirely,' said Curran, with feeling.

'I wouldn't say that,' Sally protested. 'I still re-member the nurses who looked after me when I had diphtheria.'

'Yes, Wilde,' said Armstrong, 'but my point is, what good will that do them when they're too old to work? It won't keep them out of the poorhouse, will it? If I were staying in England, I'd be fighting for the Nurses' Registration Bill, to stop unqualified people like the VADs underselling us, but I'm not, because the society clique's got nursing battened down pretty well in this country and you'll never get rid of them, or the serf mentality of people who suck up to them. I'm off to a country that'll take me on merit and won't begrudge me a decent living. '

'Why, I thought I was doing all right with twenty pounds a year and all found,' said Sally, who'd never imagined more, and so never aspired to it.

'And that's for a twelve-hour day, and being at the beck and call of the hospital for the rest of the twenty-four, if needed. Your conditions were set by the last generation, Wilde, women who were so grateful to have any job at all that they just about worked for nothing. You couldn't blame them then, they had no option and they took what they could get, but we've had our eyes opened by this war. Just think about it! For an eight-hour day in New Zealand a trained nurse can get between *fifty and a hundred*! Same in Australia. In fact, if you were lucky enough to get into the Prince Alfred Hospital in Sydney, they'd pay you between *a hundred and a hundred and twenty*! It gets even better. In Canada, in one big hospital, the head theatre sister's drawing a hundred and eighty, *and all found*! And it's not only the money. An eight-hour day gives you the chance to have a life of your own. And it's not only the shorter hours, either. The colonial nurses can hardly believe the way we're treated, it's so different in the colonies; the nurses are respected there. So tell me, my pets, where shall I go – and who's coming with me?'

There was such a buzz of excitement in the air at these dazzling possibilities that Sally and Curran were both caught up in it, and Curran and a couple of the third years volunteered themselves without a second thought.

'A hundred and eighty a year?'

'Canada, of course!'

'Some people seem to think a lot of Australia, an' all,' Sally said. 'Our Arthur's already told us that's where he's going as soon as he gets out of the army. And it's a lot warmer there than it is in Canada. But we can't go anywhere yet, Curran, it's another two years before we sit our finals.'

'That decides it. Australia it is, then,' said Armstrong. 'We'll blaze the trail, and you can come out to us as soon as you pass, can't they, girls? Fair dinkum.' Most of them nodded, quite beguiled by Armstrong's fantasy.

'Don't take them all, Armstrong,' Richmond said. 'Some of us ought to stay and fight for the Registration Bill, and I must say, that lecture we had from the Medical Officer of Health about what a Ministry of Health could do for the babies and children of this country made me think. That's something else we should be fighting for. There are a lot of changes coming, and there'll be plenty of scope here for nurses of the right calibre.'

'Yes, but the government doesn't want to *pay* for nurses of the right calibre. It wants everything done on the cheap, with women who're qualified by nothing but their titles or their bank balances in charge of it all, so that everything can roll on in the same feudal way as before. But there's another advantage to the colonies I haven't mentioned yet, especially Australia. Some of you might think it's the best thing about it.'

'What's that?' a few of the girls chorused.

'I know!' Curran was laughing. 'It's men!'

'Yes, *men!*' Armstrong declared. 'Hordes of them, a surplus of men in some places, or so I've heard. And bigger and better ones than you'll ever see in England!'

There was a grin on every face and an outcry of giggles and protests filled the sitting room.

'Terrifying thought!'

'Thrilling, you mean.'

'Just give me half a chance!'

'You can book my passage.'

'I'll apply for my passport tomorrow!'

'The colonies,' Sally mused. 'Not much chance of ending up in the workhouse there. I bet they don't even have them. Oh, but I wonder, Armstrong? I can't really see there being that much of a surplus of men anywhere, after four years of war.'

'Sure, and as long as there isn't a surplus of

women,' Curran said, 'at least we'll have a fighting chance of getting a husband.'

'And what about the Australian nurses, when we descend on them to pinch their jobs and their men? I can't see them giving us much of a welcome,' Sally said.

Curran batted the side of her head with a cushion, and Armstrong said: 'What a bloody Jeremiah you are, Wilde! I'm warning you, if you pour any more cold water on things we'll ban you from the sitting room altogether.'

'Not after tonight, you won't. You won't be here to ban me,' Sally grimaced. 'I've only just realized – this is the last time you'll be here. If they've given you a staffing job you'll be in with the sisters and staff nurses tomorrow, unless you're leaving altogether.'

'Don't be too sure about that, I just might be here again, unless *you* ban *me*,' said Armstrong, with a cautious glance in Richmond's direction. 'But I admit, nothing stays the same for long. You two, Curran and Wilde, it doesn't seem two minutes since you started, and here you are, second years already. You'll be sitting your finals before you know where you are. Work hard and make sure you pass, and Auntie and her friends will have jobs and husbands waiting for you in Australia.'

Sally opened her mouth to ask what happened if they didn't pass, but Armstrong held up a hand to silence her. 'Ah! And stow your wet blanket, Wilde. You're both coming.'

Curran was misty-eyed, entirely carried away by the idea. 'Sure, and just tell us how to get there!'

Sally gave a wry smile. 'Just get on the right boat, I suppose.'

'Oh, there'll be formalities, no doubt,' said Armstrong, and there was a tinge of bitterness in her voice when she added, 'and it might not altogether surprise you to know there's been a society formed to help British women to deal with them, and be gone. When the army demobilizes, the men who are still in one piece will want their jobs back, and the powers that be will want rid of any surplus women who might stand in their way. It'll be, "Thanks for everything, and now you can get back into the kitchen."'

'But we're not doing men's jobs,' someone protested.

'No, but there's no denying we're surplus women,' said Sally. 'Destined to be old maids, or shrivelled old spinsters, as I've heard somebody say.'

'Disgusting, isn't it?' Richmond spoke very quietly. 'Women devote their lives to teaching or professional nursing, or playing the dutiful daughter at home, and in return they find themselves the butt of ill humour and cheap witticisms.'

'Sure, and I can hardly wait to get the next two years over with,' said Curran.

'Hm,' said Sally. It was all right for Curran, she'd already made the break from hearth and home and had come to live as an exile in a strange land, among strangers who talked in different accents and had different ideas. Curran hadn't seen her family for a year, not even for one day a month. On her days off she roamed around Newcastle, strolled on the quayside, or went to Jesmond Dene, usually alone. The thought of leaving everybody she loved suddenly confronted Sally with what that must mean, and she began to see Curran with new and more respectful eyes.

Shrivelled old spinsters. The phrase came back to her that night, just before she went to sleep. A man could be a bachelor all his life and still be respected, but not a woman. Well, she'd rather be a spinster till her dying day than have anything to do with the sort of man who dealt such insults, Sally thought. And spinster she may be, but she would refuse to shrivel. She'd make her own way in the world. She'd take courage, maybe enough to cross half the world in Armstrong's wake, to seek her fortune. And she had no doubt at all that Armstrong would go, it just remained to be seen how many would go with her. They were the sort of people that a girl with no prospect of marriage should model herself on, Curran and Armstrong – sane, competent, brave, good humoured, optimistic, adventurous and altogether admirable spinsters.

A man like Dr Campbell, who everybody thought a good catch because of his profession, and his family and connections, would be a poor exchange for friends like those. Not that he was likely to be making Sally any offer of marriage, and she wouldn't have wanted it anyway, from a man who was capable of ruining a girl's life for half an hour's pleasure. And as for Will Burdett, well, if it depended on her, men like him would be left bachelors until they dwindled and shrivelled away 'entirely', as Curran might say.

Or until they learned better manners.

'Holy Mother of God!' they heard Curran exclaim, 'There's a hell of a commotion down there!' The nurses paused in their various tasks and looked at each other, and the few ambulant kids dashed towards the door. Sister Harding sent them back to bed, and then left the ward to see what the matter was.

'Listen! What's up, Nurse?' A ward full of children turned to Sally and another probationer, their eyes alive with curiosity.

'I don't know; we'll find out when Sister gets back,' Sally shrugged, but her heart leapt at the thought of what it might, just might be. If it was what she suspected, her brothers might be safe and bound for home, but what about Will?

'Sure, and I'll find out,' Curran volunteered from the door of Mary's room, 'if you'll come in and watch her for a minute. Our best girl's got a headache, and she feels sick.'

'All right, but be quick, and be back before Sister.' Sally left her place beside Louise to enter the little room where Mary was prostrate in bed. 'Do you think you will be sick?' she asked.

'I don't know,' Mary whispered, 'but I feel like it, and my head aches, and there's a ringing inside my ears.'

Her breath smelled bad, and her gums and teeth had a nasty coating. Sally put a vomit bowl within reach, and set the mouth tray on the bed table. 'I'm just going to make your mouth taste a bit better. All right, pet?' she said, already dipping a swab into bicarbonate of soda solution. 'And as soon as Sister gets back, we'll ask her for a headache tablet.'

A couple of minutes after the job was done Curran returned, with a grin that stretched from ear to ear. 'The war's over,' she announced, 'and I don't know why I'm so happy, because I was never at war with the Germans in the first place. It had nothing to do with the Irish.'

'Oh, thank God. Thank God!' Sally jumped to her feet, and grabbing Curran round the waist, danced her out of Mary's room and around the ward. Louise laughed, and clapped her hands together, and quickly stopped.

''No! Don't you do that!' Sally said, 'It hurts, doesn't it?'

'Go on, Wilde,' Curran urged. 'It was your war, you go and jig with the rest of them down there.'

'I daren't, not without Sister's permission.'

'Go and find her and ask for it, then. Sure, and we'll be all right for five minutes.' The other nurse pulled a face, but made no objection.

'All right, I will. She ought to come and see Mary, anyway.' Sally was at the ward door and out onto the top corridor almost before she'd finished the sentence, to join a crowd of laughing, chattering people who were pouring down the stairs and onto the main corridor below. She scanned the throng of patients, nurses, orderlies, doctors and kitchen staff, but Sister Harding was nowhere to be seen, and neither was Will. Instead, she bumped into Dr Campbell as he came out of theatre.

'Have you heard the news?' she said. 'Peace! I can't believe it.'

'Not quite peace – an armistice. But it's over for now, at least. Four years late, but never mind. No more men with hideous, mutilating wounds. No more lungs or yards of skin destroyed by gas, no more blind eyes. No more slaving for hours in theatre trying to save an arm or leg to see the patient die of shock, or gangrene, or tetanus! It's hard to believe, isn't it?'

'No more women made widows, or children fatherless! No more mothers losing their sons or sisters without brothers!' Sally exclaimed, 'Oh, I hope mine get home all right!'

The corners of Dr Campbell's lips stretched in a broad smile. 'No earthly reason why they shouldn't now, is there? Well, peace evidently agrees with you, Nurse Wilde! It's brought a shine to your eyes, and I'm sorry, but I can't resist. In fact, I won't resist!'

Just as she pursed her lips to ask 'Resist what?' the church bells began a joyous pealing out of the news, and his mouth descended on hers. She offered a token resistance, and then surrendered.

'Dr Campbell!' The tones of outrage came from Sister Davies, who had appeared from nowhere to poke him viciously on the shoulder. Nothing daunted, he abandoned Sally and took Sister in his arms instead, to give her a smacking kiss. Bubbles of laughter rose to Sally's throat at the sight of Sister's eyes widening in shock, and even Will Burdett was forgotten for an instant. She laughed aloud as she slipped away from them to search the chattering, cheering, bobbing, hopping, dancing throng for Sister Harding – and for a glimpse of Will, if she could catch one. She sought them up and down the full length of the corridor but seeing neither, and mindful of the time, she made her way back along the corridor. Poor lad, except for knowing his country was saved, he could hardly take much comfort in the news. His trials were only just beginning. She started up the stairs.

Sister Harding was waiting for her at the top, and halfway up Sally met her accusing stare. 'Who gave you permission to leave the ward, Nurse?'

'Mary's taken a turn for the worse. I went down to look for you, Sister,' Sally said, slowing her pace. Not the whole truth, but it would have to do.

Sister Harding was silent for a moment or two as if considering the excuse, and then gave her the news, 'Mary's collapsed. I've sent for the doctor, but I doubt there'll be much he can do. I'm going to ring the police to let her family know.'

Sally drew to a halt beside her. 'It won't be long before all her troubles are over, then, poor little mite.'

Sister's tones were icy. 'Don't give your opinion before you've been asked for it, Nurse, and don't jump to conclusions.'

For the rest of the day Sally and Curran slipped in and out of the little room to keep Mary clean, to keep turning her from one side to the other to prevent bedsores, and say a word or two of comfort to her mother, as she sat watching her child slip into a coma.

'She got diphtheria first, and then scarlet fever straight after it,' she told them, her lip quivering. 'She was in hospital six weeks. She was never really right again, and then she started with this – kidney trouble. My poor bairn.'

'Why, and she's such a good bairn,' Sally commiserated. 'I am sorry.' And she was sorry. She tried to show her sympathy with cups of tea and kind words but she saw the mother's grief with an awful detachment, didn't so much as drop a tear for Mary, and began to wonder what was happening to her. Not to feel, really feel, for the death of an innocent child, a child she'd known for over a month, seemed terrible. But she felt numb; her senses were becoming dulled by too much contact with too much suffering. This was part of the nursing routine and she was getting hardened to it. She'd soon be like Dunkley, she thought.

No. God forbid she would ever be so callous. That was something she really *must* guard against.

'Sure, and the war might be over, but dying goes on,' Curran sighed, when they got off duty that evening.

'If only she'd never caught diphtheria and scarlet fever in the first place,' said Sally, 'she'd be all right. It all started after that, her mother said. We ought to make that our next war – the war on disease. Richmond was right about public health, and I would like to get into that. It must be something really worth doing, working to stop these diseases happening at all.'

'Sure, and I thought you were coming to Australia?'

'I know, and I've been thinking about it, but there's my mother,' said Sally. 'I'm the only one she's still got at home. Will you really go, do you think?'

'If Armstrong does, I will. I'll be there as fast as I can. We could have a great life, Wilde. You can't *not* come. Leave this class-ridden old country to look after itself; it'll soon find a new set of serfs. And there's still plenty of your family here to look after your mother. Sure, and you're never at home anyway. And what would your mother do if you were leaving home to get married?'

'Hm, she'd be overjoyed at getting rid of me that way, I suppose,' Sally admitted, and the image of the younger, unblemished Will Burdett popped into her head as large as life, along with his mother's words, 'You'd have got a bonny lad for your husband – if he'd lived.'

'I wonder what they'll do?' one of the gathering in the sitting room speculated that evening. 'I wonder if they'll send the men who've been in France the longest back first?'

'That's the only fair way to do it, isn't it? They'll have done their bit, after all.'

'I bet it's the men who're needed for industry and the mines get out first,' said Armstrong. 'The ones who've got jobs waiting for them.'

'Either way, it won't be long before both my brothers are home, God willing,' said Sally.

'Are they married?' one of the new probationers demanded.

'Aye, they are.'

'No use to us then. But the Germans will be letting all their prisoners of war loose an' all, – if they haven't already. I wonder when they'll get home?'

'Soon, with a bit of luck! Hurry up and drink your tea,' said Crump, handing Curran's cup back to her. 'Maybe's I can find a bonny lad for you in the leaves, when I've done Armstrong's reading.'

'You can't read the leaves in these vulgar articles,' said Curran, replacing the cheap white hospital cup back on its saucer with a disparaging expression on her face. 'They're no good at all. You have to have fine bone china with broad rims, am I not right, Wilde?'

'How do I know? But she couldn't very well tell *you* you were going on a journey, Curran. She's said that to three of Armstrong's lot already,' said Sally. 'If she sends many more away, we'll hardly have a nurse left. Anyway, I shouldn't be having anything to do with this. I'm a chapel-goer; my mother would have a fit if she could see us now. These heathen antics would never be countenanced during Bright Hour in Annsdale Chapel, I can tell you that.' She pursed her lips in mock disapproval.

'Oh, shut up, Wilde. And if you don't like your fortune, Curran, I can't help it, but it would have been just the same with a china cup. I can tell fortunes just as well with pot as china. I had a good teacher; my Aunt Mima's been reading tea leaves for years. Anyway, with a man in uniform who's going to get very attached to you, I don't know what you've got to complain about,' Crump said. 'It's your turn, Armstrong. Drink up, and give us a hold of your cup and saucer.'

Armstrong gulped her tea down. Crump took the cup and saucer from her hands and swirled the dregs round three times to the right, and three times to the left, before inverting the cup onto the saucer. She glanced round the company then with great ceremony handed the saucer back to Armstrong and turned the cup slowly and deliberately three times to the right, before subjecting the contents to intense scrutiny. Wide-eyed and with mouths agape, the probationers watched the pair in perfect silence. Sally sat looking at the lot of them, trying to suppress the pressure welling up from deep inside her. It was no good; it finally escaped in a disrespectful burst of laughter.

'Shut up, Wilde!'

'Shut up?' Sally repeated. 'Is that the way you speak to your elders and betters?'

'It is just now,' Crump protested, almost managing to keep the smile off her own face. 'Telling fortunes is a very serious thing.' She peered into the leaves and said: 'Hm. Mmm. Yes. Yes, it's getting clearer. I see a . . . Yes, it *is* a ship. Armstrong . . .'

Someone threw a cushion at Crump's head. Everybody chorused, 'You're going on a long journey!' and then burst into laughter.

'Why, look!' Crump insisted. 'There it is, right on the rim, as plain as the nose on your face! A ship!'

'Aye, if you say so,' said Sally, and then listened in silence, yawning from time to time while Crump continued, giving another half dozen of the probationers men in uniform and three baby girls and two boys, or one girl and three boys, or various other combinations.

When every other fortune had been told Crump turned to Sally. 'I don't suppose you want yours doing, being as you're so chapel.'

'Why, of course I do. You can't leave me out, when you've done all the others. Go on, tell me I'm going to sail away on a man in uniform and marry a ship, and have lots of babies on the way.'

Crump gave her a disapproving frown as she took her cup, and with even more ceremony and solemnity than she'd afforded any of the others she swirled, upended and turned the cup, then tilted her head back and studied the leaves, long and hard. At last she shook her head. 'There's a fork. That means a terrible decision. I see a tragic foreigner in uniform . . .'

'Oh, a *foreigner* in uniform this time. That makes a change,' Sally murmured.

'Sure, and it's probably that old Belgian porter,' Curran exclaimed.

Crump's face assumed a tragic expression. '. . . There's a deep, dark place, and danger. And a death.'

'There's no shortage of deaths here,' Armstrong cut in. 'You don't need your fortune told to know that.'

Crump frowned, and then suddenly brightened and looked up at Sally with a smile. 'But here, you've got a secret admirer to rescue you!'

'A lot of nonsense!' Sally laughed, as everyone rose and began to file out in the direction of bed. She followed, thinking that Crump couldn't very well have given them all good fortunes; it would have been too monotonous. She had to throw a bit of gloom in somewhere, dream up something a bit different to men in uniform and ships and long journeys, if she wanted to be believed. Her mother was right; it was all superstition.

All the same, she climbed the stairs wishing she'd never had her fortune told at all. Disquieted in spite of herself, she undressed and lay down in bed, and the more she tried to drive it all out of her mind the more her mind drifted back to pondering on what the danger might be, whose the death, and what the terrible decision? After lights out she lay in the dark, her imagination running riot. She ought to have known better than to have her leaves read. Such things smacked of the netherworld; they opened a gateway to the regions of hell.

Chapter Thirteen

'We sent a couple of the night staff off sick last night,' the deputy matron told Sally a week later. So you'll be off duty from twelve o'clock today, Nurse Wilde. Go to dinner and then try to get some sleep. You start the night shift as from tonight.'

Sent off sick? They didn't do that for nothing. Sally had heard a rumour that a couple of the soldiers on men's medical had already died with the typical blue-black marks of cyanosis on their faces. She couldn't forbear enquiring, 'Was it Spanish influenza, Sister?'

Deputy Matron hesitated. 'I'm afraid so,' she said at last, with a look that told Sally she ought not to have asked. 'Report to the night superintendent before half past eight, Nurse. She'll tell you which ward you're on.'

It was influenza then, but why did they want to keep it a secret? It would be far better to let people know what was facing them, Sally thought. Still, hers not to reason why, and there was no time to think about that now, with patients needing to be cared for. She went into Mary's room to find her lying on her left side, barely breathing, and her mother sitting with her elbows supported on the bed, holding her hand. She raised a pair of weary eyes to meet Sally's, and smiled a greeting.

'Are you still here?' Sally asked the obvious. 'You look worn out. You should have gone home and got some sleep. I'm surprised they let you stay.'

'I think they were glad of the extra pair of hands. It can't be long now, and I want to be with her until the end. It can't be much longer, can it?'

Sally looked at the child in the bed. 'I don't know. I'll clean her mouth, shall I?'

'I've already done it,' her mother said.

'Would you give us a hand to turn her, then?

Nurse and mother stood either side of Mary's bed, and clasped hands underneath her, to lift her and lay her gently on her other side. At that moment Mary uttered a sigh. Sally began to arrange her pillows, and then realized she'd stopped breathing. She put her cheek close to the child's lips, and felt no breath, then lifted a mirror from the wall, and held it against her mouth. There was no vapour on the glass.

'She's gone,' her mother murmured.

'I'll go and fetch Sister,' Sally said.

'No, wait a minute.' Mary's mother stooped to

gather her child into her arms and hold her for a while, and then she laid her on her pillow and closed her staring eyes. 'Her last sleep,' she said. 'She was all for you, you know. She thought the world of Nurse Wilde.'

Sally felt a tightness in her throat and her chest. Tears pricked her eyes, and she knew her nose was reddening. 'Oh, dear me,' she whispered. 'Oh, dear me,' and turned away to dab her eyes and blow her nose.

'Well,' Mary's mother sighed, 'I brought her into the world, and I've seen her out of it. My poor bairn's dead. That's the worst the world can do to anybody, and it's done it to me.' She crossed to the window and, dry-eyed, stood gazing out on the still November day, at a pale sun glinting low in a blank expanse of near-white sky. 'Nothing that happens to me can ever be as bad again if I live to be a hundred.'

Sally stood beside her. 'Look at that. It looks as if we'll get some snow before long,' she choked. 'The sky looks full of it. It's cold enough, an' all. She was a grand little lass. I'll miss her.'

Mary's mother nodded, and threw the window open. 'To let her soul away,' she murmured.

At that instant something brushed against Sally's cheek, and was gone.

★

'I've checked the ward linen, Nurse, and we're half a dozen drawsheets and pillowslips missing,' Sister Harding told her. 'Before you go off duty I want you to take the book across to that laundry and ask the head laundress to look into it. She'll have to send us replacements if they can't be found. Otherwise, I'll be forced to speak to Matron. Tell her that, will you?'

'Yes, Sister,' Sally said, and thought how like Harding it was to give her a job like that the minute before she was supposed to be off duty. She raced across to the laundry block and as she entered the ironing room in her search for the head laundress Mrs Burdett, iron in hand, glanced up. The eyes that looked into Sally's were red rimmed, and full of alarm. Sally hesitated, but not daring to pause or ask what the matter was she passed on, and then the look she got from Mrs Burdett put her in mind of somebody under torture.

'I don't know what's going on here,' the head laundress told her, taking drawsheets and pillowslips off an enormous pile. 'I distinctly remember putting the key on that hook, and now I can't find it.'

'Haven't they got a duplicate?' Sally asked.

'They've got one in the admin block, but I'll get wrong if I have to go and ask for it,' the woman said.

'Oh, dear,' Sally sympathized and, errand accomplished, was just coming away when she bumped into Elinor.

'Oh, Sally, fancy seeing you! Are you still on the officers' ward?'

Sally, indeed! Sally felt a little stab of annoyance. Here, in this place, she was Nurse Wilde to everybody, even including the doctors, but Elinor had to chop her down to size by calling her Sally. She wouldn't have dared do it if Matron or any of the sisters had been there, and if she had, Sally would have got wrong off them for letting her. She ought to tell her to chalk it out and insist on her proper title. Ought to – but the thought of Elinor going home and telling them all how much 'edge' that Sally Wilde had got since she started nursing deterred her, and she couldn't force the words out. Instead, she gritted her teeth and smiled, backing away all the while, and clutching her parcel of clean linen to her breast. 'Oh, hello, Elinor. No, I'm on the children's ward. Sorry I haven't got time to talk, we're very busy.'

'Why, what a shame, Sally man. And a shame you've left the officers' ward, an' all. You might have seen our new lodger if you'd still been there, and by, he's a good-looking lad. He's an Australian, says he's come up to visit an old mate of his that's on 7a.'

Sally blanched, and returned to her ward almost at a run. Maxfield was the only 'Australian' on that ward. She'd have to find Crump before she went to bed, ask her to tell him to expect his old Australian 'mate', and hope he'd keep out of the way until the danger was passed.

'We shouldn't be in this mess very long,' Sister Davies told Sally when she and the night sister took the report. 'The war's over, we'll soon be getting some of our nurses back from France and all the colonial soldiers will be repatriated. The work'll ease up a bit then.'

Sally saw a wry smile on the night sister's face. 'Jam tomorrow,' she said. 'I've heard that cry ever since I started. We're always going to get more staff soon, but it never seems to materialize. And if ever there are fewer patients, they soon cut the number of nurses to suit. It's always jam tomorrow, and never jam today, and it'll never be any different, if you ask me.'

Sister Davies sat bolt upright in her chair. 'I should think it's true this time, though, although it hardly matters to me. They'll have to put me out to grass before long or I'll drop in harness. Well,' she turned to Sally, 'we've had one or two changes on this ward since you left, Nurse, although we've still got Lieutenant Raynor, and Major Knox, and Second Lieutenant Maxfield and a couple of others you know.'

Sally nodded. 'I'm just a bit surprised to be sent back, you know Sister, after . . .'

'Needs must, when the devil drives,' the night sister said.

'You're a good worker, Wilde, and you know the ward better than any of the others who could have been spared, that's why I asked for you. This is your first spell on nights, so I'll make it clear.' Sister Davies straightened herself up again, and with a warning glance in the night sister's direction said, 'The night staff are here to carry out the orders of the day sisters, so you do everything just as *I* like it done, and you know how that is. I'll do a round with you before I go off, and the night sister will help you if you get stuck. All right?'

Sally nodded.

'It won't be for long, and don't worry. I've had a little talk with a certain person.'

'How is Second Lieutenant Maxfield?'

'Seems very low since the Armistice. Nothing for him here, and nothing much to go back home to, I suppose. Bad job he got that letter from his wife, just when he needed her to stand by him. It must have been a bit of a blow, that, and the sight of his face, and one or two other things,' and she looked up at Sally with an expression that implied: one of them being that he found no favour with you.

With her heart in her mouth, Sally put a cautious feeler out. 'Shame he never gets any visitors to cheer him up a bit.'

'I don't know. He doesn't seem to want company, apart from Lieutenant Raynor.' Sister Davies made no reference to any Australian visitor, but went on with the report. Nothing remarkable, but there were a couple of admissions and a patient in one of the single-bedded rooms had died and the day staff had performed the last offices.

During the round those patients who knew her seemed pleased to see her back, especially Raynor, who was very jovial. Even Major Knox exchanged a few pleasantries, but when they got to Maxfield's bed he hardly looked at her. To her enquiries about his health he gave a non-committal shrug, and as soon as they passed on the next patient he took himself off into the day room.

They heard the porter rumbling up the corridor with the mortuary trolley just as the round was finished and Sister was leaving the ward. She gave Sally a nod. 'Well, I'll leave you now, and I'm sure you'll do all right. They've been warned to behave themselves.'

The porter pushed the trolley unceremoniously past them and into the single-bedded room. As Sister Davies left the ward Sally followed him to help him lift the dead officer. He covered the corpse, and as they manoeuvred the trolley out of the door Sally's eyes widened in horror at the sight of a giant of a man in Australian uniform striding towards her.

For King and Country

He opened his mouth, and she felt as if she were shooting down a steep dip on a roller coaster, leaving her stomach behind. In a fraction of a second he would announce in his loud Australian voice, for all the world to hear, 'I've come to see Lieutenant Maxfield.' She let go of the trolley and moved swiftly towards him. Before he could say anything she asked, in the softest tones, 'Can I help you?'

He grinned and leaned down, raising his hand to turn an ear towards her. Keeping her voice very low, she added, 'I'm sorry, the man in the next room has tetanus. Any noise might start a convulsion. Try to speak softly.'

'Ah! I understand, Nurse. I've come to see an old mate of mine – Kit Maxfield,' he slurred, his breath stinking like a brewery. The impostor Maxfield chose that selfsame moment to appear at the door of the day room and stand there as if he'd taken root, showing no inclination to get out of the way or go and hide himself, but staring steadily at her with his clear, hazel eye as if inviting her to betray him. She stared back with a creeping, intensifying thrill in the throb of her heart, and her eyes widened in warning. Then she tore her gaze from his and looked towards the fast disappearing mortuary trolley.

The Australian's eyes followed hers, then, 'Hawkins is the name,' he said, 'Corporal Hawkins.'

Sally's face fell into an expression of the deepest

regret. 'Oh, how terrible!' she murmured, still look-ing towards the trolley. 'Oh, I am sorry, Corporal Hawkins, really sorry . . .'

He watched the trolley vanish into the main corridor, and then turned again to Sally, evidently expecting the worst.

'I'm so sorry,' she repeated, with the sham Lieutenant Maxfield still looking at her, 'If only you'd come sooner! I'm afraid Lieutenant Maxfield is dead.' She said it with utter conviction, because it was the truth. The impostor raised his eyebrow, appearing quite detached, as if he were a mere spectator at this unfolding drama.

Corporal Hawkins seemed stunned into silence by the news. Glancing at Will, Sally said, 'I can see it's an awful shock.'

'Bloody hell, bloody hell!' Corporal Hawkins was suddenly more sober and less genial. 'When? When did he die?'

'Before I came on duty. About an hour ago, I think. From Spanish Influenza,' Sally lied.

'Poor bastard! If only I hadn't gone to the other infirmary first. If only I hadn't let them take me for a beer . . .'

'You weren't to know,' Sally said, and after a pause, 'He showed me a letter from his wife a few weeks ago. It seems she left him for another man.'

Hawkins expression darkened. 'That b . . .? She

never did him any good. Trust her to play him foul. Probably her bloody fault he gave up and died.'

'She's recorded in his notes as his next of kin, and we've no forwarding address for her. Maybe you know his mother's address.'

'He's got no family.'

'No mother and father? Nobody?'

'No. After they died, he sold everything up and came out to Australia. He's got – he had, no family.'

'Oh, dear. Nobody to write to, then,' said Sally. 'Not nice letters to write though, are they? Nobody likes to hurt a family.'

'We were his family,' the corporal said, and with a strangled sob added, 'We were his family and he never let us down.' He leaned against the wall, and wiped his cheek with his sleeve, then fished a hand-kerchief out of his pocket and blew his nose. 'He never let his mates down, poor bastard. I'd better go and have a last look at him.'

Ugh! Her heart nearly stopped altogether at that, but like lightning she blurted, 'I don't think you'd recognize him, and I'm sure he wouldn't have wanted you to see him. I think he lost interest in living after he'd seen his face.' She paused for breath, and added, in more measured tones, 'It was a terrible mess, you know. Awful.' She'd let her tongue run away with her and shot an agonized glance at Will, looking for his reaction.

He seemed unperturbed. 'Like mine,' he said softly, lifting his dressing to show Hawkins the wreckage underneath. 'If not worse.'

The corporal looked at him aghast, Sally in amazement.

It took her a moment or two to recover, then, 'He kept out of sight as far as he could,' she went on, 'hated being looked at.'

'Wait a minute,' said Will, and sticking his dressing back down he disappeared into the ward.

'Poor, poor . . .' the corporal said.

Sally touched his sleeve, and repeated, 'I'm really sorry.'

Will soon returned and put Maxfield's wristwatch, cigarette case and medal into the corporal's hands. 'If you were his family, he'd want you to have these,' he said. 'The authorities can have his papers.'

The corporal gazed at the medal for a moment. 'A lot of bloody good that did him,' he choked, tucking the things safely into his pocket. 'Thanks, mate.'

Will nodded, and returned to the day room.

'I'm sure it's better to remember your friend as he was,' Sally whispered, and added, 'If I wasn't so busy, I'd make you some tea, but we're short staffed with this awful 'flu, and I'm on my own, you see, and we have some very poorly patients. I'm going to be run off my feet getting them all settled down for the night.'

'It's all right. I think I'll take your advice, Nurse, and skip the goodbyes. The sooner I get away from this place and back to Australia, the better I'll be pleased.'

Amen to that, she thought, watching him stride out of the ward, praying to God he wouldn't change his mind and ask to see the corpse. She wished him on the boat that very minute with a fair wind behind him, before he stumbled on the truth and opened his big Australian mouth.

Such lies she'd told! And they'd sprung so easily to her lips, those inventions! And how odd was that fluttering still in the pit of her stomach, a sort of – exhilaration – and not entirely unpleasant. But she'd no time to think any more about it, for here was Dr Campbell just turning into the corridor.

Sally swiftly unwound the bandages, and ugh! that stench you could taste rose to her nostrils as she uncovered an amputated thigh with two inches of bone protruding from the slimy, disintegrating flesh.

'Oh, good God!' Dr Campbell exclaimed, and then recovered himself and looked directly into the young patient's dull eyes. 'Now then, young man, where do you live?'

'Blyth, sir.'

'You needn't "sir" me. I'm not an army doctor. Get his address, and tell Sister to send a telegram to his parents tomorrow, Nurse,' he said. And turning again to the patient asked, 'Who did this?'

'I don't know. It got lopped off with a guillotine in a Canadian hospital in Etaples. I wish I'd died.'

'You won't be dying, not if we have anything to do with it, but there's some work to be done. The nurse is going to keep syringing your stump with hypochlorite solution tonight, and tomorrow we'll take you to theatre and put an antiseptic dressing on. As soon as we get the flesh healthy and clean a *competent* surgeon will re-amputate – either me, or the chief. Irrigate every four hours, Nurse, without fail, and do all the usual observations.'

'Yes, Doctor,' said Sally, glad to play her part. Whatever else he might be, Campbell was a brilliant doctor and inspiring to work for. Nothing could take that away from him.

He looked again into the patient's pale face. 'Don't worry; we're going to get you right. And whoever did this will be brought to book. I'll see to that.'

'What a disgusting mess,' he told Sally, leading her, as the chief was wont to do, away from the patient's bed and towards the fireplace in the centre of the ward, there to discuss the case. 'Whoever did that must have been drunk, or blind. He ought to be struck off.'

'He's from Blyth,' said Sally, thinking of the

patient, 'so his parents live quite near. They should be able to come and see him pretty regularly. And the other lad's from Benwell – even nearer.'

'Well, the war's over now, Nurse. No reason not to send them to the nearest hospital to their homes, is there?'

'Their families aren't going to delay their recovery then, now we've signed the Armistice? '

'I suspect not. There isn't the same incentive to drag convalescence out forever, and only a fool would desert now the war's over. '

'So we'll get more and more local lads.'

'Yes. All those released from German prisoner of war camps, of course, and some transferred from other hospitals. Now don't look so worried. We're bound to lose some in the exchange.'

She nodded, but her expression didn't brighten.

'We will get that young man's leg right, you know,' he assured her.

'I hope so,' she said. 'Anyhow, it'll not be my fault if we don't.'

He nodded, and there was a hint of reproach in his voice when he said, 'I thought you might have asked me about my cousin.'

She looked swiftly up at him. 'I thought he was doing all right.'

'His recovery hasn't been uneventful, I'm sorry to say. He's had myocarditis.'

'Myocarditis. Inflammation of the heart muscle. Oh, dear. That's really bad, isn't it?

'It is. Bad enough to be fatal, in many cases.'

'Poor little Kitten. But he's not . . . He's not going to die?' She'd felt near to tears since Mary's death, and now . . .

He put a reassuring hand on her shoulder, his eyes softening in sympathy. 'What a tenderhearted girl you are! But no need for such concern. He will get better, just not as fast as we'd hoped.'

She stepped back slightly, putting herself just out of reach of his consoling hand. 'I'm sorry,' she said and, seeing Will's eye upon her as he returned to bed, she was again gripped by that irrational idea that if Kitten died, then so would he.

There was no orderly on duty, so she wheeled the bedtime drinks trolley into the ward and left it, to speak to Night Sister before she started her ten o'clock medicine round. The patients would have to help themselves, and each other. As she'd hoped, Maxfield and a couple of other patients were busy at the task on her return to the ward. With luck, they'd collect the cups in as well, and free her to attend to the lieutenant with the botched amputation. They did, and by eleven-thirty almost everything was done, and the patients settled for sleep. Just the water jugs to collect now, and all the fluid balance charts to tot up.

Then everything on Sister Davies' list would be done, and there would be nothing else to do but filling in jobs, the interminable cleaning of cupboards, making of dressings and rolling of bandages.

She left the charts in the office and pushed the trolley full of water jugs into the kitchen where she stood at the sink washing them, hoping that Maxfield would follow her. A patient from Blyth, and one from Benwell – they were coming from nearer and nearer. Clean, well-fed, and with all the sepsis gone from his facial wound, Maxfield was looking exactly like the old Will when you looked at the right side of his face, and anybody who knew him would be certain to recognize him in spite of that ugly moustache. It was only a matter of time before they admitted someone from Durham, maybe even from Annsdale itself, and then he'd be done for, and so would she.

His eye was closed when she went silently round after midnight with the water jugs and the new fluid balance charts. She nudged him, and kept her voice low. 'Lieutenant Maxfield?'

No scribbled note this time. Instead, he trapped her hand in his and kissed it, but when she walked pointedly to the top of the ward and into the treatment room he didn't follow. She cleaned and tidied the room, swabbed her trolley down, and got everything ready for the next wound irrigation. She did it at two. That would start a nice, regular routine for the Lieutenant from Blyth: irrigations at two, six and ten, round the clock, until he went to theatre.

Job done, she went back into the ward and saw Maxfield out of bed, putting coal on the fire. She'd left her raggy old cardigan on one of the chairs beside it, and went to put it on and pull it close around her.

He looked up. 'Cold?' The word was barely audible.

She nodded, murmuring, 'Aye, it gets cold, the further you get away from the fire. The two new patients are local lads, you know. One's from Benwell. The other lad, the worst one, he's from Blyth. Pity it's not the other way round, it would be easier for his parents to get here. I'll have to do his wound again at six. Maybe you won't mind helping with the tea, and the washing bowls.'

He nodded slightly, but nothing more, and sat down with his blind and wounded side facing her, with some of the purple scar visible round its smaller dressing. Did he understand the danger he was in, she wondered? Would she have to spell it out for him? She pondered for a moment or two, and decided that she would. 'There'll be more and more local lads soon,' she said. 'The wards'll be full of lads who live round here.'

Still no response. My God, she'd need a hammer and chisel to get the message into his thick skull? She sighed. Better leave it for now, and start on some of the filling in jobs, before the work began again in earnest. She'd start by totting up the fluid balance charts, and she might as well do them beside the fire where it was warm, and she could keep an eye on the patients. She went to the office to collect them, looked in on the patients in the single-bedded rooms, and when she returned to the main ward she was glad to see that Maxfield was in bed.

'Why, are we not going fetch him in, like? Will nobody give us a bit hand to fetch him in?' the one-pip TG from Benwell suddenly shouted as she passed.

'Fetch who in?' Sally stopped to ask, and then realized he was still asleep.

'The corporal! listen, man . . . listen . . . he's screaming his bloody head off!'

'No. No,' said Sally, firmly. 'He's not screaming now. He's gone to sleep.'

'Dead.'

'No, not dead,' Sally said. 'He's had some morphine. He'll be all right.'

'All right . . .'

The lie seemed to do the trick and the second lieutenant turned over, his slumbers calmed. Sally shuddered and pulled her old cardigan round her, and then determinedly casting his nightmare out of her mind, she sank into the comfy armchair. The ward was quiet now, and it was cosy by the fire. She settled to the simple arithmetic on the charts, to the making of swabs and rolling of bandages – and began to reflect on the glib lies she'd told the Australian corporal. She smiled, too exhausted by this time to feel the terror that ought to have gone with the remembrance.

Three o'clock came and the patients were all asleep, the siren sounds of their gentle, rhythmic breathing luring her to join them. Despite all her efforts to keep them open, her leaden eyelids drooped and fell. Her head felt so heavy . . . she ached for sleep. She would just rest her head against the back of the chair for a moment until . . . the bandage fell from her hand and unrolled itself unheeded along the parquet floor.

'Why . . . bring him in . . . not? Cannot stand . . . screaming, man . . . give us a hand?' Agonized supplications from the lad from Benwell at last penetrated the murk of her fatigue. 'Listen! Can you not hear? I cannot stand . . .'

'Shut up, shut up, shut *up*!' someone shouted, and she opened her eyes to see gentle Raynor clumsily hurl a slipper at the tortured dreamer. She pulled herself up and with her mind still numbed by tiredness she moved towards them to soothe Raynor, and rescue the phantom corporal once more.

Peace restored, she went to the kitchen and turned the cold tap full on, shivering as she cupped her hands under it and doused her face again and again and again. When she looked up, Maxfield was beside her, handing her a towel. 'Half dead for lack of sleep,' he said. 'There isn't a soldier in the British Army doesn't know what that's like.'

She took it from him and slowly rubbed her face. 'I suppose not. I'm glad I don't have to pass any empty beds. The pillows look so tempting I think I'd get in.'

He stood closer. 'You can get in mine and welcome. I'll keep you warm, an' all.'

'No thanks.'

'You would rather get in with Dr Campbell.'

'No, I wouldn't.'

'You like him, though.'

'He's a very good doctor.'

'You like him. I saw you in the corridor with him on the day the Armistice was declared, and Sister Davies had to put a stop to what he was doing, but you didn't seem to mind it, you were laughing all over your face.'

'I was looking for you.'

'Aye, well, you found him. And he's very interested in you.'

'If he is, I don't know why,' she said, and thought, another lie. It's becoming a habit.

'You've an eye for a good-looking feller.'

'No, I haven't!'

'Yes, you *have*.'

'Stop talking, Will, and go to bed. It's past three o'clock, and you should be asleep.'

'I haven't slept a wink all night. How can I, with you in the ward? And anyway, I don't go to bed when I'm told, like a good, obedient little probationer.'

'No you don't, although I'd have thought you might want to make things a bit easier for me, especially tonight.'

'*After all I've done for you*! Is that what you mean? Because you snatched me from the jaws of death, disguised as an Australian corporal? Well, I'm very grateful, and I'd have been even more grateful before I got a good look at my face. Now I'm not so sure. Maybes you shouldn't have bothered. When Nurse Crump told me he was coming I just thought, oh well, that's the end of it, then; we've all got to die sooner or later, so maybe the sooner the better.'

'That's a wicked thing to say.'

'True, though. Normal men like women; there's an infirmary full of cases of venereal disease in this city alone to prove it. I'm a normal man, but I doubt there's any woman will like me back, not with this,' he said, pointing to his broken face. 'The best I can expect is to live half a life, rotting away out of everybody's sight in the back of a photographer's shop in Staffordshire. And unless you manage to get Dr Campbell up the aisle, which I doubt, the best that can happen to you is to live half a life here, letting them treat you like an overgrown kid, and call it your *vocation*.'

For King and Country

'I wanted to help you, Will, and I stuck *my* neck in a noose to save *yours*, but you're so wrapped up in yourself you've no thought for anybody else, not even your own mother. I'm fed up with you. You're a pain in the neck.'

'A pain in the neck!' he snorted. 'You know, Sal, life's a bloody jest. It's nothing but a sickening farce. I went to war because I wouldn't have a lass I was over heels in love with making out I was a coward, and now, when it's too late and I come back like this, I find out she never did give me that white feather in the first place. It took days for that to sink in. Now, when I've got no face, no name, no job, no marrers, no brothers and no home I dare go back to, she calls me "a pain in the neck".'

'I don't believe you were ever over heels in love with me, Will. You weren't the sort to fall over heels in love; you were the sort to make other people fall over heels in love with you. And you've still got your mother.'

'Aye, I've got my mother, and she'd have been better off never born, the way I look at her now. She'd be better off if she'd never had any of us, either.'

'Why, maybe there *is* something to be said for being a shrivelled spinster, then,' Sally gibed.

'No, there isn't,' he contradicted himself. 'There's nothing to be said for it. God made women to be wives and mothers. They were never intended to live lonely lives with nobody to love, and men weren't, either. I don't know how anybody can stand the thought of going through life like that. I know I can't.'

She shivered, and reached for the kettle. Standing arguing in the kitchen like this, it would be a wonder if they hadn't been overheard. 'What time is it?'

'Nearly four o'clock.'

'You'd better get back to bed then, and stop making a lot of rattle that somebody might hear, unless you *want* them to catch you. Night Sister'll be coming before long, to do the morning round.'

'All right, I'm going. But you think you've got me taped and you haven't, and that's where *you're* a pain in the neck. I *am* the sort to fall over heels in love. I've done it plenty of times.'

Only it never lasted very long, she thought, watching him pad out of the kitchen. Awake now, and cold, she willed the kettle to hurry up and boil so she could have a cup of tea and put her feet up by the fire and enjoy it while she had the chance, because the next frantic stretch of work would start in an hour, and she wasn't sure she had the strength for it.

Chapter Fourteen

It seemed strange to sink exhausted into her lovely bed the following morning, to close her eyes and rest her aching limbs, her work done, just as everybody else was starting theirs. She yawned and snuggled further down in the bed, picturing them all haring round the wards while she lay idle. It was nice. Very, very nice ... A picture of the Australian corporal wiping his tears on his sleeve floated into her mind. 'He never let his mates down, poor bastard ...' He never let his mates down ... she wondered fleetingly if as much could be said for Will.

She slept like the dead, and waking at about six o'clock looked out of the window. There was a full moon, enough light to see by, and it would be over two hours before she had to be on duty again. There were plenty of people about, so she decided to get dressed and go for a brisk walk on the Leazes.

★

'Two minds with but a single thought, Nurse Wilde. What a coincidence!' Dr Campbell exclaimed.

'Not really. I come out for a stroll quite often. It's nice to get a breath of fresh air now and again.'

'Quite. Your man from Blyth was the last on the list today. We've bipped the stump and put a dressing on that should last a week, so you should have an easier night if you're on that ward tonight.'

'I suppose it'll give him an easier night, as well.'

'It will. And how often is "quite often", Nurse Wilde? I've never seen you here before.'

'Why, no. Maybe not *quite* often, but whenever I get the chance. I used to go up to Jesmond Dene sometimes in the summer, before August when the big push started and we got so many casualties. It's lovely up there.'

'But now it's the middle of winter. Aren't you frightened to wander about on your own, in the dark?'

'Not really. It's so peaceful, under the stars. You wouldn't think there was anything wrong with the world.'

'Well, perhaps there isn't now the war's over.'

'Except that the war will take a lot of getting over for some people. And some will never get over it.'

'You're right. But all things considered, I don't think you should be wandering about alone. I'll walk back with you.'

For King and Country

'But I like to walk on my own after dark,' Sally said. 'When I look up to the sky and see all those other worlds it makes me think that however awful things seem, nothing down here matters very much. We're all just specks of dust in this vast universe, but we're all a part of it at the same time. It's very mysterious, and comforting in a way. It's hard to explain, but when I look at the stars I understand eternity. I know that in the long, long run, everything will be all right.'

'Don't they make you feel frightfully romantic?'

'No. They make me feel . . .' she searched for the word, and found it. 'Distant,' she said, triumphantly. 'That's it. Daft, isn't it?'

'Oh, dear,' Campbell said, 'not "daft", perhaps, but not quite what I was hoping for. You're a strange girl, Nurse Wilde, a bit of a mystic. Not like any girl I've ever met before.'

'No girl you ever meet will ever be like any girl you ever met before unless she is one of the ones you've met before. It stands to reason. Everybody's different, men and women alike.'

'And now you're beginning to sound like your Irish friend.'

'How do you know I've got an Irish friend?'

'Hospitals are hotbeds of gossip.'

'But not about probationers. We're not important enough for anybody to gossip about.'

'You'd be surprised how much doctors talk about probationers, especially the housemen.'

'Maybe I wouldn't be surprised at them talking about *some* probationers, but I'm surprised I've ever been mentioned,' said Sally, thinking of the ones who were good-looking, or who, in her mother's words, had a bit of go in them.

'Of course! You're such a conundrum. Do you know how Dr Lowery described you? "A little sugar stick of a housemaid." That's what he said. I wonder what you'd say about him? He's quite a handsome chap, isn't he?'

Was Dr Lowery handsome? Maybe she'd thought so once. Maybe in truth he was handsome, but then she'd seen an ugly side to him, and had begun to think of him as ugly, and had thought of him as ugly ever afterwards. But she could hardly insult Dr Lowery to his cousin's face.

'Now why don't you tell me what really happened in their household?'

'It sounds as if you already know.'

'But only something of their side of it – Dr Lowery and my aunt.'

'And what was your aunt's side?'

'Oh, she feared for her husband, without a doubt. She told my mother she was convinced you were deliberately enticing him away from the bosom of his family – and succeeding. So naturally, when I heard you were working here, I decided I must get to know this *femme fatale* for myself, and find out what the attraction is.'

'And what is it?'

'Not at all what I'd been led to believe, but there is something. Like your attachment to the stars, it's hard to explain, but Lieutenant Maxfield seems to feel it very strongly. I think he's languishing for love of you. And how is it, Nurse Wilde, that with you I always start as inquisitor, and end by being quizzed?'

'I don't know, Dr Campbell,' said Sally, turning to face him as they neared the hospital. 'Do you?'

Campbell started. 'Well, speak of the devil! See? Over there? I'm certain that's Maxfield, standing with that woman. I say, what do you suppose they're doing?'

Sally looked over to where Dr Campbell was pointing and saw Will deep in conversation with his mother. She felt her stomach lurch and her heart beat a little faster as they walked towards them and the nurses' home, but to change direction now would have seemed too odd. 'I'm no wiser than you, Dr Campbell,' she said. 'What do men and women do when they meet in parks?'

He chuckled. 'Well, talk about the stars and the vastness of the universe, if the man is very unlucky,' he said. 'But sometimes they indulge in amorous dalliances, or so I'm told.'

'The sort of thing an old admirer of yours was fond of,' said Sally.

'An admirer of mine?' he exclaimed. 'And who was that?'

'Well, you've had so many, haven't you? But I was thinking of Rosie Ramsden,' said Sally, all her nervous tension suddenly evaporating in a fit of the giggles.

'Rosie Ramsden? Who's . . . *Rosie Ramsden*!' he exclaimed. 'You've been talking to Nurse Armstrong!'

'Not necessarily. But you said it yourself, Doctor. Hospitals are hotbeds of gossip.'

They were passing Will and his mother now and, seeing them, he pulled his mother back into the shadows. With laughter in his own voice Campbell protested, 'Sally, you shock me! I begin to see it now. There's a decidedly wicked streak in you that only becomes apparent on closer acquaintance. And you've got a sense of fun. I never suspected that.'

Nerves tickled her stomach again, and another gurgle of merriment was his only reply.

'And what do you think of your admirer, Sally, now you've seen what sort of company he keeps?' he asked, as soon as they were safely out of earshot. 'I must say, if he wanted a lady of the town, he could have chosen a better example. Beside her, even Rosie Ramsden would look healthy.'

'Nurse Wilde to you, Dr Campbell. I've got a

living to earn, and I can't afford to be sacked for
familiarity with the doctors. And anyway, maybe he
didn't choose her. Maybe he was just asking the time.'

'But how could he, if he can't talk?'

'Ah,' said Sally, realizing her mistake and suddenly
sobered. 'Why, you've got me there, Dr Campbell.'

'I have, haven't I?' he said, and in such a thoughtful
way that shivers ran down her spine. 'It begins to look
as though the chap's a fraud, doesn't it? I shouldn't
be surprised. Shocking reputation for desertion and
indiscipline some of these Australians have got.'

They left the park and walked on in silence for a
little way, then Sally said, 'But he's got the DCM or
something, hasn't he?'

'Yes. Quite a puzzle. His physical wounds put
any return to active service out of the question, and
there's some nerve damage to the right arm as well as
the head injury, but even so . . . Do you know, I'm
more and more convinced that the mutism is nothing
to do with the head injury. It's voluntary. I wish we'd
listened as we passed them; I'd like to bet that he was
talking to that woman all right. So! just as the enigma
of Nurse Wilde begins to unravel we have another
enigma in Lieutenant Maxfield,'

'Well, it's not worth bothering about now, is it?'
she said as they crossed the road to the nurse's home.
'He's not fit for active service, and the war's over
in any case. Anyhow, I'll have to go in now.' She

hastened towards the nurses' home, leaving him standing.

'Wait a bit!' he called. 'I've only just realized – you still haven't told me your side of the Lowery business. I haven't solved the enigma at all!'

She gave him a brief wave and escaped through the door, closing it thankfully behind her, hoping to God she'd managed to deflect him from any more unravelling of Will. But the look on his face when she'd mentioned Rosie Ramsden had been something to behold, and she smiled. That was another thing about Dr Campbell that redeemed him a bit. At least he could take a joke against himself.

'Sorry.' The lad from Blyth had kept being sick ever since he'd come round from the anaesthetic.

'I'm sorry to be such a nuisance,' he repeated, as Sally removed the vomit bowl. 'I'm sorry. Oh, Nurse, I've such a pain in my leg, it's unbearable.'

'It's nearly ten,' she said, taking a cloth to wipe beads of sweat from his forehead. 'Sister'll be along in a minute to do her round. I'm sure she'll give you something for it. Can you wait till then?'

'Aye,' he said. 'I can wait till then.'

Sally left him to empty the vomit bowl and on her return found Will there, very subdued. He took the clean bowl from her with a nod towards the lad from Blyth, meaning that he would keep a watch on him.

She left them to get on with the rest of the work knowing that the lad would be well looked after, but worrying about Will's recklessness in leaving himself wide open to discovery.

Two o'clock, and all the patients were quiet. Even the lieutenant from Blyth had fallen into a drugged doze when the night sister came to do her second round, and Maxfield had gone back to bed.

'He seems all right, now, Nurse.'

'Yes, Sister,' said Sally, easing her shoulders. 'He stopped vomiting about an hour ago. He must be worn out.'

'Are you all right, Nurse?' asked Sister, watching her pull at the muscles of her neck.

'Yes, Sister. Just a bit of an ache. I slept like the dead before I came on duty, and I think it must be the way I was laid.'

Sister nodded. 'Send for me at once, if he complains again.'

'Well, I take it all back, Sal,' Maxfield told her, intruding on her peace as she stood in the kitchen waiting for the kettle to boil for her well-deserved cup of tea. 'I didn't give you enough credit. Maybes you're not going to end up an old maid after all. Dr Campbell likes your wicked streak and your sense of fun, and you like his, by the sound of it. You were just about splitting your sides when you passed us.' A frown darkened his face. 'You want to be careful, though, and make sure you get that ring on your finger before you let him get too wicked. And be careful of Nurse Dunkley, an' all, or you might not live to see your wedding day. There's many a slip twixt the cup and the lip, hinny.'

'Would you like a cup of tea when the kettle boils, Lieutenant Maxfield?'

'Aye, I would. So, he's got a nice little routine going. He spends his days ogling Nurse Dunkley on the ward, and his evenings getting wicked with Nurse Wilde.'

'Hardly that, Lieutenant Maxfield. I'm a shrivelled old maid, remember?'

'You won't be a maid of any sort for long, if he has anything to do with it.'

She leaned against the sink and looked him up and down. 'It sounds as if you're jealous.'

'Of course I'm bloody jealous. You'll go walking on the Leazes with him, but you won't go with me. I don't know why not. Nobody can see my ugly face after dark.'

'I didn't go walking with him, Lieutenant Maxfield, I went for a walk on my own. I just happened to bump into him. And you want to be careful, yattering to people where other people might hear you. You'll get yourself gaoled before you've finished.'

'Well, it's a chance I'll have to take, isn't it? I'm surprised the bloody Australian Army haven't cottoned on to me before this time. It's a miracle. I wish this bloody arm would heal. You wouldn't see my backside for dust if I knew it would be all right; I'd be out of the way altogether.'

'Where to?'

'Staffordshire, maybe. The darkroom beckons, and there's nowhere else I can go. I'll crack on I've been a prisoner of war in Germany.'

'That might be all right, as long as you don't come across somebody who really has been one, and realizes you weren't. What then?'

'I'll refuse to talk about it. Plenty do. The sooner I'm off, the better. I'm fed up of hanging round here watching you with Campbell. My mother got a good look at him. "She's got herself a good-looking lad," she said, "but he's not half as bonny as you used to be."'

She took a couple of steps towards him. 'Get this straight, Will. Dr Campbell's not interested in me, and I've got no interest in him at all.'

'Haven't you?' said Maxfield. 'Swear it, then. Swear it on your mother's life.'

There was a shout of alarm, followed by a crash. 'Sounds like your cue to rescue the corporal again,' he said, tilting his chin towards the ward.

Damn, and the kettle had just begun to boil. If he'd

been in a better mood she might have asked Maxfield to go and see what was wrong, but not now. With a sigh of regret for that delayed cup of tea she turned off the heat and an instant later was beside the dreamer from Benwell. He was in the trenches again – and stretching Lieutenant Raynor's nerves to breaking point. Sally soothed and calmed them both, picked up the spilled urinal and mopped the floor. After that, the lieutenant from Blyth started calling for her.

'She could have done this herself, instead of dragging me out of bed,' said Dr Campbell, tossing the empty syringe into the receiver, in none too pleasant a temper.

No doubt Night Sister would have done exactly that on any of the other wards, Sally thought, but this was the officers' ward, a different kettle of fish entirely. 'I suppose she had to be sure there was nothing really wrong, Doctor,' she said.

'Hm. Well, there isn't. But now I'm up, I think a cup of tea would be in order, Nurse. Bring one for yourself, as well,' he ordered her, and snatching up the patient's notes he disappeared in the direction of the office.

She turned to the patient. 'You'll be feeling a bit better before long,' she assured him.

'I am, Nurse. I'm feeling a bit better already.'

'Pain always seems to be worse at night, you know,

when you've nothing to take your mind off it. That's what the Doctor thinks, anyway. You should be able to get some sleep now.'

She left him and made for the kitchen. Tea, at last. She'd be glad to get a drink and sit down for two minutes. Her shoulders were stiff, and her head was beginning to throb.

Dr Campbell had finished writing up the patient's notes when she went into the office. He cleared a space on the desk for her to put the tray on.

'I'll have to go in a minute, and make a start on the ward,' she said.

'Sit down and drink your tea.'

She poured the tea and sat down.

'Thanks for this,' he said. 'I'm sorry if I seemed churlish, but I'd just got back to sleep after going to see an admission on women's surgical, a rather lovely young thing, and thinking about her had kept me awake for quite a while.' He leaned towards her a little, and grinned. 'I suppose I shouldn't tell you this, but it's such a gem I can't keep it to myself. I was sitting beside her bed taking a careful history, and I asked her, as one does with young women, "And tell me, my dear, when you're having your monthly period, how much do you lose?" She looked at me as if I were talking Greek, and then the light dawned. You'll never guess what she said.'

'What?'

Dr Campbell's eyes danced, and his grin widened. 'She tilted her head to one side, rather as you do, as a matter of fact, and she thought for a bit, and then she said: "About twenty quid a night, Doc!" Ha, ha, ha, ha! I don't know how I stopped myself laughing out loud.'

Sally's eyebrows shot up, and she felt a flush rising to her cheeks. She felt hot all over, and her head was pounding. She had a sense of unreality but gave him a glazed smile, and heard herself say, 'That's one for your collection then.'

'Yes?' Dr Campbell said, but his eyes were raised to somebody behind her. She turned to see Will, standing at the open door of the office gazing silently at them. He must have come to fetch her to the lieutenant from Blyth. She tried to get to her feet to follow him.

'Oh, Will . . .'

'I say, Nurse Wilde, are you all right?' Dr Campbell was looming over her, his face full of concern.

'No,' she whispered. 'My head's splitting. I'll have to get some aspirin.' But it wasn't just her head that pained her, it was everything; she ached everywhere.

A minute later, Dr Campbell was putting a thermometer under her tongue, and taking her pulse, with Will looking on, like a man condemned.

Chapter Fifteen

'Mother, why did you light a fire?' Sally asked, watching the firelight flickering in the centre of the surrounding gloom.

'I've had a fire in here since we brought you home from the hospital. You've been delirious for the past three days.'

She must be on the point of death. Her fever, her headache, her closing throat and all the sensations of pain that racked her body told her so, and the bedroom fire confirmed it. Whoever had a bedroom fire, unless somebody was dying? Her heart felt so heavy, heavy with the burden of Mrs Burdett's fear and grief, laden with the weight of Will's anger and misery. It was impossible she would live to see the morning.

Poor Mrs Burdett. Poor Will. What would to happen to them now? He frightened her. He'd given up hope and would give himself up before long, and that would be the end of his mother. Sally gazed into the fire and saw Old Death with his scythe writhing in the flames, waiting to cut off all their days.

She felt suffocated. She was too hot; she couldn't breathe. She pushed the heavy blankets off and her mother reached for a towel to wipe her sweat-drenched skin before the moisture turned to ice and made her shiver. She was dying and she couldn't help it, and yet it seemed such cowardice, such a treacherous, feeble thing to die now, when he needed her more than ever.

'Where's Will?' she asked.

Her mother touched her cheek. 'Oh, Sally,' she choked. 'Will's dead!'

'Dead! So soon?'

'Soon?' her mother echoed. 'He died in France, months ago. Do you not remember?'

'Oh, yes. I'd forgotten.' They hadn't told her mother then, that Will was still alive. That was good. Most people didn't know how to keep their mouths shut, even people like her mother. The fewer who knew, the safer for him. She watched her mother sniffing back tears as she left the room.

She was alone. The light was failing and the night drawing in, and the blackness around the fire grew ominous and filled her with horror. It concealed so many lurking demons, and every one of them intent on trapping them, her and Will. Frightful, malevolent spawn of the devil, all cunningly, patiently, setting their snares.

The light blazed in, hurting her eyes and blinding her, and for a moment she shut them tight and turned away, and then, shielding them with her hand, she slowly turned her head to see Ginny silhouetted in the window, still holding Arthur's old billiard cue she'd used to push the curtains back. She stood the cue in its resting place in the corner by the window, and came to sit on the bed and stroke Sally's hair.

'How are you today, Sal?'

I can feel my life ebbing away, and I'm so short of breath I can hardly speak, Sally thought, and heaved a sigh. 'I'm dying, Ginny,' she said at last, and saw from the look on Ginny's face that it was true.

But she denied it. 'You're doing nothing of the sort, Sally man. We're not going to let you.'

Sally squinted up and saw a flicker of fear in the depths of Ginny's jet eyes. She can't stop me, she thought. I'm dying, and Ginny won't be able to stop it; nobody will. She tried to sit up but her legs wouldn't move. They were like lead, and the sensation was familiar. It broke her dream. She'd been running, running with Will, but her legs wouldn't move, and she'd slowed him down until . . . But her sister was getting too near, leaning right over her.

'Keep away, Ginny.'

'I won't get it, hinny, never bother. We had the three-day 'flu last spring, me and me mam. We'll be all right. Our Emma's keeping away though, because of the bairns. And Kath the same. The school's shut because of the 'flu.'

'Where's me mam?'

'Out, to get some messages. There's nothing in the house; she's run out of everything. I've come to keep an eye on you until she gets back.'

'Ah,' said Sally, and wondered why that would be, unless she was at her last gasp. Her body felt as dead as her legs, her chest hurt, but worse was the shortness of breath, and a fierce thirst.

'You've been in bed six days, Sally man. Mrs Burdett wants to come and see you, as soon as you start to pick up a bit,' Ginny told her.

'Why then, she'd better come now,' said Sally, 'or she'll be too late.'

But an hour later, just as her mother and Ginny were helping her to sit up she had a curious sensation, like a wave washing through her, sweeping sickness and pain before it, and away.

'I thought my time had come,' she told her mother and Ginny as she sat in the tin bath in front of the kitchen fire, holding a flannel to her face while her mother rinsed her hair with the jug.

For King and Country

'You're not the only one,' her mother said. 'I walked into the bedroom yesterday afternoon, and I got the fright of my life. The way you were staring into that fire, I thought you'd gone. I'd just lifted my hand to close your eyelids when I saw them flicker, and your lips moved. I was never as relieved in all my born days.'

And that's a mother's love, Sally thought, watching and tending, loving unto death, and beyond it. Pity Mary's mother, pity any mother whose child is ill, or hurt, or hunted.

'Mrs Burdett's been asking after you. She wanted to come and see you, but I wouldn't let her, in case she caught it,' said Ginny. 'And our Arthur might come by a bit later on.'

'Our Arthur?'

'Aye. He's been home since the day before yesterday, and he's grinding ginger because he reckons he should have been demobbed, but he's got to go back.'

'Poor Arthur,' Sally said. 'What day is it?'

'Monday.'

Monday! Sally's face fell. 'Why, I've been at home a whole week, then,' she said. 'I'll have to get back to the hospital. We're short staffed.' Anything could have happened to Will in a week, and the sooner she saw Mrs Burdett the better.

'You're going nowhere near the hospital yet.

You're not fit.' Ginny told her, politely turning away while Sally struggled to pull herself out of the bath and into the towel her mother was holding out for her.

It took her all her strength to stand. Ginny was right, she wasn't fit. She was glad to get back into bed, between fresh sheets and sit there combing her hair for a while, glorying in her cleanliness. After a week of sweating and shivering in bed, it felt grand.

Mrs Burdett sat as far away from Sally as she could, and remain in the same room. 'I'm sorry, but I don't want to catch the 'flu. I need to keep my job. As long as Will's there, anyway.'

'Why, I don't want to give it to you, Mrs Burdett,' said Sally. 'Have you seen him? How is he?'

There was a long pause, and then a doubtful, 'All right.' Soon followed by a sharper, 'As all right as he ever will be from now on, I suppose.'

'How's his arm? Is it healed yet?'

'No. He says they're still picking bits of bone out of it. He says if it weren't for trying to get that right, he'd have been off weeks ago.'

'Where to?'

'Staffordshire. I've written to Dad. We're both going there, to start afresh, where people don't know us so well. Where people aren't as likely to start putting two and two together,' Mrs Burdett said, and added, sharper still, 'I saw you with your doctor friend, in the park. He looks a bonny lad, from what I could see of him.'

'Hm,' said Sally, not willing to get into any discussion about 'her doctor friend', because Mrs Burdett sounded like somebody who was grinding an axe.

'Hm,' Mrs Burdett repeated. 'It was all different before Will went to war though, wasn't it? You wouldn't have thrown him over so easily then! He always had a string of lasses chasing him, and he'd brought a few of them home. Any one of them would have been glad to be his wife, but you – you were the only one he was interested in. I knew it was different with you, it was serious, and he thought you liked him. Still, we can all see he's not the same lad now as he was then, and now you don't like him any more. Now his looks have gone, you've got a new one. Off with the old love, and on with the new.'

'Mrs Burdett,' said Sally, 'why did you come to see me?'

An angry flush suffused Mrs Burdett's face, and a thick vein bulged in her forehead. She jumped to her feet and with her fists clenched by her sides rapidly moved a few steps closer. Sally flinched, almost expecting a blow.

'Because he said you called him a coward!' she exploded. 'I can tell you he's *not*. He's never done a cowardly thing in his life, so get that straight. None of my lads have.'

Sally stared at her, and kept quiet.

'He deserted,' Mrs Burdett began, and then stopped, moved to the open door and looked out onto the landing before quietly closing the door. All fear of influenza apparently gone, she stood right over Sally, eyes burning. 'He deserted because I told him to,' she said, her voice low and urgent, 'in the same heart-broken letter I sent telling him about our Henry getting killed. Three lads! I'd lost three! That's more sacrifice for king and country than any mother should have to make, and I thought they'd taken more than enough from me! I got my first buff envelope after the first of July 1916, when just about every family in the village got a one as well. "Dear Mrs Burdett, it is my painful duty!" Not as painful for them as it was for me, by a long shot! And I had to go two better than everybody else, they kept coming to my house until I had three, until I only had Will left. I told him so, and I told him to get out of it, before it was too late, before Lloyd George and Haig, and all the rest of the warmongers got him killed as well, and lost me all my sons. And now look what's happened! The war's over, and my family's done more than its fair share, but my poor lad'll have to spend the rest of his life looking over his shoulder, hiding from the police, scared that somebody might recognize him and give him up.'

'I'm sorry,' Sally whispered.

'Sorry!' Mrs Burdett's eyes were wild, her face a mixture of fear and fury. 'But some people might say he got what he deserved.'

'I don't know anybody who'd say that,' Sally said.

'I thought *you* might.'

'Well, I wouldn't,' Sally said. 'And I don't know anybody who would.'

'Liar! You talk as if you were born yesterday. They're not far to seek, people like that. Your Arthur's wife would say it for one. She's just the sort, and the postmistress.'

'Mrs Burdett,' said Sally. 'I would never give Will away, and I'll do anything I can to help him.'

Mrs Burdett stared at her for a moment and then put both hands to her face and began to howl. She turned away from Sally, went back to her chair and sat down, fishing in her pocket for a handkerchief to dab her face and calm herself. 'If I'd known the war would be over so soon I'd never have put the idea in his head, and then he might be home by now,' she sniffed, her nose reddening and her voice thick. 'If I hadn't done that, he might be all right today.'

'Or he might be dead,' Sally said. 'Or worse injured. And what's the use of thinking about what might have happened, anyhow? We have to get on with what we're faced with, and make the best of it. Only be careful about talking about him, Mrs Burdett.

If we got caught, if I got sent to prison for helping him, it would just about kill my mother.'

Mrs Burdett gave her a look of scorn. 'All you think about is your own skin, and your mother doesn't know how lucky she is.'

Sally didn't want an argument; she wanted her visitor gone. She wanted to be left to her own thoughts, to let what she had learned sink deep into her being, to feel the gladness of it. 'Didn't you hear me, Mrs Burdett? I said I'll do anything I can to help him, and I mean it. And my mother's well aware how lucky she is.'

After her visitor had gone, Sally lay back on her pillows, her feelings in turmoil, her head spinning. 'You were the only one he was interested in . . . it was serious.' So he had loved her, after all. And it wasn't cowardice that drove him to desert, but that letter from his mother. She ought to have guessed it might have been something of the sort. At school he'd always been the leader of the pack, and the rest of them hadn't followed him because he was a coward, they'd followed him because he was the brightest and bravest among them.

Shame on women, she thought, that such things mattered to them, that they could blame a man for an all too natural love of his life. What was it Curran had said? 'Judge not, that ye be not judged?' But she'd judged Will, and misjudged him, too, and had been so lacking in courage herself she had actually contemplated turning her back on him in his hour of need. Shame on her for such treachery, for being so quick to judge. By rights, she ought to hang her head in shame.

She did no such thing. 'Oh ye of little faith,' she murmured, and gave heartfelt thanks for the chance to make amends. She could have loved Will even with feet of clay, and would have done – but what a relief it was, what a weight lifted off her, to know he was a worthy idol, after all.

She couldn't lie in bed a minute longer. The house wasn't big enough to contain her, or this sudden burst of energy within her. She got up, threw on her clothes, and went downstairs. Snatching her coat from the peg, she told her mother: 'I need some fresh air, Mam. I'll not be more than a few minutes.'

'Are you out of your mind? It's freezing outside, and it's nearly dark. Get back to bed this minute!'

'Just a few minutes,' she repeated, and escaped through the back door and into the cold twilight. The stars were out, and the moon was rising, and in its last quarter. She got to the end of the garden path and out of the gate, and hearing the back door open glimpsed her mother sillhouetted at the top of the steps with the mellow light of the kitchen behind her. 'Sally, Sally! Come in!'

'Just a few minutes!' she called, directing her steps

towards the path through Annsdale woods until she was out of earshot of the house. With renewed life surging through her she lifted her arms and threw back her head to gaze at great galaxies of stars, full of gladness and, for the moment, ecstatically alone.

She'd walked to the last of her strength, and it was beginning to rain, when her brother Arthur came striding towards her.

'Hello! I was just coming to see you, our Sally. I thought you were supposed to be at death's door.'

'I was, and then the fever broke, and I've been in bed so long I wanted some air. But I wish I hadn't come so far.'

'You'll end up with pneumonia, before you've finished.'

'I hope not. I'm so thankful to be alive.'

He offered her his arm. 'Away, then. Hold onto me, and let's get you back home.'

'I should be out of the army now, this minute. I shouldn't have to go back at all now the bloody war's over, but I've got to, for nothing better than guarding bloody prisoners and scrubbing pots and pans. I've a bloody good mind to hop it.'

'Don't,' said Sally.

'Why not? Why shouldn't I?'

'Because they can shoot you for it, and even if you

don't get caught, you'll spend the rest of your life looking over your shoulder, hiding from the police, scared that somebody might turn you in. And people say they never stop looking for you.'

'They'll have to look a bloody long way to find me, then. I'm going to Australia as soon as I get loose.'

'What's Kath say about that?' their mother asked.

'It doesn't matter what she says. We're going.'

'But you can't make her go if she doesn't want to, Arthur,' Sally said.

'And you can't go and leave her and the bairns,' their mother said.

Arthur sat staring at the fire for a while, his jaw tense. 'I bloody can, though. I'm sick of having her bloody family interfering in our business, sticking their noses in where they're not wanted.'

Sally gave a little cough. 'Kath seems to want them, though.'

She would have been wiser to stay out of it. He scowled at her. 'If she thinks more about her family than she thinks about me, she can bloody stop with 'em. They can have her altogether.'

'What's so good about Australia, anyway, Arthur?' their mother asked. 'They've got a awful reputation, some of the Australians. There's one in the paper today, Francis Jesset, an Australian soldier, in court for stealing a linen collar and a pair of . . .'

'Aye, there's one in court, and there's hundreds

dead and wounded in France and Turkey and Pales-
tine and Italy,' Arthur flared, 'defending the bloody
Empire, but they don't get a mention, and there's no
better lads on this earth. They'll stand for no old bull
from the so-called upper classes, though, and that's
why *they* can't stick 'em. I'm sick to the back teeth of
England, and English courts and the English bloody
class system. And I'm sick of the way our lads were
treated in France, living in pigsties half the time, fed
on dog biscuits and bully, and tea that tasted of petrol,
and only a bob a day to take to the *estaminet* if you
were in the rear, to buy a few chips or an egg, or a
glass of watered down beer while the officers were
living off the fat of the land. The Australians showed
our lot the road home, though. Do you know what
they got paid?'

'Four shilling a day,' said Sally.

'How do you know?'

'I've heard a bit of talk about some of them getting
themselves into trouble with it. The sort of trouble
our lads couldn't afford to get into.'

'Why, that doesn't make them any worse than
anybody else, does it? Their government treats them a
lot better, though. Did you know that the Australian
government wouldn't stand for any of their lads
getting shot?

'Aye. I've heard some of the officers arguing about
that at the hospital.'

'Have you heard of field punishment?

'Yes,' Sally said. 'Some of the lads in hospital told us about it.'

Arthur stared at her, brows drawn together, expression black and brooding. 'Aye, well, I got a dose of that, last year, in the middle of summer. The bloody sun scorching down, and they spread-eagled me against the gunwheel and knotted me up with my hands about a foot above my head within range of the enemy guns – and left me there with all the bloody flies crawling all over me, until some Australian lads came by and cut me down. The sergeant daren't tie me up again, either, because they'd threatened him with all sorts. And I was supposed to have been tied up for two hours every other day for a fortnight, but it didn't happen. So that was the end of that, except for being robbed of me pay and being put down the leave roster, and I still had to do all the shit-shovelling and extra fatigues that go with "field punishment". Oh, aye, I still had that to face, but there was no more getting knotted up to gunwheels, to bake in the bloody sun for hours at a stretch. The Australian lads put paid to *that*.'

'Why, you must have done something to deserve it, I suppose, field punishment,' said their mother.

'Aye, I did. I called the officer something I won't repeat, and to his face, and I meant it, too. And I still mean it because he is one, and if I ever lay eyes on

him once I'm out of the army, he'll know about it.
And that's why I like the Australians, do you see,
because they're men, and they make bloody sure they
get treated like men, and they treat other people the
same way, and they kowtow to nobody.'

Well, there was no denying it. Australia and Arthur
would certainly suit each other, Sally thought, and
she couldn't help smiling. 'A few of the nurses at the
hospital are talking about going to Australia,' she said.
'They want me to go with them, help solve England's
surplus women problem, like, by getting ourselves out
the road. They were saying the same sorts of thing
as you, about the wages being twice as much as we
get, and everything.'

Arthur's eyes lit up. 'It's not just that, Sally man,
not just the money. The Australian government treats
its soldiers like human beings, not just bloody cannon
fodder. And I'll bet it's the same with their women.
You should come, Sal. Come with us. Come with
me, if I end up going on my own. I'll see you right
till you get a job and get settled. We'll get on a lot
better in Australia.'

'I'll be another two years before I'm qualified,
Arthur. I couldn't get a job in Australia yet.' Their
mother's face fell, and Sally saw it. 'And anyway,
I told 'em I could never go and leave me mam,' she
added.

He gave her a challenging stare, and tipped his chin

towards his mother. 'You've left her already. You're never here anyway; you're a slave to that bloody hospital, by all accounts. If me mam ever needs any help, it'll have to be our Ginny or Emma that helps her, or our John when he gets back. One day off a month? How are you going to look after her, with one day off a month? It's bloody serfdom, man.'

'You're not the only one that's made that comment,' said Sally. 'But I'm happy nursing, and I want to get back to that "bloody hospital" as you call it, as fast as I can, or they'll make me make the time up before I can take my finals.'

'Why, come away out with us,' Arthur had insisted, on her last night at home. 'I'll pay you into the pictures. It'll do you good, get you away from the same four walls.' And he'd been so determined to do her a good turn she'd let herself be persuaded to go with him and Kath.

But she ought to have known better. He'd been aggressive enough at times even before he went to France, but now his mood could change in an instant, and it only took something like this to bring him to flashpoint.

'Make me, then,' he goaded the usher, his voice loaded with menace. '*Make* me stand up.'

Sally and Kath were already on their feet for the National Anthem with the rest of the cinema audience. Sally reached around Kath and gently touched her brother on the shoulder. 'Away, then Arthur,' she cajoled, 'we all have to stand up for the king.'

Arthur stayed contemptuously in his seat. 'We all *don't*,' he said.

Kath sat down again beside him, and seeing her teeth glint in the darkness, she guessed Kath took some pleasure in Arthur's show of independent masculinity, but Sally quailed as the usher began to jab Arthur in the shoulder.

He reacted instantly, starting round with fists clenched and shoulders hunched, and Sally could well imagine the look of naked aggression that would be confronting the usher. 'I'll see you as soon as this is over,' he swore, 'and I'll knock your bloody brains out, poking me. You'll be swilling 'em off the bloody pavement, mate, when I get you outside.'

To Sally's horror, people were turning round to see what the matter was, but that was immaterial to Arthur, and Kath seemed to revel in it. Something about Arthur's expression or the tone of his voice must have convinced the usher that the threat was not an idle one and Sally was relieved to see him back away, and vanish. It was not until the last note of 'God Save the King' had faded into silence that Arthur and Kath stood up, and they filed out with the rest.

For King and Country

How on earth had she imagined that four years of war would mend him? If you want to be made a public spectacle of, come out with our Arthur, she thought. What had possessed her to do it? To have everybody's eyes on her, to be a person who might be remarked on or pointed out by anybody was something she'd always hated, and now she wanted to avoid it more than ever. In a situation like hers, it was better to be invisible.

But Kath took a bit of fathoming. One minute she was denouncing Arthur to all her friends and relations, and the next they were as thick as thieves. One minute refusing to emigrate with him, the next taking his side in an argument, solid as a rock, glorying in his dominance. And he was the same with her. Whoever said 'never interfere between man and wife' was right, Sally thought. They're more 'one flesh' than outsiders might imagine, to hear them talk. A closed book to everybody but themselves.

She looked at her brother, a bit calmer now he'd asserted himself, and thought that all the qualities of the born warrior were summed up in him, the dominant male. How odd it was that he was the only one to encourage her to strike out for herself in the world, and believe she could do it.

Chapter Sixteen

The sitting room was empty, so Sally took the armchair nearest the fire. With a bit of luck the seniors would let her keep it, considering she'd been so ill. Crump was first up from the dining room, arriving even before the tea. She flung herself into the chair opposite, and then leaned eagerly towards Sally.

'I'll tell you who was floored when you went off, Wilde, as if you couldn't guess,' she burst out. 'Lieutenant Maxfield! I knew there was something wrong as soon as I went on duty just by the look on his face, before ever Sister told us you'd been taken bad. By, but we had some work to get through that morning! I don't think half the patients got washed. I'm surprised you're back so soon, though, and I'm glad, an' all.'

'You'll not be glad when I tell you the doctor won't let me start work. He says my chest's not right, and he's sending me home again. Matron says I'm overdue for the two weeks off I was supposed to get at the end of my first year, so I've got to take them now, and see how I am after that.'

'Silly old dodderer. They ought to sack him, and let Dr Campbell look after us,' Crump grinned, with a wicked expression on her face. 'He'd be more like it. I wouldn't mind him listening to my chest.'

'That's why they picked the old dodderer, I suppose,' Sally smiled. 'He'll be a lot less trouble in the long run.'

Crump rolled her eyes heavenward. 'Hm, maybe,' she said, and then scrutinizing Sally, 'I've got to admit, you do look a bit whammy, Wilde. Maybe the old doc's right. You'd better stay off for a bit. You'll be going home again, then.'

'Aye, but not today. I'll have a walk round Leazes Park this afternoon, and I'm staying in Jesmond with a friend of my sister's tonight. And tomorrow, I might have a walk in Jesmond Dene. Get plenty of fresh air.'

'Genteel Jesmond! I didn't know your family mixed with the elite, Wilde! I think Jesmond Dene's the bonniest place in the whole of Newcastle, except we never get much chance to enjoy it. You don't want to catch a chill, though,' said Crump, jumping up at the sight of the tea trolley. She was first there, but the other probationers began to troop in before she sat down again, and after handing Sally a cup of tea Crump perched on the arm on her chair, while they brought her up to snuff with all the gossip. How good it felt to be back.

'Well now, how did I know somebody would tell you I was better?' Sally laughed.

'Because you know Nurse Crump's the sort of good-hearted lass that cannot hold her own water,' Will said. 'And she fancies herself a bit of a match-maker, an' all.'

'You're right. That's why I was careful to let her know I'd be on the Leazes. Your face is healed, Will. You've got the dressing off.'

He raised a hand to shield the scar. 'Horrible, isn't it?'

It was horrible, but, 'It doesn't look so bad,' she said.

'It's getting dark. You'll think it's bad when you see it in broad daylight. I look in the mirror, and a gargoyle looks back.'

'That purple colour will fade. It'll not look so bad in a few months. I'd better not stay long, somebody's bound to see us.'

He offered her his arm. 'No, they're not. And I thought I'd seen the last of you a couple of weeks ago, so you're not getting away that easy, now. Away, and let's have a stroll round the boating lake.'

'But there'll be other people there.'

'It'll be pitch black before long, and then nobody'll be able to see us. Come on, you can tell me how you've been, and how they're all going on at home.'

'If you mean your mother, she's all right. She's not all that fond of me, though. Why didn't you tell me it was her told you to get out of it – to desert?' she asked him, her voice low.

'Why should I? That was the turning point, but it was still my own choice. I could have said no, so I'm not going to make her an excuse for anything I've done.'

'Too proud.'

'Aye, if you like. Too proud. And I thought the same way as her anyway. Three lads is enough of a sacrifice from one family. Let some of these buggers who make money hand over fist out of wars send some of their sons to the slaughter for a change. I'd had enough of it.'

'Oh, Will,' she sighed.

'Oh, Will nothing. As soon as I got that letter telling me our Henry was dead I started to turn it over in my mind, how I could get loose. The safest, easiest way is to wait until you get your leave and then forget to go back, but there wasn't a cat in hell's chance o' that. Nobody was getting any leave, although some of us had had none for a year. We were told nothing, but you'd have had to be blind not to see they were getting ready for the finale, what with all the work that was getting done behind the lines.' He paused, staring into the water, jaw clenched.

'Why, go on, then,' Sally prompted.

'Oh, aye,' he said softly, his voice no more than a murmur. 'They were getting ready for the final showdown, no doubt about that, what with railways being laid, and water supplies, and everybody working to get the roads right, and ammunition getting piled up, and everything else going on. And they were expecting plenty of wounded, that was plain to see. There were half a dozen casualty clearing stations got ready that I know of, and as many ambulance trains to start shifting wounded out. And they're not small undertakings, you know. They're like hospitals on wheels, man, there's even carriages used for operating theatres, fitted out with everything. Oh, yes,' he emphasized, 'they were expecting some bloody carnage. And the cages that were getting built for prisoners, they were preparing for a good harvest of them, an' all.

'Well, the Germans must have got wind of something, because the first week in August – the nights that we were getting the attacking units together – they started sending gas shells over, one after the other. Then we heard they'd raided a couple of units near Morlancourt, and gained about eight hundred yards. They took over two hundred prisoners, an' all. It would have been a sight better for me if I'd been one of 'em.'

'Might have been a sight worse, an' all,' Sally said. 'I've heard they sometimes kill the prisoners.'

Will snorted. 'Not only them. There's plenty of that goes on, on both sides. Anyway, the night after that they started a heavy bombardment and they managed to destroy a quarter of our tanks, with zero hour fixed for twenty past four the next day. Not a good omen, I thought.'

'So that's when you deserted.'

'No. I was there with the rest, waiting for the attack.'

Sally shivered. 'It must be terrifying.'

'Something like that. Keyed up. It's a funny feeling. Your stomach's a knot of nerves, wondering what you'll be running into when the whistle blows, wondering whether there'll be one with your number on waiting for you. Not so much terrified, a really intense feeling.' He dropped his arm, and taking her hand, gave it a gentle squeeze. 'I can't describe it, except it's more like that feeling men get about women than anything else, something like wanting a woman and knowing she's here, and thinking she might let you, just might . . .'

Sally flushed, but did not withdraw her hand. 'Might what?'

For King and Country

A sudden tight squeeze on her hand felt like an electric shock. 'You know what! It's that same life-or-death feeling. You could call it excitement, but it's a sort of calmness at the same time, with your heart going boom, boom, boom, but quite steady, and your eyes and ears wide open, everything alive, you've never felt so alive. I don't know how anybody could understand it, unless they've been there in that silence waiting for zero hour, getting the guns into position, listening to the drivers whispering to their horses, maybe hearing a stray bullet whistling over-head, or a shell. Waiting and listening, and keeping silence, knowing that a few yards away other men are probably doing the same thing, as intent on your destruction as you are on theirs.'

But she did understand it, she'd felt a pale shadow of that same excitement, and gave his hand a return squeeze, quite unconsciously. He pulled her close.

'Aye well, our guns opened up, my eardrums nearly burst, the earth shook under our feet, and we could see nothing but smoke and flames, and the men in front. Lucky for us there was a mist. That helped us, and our artillery held the German guns off. It was amazing. We were over their front line in a morning, and the amount of prisoners we took, I couldn't believe. And they seemed only too happy to give themselves up a lot of them; they must have been even more sick of the war than us. It was a cakewalk, and I thought, if this goes on, it can't last much longer. They were surrendering in droves, giving the officers plenty to do, and that's when I beat it. I thought: aye, well, the Burdetts have done their bit now, and more besides, so I got out of sight, and as soon as it was getting dark, I was off. As luck would have it, there wasn't much of a moon, so I got as far as I could while I could see enough. I started again as soon as there was enough light to see by the following morning, because I knew I wouldn't dare travel in broad daylight, and I was just setting off when I just about fell over a dead Australian.

'Well, it all went through my mind like lightning. I thought, if I get caught, and court-martialled for deserting during a battle, I'm certain to get shot, and if that happens, I want it to be as somebody else. I didn't want to bring any disgrace on my mother, and I didn't want to risk them doing her out of her pension, either. And there was this dead Aussie in front of me like the answer to a prayer, because it doesn't matter what they've done, everybody knows the Australians can't be shot, regardless. So I swapped his rig-out for mine – ugh, and when I came to pull one of his boots off, his foot came off with it, but never bother, we'd got so we weren't all that fussy in France. When you've drunk water out of shell-holes you've seen rats swimming in, and you know they've been feeding on corpses, well . . . anyway, the boots were all right, nice soft leather, and not too tight either. I hesitated a bit about taking the necklet with his dead meat discs; I wasn't sure I wanted to be identified as anybody in particular. But then I thought that unless you get your head blown off you can't very well lose them, and not having them might look even more suspicious, so I took them, and I remembered his name. Then I thought if I've got the discs I might as well have his papers, and I had no hesitation about his money, and then I was off, but I can't have gone ten yards before . . . Bang! I got my bloody face cracked open and that was the last I knew until I woke up on the ambulance train.'

She raised her hand to touch that crater that was once an eye and a cheekbone, and held back, saying nothing for a moment, and then, 'It's nearly dark now.'

'Aye,' he said. 'Darkness, the refuge of criminals and fugitives.'

'And lovers,' she said. 'You mind the start of that poem, Will?' she asked.

> Out of the night that covers me,
> Black as the Pit from pole to pole,
> I thank whatever gods may be
> For my unconquerable soul.

'Aye, I do,' he said, 'and the end:

347

Annie Wilkinson

'In the fell clutch of circumstance
I have not winced nor cried aloud.
Under the bludgeonings of chance
My head is bloody, but unbowed.'

She lifted her face to his, and very gingerly
touched that dread disfigurement. 'The bludgeonings
of chance! Oh, Will, how could you have believed
I would give you a white feather?'

'How could you have believed I was a coward?'

She bowed her head, and felt a pain tightening
in her throat and round her heart. 'We know each
other better now, I hope.'

Bundled up against the biting cold with layers of
underwear beneath her dress, wearing a cardigan,
thick coat, and scarf on top, and a woolly hat pulled
around her ears, Sally walked through Jesmond Dene.
In early summer, when she'd come up from the
hospital to spend a rare free hour or two here she'd
thought there could be no more beautiful spot on
earth. And then the August Offensive had crammed
the hospitals with casualties, putting paid to afternoons off for a time.

Now a glittering layer of frost covered boughs of
naked larches, walnut and tulip trees, the leaves of the
yew and holly, and the mosses and ferns on the stony
outcrops either side of the Ouseburn. She'd intended

to follow it no further than the old watermill and then turn back, but the air smelt so fresh after days indoors, the day was so bright and crisp, the place such a delight that she walked on, despite the cold chilling her cheeks and fingers, and in defiance of all warnings of dire consequences should she stay out too long, outrun her strength, and get frozen. The dene breathed enchantment; it held an atmosphere of magic, and the cold was as nothing. She was too drunk with love to feel it. She felt as if she were walking through a fairytale, a wonderland where miracles might happen. 'That arm's got to heal,' she muttered to herself. That arm must heal. It was the only stumbling block, the only barrier to his escape. She heard a sharp *tik* and glanced up to catch the white wingbar and undulating flight of a hawfinch, a rare sight. It couldn't hurt to go on for a few minutes, maybe as far as the ivy bridge, and then turn back, but oh, if only Will were out of that ward and here with her, to love it all as she did, to share the pleasure of it.

At the bridge she stood for a few minutes lost in reverie, gazing at the waterfall and the deep pool at its base. She'd walked too far, and she'd be exhausted before she got back. Better make a start.

'Sally! Sally!' Little Kit Lowery was running towards her, his bright hair glinting in the sun. He slowed to a walk as he neared her, and behind him she saw Dr Lowery striding along, with his wife hurrying at the rear. Her heart sank. If only she'd been alert enough to spot them all while she still had a chance of escape. She was glad to see Kitten, and could have suffered his mother, but the prospect of a meeting with Dr Lowery again turned her stomach. She'd have given anything to avoid it, but no escape was possible, and so she forced a smile.

'Why, Kit, you're running! You must be feeling a lot better.'

Kit was breathless and hesitated a few feet away from her, suddenly shy.

'I know I am,' he said. 'But I was in hospital a long time, Sally.'

'I know. I kept looking for your number in the *Chronicle*, and I was that glad when it started to say 'improving'. But what are you doing here?'

'It's my birthday! But did you really, Sally? Did you look for me?'

'I did. And your cousin sometimes told me how you were getting on.'

'I was fed up of the hospital. I'm very bucked to be out of it. Doesn't the frost make everything look lovely?'

Two laughing eyes looked into Sally's, and the pleasure on his face would have compensated her for the loss of a thousand nights' sleep. He hadn't changed towards her in spite of that awful scene, and the thought that she'd been there when he needed her elated her.

'It does! Away then, my canny lad,' she exclaimed, throwing her arms wide. He hurled himself into them and, lifting him off his feet, she span him round. He seemed scarcely heavier than he'd been over a year ago, but she lacked the strength she'd had then, and sobered by the approach of his parents, she put him down.

'It'll soon be Christmas, Sally!' Kit's voice was full of excitement.

'Why this is only the first Sunday of Advent, so we've a while to go yet, bonny lad.'

'You seem to be doing very well at the hospital, Sally,' Dr Lowery hailed her. 'I'm very proud of my protégée. Of course, I always knew you'd make a first-rate nurse.'

'Thank you,' she said, without enthusiasm.

'You're convalescing from the 'flu, I hear. But your mother lives in Annsdale, surely.'

'She does. But I'm staying with a friend of my sister's for a day or two. She only lives a few minutes walk away.'

Four eyebrows uplifted slightly as Dr and Mrs Lowery took in the news. 'In Jesmond? Your sister's friend, living in Jesmond! What a coincidence. Beatrice has cousins in Sanderson Road,' said Dr

Lowery. 'Perhaps they know your sister's friend. What's her name?'

'They call her Brewster. Miss Brewster,' said Sally.

'*Miss* Brewster. Where exactly does she live?'

Sally described the place.

'A maiden lady, living among the industrialists, and the shipping magnates, all the most respected citizens of Newcastle! And she's your sister's friend!' Dr Lowery exclaimed, not attempting to swallow his surprise.

But Mrs Lowery's interest appeared to have faded with the realization that Sally's acquaintance was a mere spinster. 'No, I don't think we know her,' she said.

Dr Lowery's brows creased in puzzlement. 'Miss Brewster lives with her parents, I daresay.'

'No,' said Sally. 'She lives alone, but I don't think she mixes much, apart from going to St George's on Sundays. But I'm surprised to see you in Newcastle, Dr Lowery.'

'The practice, you mean? I was lucky enough to get a locum for a couple of days, no easy matter these days, but Kit wanted to spend his birthday at his aunt's, and we gave in. We indulge him rather too much, since his illness.'

'I'm not surprised. Happy birthday, Kitten,' Sally said, and remembering his last one added, 'and will you be having chocolate cake again this year?'

'I hope so. Why did you go away, Sally?' he demanded. 'I wanted you to stay with us.' He looked at her with a child's directness, calculated to cut through all polite evasions.

But polite evasions were essential. 'So I could go to the hospital to look after boys like you who get poorly,' she said, 'and help to make them better.'

'The Lord works in mysterious ways his wonders to perform,' Mrs Lowery murmured.

'Indeed,' her husband agreed. 'Well, we must be getting along. I hope you'll be better soon, Sally. Keep up the good work.'

With a nod to Sally they moved off, and then suddenly, with the brightest of smiles Mrs Lowery turned back. 'Oh, Sally! I meant to tell you – that young man who came to the house while you were out that time – I saw him the other day, walking on the Leazes. But I suppose you must have seen him.'

Sally felt the colour drain from her face. 'No, Mrs Lowery, I haven't, and neither have you. You couldn't have. His mother had a letter – he was killed three months ago.'

'But I could have sworn . . . well, I admit he had a moustache, and a rather bad facial wound, but it was the same face, and the same way of walking.'

'Whoever it was, Mrs Lowery, it couldn't have been Will Burdett. His mother had all his things sent back to her.'

Mrs Lowery looked very dubious. 'But I could have sworn . . .'

'That's odd,' said Dr Lowery. 'I remember your telling me, and it's not often you're wrong, is it? My wife has many faults, but failing eyesight isn't among them, and she has a phenomenal memory for faces.'

Sally stared at them, leaning against the bridge for support. Her husband's meagre praises seemed to please Mrs Lowery, and she approached Sally with a half-smile. 'Of course, he was your sweetheart,' she said. 'You look quite ill. I'm so sorry, my dear, but I could have sworn . . . But it was getting dark. I suppose I must have been mistaken.'

Was there a tinge of malice in that voice? A touch of malevolence in those oh, so gentle fingers on her arm?

'There's no other explanation, Mrs Lowery,' Sally whispered. 'Will's dead; and what'll grieve me to my dying day is this: he died believing I'd given him a white feather. '

Mrs Lowery withdrew her hand, and the look in her eyes told it all.

'Will's dead,' she'd told them, with her knees buckling under her. The wicked witch and the warlock had cast their evil spell, and thrown a shadow over the enchanted land. Sally shivered and turned for Miss Brewster's house. If only she hadn't insisted on coming out, she might never have met them again, those birds of ill omen. She hardly knew which of them was worse, him or her. It was cold, cold, cold, and she wanted to be back inside, but hadn't the energy to walk at more than a snail's pace. This was no good. She began to hum a ragtime tune to revive her flagging steps, and was soon moving through the lovely wooded gorge of Jesmond Dene at a quicker pace.

She had been a hard taskmistress, Mrs Lowery, and a spiteful one at times. When she'd first gone to work for them Sally'd had no doubts about who was to blame for all the friction in their house; it was her. She'd sympathized with this poor man with his demanding, unreasonable wife, and had helped him in the surgery because his wife refused. And so she'd slaved for both of them and might have killed herself with overwork had he not tapped on her bedroom door that night and, before she'd had a chance to answer, stepped inside.

She blushed from head to toe at the remembrance. How could he have so mistaken her as to think . . . She'd admired him, certainly. She'd been flattered that a man of his standing should think a housemaid worthy of instruction, of intelligent conversation. She was ready to admit that she'd worshipped him from afar, and that was how he should have stayed, a romantic hero in a silly young girl's head, nothing nearer and nothing more. She'd never given him any sort of encouragement to . . . any reason to think . . . and he knew it.

And then he'd walked into her bedroom spouting all sorts of rubbish while she sat helplessly in bed in her white, virginal nightie, and two minutes later his wife had burst in on them. What must it have looked like? What must she have thought? Sally had pulled the sheet up to her neck and looked at the pair of them, appalled at finding herself in the middle of this scene from Bedlam, with the doctor telling his wife it was no wonder if he was tempted to stray, it was all her fault, and Mrs Lowery crying and incoherent, blotchy-eyed and raving, until six-year-old Kit awoke at the noise, and came up the attic stairs, adding his wails to his mother's.

'Don't go, Daddy!' Clinging on to his mother's skirts he'd screamed it, and Sally had stared at them open-mouthed, utterly bewildered at this scene of accusation and counter accusation, of tears and gnashing of teeth. 'Don't go, Daddy!'

Go where? Who with? Nothing of the sort had ever been contemplated, not by Sally, at any rate. She'd looked at Dr Lowery for an explanation and had been amazed to see him absolutely in command of himself, with a tiny smile playing at the corner of his mouth, and a light of satisfaction gleaming in his eyes. It dawned on her then that he was enjoying the drama he'd caused, loving being in the centre of it, and she'd thought: this is not about me at all. It's about the two of them, and he's using me in some cat-and-mouse game he's playing. He's torturing her, and enjoying it! He's feeding off the misery he's causing, like a vampire feeds off blood.

She got dressed as soon as they left her alone and packed her bags, and sat sleepless on her bed until day broke. Then she said a final goodbye to Dr Lowery in the doorway of his house. Mrs Lowery did not appear; Sally would have been surprised if she had, but at the very last moment Kitten had come bounding down the stairs, had thrown his arms round her legs, rested his cheek against her stomach and squeezed tight.

'Don't go, Sally! I don't want you to.'

'I have to go, Kit. Your daddy always said I'd make a good nurse, and now's the time to start.'

'I'll write to Matron and put in a good word for you, if that's what you want,' Dr Lowery said, then added, as if nothing had happened, 'but you needn't go, you know. It's not necessary. My wife's given to bouts of hysteria at times, that's all.'

What was he talking about? She could hardly look at him, this handsome, clever man who'd been her hero. She'd witnessed the ugly cruelty of him, and now she thought of him as ugly, felt his appalling ugliness at her core, and his handsome face and cleverness, and his glib tongue had lost all hold on her.

She gave the child a tearful smile. 'Goodbye, Kitten. I'll miss you.' She touched his cheek then turned to Dr Lowery, her manner distant. 'Goodbye, Doctor.'

She saw he was not pleased, but left then, feeling as if she'd escaped a madhouse. There was a tightness in her throat and tears threatened, not for him, but for the child she'd been fond of, and her shattered illusions, and for the part she'd played herself in ignoring all the little slights he'd dealt his wife, for being such a willing pawn in his game with Mrs Lowery. But when a man makes such disparaging comments about his wife they make you squirm, what else can you do but pretend you haven't heard, or make no comment if it's obvious you have? She could hardly take him to task, her employer. But in her heart she'd made excuses for him because his wife was difficult, and he'd managed to make himself appear so misunderstood, so patient and good, and kind, and noble.

He was none of those things. She wanted no favours from him and would have liked to tell him so. She'd have liked not to have to depend on Dr Lowery for anything, or his wife for that matter, but there was the bogey of employment and references, always there to force a servant girl to eat the bread of humility, if she wanted bread at all.

For King and Country

And so she'd held her tongue. There was only one person who would be blamed for that nasty little performance, she'd thought, as she walked towards the station with just enough money in her pocket to get her back to Annsdale and her mother. It would be the housemaid, and none other. Dr Lowery had plenty of surface charm, which kept the uglier depths of him well hidden. No doubt his wife could have told many a tale about those ugly depths if she'd wanted to, if she'd clung to her own judgement rather than let herself be bullied and seduced into seeing things through the distorting lenses of his eyes, with him always the hero of the piece, the coveted prize of every woman breathing. But Mrs Lowery wouldn't want to tell such tales; she'd want to blame anybody but him, and Sally had known only too well from living near him day by day how that had come about, how easy it was to be drawn in, until there was only one way of seeing the world – his way.

Will had stopped writing to her, and the demigod she'd idolized had shown his feet of clay, and hurled himself off his pedestal. Well, love and hero-worship had been a washout. She gave a cynical little laugh. In romantic novels, men run off to join the Foreign Legion after disappointments in love, and women go into convents. Nursing, she'd thought, would be pretty much the same thing.

★

Annie Wilkinson

The sight of Miss Brewster's gabled porch conjured thoughts of a roaring fire and steaming coffee, and dispelled her reverie. The Lowery episode was all in the past, and better left there and forgotten she thought, as she approached the gate. What she was faced with now was that Will was trapped in that hospital until his left arm healed, with every day bringing fresh dangers of discovery. She had to see him as soon as she could, to warn him about the Lowerys.

Chapter Seventeen

Shivering and with teeth chattering, Sally stood on the scrubbed white doorstep and raised her hand to the polished brass knocker. She had hardly let it fall before Miss Brewster opened the massive oak door and stood there, tall and angular, frowning like the Wrath of God.

'Where on earth have you been? You were only going to be five minutes!' She ushered Sally into the hallway, touched her frozen cheek with the back of her strong, bony fingers, and nodded in the direction of the drawing room. 'You're frozen to the marrow! Get your things off and get in there this minute. I'll make you a mug of something hot.'

'Don't put anything in it, will you? Remember, I've signed the pledge!' Sally said, watching her hostess disappear down the hall and into the kitchen.

The drawing room fire was roaring up the chimney back, a welcome sight. Sally crossed the thick Persian carpet and perched on the padded red leather seat of the brass fender until the heat drove her back a little, half scorched now, as well as half frozen. Still shivering she dragged the leather pouffe as near to the fire as she dared and sat on it, and staring into the flames wondered what Will was doing, and how long it would be before she could get back to the hospital.

Miss Brewster handed her a mug of steaming coffee. 'There, get that down you.'

Sally took it and gave it a surreptitious, suspicious sniff. 'You've put something in it.'

The older woman bared her large, yellowing teeth and laughed. 'It won't hurt you. It'll do you a power of good.'

Sally was not convinced, but it was near impossible to get anything to drink in this house that wasn't laced with alcohol, and Sally's protests that she was teetotal ran off Miss Brewster like water off a duck's back. The stuff was 'medicinal'.

'I wonder you dare carry on like you do, Miss Brewster,' she said. 'I wouldn't, for my soul. If I were in your shoes, I'd be frightened of the police and the customs men catching me.'

'Ach, you worry too much; those people aren't half as clever as they want you to believe. But if I went about looking as nervous as you do just now, I would be frightened, because my face would tell them I was up to no good. But I don't, I live the sort of life that puts me beyond suspicion. I was at church this morning, dropping my mite onto the collection plate and sitting through the sermon, and then I loitered about the place with some of the righteous afterwards, deploring the state of the nation's morals and the youth of today, and wondering what the world's coming to. And it'll soon be Christmas! It only took us five minutes to establish that, after the clue the vicar gave us about it being the start of Advent. He's honouring me with a visit on Tuesday for afternoon tea, by the way.'

Miss Brewster clasped her hands in front of her breast in what Sally supposed must be the vicar's manner, and went on, '"And ah, ahem, perhaps you'd care to make a contribution to my little fund for the moral welfare some those wretched women who tramp the Quayside, Miss Brewster?" I felt like telling him if it weren't for his congregation, half the lasses on the Quayside would be out of business. But I nodded, and smiled, and tut-tutted, and he wants to get me on the Board of Guardians, now! How could I make myself any more respectable? And old maids have nothing very important to do, so better find them some useful occupation, as long as it's unpaid, of course.'

'Oh, Miss Brewster!' Sally reproached her, 'You'll cop it, one of these days.'

'What? Never. If anybody ever comes nosing about, then there's enough glass in that coping on top of the back garden wall to put them off. I can't see anybody wanting to hop over that, can you?'

Sally shook her head, more at Miss Brewster's shocking hypocrisy than at the thought of the wall. But no, she certainly wouldn't like to try 'hopping over' a seven-foot high wall to cut herself to ribbons on those enormous shards of broken glass Miss Brewster had had set into the thick layer of concrete at the top. And as if that weren't enough, there were the dogs. Scutum, the mastiff, who might have been the model for *The Hound of the Baskervilles* and whose bark would awaken the dead, and the surly bulldog, Gladius – both lived in the outhouse and had free run of the shrubbery. They would be more than enough to deter even the most determined uninvited guest.

Miss Brewster gave Sally a broad, confident smile, and echoed her thoughts. 'And then there are the dogs, of course. Mastiffs have strength and courage, no danger to the mistress or her property while they're around. They're the most powerful fighting dogs in the world; the Romans used to use them to fight wild animals in the arena. My father told me that an English mastiff once killed a tiger in India in single combat, and Scutum's the best of the breed.' She paused, the light of battle in her eyes. 'That bulldog's pure bred, as well,' she said. 'He'll go straight for a man's head, rip his face off without a sound, and he'll hang on till he's killed.'

She looked as if she relished the thought. Quite appalled by this bloodthirsty exhibition, Sally lifted her cup to her lips to hide her horrified face.

Miss Brewster grimaced, and gave an expressive shrug. 'A timid old Christian lady living on her own, you know – nobody could blame her for trying to protect herself, could they? No, my dear, don't worry your head about policemen and customs officers catching me. I've run my little enterprise for many a long year. It's served me well, and I've never come a cropper yet. I'm as safe as the Bank of England.'

Timid old lady were hardly the words Sally would have chosen to describe the middle-aged battleaxe facing her, but Miss Brewster wasn't as safe as she imagined, and neither was Ginny, who, Sally had been shattered to learn, was complicit in the illicit 'little enterprise'.

'But you're not safe,' she said. 'There's always people with loose tongues, and somebody's sure to give you away, sooner or later.'

'Pouf!' Miss Brewster gave a little exclamation of contempt. 'Impossible. I only deal with people I'd trust with my life.'

'Hm, that's what our Ginny says,' said Sally, far from convinced but deterred from further argument. Despite her posturings of religion and genteel timidity, regardless of her age, Sally suspected that the law would have little mercy on Miss Brewster, if it ever got wind of her.

But there was a more immediate problem, one she must tackle as soon as it began to get dark. 'I'm going into Newcastle after tea, Miss Brewster,' she said. 'There's something I've got to do.'

'What? You'll do no such thing; you look half dead. I should never have let you persuade me to let you out this afternoon. Ginny'll have my liver if anything happens to you.'

Sally swallowed a mouthful of coffee and smiled. She saw no point in arguing; she would be going, regardless. Good heavens, Miss Brewster's beverages certainly warmed you up as they went down, she thought. Heat scorched her throat and began to seep though her whole body.

She made her way to the place she'd seen him with his mother, and there he was, waiting. Fearing any watchful eyes she suppressed the impulse to run to him and strolled in his direction.

'Lieutenant Maxfield!'

'Why I wasn't expecting to see you, Nurse Wilde! But it's a nice surprise. I thought my mother would have been here by now. I don't know where she's got to . . .'

With only one thought on her mind, Sally cut in, keeping her voice very low. 'You've got to get away,

Will. Now. Leave the hospital now. I got the shock of my life. That woman I worked for, that b ... Mrs Lowery, she told me she'd seen you here, on the Leazes. If she hasn't told Dr Campbell already she soon will, and he'll start asking questions.'

'Leave the hospital? What, before I get this arm healed?' he gave a muffled snort. 'Huh! I'd rather take my chance at a court martial than risk that. Have you seen the way Raynor struggles?'

'He manages.'

'He doesn't. He has a job with everything; washing, dressing, eating, the lot. We've had a couple of new patients since you went off, and one of them's an officer from Gosforth ...'

'Oh, Will, they're all local lads now. Somebody's bound to recognize you before long!'

'Gosforth's never been local to me, and never likely to be, nor anywhere like it. Anyway, listen to what I'm telling you about Raynor. Him and this new officer are in the same fix, and I heard him asking Raynor if he ever thought about doing away with himself. And do you know what Raynor said? "Only when I want to cheer myself up!" When the doctors and nurses come round, though, he's always "all right", like we all are, but he'll never be all right again. What he "manages" is to put a brave face on it most of the time, and it's a good job for him he's from a class of people who don't have to earn their living by the labour of their hands. Raynor's educated. He comes from the sort of family who can help him get into the law, or shipping, or accountancy, any one of a hundred jobs a man can do sitting at a desk – or into some job giving the orders, telling other people what to do. Well, I'm glad for him, because he'll probably be right enough in the end, but I'm in a different class altogether.'

'But you can learn photography.'

'Even for photography, you need two hands, Sally man. And a working man without the use of his hands is buggered. He's useless. So when you say my life's at stake, you're right. My life depends on my two hands.'

She couldn't dispute it. Although the loss of a leg was a bigger shock to a man at the time than the loss of an arm, it was far less of a disability when it came to earning a living. The surgeons would amputate a leg if the case seemed hopeless and the pressure of work was heavy, but they'd move heaven and earth to save a man's arm, even if it meant keeping him in hospital for the best part of a year.

'There's a world of difference between me and Raynor,' Will continued. 'He'll get a decent pension for his disability, but not me. I'll get nothing, remember. I've disqualified myself from getting any help from my country.'

There was no denying it. If he couldn't earn, it

would be a straight choice between starvation and charity, and she couldn't see Will wanting charity. Her face fell.

'So what am I going to do?' He looked at her, clear-eyed, frank, quizzical. 'Sit in a back room in Staffordshire, living off my mother and her dad?' He shook his head. 'No. If I've no hope of a decent life, I'd sooner finish it altogether.'

She placed a forefinger on his lips and pressed hard. 'Shush. You won't! You can't say things like that, Will. There's always hope; and these days women can work, an' all.'

He stretched out his right arm and pulled her into him, to kiss her forehead. 'What is a man, Sally, when you come to think? What makes a man a man? I used to think it was being part of a family, brothers, friends, village – knowing where you belonged, but that's all gone, all but my mother. Why, having a face fit to show the world, then, to wink at the lasses, and know they're thinking, why, he looks all right! I wouldn't mind an hour or two on the back row at the pictures with him! Well, that's gone an' all. All right, then, I'll settle for a good wife and a pair of strong arms to earn a living for her, and respect from the men I end up working with. If I can get that, I can still think myself a man.'

'You're still you, whether you lose your arm or not,' she snuffled, laying her head on his shoulder.

'What difference can it make to that? You're still a man!'

'I'm not! It changes you, Sally, you're not the man you were before, and if I lost my arm I wouldn't be the man I want to be. What use is a man who can't earn a living? He's no good to man nor beast. I'd be a sight better out of the world than in it if that happened, for everybody's sake.'

She stood back and grasped him savagely by the shoulders, scowling like a demon. 'Why what about your mother, then, you selfish . . .? You were going to make sure she gets her pension, but if anything happens to you, she won't need a one. It'll be the last straw; it'll finish her off altogether, so stop – talking – like – that.' She accompanied her words with violent shakes, and all the ferocity she could muster.

'All right, hinny! Steady on,' he laughed, but there was no mirth in the sound. There was something in his voice she'd have been hard put to define, but it opened a void in her and made her sick with fear. He was near the limit of endurance and another blow, a blow like an amputation would tip him over the edge. She felt ill, and powerless, angry with him for his defeatism, and near to tears.

She put both arms around him and squeezed him fiercely to her, listening to the beat of his heart, then releasing her hold a little, she said, 'Don't talk like that Will. Don't even think like it.'

For King and Country

You're still you, she'd said, and she'd meant it – but it was a lie. He was no longer the laughing optimist she'd known at school, nor even the cheerful, dauntless young man who'd kissed her dreams and hopes to life. He was deeply, fundamentally changed. War had destroyed his family and shattered his illusions; desertion and mutilation had darkened his life and his future. Nothing would ever, could ever, be the same, not for them, nor for anyone else washed in the Great European Bloodbath.

On Saturday night she was taking the report from Sister Davies when her heart leapt into her mouth at the sight of Mrs Lowery at the office door, accompanied by another woman.

'Goodness, Sally! Back at work so soon! But you're very pale, my dear.'

Was that mock or real concern? 'I'm all right, thank you, Mrs Lowery,' said Sally, paler still at the sight of the doctor's wife.

'Show the ladies to the new patient, Nurse,' Sister said. 'Top bed on the right-hand side.'

Sally obeyed. Will was lying quietly on the farthest bed on the same side, looking at his paper, oblivious of the danger. She hoped to heaven he stayed there, because she daren't draw attention to them both by going the full length of the ward to warn him, so she returned to the office.

Closing the door behind her, she took the seat by Sister Davies' desk.

'What are they doing here, at this time of night?'

'Got permission to visit a new patient, a cousin or nephew of theirs, I think. Shrapnel wound in his thigh.'

'But it's not visiting hours.'

Sister Davies' expression was sardonic. 'Ah, but they're doctors' wives Nurse Wilde, and doctors and their wives are a law unto themselves. I thought you'd have realized that by now. Exceptions can always be made for them. They're sisters. The eldest's Dr Campbell's mother. You seem to know the other one.'

'She's his aunt, the woman I used to work for before I started nursing.'

'I see. Not a happy time, judging by the look on your face.'

'Not really,' said Sally, in agony to get the report over with and get out onto the ward.

Mrs Lowery and her sister were sitting quietly by their relative when Sally and Sister Davies entered the ward. Will was still lying on his bed at the bottom with his left arm encased in plaster of Paris, still looking at his paper with his blind side facing them. Sister started with the patient in the first bed on the other side, proceeding in the usual clockwise direction. With any luck, Will would stay in his bed and Mrs Lowery and her sister would be gone by the time they'd finished. Sally smiled, and listened, and did her best to absorb the details of every patient's progress, with scant success. At last they got to Will. His face expressionless, he nodded or shook his head in answer to their questions, betraying nothing.

'He got his wound debrided and redressed a couple of days ago. It's looking much better, so they've put a pot on it this time,' Sister said. 'He's making good progress.'

'Don't you think he looks a bit feverish, Sister?' Sally asked, flashing a warning at Will as she reached for the thermometer. 'Maybe I ought to take his temperature.'

'No need to make work,' Sister Davies protested. 'It was all right a couple of hours ago. We'll finish the round.'

Sally returned the thermometer to its holder, and went on with the round to the last patient. The gentle chinking of cups and glasses announced the arrival of the orderly with the trolley of bedtime drinks, but neither Mrs Lowery nor her sister showed any sign of leaving. She gave Will a last glance before returning to the office with Sister Davies. Suddenly she saw him fling on his dressing gown and cross the ward to show Raynor something in the paper. And with growing alarm, Sally noticed that Mrs Lowery had seen him too.

Sally began the medicines as soon as Sister left the ward, dispensing them as calmly as she could, her flesh creeping at the sensation of Mrs Lowery's eyes on her, and then on Will, and then again on her. She passed Will and Raynor, thankful when they barely acknowledged her, but was shaken a minute later when she saw Raynor pick up his glass of port and Will his beaker to stroll together up the ward. Mrs Lowery was watching Will like an eagle. They were just halfway when she jumped up from her seat and crossed to the window on the opposite side of the ward, purporting to look out of it, but turning to scrutinize the unblemished side of Will's face as he passed. With his attention wholly on something Raynor was saying, Will accompanied him out of the ward and along to the day room, oblivious of Mrs Lowery's scrutiny. She returned to her chair, murmuring to her sister and casting occasional glances at Sally.

Outwardly composed, Sally continued with her task and when she reached the new patient, very civilly asked the ladies if they'd like the orderly to bring them a drink from the trolley.

'No, thank you,' Mrs Lowery replied. 'It's time we were going. Nurse Wilde, that man who's just left the ward – he's the same person who came to see you that day.'

'Which man, Mrs Lowery? There were two of them.'

For King and Country

Mrs Lowery looked at her intently. 'The man with the scarred face, of course.'

Sally shook her head. 'You must mean Lieutenant Maxfield. But he's an Australian, Mrs Lowery, with an Australian wife who writes letters to him from Australia. How could he be the same man? The man who came to see me was the last of four brothers. The others were all killed in France, and straight after he'd been to see me, Will joined up an' all. His poor mother got the buff envelope when the August Offensive started. They sent his identity discs and all his bits of things back not long after. No, Mrs Lowery, it's not the same man you saw in Darlington. Not the same man at all.'

Sally gave a little shrug, and spread her hands in a gesture of helplessness. 'I don't think I can tell you anything else, Sergeant,' she said.

He gave her a penetrating stare. 'Are you sure about that, Miss?'

The sergeant and his constable were conducting interviews in the day room about the disappearance of one Christopher Maxfield, Second Lieutenant of the Australian Imperial Forces. The night sister and night superintendent had already been questioned, and Sally had been detained for interview as well.

She turned two weary eyes upon him and held his gaze, noting the flaking skin around his eyebrows, and a couple of blackheads on his rather bulbous nose. 'Quite sure,' she said.

The sergeant looked at her steadily for what seemed an age, then said, 'We've been informed that he was very attached to you.'

Sally stared as stolidly back, eyes blank and face expressionless. 'Well, I had no attachment to Lieutenant Maxfield.'

'If he was Lieutenant Maxfield,' the younger policeman cut in. 'There seems to be a difference of opinion about that.'

The sergeant nodded. 'We've got it from a very reliable source that his name wasn't Maxfield at all. He was a fellow that you knew, called Will.'

Sally's eyebrows lifted then, and her mouth turned down in a fleeting grimace of mild derision. Her breath escaped in a resigned, regretful little sigh. 'Your so-called "reliable source" is Mrs Lowery, then,' she said, and paused, gazing out of the window for a moment or two before adding in low, reluctant tones, 'but I'm sorry to say I wouldn't call her reliable . . . exactly. Her husband doesn't. She accused me of carrying on with him while I was their housemaid, and I left straightaway. Lasses in my position need their good name, and I couldn't afford to stay there until she'd destroyed my character with her flights of fancy. Her husband told me she's given to bouts of hysteria.'

'Oh, he does, does he? Well, it might interest you

to know that our reliable source is Dr Lowery, and not his wife.'

'Dr Lowery himself?' Sally repeated, her eyebrows well up now. Dr Lowery had never laid eyes on Will as far as she knew, and it was on the tip of her tongue to say so, but maybe the less she said, the better.

'Well?' There was a glint of suspicion in those black beads, which bored into her face from their puffy, wrinkled eyelids.

She stared into them. 'Well what?'

'Well, what have you got to say about that?'

'Nothing, except that as far as I know Dr Lowery never saw Will. His mother knew him pretty well, though, and she got a letter telling her he was dead, so if you've got him listed in your gazette you might as well cross him out again. Lieutenant Maxfield might have had a bit of a look of him, but he was nothing like the Will Burdett I knew.'

'*Have had*? *Was* nothing like? What do you mean by that, Miss?'

Her eyes suddenly brimmed with tears. 'I don't know what I mean by it, really,' she said, sniffing and lifting her apron to fish in her dress pocket for a handkerchief. 'Except that the last time I saw Lieutenant Maxfield he was in a funny mood, and he said if his arm wouldn't heal he'd be better off the earth. "I'd think nothing of jumping off the Tyne Bridge," he said. "Why prolong the agony?" That's exactly what he said. I'm sorry, I'm tired, and I've just got over the 'flu, and I'm not picking up very well. I seem to cry at anything.' She dabbed her eyes.

'Are you saying he's done away with himself, Miss?'

'Oh, I hope not,' she said. 'I'm just repeating what he said.'

'Just wait outside, Miss,' the policeman said. 'Sister will let you sit in her office. We may want to speak to you again when we've interviewed some of the others.'

'But I've been on duty all night, Officer,' Sally protested, 'and I'm on again tonight. I'm dead tired, and I want to go to bed.'

'Just wait in Sister's office, Miss.'

She got up and wearily made her way to the office, passing Raynor, who was the next to be questioned. He gave her a smile and a nod of acknowledgement. It was then she realized her mistake.

Dunkley was in the office, getting the patients' notes ready for the round. 'Go down to the porter's lodge and get the notes for the new admission,' she commanded, without as much as looking up.

'I'm off duty, Nurse Dunkley. I finished my night shift an hour ago,' Sally protested.

Dunkley rounded on her. 'Do as you're told, Nurse, and don't answer back. And don't imagine I don't know what's going on between you and Iain, either,' she said, her pretty face contorted and ugly with jealous passion.

'Iain? I suppose you mean Dr Campbell. I didn't even know his first name,' Sally said, meeting her opponent's eyes with less sympathy than she'd have felt for an insect on a pin. She didn't care a straw for Dunkley's petty jealousies now, or for 'Iain' either.

'Didn't you? I don't believe it,' Dunkley snapped. 'But I haven't got time to bandy words just now. Go and fetch those notes Nurse, and get a move on. And I'll tell you this much – when I get into that day room, I'll tell those policeman that still waters run deep, and our Nurse Wilde knows a lot more about Lieutenant Maxfield than she's letting on.'

Sally hesitated for a moment or two, and then sauntered out of the office.

On her return with the notes she almost bumped into Raynor, who was just stepping out of the day room. He gave her a cold and distant look, far from his usual friendly manner.

'That took longer than anticipated. They seemed awfully keen to know whether he could talk or not. Said *you'd* said he could.'

'I never did. I said no such thing,' she said, her face impassive. 'If they're saying that, they've got hold of the wrong end of the stick, or they're fishing. What did you say?'

'I told them,' he said, 'that I've spent more time with Maxfield than anybody on this ward, and as far as I know he's never spoken a word to anyone.'

'Me neither,' Sally said, in tones as frosty as his. They parted company at the door of Sister's office, when Sally entered and put the notes in front of Nurse Dunkley. She was rewarded with a curt nod.

'Good,' Dunkley said. 'Now you can go and clean the doctor's sink before the start of the round. Make sure there's a clean towel, and that the nailbrush and soap are clean as well.'

Nine o' clock already, and she should have been off at eight, but with no further protest she went and scoured the sink, and was rinsing and drying it when Knox returned from the day room. Bristling with irritation, he went to unburden himself to a patient nearby.

'Pair of cwetins!' he scowled, jerking his head in Sally's direction. 'Some cock and bull stowy about the fellow being the girl's sweetheart, and *English*. Girl wouldn't have anything to do with him! I told them – the fellow's an Austwalian – no doubt about it. I can wecognize 'em a mile away, insolent blighters! Not the slightest bit surpwised he's wun off! I told them, look on the first boat back to Austwalia – that's where you'll find him.'

Half an hour later, after more interviews, Sally was called back.

'You told us something interesting,' the sergeant said. 'You said,' he looked at his notes for confirmation, 'you said: "He said if his arm wouldn't heal he'd be better out of the world than in it. That's what he *said*." Now most of the other witnesses have told us the gentleman never spoke. One said he was mute due to shell shock. So can you explain how it was that he spoke to you, Miss?'

'He didn't speak to me.'

'You distinctly told us he did.'

'Can I have a look at your notebook, Officer?' she asked.

'I'm sorry, Miss, you can't.'

Sally took a notebook from her own pocket and scribbled in it, then passed it over to him, asking: 'What does it *say*?'

'It says: "I'd be better off the earth."'

'Well, that's what I meant. Like people might say, "It says in the *Chronicle*," or "When my bother wrote to me, he said this and he said that", meaning in his letter. Like it *says* in your notebook what all the witnesses *say*. You wouldn't say he *wrote* that a thing happened, you'd say he *said* it had happened. I would, anyway. I can't explain it very well, but anybody would know what I mean. He said it in a note. He was *always* writing notes,' she emphasized, marvelling how easily the lies rolled off her tongue.

The policemen looked only half convinced. 'I see,'

he said. 'Well, perhaps there's been a misunder-standing. You can go for now, but we may want to question you again.'

Sally rose from her chair. 'Thank you,' she said, and turned to go. After a moment's hesitation she turned back, and with great dignity, said, 'I'm not in the habit of telling lies, Officer. I was too well brought up for that. I think most of the people in authority here would give me a good character if you asked them, and everybody in Annsdale, as well.'

They looked up at her, met her gaze for a moment, then the sergeant spoke. 'All right, Miss. You can go.'

All right, Miss. A bit more conviction in that, unless she was deluding herself. She'd have to report off duty now, even though it was two hours after the proper time, or Dunkley would be sure to kick a stink up. But it was Sister she found in the office, who looked at her with sympathetic eyes and shooed her away with that familiar sweep of her right arm, outraged that she'd been kept up so long. She was to go off this minute, and get straight to bed.

Sally went off, but not to bed. She went straight to Matron's office, and rapped on the door.

At a bench littered with a mass of paraphernalia, peering down a microscope so intently he was oblivious of her presence, sat the pathologist. Ridged bottles with ground glass stoppers, racks of test tubes, pipettes, tripods, Bunsen burner, specimen jars, flasks and Petri dishes surrounded him, along with instruments whose purposes she couldn't even guess at.

She gave a little cough. It had no effect. She gave a much louder cough, and got no response. She spoke up. 'Excuse me, Professor, I'm Sarah Wilde. I think Matron just telephoned you about me.'

'Ah, yes,' a voice responded, and a hand reached above the bench to pick up the pipe which was smouldering in an ashtray on the window ledge. The hand was thin and long-fingered, the veins prominent, and the man who turned with his pipe between his teeth to face her was fortyish, almost skin and bone, his dark hair swept back revealing deep creases in his forehead. 'Ah, yes,' he repeated, after several puffs. 'So what makes you think you'll be any use to me?'

'You've got a vacancy, and when you gave us a lecture three or four months back you said you thought women were "eminently fitted for pathological work".'

'Hm.' He stuck his pipe between his teeth and sucked a good draught of smoke into his lungs before removing it again. 'What else did I say?'

'You said the work needs people who are keen, dexterous, and good at figures, for working chemical reactions and statistics out. Well, I fit the bill.'

He gave her the ghost of a smile. 'You're sure

about that, are you? But will you stick it? You don't seem to have stuck nursing long.'

'I'll stick it if I get into laboratory work.'

'Why?'

'Because I'm interested in microbes, and how they cause disease, and what we can do to stop it,' she said. 'And to be truthful, I'd be earning better money, the hours are shorter and I'll get a half day on Saturday and Sunday off every week, so I could help my mother more. I'll like the work.'

'Don't you like nursing?'

'I like it a lot but the work's heavy and the hours are long, and since I had the 'flu I haven't got the same stamina. And I've got responsibilities at home,' she lied.

The pipe went into his mouth again, and he sucked it thoughtfully, his eyes never leaving her face. 'Well, you don't need to be particularly robust for our sort of work, and I'll guarantee your night's rest won't be broken by an aching back or painful feet. You can stand or sit to your work, just as it suits. You'll certainly find it a lot easier physically. But you might want to go back to nursing as soon as you feel fit, and then the time and effort I've spent training you will have been wasted.'

'If I get the chance to work in the laboratory, I'll do well at it, and I'll stay.'

'All right,' he said, after some consideration. 'We'll

start you on the bottom rung of the ladder and teach you as you go. I'll give you a fortnight's trial and keep you on if you show enough aptitude. It's Monday now. How soon is Matron willing to release you?'

'When I've worked the week out. So next Monday morning.'

'Monday morning then, half past eight sharp.'

She nodded. Good. She'd soon have the free time she needed to be able to tend to her own business as well as the hospital's, so that was the first hurdle over. She left the laboratory mindful of another one she'd have to surmount. That challenge would come tonight, but she was in it up to her neck now, and there could be no turning back. She felt some trepidation, but no pricks of conscience, no sense of guilt. Rather die than tell a lie? Like hell! Rather not, nor let anybody else die either, or spend miserable, shaming years in gaol, if she could help it. Truth was all very well unless it was set to destroy people who'd already suffered enough, and who hadn't deserved their suffering in the first place, like Will and his mother. In cases like that, lies must be justified. Lying done in a just cause and for a higher good, you could even think it a virtue. The more she thought about it the more she was convinced, so since she had to live a lie, she'd live it boldly.

She was treading the parquet back to the nurses'

home when the porter pulled a patient out of the ward, with Crump trotting at the back of the trolley. 'No rest for the wicked,' she said, as they passed each other. 'What about Lieutenant Maxfield then? What's happened to him, do you think?'

Lifting her hands palms upwards, Sally shrugged with well-feigned indifference. 'Anybody's guess, I suppose,' she said, and saw Crump's face fall in the second or two before she passed.

Poor little Crump, she was feeling sorry for Maxfield. She was as good as gold under that crust of dry cynicism. At the memory of the good times they'd all had, Sally's face fell, too. It would be awful when it came to it, to part with them all – like a little death to separate herself from all these good lasses she'd been happy among, knowing they were carrying on the great business of healing without her, and she no longer part of it, or them. And what would her mother say when she told her she'd left nursing, Sally wondered? I told you so? She wouldn't put it past her. But maybe it would be better not to tell them anything at home, and then she'd be free to come and go as she pleased, without any explanations to anybody. A few strides further on she was filled again with elation, a bubbling excitement at something new and unexpected in her life, a tingling apprehension at the thought of the dangers confronting her, of fresh tests of her new-found capacity for deception, of such tests of wit and courage as she'd never imagined having to face in her life.

Chapter Eighteen

D r Campbell appeared when she was halfway through her evening's work, to check on a patient, he said. Sally led him to the bed.

'It looks as if he's asleep,' she murmured. 'Shall I wake him up?'

'No. Sleep will do him good. I'll see him tomorrow morning. I'll have a word with you in the office, though, if you don't mind.'

'Not at all, Doctor,' she said, thinking there was hardly any point coming to see the man at all if it could wait until tomorrow morning; the patient was just an excuse.

He closed the door behind her and, making himself comfortable in Sister's chair, motioned her to sit down. She did so, and found herself subjected to a full minute of silent scrutiny. Crump would probably have asked him if he was sure he'd got an eyeful, and a faint smile played around Sally's lips at the thought, but fully determined to withstand it all and give nothing away, she kept her own counsel.

In the end he said, 'I have the solution.'

'The what?'

'The solution. To the enigma of Nurse Wilde, I mean. You gave it away the night you were taken ill. I wondered what you meant, and now I know.'

'What I meant?'

'Yes. But perhaps I should say *who* you meant. The Will you spoke to the last time we sat in this office together.'

Her eyes held a glint alarm for a fleeting second, then dulled into blank incomprehension.

'That night you sank into delirium, Nurse Wilde, just before I had to send you off to the sick room,' he prompted. 'I remember it vividly. Lieutenant Maxfield appeared in the doorway, and you said, "Will, oh, Will." And I was wondering, who the devil's Will? Is the girl having hallucinations? But since I've heard Mrs Lowery's version of events, since we had the visitation from the police, I've realized you weren't.'

She rolled her eyes upwards, frantically casting her mind back to that point before her collapse. 'Oh, yes,' she said. 'I remember now, I had a terrible headache. The last thing I remember is asking for an aspirin. I was saying, *will* you get me an aspirin.'

He gave her a disbelieving smile. 'My aunt thinks otherwise, and our Lieutenant Maxfield's reaction to your illness seems to support her theory. The chap was distraught. All together, Nurse Wilde, there's as little doubt in my mind about his identity as there is in Mrs Lowery's. He's your young man. Your sweetheart. Admit it.'

She assumed a brusque, no-nonsense attitude. 'I'm sorry, Doctor, I haven't got the foggiest idea what you're talking about. But I *have* got a ward full of patients waiting for their medicines, and then I've all the obs to do. Can I go, now?'

'Give it up, Nurse Wilde,' he urged her, with a look of a man cheated of a prize. 'The game's up! It's solved at last, that riddle of Maxfield's attachment to you, if not Dr Lowery's.'

She repeated, 'I don't know what you're talking about, Dr Campbell.'

'You're in no danger from me, Nurse Wilde, and neither is your Will. I've nothing to gain from meddling in your intrigues. My interest's purely academic, but I'd like to have my hypothesis confirmed.'

She looked at him, and it must have been something in her eyes that prompted him to say, 'I told Dr Lowery there was no point in informing the police, you know. Maxfield – or Will, as you know him – will never be any use to the army again. I don't know why Lowery didn't let well alone.'

Sally grimaced, for how could a man of Dr Lowery's temperament be expected to let well alone when presented with a golden opportunity to make himself the centre of a juicy little drama? 'But if he thought Lieutenant Maxfield was a deserter, it was his public duty to inform the authorities, wasn't it?' she said, with mock approval. 'It's a bad job for Private Burdett's mother, though, having the police going to see her, getting everything raked up again when the poor lad's been dead for the past four months. It's a bad job for the police an' all, running about on a wild goose chase. It's all been a sheer waste of everybody's time, as it turns out, but Dr Lowery wasn't to know that.'

'All right, Nurse Wilde. I won't argue any further. I can see it'll get me nowhere. I give up.'

'Well, in that case, Doctor, I'll go and get on with what I'm supposed to be doing, and then all the patients can settle down for a night's sleep.'

So, by his own account Dr Campbell had tried to put Dr Lowery off going to the police. She believed him, and would have thanked him, had she dared. But she was resolved that no word would escape her mouth that might incriminate either her or Will. She got through all the work and managed to get the fluid balance charts totted up before Night Sister came, ready to be hung quietly back on the wall by each patient's bed as they did the round. After Night Sister had gone the ward was as quiet as the grave, and Sally sat down for five minutes and stared into the glowing coals of the ward fire. It was almost three o'clock, that time of night when the night nurse's eyelids droop and sleep seems irresistible, but she was wide awake, much too keyed up for slumber. She went to the ward cupboard and groped inside for lint and a roll of gauze, but instead of cutting dressings she put them in the pocket of her dress, and felt for the jar of BIPP ointment. She found it, and opened it by the light of the fire. It was empty.

She felt winded, as if she'd fallen from a great height and had all the breath knocked out of her. If she couldn't get the ointment it would spell disaster, because they wouldn't dare ask any doctor or hospital for help, and she had only two more nights to go before she lost the chance altogether. She racked her brains for a solution. There would be no hope of getting any from the dispensary at this time of night. It would be locked, and she could hardly ask the night superintendent for the key. She'd have to wait until tomorrow night. But what if there were no fresh jars tomorrow night? Or the night after? She might never have another chance to get any.

Unless. Unless she went to theatre, where they kept plenty of the stuff. But to get caught there, that would be the end of everything. Unable to sit or settle to anything she got up and flitted silent as a ghost round the darkened ward, checking the gentle breathing of every patient. They were all sound asleep, for once. She looked towards the ward door, wondering how long it might take. None of the patients were critically ill, and she could be there and back in ten minutes, surely? Ten minutes at the outside. She hesitated, but remembering that he who hesitates is lost she left the ward and went to look up and down the main corridor – silent, still, and empty.

It's one thing in a place you're familiar with, but to grope for things in the dark in a place you've only visited occasionally is a different proposition. Turning the light on was out of the question, and so she had no alternative but to feel her way round the walls of the anaesthetic room until she came to the cupboard. Thank heaven the key was in the lock. She turned it, cringing at the sound it made, and the squeak of the hinges when she opened the door. Glass shelving, too, everything she touched made a scrape or a rattle, the sound magnified in her mind by her fear and the stillness of the night. At last she put her hand on the jar of BIPP on the bottom shelf. There was just enough light from the corridor to make it out as her eyes became adjusted to the darkness. She knelt to unscrew the lid and fished in her dress pocket for the little container she'd brought and the wooden tongue depressor she would use to scoop the BIPP out.

The lights went on. Like a startled rabbit she looked up, jar in hand, and met the tired blue eyes of

Dr Campbell. 'What *are* you doing down there, Nurse Wilde?' he mocked. 'Saying your prayers – *again?*'

She looked at the jar under her hand, and then back at him, and blanched. A thousand excuses rushed through her brain, and every one of them hopeless.

He tut-tutted at her, and shook his head. 'You mistook the anaesthetic room for the chapel,' he said, looking down at her. 'Is that it? No, of course not. But whatever can you want with *that* in the middle of the night, when none of your patients need dressings done, Nurse Wilde?'

I saw the ward had none when I was tidying the cupboard, so I decided to get some, sprang to mind, but it wouldn't have washed. There were proper channels for obtaining supplies, and abandoning a ward full of patients to raid the cupboards of other departments in the middle of the night was not among them. At a loss for any other answer, Nurse Wilde kept her mouth tight shut.

Campbell gave her a wry smile. 'You must want it very badly. How badly, exactly? What's a jar of BIPP worth to you, Nurse Wilde?'

She returned the jar to its cupboard and shut the door, then glanced up at him. A strange half smile was playing on his lips, and she thought she saw derision in those eyes that fixed hers.

'Oh, this is a difficult one to extricate yourself from, *n'est-ce pas?*' he taunted. 'I think the riddle of the little sphinx is solved at last! Finally, and without a shadow of a doubt. What other explanation can there be?'

She froze, as helpless as a butterfly on a pin. He walked towards her, his smile broadening and his eyebrows lifting as he looked into her eyes and answered for her. 'None. There is no other explanation. Which brings me back to the first question,' he said, stooping to catch her by the wrist and haul her to her feet. 'What's a jar of BIPP worth, Sally? A kiss, at least, I should say.'

He ran his fingers very gently down her cheek to the point of her chin and lifted her face to his. 'More than a kiss? I fancy I might ask for more than a kiss, under the circumstances.'

Images of ruin and disgrace raced through her mind, of nurses sacked and sent down the drive with their suitcases, of unmarried mothers shut away in the workhouse, of girls who'd tried to hide their shame dying grey-faced of stinking, septic abortions, and of mad, disgusting old women in the last stages of syphilis. Those were the results of giving men 'more than a kiss'; the warnings were everywhere you looked, and they horrified her. She'd steeled herself for lies and deceit, and even theft, but not that! Not prostituting herself. She blushed, felt her nose going red and her eyes filling with tears.

That expression of mockery left his eyes. He let

her go, and stepped back a pace. 'Dear me,' he sighed. 'Dear me! Is the thought so distressing? Just a kiss, then. Here.' He turned his cheek towards her, tapped the middle of it with his forefinger, and waited.

She was leaning forward with lips puckered when Dunkley's voice rang out, clear and peremptory: 'What's going on here exactly, might I ask?'

'Thank you for looking after him,' Sally said with barefaced coolness when Sunday morning came and, her nursing career at an end, she put her suitcase down in Miss Brewster's hallway. She'd had an odd feeling that she was being followed all the way from the hospital, but there was no time to think about that now. There was Miss Brewster to deal with, and her manner was icy.

'You've put me in a very bad position.'

'I know,' said Sally, with no apology in her tone. 'I had nowhere else to go. There was nothing else I could have done.'

Never in her life before would she have put anybody in a 'bad position', especially not a person who had done her a kindness, but after Mrs Lowery's visit to the ward she'd sent Will to the deserted laundry and there he'd stayed, safe enough and warm enough all day Sunday, until it got dark. Then she'd spirited him to Miss Brewster's house and left him there, returning to the hospital without a qualm to start her night shift. And when before leaving she'd looked Miss Brewster straight in the eye and said, 'You won't give him away, will you?' her words had been a threat as much as a plea.

Now she discovered within herself a core of steel, a ruthlessness, a determination to bend this woman to her own purpose, and Miss Brewster seemed to sense it, to understand Sally's veiled threat without the need for words. Resentment burned in the eyes that met Sally's impassive gaze, but the older woman was the first to look away. Sally knew too much about Miss Brewster, and now Miss Brewster knew too much about her and Will. It would be better for all concerned if nobody said anything about anybody. If Miss Brewster stayed quiet and played the game, she would have nothing to fear, and neither would they.

'I'll make sure you're not out of pocket, Miss Brewster,' she said. 'I'll be getting a decent wage soon. And I'll be able to help in the house.'

An angry colour rose to Miss Brewster's cheeks. She hesitated, drew in her breath as if to protest at this presumption that Will would be staying any longer and that Sally would be staying too, but after a second's consideration, merely said, 'The daily woman will do the housework, and he's lucky she didn't see his shaving tackle lying on the bathroom window sill. Lucky for him I spotted it and moved it before she went in, wasn't it? All right. You'd better take your case upstairs, and get some sleep. It's ten o'clock already.'

'No, I won't go yet. I'm starting in the laboratory tomorrow morning, and if I go to bed now I'll be awake half the night. Where is he?'

'I've given him some work to do. He'd better earn his keep while he's here.'

Sally thought of Will's damaged arm, and her eyes narrowed. 'Where is he?' she demanded.

Her expression sour, Miss Brewster said: 'In the shrubbery, attending to the business. He'll be there for a while. I'm going to church.'

Under the shrubbery would have been more accurate. Under the watchful eyes of the dogs Sally followed the path to the twin 'compost bays', hidden behind an ivy-clad wooden screen and bounded at the back by the garden wall. One of the bays was clear of debris and a hinged wooden lid was propped against the wall, leaving the mouth of an old mine shaft gaping wide and dangerous. Undaunted, Sally hitched up her skirts and clambered onto the ladder to start the long descent into an old bell pit, that sphere of light above her shrinking smaller and smaller the further she went. Three quarters of the way down her heart began to race at the sudden thought that all Miss Brewster had to do was jam the lid on the shaft for long enough and she would be rid of her unwelcome guests for good;

nobody would ever find them here. She stopped, and clung onto the ladder until her panic subsided. Of course somebody would know. Ginny knew she'd stayed at Miss Brewster's, and she knew about the mine. She'd soon start asking questions Miss Brewster wouldn't want to have to answer.

'Sally? You silly lass! Go back up!'

'No fear, not when I've risked my neck to get so far. I think this is the longest ladder I've ever seen. How deep do you think it is?' Her eyes becoming accustomed to the gloom, Sally continued her descent until she reached the bottom.

'About two hundred and fifty feet, at a guess. Maybe three hundred. About that.'

'Why, I might as well have a look at Miss Brewster's secret, now I've come so far.'

'Miss Brewster's secret's bloody dangerous, Sally man. Go back.'

Sally looked down into a large underground chamber and saw three large barrels, and some strange examples of the blacksmith's art, with pipes and columns poking out of them at all angles. Illuminated by a couple of miner's lamps, Will was hunkered down beside a contraption that looked like a pot-bellied stove with a small open fire underneath it.

'What's in the tubs?'

'Sugar water and brewer's yeast, in three different stages of fermentation. She keeps it just warm enough down here for the yeast to work. One lot's ready now, the next will be ready next week, and the other the week after. She has it on the go all the time, Sally man. A few days after she's distilled one lot, the next lot's ready. She's just left me to siphon a load of it into this pot still, and then I'll have to keep a watch on it, get the temperature up and then keep it right. She reckons it'll take about three hours to run through, and she'll be back before it's finished. Go back up, Sally man. Get out of the way, in case it all goes up in flames.'

Sally looked at the huge barrels. 'Why, it hasn't gone up so far, and she's been doing it long enough. How on earth did she get them down here?'

'I asked the same question, and she says she didn't. Her father did, when he found the old bell pit, soon after they'd bought the house. Or maybes he knew about it before, and that's why he bought the place. She said he learned about distilling when he was soldiering in India. She's not fond of me, though, Sally man. She'll be chucking me out before long, or telling the police to come and get us.'

Sally climbed down the last few rungs of the ladder. 'She's not fond of me either, any more,' she said, 'but I'll be staying here as well, now I've finished nursing. It'll be handy for the hospital, and she won't chuck us out, or tell the police.'

'How will she not?'

'We know about the still, don't we?'

'You mean ... blackmail?' He sounded incredulous. 'I'd never have believed *you* ...'

Sally shrugged. 'Why, needs must when the devil drives, Will, and if you're a hypocrite, you lay yourself wide open, don't you? And she is a hypocrite, and not only with the distilling either. She's let you struggle down that ladder with your arm in plaster, and she's left you down here with all this, and she's put her sweet old lady hat on and gone to church, the old sinner.'

'Blackmail, though, Sal. That's wicked.'

She answered him with another shrug. 'Maybe, maybe not, but in for a penny, in for a pound. And that plaster's going to be filthy before you get back to the surface. I've a good mind to ask her for something for your labour an' all, while I'm at it.'

'I'm beginning to see an altogether different side to you.'

'So am I.'

He gave a bark of a laugh, and the sound echoed from wall to wall, startling them both. He lowered his voice. 'You're dangerous,' he said, 'as dangerous as what's she's doing down here. What comes out after this run will be about forty per cent alcohol, and it's got to go through the still three more times before it's ready. She reckons it'll be over ninety per cent at the finish. It'll catch fire as easy as petrol, and I don't want to be trapped down here if that happens. It'll

explode, with all the alcohol fumes in the air. It'll
be like the time we were trapped in a trench when
the Germans came with their bloody flamethrowers.
I've seen men alight, screaming like banshees, lighting
up the night sky like torches. That's what it'll be like
for anybody trapped down here if that goes up; you'll
end up like a bloody torch, man. It's a miracle she
hasn't gone up in flames before the day.'

There was an edge to his voice and she could
see tiny droplets of sweat glistening on his top lip.
The realization of his fear shocked her, but she
wouldn't – couldn't – say anything. He wiped his face
with a handkerchief, and thrusting it back into his
pocket, said, 'She's got guts, I'll say that for her, and
so have you.'

'And so have you.' She stressed the words.

'A lot of people wouldn't think so. She doesn't.
She despises me. I can feel it.'

Sally changed the subject, and nodded towards his
left arm. 'How've you managed?'

'I've managed all right. It seems all right.'

'Maybe if you can help her, she'll come round.'

'She's never going to come round, no matter what
I do. I'll be glad to get out of it.'

'Well, it cannot be helped, Will; this is the safest
place, for now. We'll go as soon as it's safe to go. Till
then, she'll have to put up with us, whether she likes
it, or not.'

Annie Wilkinson

'Have you seen my mother?'

'No, I haven't. She hasn't been at work for a day or two, but don't you go looking for her, or you'll end up in clink, and that'll be the finish of her,' Sally said, quite snappishly.

It wasn't quite a lie, and it wasn't the truth, either. Ginny had written to tell her the police had been to see Will's mother, and she'd had a slight stroke. If his mother got any worse, if she died, he'd hate her for keeping it from him. But if she did tell him, he'd be silly enough to go dashing away to Annsdale Colliery where he'd be recognized, and probably arrested, and his mother wouldn't want to be the cause of that. So she decided to leave it, give the police a chance to lose interest in their search, and hope that with help from friends and neighbours his mother would rally.

'I wonder what's wrong,' he said. 'Will you go, Sal, and find out?'

'I'll go as soon as I can. It won't be long. I'll go on Saturday afternoon,' she promised, and then looked pointedly at the still. 'Well, she's been distilling for many a long year as far as I can make out, Will, and it hasn't gone up yet, so she must have a pretty safe way of doing a dangerous thing. It just goes to show what shrivelled old spinsters are capable of when they put their minds to it, doesn't it?'

★

For King and Country

'He's not a very chatty soul, as a rule. He's usually in a world of his own, lost in his work. Forgets everything else, doesn't hear what you say to him, doesn't notice the cold. At times, he even forgets to go for his dinner. And if we have a lot of work on, he forgets to go home,' the senior technician told her on Monday morning, as he looked over her shoulder, watching her sowing culture media with the discharge from a wound. 'Funny sort of gardening this, isn't it? But it's better than any allotment as far as the prof's concerned. Right, put that to one side and look at these, after a couple of days' culture. Now there's a healthy growth for you.'

Sally looked at the glass dish, the reddish culture medium almost covered with a growth of bacteria. 'From a septic wound?' she said. 'I don't think that's very healthy.'

The technician laughed. 'I was talking about the bugs, not the bugger they've made their home in. We look at things a bit differently here. We're more concerned with the advancement of science than with the treatment of any particular patient, but it's thanks to us that for the first time in history we've had a war that hasn't killed more men from infection than from their injuries. There'll be no stopping laboratory work now. Away, and see them through the microscope.'

She peered down the microscope, and the clusters

of tiny blobs she saw reminded her of frogspawn, or boiled tapioca.

'It'll be one of your jobs to prepare the plates with culture medium so that we can grow these beasts, and you'll have to be careful not to contaminate them with your own bacteria. Don't worry; it's no more difficult than mixing custard for your mother, but you've got to get it dead right. Once we've grown them, we can dye them. I'll show you how to spread films, and later maybe stain them. Gram staining helps to classify bacteria; some are Gram-positive, some Gram-negative. Look at these little darlings.'

Sally looked down the microscope at one slide after another, of bacteria with their beautiful purple stains, arranged like bunches of grapes, or in chains. She began to see the fascination with 'this funny sort of gardening'. 'Bonny, in a way, aren't they?' she said.

'There speaks the budding scientist,' the technician grinned.

'Bonny, but deadly,' Sally breathed, and a picture of Dunkley and the Lowerys unaccountably popped into her head. 'It's amazing stuff, isn't it, BIPP? To stop the wounds going septic, I mean.'

'And cleans them up if they are. Yes, it provides a very unhealthy environment for these little chaps, just the opposite to the culture medium. It kills them before they kill the patient, but the BIPP nearly killed one or two of the patients when they first started using it, you know,' he chuckled. 'They never told you that, did they? Bismuth poisoning, from over-generous use. They only put a smear on now, of course, and it seems to work just as well.'

She peered down the microscope again, glad of the little protection her white coat afforded, and wondered which of these 'little darlings' might be lurking under Will's dressing, and how many of them. The chief liked to leave wounds to heal under one dressing, if possible, but fractured limbs with inflamed, infected bone presented quite a challenge. Inflammation destroys the bone, and where there's dead bone there's always sepsis, Dunkley had told her, and pieces of bone that won't unite can be dying and coming away for a year. Will's arm would never mend until all that was shifted. Thank heaven it had been debrided and BIPP'ed just before he'd had to leave. She wouldn't take the dressing off for another month, unless he started complaining. Hope to God it would be all right by then.

He'd said it felt all right. What might happen if it wasn't, she didn't like to think.

The hallway of the administrative block was empty, except for Nurse Dunkley. Sally tried to escape, to slide out of the front door without a confrontation, but too late. Dunkley was in front of her like lightning, blocking her exit.

'Ah, Nurse Wilde!' she challenged. 'Oh no! It's *Miss Wilde* now, isn't it? Strange coincidence, though. The minute the lieutenant disappears, you move out of the nurses' home!'

'Life's full of coincidences, Nurse Dunkley.'

'And some of them are too big to swallow, but you bat your shifty little eyelids at people and look at them as if butter wouldn't melt in your mouth and tell them you've nothing to do with him – and that's just what they *do* do, they swallow it whole!'

This nasty bitch's bonny blue eyes miss nothing, thought Sally, but her expression was impassive and her tone flat when she said, 'Excuse me, I've got to go.'

Dunkley refused to move. 'Still waters run deep. Dr Lowery's right about you. The quiet ones are always the worst.'

'Dr Lowery knows nothing about me.'

'Dr Lowery knows everything about you, and so does his wife. You were with them long enough. But you'd better watch your step. I've got my spies and I'll strip that innocent mask off you before I've done, and then they'll all see what your game is.'

'I've got no game,' Sally protested, doing her best to sidestep Dunkley, and failing.

'Haven't you? I'd say you've got two. Helping deserters, and helping yourself to my fiancé.'

Very coolly, very deliberately, Sally turned the

thrust of the exchange away from deserters. 'I didn't realize you were engaged,' she said. 'Iain didn't tell me that.'

'Iain!' Dunkley jumped as if she'd been stung, and rasped, 'You'll forget Iain, if you know what's good for you.'

'I'll *never* forget Iain,' Sally countered, but the reaction was more than she anticipated.

Dunkley started towards her with such menace that she jumped, but too late; her hat was half off and Dunkley's fingers were tangled in her hair. Sally put a hand around her wrist and wrenching herself free ran through the massive front door of the entrance hall, out into the safety of a wet December night. She looked back and for an instant saw her adversary framed in the doorway like malevolence made flesh.

A shudder ran down Sally's spine. She shook herself, ruefully rubbed her scalp and straightened her hat, and after a moment or two put up her umbrella and took the road to Jesmond.

It was true, though. She would never forget Iain, or the change the sight of her distress had wrought in him. His protectiveness towards her during that horrible little scene in the anaesthetic room, his shielding of her when Dunkley had threatened to report her to Matron, had left her stunned.

'I warn you, if you say anything about Nurse

Wilde, there's plenty might be said about you,' he'd warned her.

'I've lost my good name because of you,' she'd told him, 'and now you're betraying me.'

'I'm not betraying you, and I won't – unless you force me.' He'd looked as if he meant it, and it had shut Dunkley up, for the moment. Whatever Dr Campbell might have done in the past, that one shining deed, that kindness towards her in her hour of need redeemed him for ever in Sally's eyes, and she loved him for it.

But there had been such venom in the glance Dunkley had shot at her. Poor Dunkley! How she must be suffering! During her half-hour walk back to Jesmond, Sally began to think of everything she should have said in the hallway, and berated herself because she hadn't. 'Don't speak to me like that. I'm not your little probationer now!' would have been a good start. Never mind, she'd save that for next time. Her scalp was sore but her step became jaunty, and her lips parted in a smile.

Dunkley had dished plenty of pain out to other people, in her time. Let *her* suffer, for a change!

'It's a good thing for the nation that not all its soldiers ran away,' Miss Brewster said, revealing her large yellow teeth in a smile of derision as she leaned forward to pour Will another glass of her Christmas batch of home distilled 'whisky'. 'Lucky for us that some men had the guts to fight for England and see the thing through to the finish. At least we've got some heroes to boast about.'

They had maintained an uneasy truce for the past few days, but Miss Brewster had made quite an evening of sampling her Christmas batch, and after holding forth about her father's exploits in India and the decorations he'd received, had moved on to the topic of the war in France, evidently in the mood for baiting him again.

Unfortunately Will also had a fair quantity of homemade spirit inside him, and was in no mood to knuckle under this time. Flexing his fists he turned to Miss Brewster, an angry flush spreading over his face, the veins becoming prominent on his forehead. 'Aye, my three brothers were among the lads who fought for England,' he snarled, 'but they didn't see it through to the finish either. The war saw them through to the finish; they're all dead. I was with our Jack when it was his turn, and I can tell you there was nothing bloody heroic about it.'

He took a gulp of spirits. 'I'll tell you about men who've got the guts to fight for England, if you want to know something about heroes,' he said. 'I'll tell you about the attack that finished one of my brothers. We got sent over the top in broad bloody daylight, and we had to go for the German position in extended order with a gap of about five or ten feet between us, over ground churned up by bombardment and littered with all sorts. My bother went over in the wave before me, and we never fired a bullet. We never saw a bloody German to fire at, but they saw us all right, because we walked into one continual hail of bullets and shrapnel. We never got the chance to shoot at all. We could see nothing to shoot at.

'I saw our Jack spin round and fall in front of me, though, and I was supposed to leave him and go on for the attack, but I didn't. I dropped, and crawled over to him and flattened down beside him, bullets and bloody shells dropping everywhere, man. He'd got a one in the chest, and he couldn't move, neither hand nor foot. So I was looking round for some cover, and there was a dead mule a few yards off, and I thought, if I can get him behind that he might be safe until we can get back to him. So I had to drag him there, poor lad, and he never made a murmur. Then I scrambled forward with the rest. We kept on for about six hundred yards, and after we'd lost hundreds of men and gained nothing, we got the order to go back.

'England's "heroes" died like bloody cattle, worse than cattle, and not for England, either, if you want my opinion — not for any of the people *we* know in England, anyway. More for money people, and bloody politicians, and brainless generals. And that's the way all my brothers went – their lives were thrown away.'

A strangled sound, something between a bellow of rage and a sob escaped him. Startled, both women looked at the pain-contorted, ruined face, and looked away again. The silence grew heavy, broken only by the relentless ticking of the grandfather clock.

At last, Sally asked, 'What happened to Jack?'

'Why, he got left there! What else? The stretcher-bearers bring the ones in who've got a chance first, like, and he had none. So they left him the first time and he was dead by the time they went back to him. He got fetched in with the rest of the dead, and piled up outside the dressing station. A couple of days later I was with the fatigue party that shovelled him into the mud, along with a lot more. No wonder my poor mother thought she'd made enough sacrifices for England.'

'She made three too many,' said Sally, directing a warning glance at Miss Brewster. It was unnecessary. The smile had been wiped right off her face.

Silence again, save the ticking of the clock. Will was scowling into his glass, but Sally sensed that he was near to tears. She attempted to cheer him.

'It'll be Christmas before long, the first Christmas of peacetime. That's something to be glad about.'

'There's too many people not here to see it,' Will said. 'Like my three brothers. Christmas has come a bit late for them, like. I've got nothing to be glad about, or my mother, either. Three good sons. Three canny lads – all slaughtered, and another one that'll be good for nothing, unless this arm heals. Nobody knows the torture they went through, all our lads, day after day and night after night. Nobody'll ever know, because the more they suffered, the less they want to talk about it. People in England have no idea. You daren't write home and tell anybody, they'd have had you up in front of a court martial. And anyway, you couldn't describe it. Nobody could imagine it, unless they'd been there.'

He seemed to slump, and his anger turned to grief. He took out a handkerchief and blew his nose, all the fight gone out of him.

'Oh, dear me.' Sally heaved a sigh, wondering how his mother was, hoping she wouldn't have to bring him news of another bereavement after her visit to Annsdale. She had an overpowering desire to put her arms round him, to try to comfort him, but not here, not with Miss Brewster looking on. Will wasn't known in this locality; they might risk a short walk. She crossed to the window and held back the curtain. The street was lit by a full moon and a few people were about, including one she'd seen before, a young lad leaning against a lamppost opposite the house. With a sudden qualm, she remembered Dunkley's threats of vengeance, and looked more intently. What was he doing, hanging about in the freezing cold?

No, she was giving way to hysteria. It was just some lad waiting for a sweetheart, or a friend, she thought, and dropped the curtain. Still, better stay inside, just in case. She would go into Will's room tonight, after Miss Brewster had gone to bed. She'd never realize. She'd drunk enough to knock herself out for a week.

Chapter Nineteen

His curtains were open, and she could see him from the open door still dressed and lying at full stretch on the bed staring at the ceiling, his injured left arm in its sling. 'Come in, Sally.'

'How did you know it was me?'

'Why, it's not likely to be *her,* is it? Come in, and shut the door.'

She left the door open, and with her dressing gown wrapped tightly around her, went and sat beside him.

'You know what Raynor says?' he demanded. 'He says war's a racket. There are people who want wars, people who get fat on them, like international bankers, and arms dealers, and corrupt politicians. So they start the wars, and then they send fools like us to get maimed and slaughtered. Then at the finish, we come out of it limbless and faceless, and they come out of it rich. I believe him, an' all.'

'Why, maybe he's right, I don't know. But why don't you get into bed? You must be freezing.'

'It's not that cold. Not with these radiators she has going.'

'But they're cold. She doesn't stoke the boiler all night. She couldn't get the coal.'

'She gets plenty. It seems as if you can get anything you like if you know where to go, and you've got the money to pay. I keep wondering how she's managed to get all the sugar she uses for making the booze, but she won't tell me. She gets it, though.'

'She went too far tonight. I told her to shut up about it in future, after you'd gone to bed.'

'That would do a lot of good. Anyway, I've taken no hurt.'

'Are you sure?'

'Aye, I'm sure. I don't get patronized, I don't get pitied, and I get no quarter. She's maybe doing me some good.'

She moved nearer to him. 'I'm cold, even if you're not.'

He looked up at her, his teeth glinting in the darkness. 'We'll get into bed, then, shall we?'

'No. But we could get off the quilt, and put it over us.'

'That's better,' he said, after they'd arranged the eiderdown over themselves. 'Now cuddle up to me.'

Sally complied, and he raised his right hand to stroke her hair. She winced, and pushed it away.

'Why, what's the matter?'

'I've been in a battle an' all, or more a catfight, like, and I've lost a bit of hair there.'

'What? Who with?'

'Nurse Dunkley. She never liked me, and she got a hold of me just as I was leaving the hospital.'

'Why, I never liked her, but I wouldn't have believed she'd sink to a catfight. I'll bet I know who it was over, though.'

'Who?'

'Dr Campbell. She knows he's sweet on you.'

'No, he isn't.'

'He is, and many's the time I've thought you were sweet on him an' all.'

'What do you think now?'

'I think if you liked him all that much, you wouldn't be lying here beside me.'

'Is that right?'

With his lips almost touching her ear he murmured: 'Women have got an awful power over men, Sal.'

'Have they?'

'Aye, they have.'

'And did you feel that power when you were in France, Will?'

'You feel it everywhere, but in France I didn't see many women. I was with a company of men, most of the time.'

'What about when you were in the rest areas?

There were women there, or so I've heard. The sort of women that a lot of men like to carry on with.'

'Ah.'

She pulled back, and turned to face him. 'Ah, what?'

'Just — ah!'

'Ah!' she leaned over him, gazing intently into his face. 'That's not an answer.'

'Why, if the question is was I one of the men that carried on with that "sort of woman" in France, the answer's no.'

'Are you sure?'

'Of course I'm sure.'

She lay back and relaxed against him. He nuzzled her cheek, and the feel of his warm breath on her neck sent a thrill of desire through her, making her guarded. That feeling wasn't to be trusted; it must be the selfsame one that had driven Dunkley to throw her reputation away for the sake of Dr Campbell.

'Let's get into bed, Sally.'

'No.'

'Why not?'

'Because if we do, something might happen that I don't want to happen. Not yet, anyway.'

'Why not? You're safe with me. You'll be all right. I love you.'

She stroked his cheek in answer, but otherwise lay silent.

For King and Country

He pulled her closer. 'Why not? Why not?' he urged. 'Nothing will happen, and if it did, she'd never hear us. She's had enough to fell a horse.'

Sally shook her head slightly, but said nothing.

'You're a funny lass, Sally. I don't really know where I am with you. You move heaven and earth to get me out of harm's way, but when it comes to anything else, you push me away. You can't stomach me because of the mess my face is in. That's the top and bottom of it.'

'It's not. If you want to know what I think, it's a better face for you than the one you had before.'

'Why, how do you make that out?'

'The one you had before made you too vain. Too full of yourself.'

'Hm. I had something to be vain about, with that face. And maybe you'd never have been interested in me if I hadn't had it.'

'I never was interested in you, remember.'

'Aye, I do remember. I wanted to be your knight in shining armour, and you were the only lass in the village that didn't want a one.'

'Oh, I wanted a knight in shining armour,' she said, 'but you had too many princesses. You were in love with them all, and I didn't want to be one of a crowd.'

'I was in love with everything once. You mind that bonny day we bumped into each other in the park, long before your Lizzie's wedding? I was in love with the sunshine on your face and on those little golden hairs on your arms. I was in love with the clouds, and that little lass with her cough drops. She wanted to give us a one; do you mind that? I was even in love with the feel of the grass prickling through my shirt and that tune the band was playing. What was it now?'

'I forget.'

'How can you forget? I haven't forgotten,' he said, and hummed a few bars.

'"Tales from the Vienna Woods",' she said, and slipping her arm under his waist and pulling him close, she kissed his unblemished cheek. 'What are you in love with now?'

'Only you.'

'What else, then?'

'This is a dark place, Sally. There's nothing much to love here, except you.'

A cloud drifted over the moon, obscuring its light. Sally watched it for a moment, then said: 'I'm a virgin, Will, and virginity – well, it's something you can only give once. When I give it, if I give it, I want it to be to my husband.'

He turned to face her. 'I'll be your husband, if you'll take a husband with a face people will cross the street sooner than look at.'

She kissed his cheek again and sat up. 'I'd better go.'

He held her back. 'No, don't. Stay with me. I'll keep you warm, and never bother, I'll show you what a good lad I can be, if that's what you want.'

'Mutti!'

The heavy curtains were still open, and a grey dawn was peeping through the window when she was awoken by a cry. She turned to see anguish on his face, and squeezed his hand.

'Will, Will!'

'Oh, oh,' he gasped, his eye wide and staring until he saw her and came shuddering to himself.

'You were dreaming.'

'Was I?'

'You shouted "muddy!" Just like the night nurse said you did, when they thought you couldn't talk. Only it sounded more like "mutter!"'

He sat bolt upright and shook himself like a dog shaking water off its coat. He looked at her, still shuddering from time to time, as if throwing off some unseen horror.

She sat up. 'What is it, Will?'

'Ugh,' he breathed. 'Ugh,' but gave her no other answer.

She put her arms around him and rested her cheek on his shoulder. 'Don't think about it.'

After a while he said: 'It was a few weeks after our Jack copped it. We were mopping up, after taking a trench. Before the war, nobody would have believed what that entails. You sling smoke bombs in the enemy's dugouts, so they have a choice between choking to death and coming out. So they come out, and as soon as they do you shoot them, or put them to the bayonet. Well, that was the job I had this time, and I was all keyed up and baying for blood. "Come on out, you buggers, let's have you," I was yelling, but there was only a couple came out, with their hands up, jabbering, "*Kamarad, kamarad!*" like they do.

'"I'll give you bloody *kamarad*," I said, and I put the first one to the point. But the one behind him was younger, and when it was his turn, when I stuck the bayonet in – he was only a kid – he looked – straight into my eyes as he fell, and he said "*Mutti!*"'

He stared straight through her and gave an awful groan, and then placing his hands behind his head he curled himself into a ball.

Sally sat beside him, horror-struck at the thought of those lads and the German muttis who would never see their sons again. Then came the tears, welling into her eyes and dropping onto the killer of their children, her ordinary village lad turned murderer. She murmured choked words of comfort he seemed not to hear, and stroked his hair.

The scars on his face were bad enough, but now she saw the scars within, deep and ugly – scars that might never heal. They filled her heart with dread, and her mind was overwhelmed by doubt that she would prove strong enough to take on the burden of a broken man.

'She can still talk,' the neighbour said, her bright brown eyes looking inquisitively into Sally's as she prattled on, seeming quite oblivious of Mrs Burdett's presence. 'She's paralysed all down one side, and her speech is slurred, but you can just make out what she says, if you listen hard enough. Me and the lass across the road, we keep coming in to have a look at her, try and get her to eat a bit. Help her to use the bucket, like. She hasn't had one wet bed, so far. We're expecting her father today, he's coming to look after her, and I'm not sorry. I've got my own family to see to, but poor lass, you couldn't see her stuck. Your Emma and your Ginny and your mother keep bringing her a bite to eat, and now you're here! I never realized you were all so friendly, although I know you knew the lads.'

Sally nodded, and the woman's gaze became more intense.

'It was after that bobby was down asking her about their Will that she took the stroke. They reckon he's not dead at all; he's a deserter! By, that must have been a shock for her!'

'Will's dead,' Sally insisted, 'and they'd have done a lot better to leave her alone.'

'Oh, aye, I'll agree with you there,' the woman said, but Sally said no more, her attention was focused on the woman in the bed, who was struggling to speak.

Half reluctantly, the neighbour said, 'I'll get off now, then, shall I?' Sally nodded, and saw her out, locking the door behind her before returning to Mrs Burdett's bedside.

'Good neighbour,' she slurred, giving Sally a lop-sided smile. Sally smiled back and nodded agreement, detecting a trace of irony in the words.

Now feeling the scrutiny of Mrs Burdett's searching eyes she sat down and took her limp, cold hand. 'Never bother. He's safe, and I'll keep him safe,' she promised, giving it a squeeze.

Mrs Burdett closed her eyes, and released her pent-up breath in a long sigh.

'It's a good job you told us where to find the key to the laundry,' Sally went on. 'He passed the first night there, well out of the way, lying beside the ironing stove with plenty of blankets to cover him up. He said he'd had many a worse billet in France, anyhow. I've got him staying with a friend of our Ginny's just now. He's all right,' she emphasized, 'they'll never get a hold of him there. He'll be all right.'

Mrs Burdett spoke, but in so garbled a fashion that Sally couldn't be sure she'd heard her right.

'Did you say "Marry him?"' she asked. 'Why, Mrs

Burdett! And are you sure you want me for a daughter-in-law, like?'

Mrs Burdett nodded, and with a great deal of effort said something that sounded very much like, 'He'll give you bonny children.'

Sally gave her an embarrassed smile. 'I can do a bit of nursing now, you know. I'll wash you and change your bed while I'm here.'

'When I die,' Mrs Burdett struggled to say, 'everything's for you. Marry him.'

Sally raised her eyebrows, and protested, 'You're not going to die, Mrs Burdett. People can get better from strokes, and your dad's coming to look after you.'

'For you,' Mrs Burdett repeated.

'For me, for Will? Is that it?'

Mrs Burdett nodded, and Sally gave her a pitying look. Poor woman, she was as poor as a church mouse. She must be going wrong in her mind. When Mrs Burdett died, it would be a miracle if she left enough for a decent burial.

Best to humour her, though. 'All right then,' she smiled. 'It's all for me.'

Matters were not quite as bad as the neighbour had said. Mrs Burdett still had some use of her right arm, so bathing her was easy, and she'd lost so much weight that getting her out of bed to change the sheets wasn't too much of a job either. Sally had just tidied everything away and was combing her patient's hair when they heard the expected knock on the door.

Mrs Burdett's eyes brightened. 'Dad.'

'You'm Sally Wilde,' Mr Hibbs said, when she opened it. 'Nurse Wilde. I ent forgotten.'

She led him in, pleased to have washed his daughter and dressed her in clean linen before he saw her, hoping it might lessen his shock at the sight of her lolling body and her palsied face.

It didn't. Stricken, he dropped his suitcase on the floor. 'Oh, Bessie!'

Sally escaped into the kitchen, leaving them to their greetings and explanations and mild recriminations, and kept out of the way until the kettle boiled.

'Send him to Stafford,' the father said, when she eventually took the tray into them and poured the tea. 'I'm taking Bess home, as soon as she's fit. Send him to Stafford, or I'll come back for him when she'm settled with her sisters. Nobody'ull remember him there, except his own family, and they'm not going to let on. He'll be another prisoner of war who made his way back from Germany, and nobody to say any different.'

'He'll be safer where he is . . . for now,' Sally said.

'He'll be better off in Stafford,' the old man insisted. 'Men like to be their own masters, I know that, and you can't drive 'em to anything they don't want to do, but if he takes my advice, he'll let his uncle teach him the photography business. It's a good living. But if he wants to stay in the pits, we've got pits in Staffordshire. He can work in one of them.'

'I can't see anybody in their right mind going down the pit, if they've got the chance to be a photographer,' said Sally. 'I'm sure he'd rather do that. But I'm not sure he wants to go to Stafford.'

Mrs Burdett reacted instantly. 'Yes! Tell him! Go, go!' she slurred, gesticulating with her good hand, 'Marry him, go!'

The old man lifted his eyes to Sally's as she handed him the cup. 'She might not be as sweet on Will as you'm told me he is on her, Bess, and he's got nothing to keep a wife on. And she might have got a chap with better prospects in mind,' he said, his eyes still on Sally. 'But send him to Stafford for Christmas. Give us six months with him, and when you get some holidays next summer, come and see us. See what his prospects are then.'

Sally answered with a nod, and a troubled smile. 'Aye, all right. I'll ask him if he'll go, anyway.'

'Well, it's the twenty-first of December already,' Ginny said, when Sally arrived at the Cock Inn. 'Another four days, and it'll be Christmas Day. It's a pity you don't take a drink. If you're up anywhere near Miss Brewster's, you'll have enough to make merry on. But I suppose you'll be working.'

'Why, Christmas Day's always the patient's day, Ginny. Always has been. On Christmas Eve they put the lights out on the wards, and the nurses go round with candles singing Christmas carols, until they've been round every ward. It's lovely.' She gave a nostalgic little sigh, regretting that she wouldn't be a part of it this year.

Ginny gave her an old-fashioned look. 'Why then, that's something to look forward to.'

'Aye, it is. And then on Christmas Day, the consultant comes onto the ward when the dinner comes up, to carve the turkey for the patients. Oh, yes, they're well looked after on Christmas Day, the patients are.'

'And you'll be there, doing your bit, I suppose.'

'Why, that's what the nurses are there for, Ginny man.'

'Come on upstairs. It's half an hour before opening time. We'll have a cup of tea. How's Will getting on?'

Sally followed her sister through the empty bar and up to her living quarters. 'All right, as far as I know.'

'They keep you fastened in that nurses' home, I suppose.'

'Aye, they keep the nurses on a bonny tight rein, Ginny.'

Halfway up the stairs, Ginny turned round and looked at her. 'Why, tell the truth and shame the devil, our Sally. This is your own sister you're talking to, and I know for a fact you've packed nursing up, and you've been living at Miss Brewster's for over a week, *and* you're blackmailing her into letting Will stay there. But if you report her, there's nothing to stop her reporting me. Have you thought about that?' she said, resuming her ascent of the stairs.

'She won't report you,' Sally said, her jaw set in an obdurate line. 'And if she does, you just deny it. She can't prove it. You never gave her any receipts, did you?'

'I can't believe you, our Sal, the way you're carrying on. I suppose you've had to lie to shield him, but I'm glad your mother's not here, listening to the fibs you're telling. You want to be careful you don't end up a habitual liar, especially not with your own. And Will's in the wrong place there. She's a spinster, used to living on her own and having everything her own way. It's not fair to put on her. Bring him here. He'll be all right upstairs. His mother'll be able to come and see him then.'

Sally followed her sister into a kitchen bright with winter sun and filled with the scent of brandy and spices. 'How can he come here?' she demanded. 'People are in and out of this place all the time, and I thought you said our Lizzie's husband might be coming an' all, and him a captain?' She lifted the wooden spoon and began idly stirring the bowl of mincemeat on the top of the stove while Ginny began to fill the gleaming copper kettle. She raised her voice a fraction above the rush of water. 'Why, he's not likely to have much sympathy for a deserter, is he? And Will's mother has a job to walk, so how's she going to get here? And then up all these stairs?'

'We'll carry her up. How else?'

'Why, that might look a bit suspicious, don't you think? You suddenly starting fetching her here, when she's never set foot in the place in her life before? She's got plenty of nosey neighbours who'll soon start asking each other what that's all about. Anyway, her father's taking her to Stafford as soon as she's fit to go, and he wants Will to go an' all. He's given me a letter for him, and money for the fare.'

Her lips compressed and her dark brows drawn together in a slight frown, Ginny turned off the tap and set the kettle on the stove. 'If Mrs Burdett doesn't see Will soon, she might never see him at all, the way I look at her,' she said.

'Will's had too many narrow squeaks already, and the police haven't given up looking for him. If he does come to see her, he'll probably get caught, and then we'll all cop it, and what good's that going to do her? And Miss Brewster's house is like a fortress, Ginny man, you know that yourself. Nobody'll ever catch him there. He's better off where he is, until his arm heals. Anyway, I've seen people a lot worse than Mrs Burdett after a stroke, and they've lived to tell the tale.'

Ginny gave up the argument. 'All right. Please yourself.'

'I will,' Sally assured her. 'And if you haven't already told me mam I've moved out of the nurses' home, don't. Don't tell her about Will, either.'

Ginny reached up to the shelf for the tea caddy, and put two spoons of tea into the brown teapot. 'I haven't. It would be nice if you could get here for the New Year, though, Sal. We've just heard our Arthur's getting demobbed. I hope he'll be here in time to be the Cock's first foot.'

'I hope he will,' said Sally. 'And you'd better make the most of it; it might be for the last time. He'll be on the boat to Australia, the first chance he gets.'

'Try this.' Miss Brewster handed Will a cut-glass goblet full of ruby coloured liquid.

He raised it to his lips and, very hesitantly, took a sip. 'Aye, it's lovely, Miss Brewster. A bit sweet for me like, but it's nice.' The smile he turned on her had something of the old charm, despite his ruined face. Sally caught her breath at the sight of it, and looked away.

Miss Brewster had melted a bit towards him since his outburst about England's heroes, and he evidently had every intention of helping the thaw. She beamed back at him for a moment, and then handed a glass to Sally. 'Now you.'

Better forget she'd signed the pledge. Sally took the glass and sipped a little. 'Mm,' she said, 'It's lovely. You're deliberately leading me astray, Miss Brewster.'

'Nothing pleases me more,' smiled Miss Brewster, 'than to . . .'

There was a hammering on the door, and her expression changed to one of irritation. 'Now who the devil's that, on Sunday? Not that accursed vicar, I hope, come to clack his false teeth at me again. Better go into the kitchen, you two, and take the bottle and the glasses with you.'

They jumped to obey. Snatching up the parish paper and her reading glasses, Miss Brewster followed them into the hall. En route to the kitchen they heard her open the letterbox to demand: 'Who is it? Who's that, disturbing people on the Sabbath?'

'It's the police, Madam. We have reason to believe that you may be harbouring a deserter.'

'Harbouring a deserter!' exclaimed Miss Brewster, her tones rising from sharp to razor-edged. 'Me, the only daughter of a decorated army major? Do you know where you are? This is *Jesmond*!'

'Jesmond or not, Madam,' the policeman insisted. 'We have a warrant to search the premises.'

'Good heavens, this is an outrage! Show me the warrant. I demand to see it.'

For King and Country

On hearing the word 'deserter', Sally knew exactly what she had to do.

She was in the shrubbery, turning the compost heap when Miss Brewster, came outside to open the door in the garden wall to let the police through. The mastiff began to bark and the bulldog snarled as the sergeant and the constable invaded their mistress's territory. Both men backed away.

'Are you sure you can't find the front door keys, Madam?' the sergeant asked.

'I've told you, haven't I? Well, don't just stand there. You've insisted on being let in, so come in,' Miss Brewster urged.

'I'd rather you chained the dogs, Madam.'

'Quiet!'

The policemen looked startled. The dogs fell silent, and there was a tinge of contempt in Miss Brewster's voice when she said, 'I meant the dogs, not you. They won't hurt you; I'll answer for it. Come in. This is Miss Wilde, my entirely respectable companion.'

'We're already acquainted with Miss Wilde, Madam,' said the sergeant, 'but there seems to be some doubt in some people's minds about her respectability.'

Sally stuck the garden fork in the ground and lifted the watering can to sprinkle the heap. 'We meet again, Officer.'

'That's a funny thing for a Methodist girl to be doing on the Sabbath,' the constable remarked.

'I help with the garden to oblige Miss Brewster. I'm shut in a laboratory all week, and the fresh air does me good, so I don't think God will mind all that much,' she said.

Miss Brewster slowly turned towards her, and the look she gave her made Sally's blood run cold. 'I hope, Miss Wilde, that there's nothing in this accusation. It would disgust me to think I'd dishonoured my late father's name by sheltering anyone who'd helped a *deserter*.'

Sally returned her gaze with one just as piercing. 'You can set your mind at rest, Miss Brewster. I've done nothing of the sort.'

'I'm very pleased to hear it.' Her tones were icy.

'I'm afraid, Madam,' said the sergeant, 'that we'll have to search the house.'

Miss Brewster continued her *grande dame* act. 'This is an appalling intrusion into the private home of a respectable lady. I shall write a letter of complaint to the Chief Constable directly you've gone.'

The sergeant began to look uncertain. 'Why, maybe we'll just have a quiet word with Miss Wilde, and leave it at that.'

'No!' Miss Brewster contradicted, very decidedly. 'You'd better make your search, and search thoroughly, from the attic to the outhouse, or the finger of suspicion will be forever pointed at me. I insist you do it. Show them in, Miss Wilde.'

Sally remembered the three half full glasses of sloe gin she'd left in the sink, and all Will's clothes, and his shaving gear upstairs, and her heart sank. 'Are you sure, Miss Brewster?' she asked, her manner truculent, her words a threat as much as a question.

The temperature plummeted further. 'Of course I'm sure! From the attic to the outhouse. Pull the mattresses off the beds, tear up the carpets, ferret under all the floorboards. Don't leave a splinter of skirting board or a flake of paint undisturbed. Go! Unless, of course, you *have* got something to hide?'

Sally blushed, and without another word led the officers inside and up the stairs, noting on her way through the kitchen that only two of the glasses remained. Upstairs, Will's nightshirt was gone from his bed.

The constable opened the wardrobe. 'Hello. This is full of men's suits.'

'They belonged to Miss Brewster's father,' Sally said.

'Hm.' They left the bedroom, and her heart almost stopped as they opened the bathroom door. But there was neither razor, nor soap, nor shaving brush to be seen. The constable began to rummage in the cupboard.

'What's this, then? It's still damp. I reckon it's not

long since this was used.' He held out the shaving mug and all its contents, right under her nose.

The beady eyes of the sergeant were upon her. She tore her eyes away from the razor and shaving brush, and fixing them on the blackheads on his nose, her lips curved in a supercilious smile. 'Miss Brewster's. Some older ladies, you know, are troubled with a . . . a few whiskers . . .'

'On their chins,' the constable added, with an ungallant snort of mirth.

'Yes,' murmured Sally, her stomach in turmoil, but her gaze steady. 'Perhaps you'd better ask her about that.'

'Righto. Downstairs, then,' the sergeant said.

But the downstairs search was even less fruitful than the one upstairs. In the drawing room the sergeant said, 'Have you anything to add to your previous statement, Miss?'

'There's nothing I can add, Sergeant.'

'Are you going to ask the old lady about the shaving tackle, Sergeant?' The constable smirked at Sally.

The sergeant quelled him with a look.

Miss Brewster was waiting for them in the kitchen, her expression baleful. 'Search all the cupboards,' she demanded, sweeping her arm in the direction of a green painted door on the far side of the room, 'and look in the pantry, do.'

For King and Country

The constable headed for the door. Miss Brewster's eyes flashed fire. 'You'll see a galvanized tub in there,' she said, 'full of our unmentionable garments waiting to be sent to the wash, but don't let that deter you from your duty. Rummage through them, by all means.'

'That won't be necessary, Madam.' The sergeant closed a cupboard door. 'Come along, Constable.'

Miss Brewster ushered them out of the kitchen door. 'Gladius! Scutum!'

The officers blanched as the dogs leapt to her side. 'You'd better look in the outhouse. It reeks of dog rather, but I suppose a deserter could make himself fairly comfortable in there, once he got used to the smell.' Her voice was full of scorn.

'I doubt it, with those animals for company,' the sergeant remarked. 'But you'd better have a look, Constable.'

As they watched the constable drag his unwilling feet over to the outhouse Miss Brewster gave a grim smile. 'I doubt it too.'

He soon returned, shaking his head.

'It looks as if an apology's in order, ma'am,' said the sergeant. 'I hope you'll excuse the intrusion, but we're obliged to do our duty.' He looked as if he were trying to nerve himself to say something else, and failing.

'Hm,' Miss Brewster said, 'and now, I hope you're

satisfied. But I should very much like to know who Miss Wilde's accusers are.'

'I don't know as I'm at liberty to say,' the sergeant said. 'Maybe you'd better inquire of my superior. But we had the information from what's called a very reputable source.'

He wasn't going to ask about the razor, Sally decided, sizing him up.

Miss Brewster looked down her long nose. 'A very *dis*reputable source, you mean, and a cowardly and underhanded one, too, in my opinion. I certainly shall "inquire of your superior", as you put it.'

The sergeant's eyes locked with Miss Brewster's for one brief moment. He glanced away and opened his mouth and Sally knew then he was actually going to come out with it. Miss Brewster started as she suddenly snatched up the fork and began turning the compost heap, her movements swift and vigorous, her expression that of one who might be dangerous to trifle with.

'We did find some shaving gear, though, in the bathroom cupboard,' the sergeant remarked, adding, very warily, 'and it was *damp*.'

Sally turned and looked Miss Brewster full in the face. Give him away, you old battleaxe, she thought, and I'll make sure you give yourself away in the process. These two will have a field day, catching a deserter and an illicit still in one swoop.

Miss Brewster seemed to understand. 'That was my father's,' she snapped, 'and he's been dead for years. Of course it wasn't damp!'

The policeman hesitated as if half inclined to press the point, but before he got the chance to open his mouth, Sally thrust the fork into the ground and cut in, 'I don't need to ask who my accusers are, I already know, and I can tell you it was done for nothing but pure spite. Talk to Matron. Talk to the minister in Annsdale Colliery. They'll give me a good character, or anybody else who really knows me.'

'We already have, Miss, and they did,' the sergeant admitted.

'I'm just sorry you've wasted your valuable time.'

'Yes, Miss. So are we,' said the sergeant.

And although the two policemen passed within inches of Miss Brewster on their way out of the garden door, they failed to notice the fine down still covering her face and chin.

No marks for observation there.

Chapter Twenty

'I couldn't eat another thing. I'm as full as a gun.' Sally forced down the last crumb of Christmas cake, along with the last morsel of marzipan.

'Why, I couldn't, either. This is the second big meal I've had today. I did a Christmas dinner for my mother and my sisters and their families before I came away and left them to their own devices. They probably think I'm down at your house, playing ludo,' Ginny said, with a wink at Mrs Burdett. 'I don't know what they'd think if they could see us all having tea with the cream of Newcastle, like.'

From the head of a table strewn with the wreckage of Christmas tea, Miss Brewter spat contempt. 'Cream of Newcastle my eye! I usually entertain a few representatives of the cream of Newcastle at this time of year, respectable clockwork people with their respectable clockwork lives, and damned dreary bores they are – or power maniacs. I know whose company I'd rather have.'

'Why, who's is that, Euphemia?' asked Ginny.

It had been on the tip of Sally's tongue to protest, but I'm in and out by the clock, Miss Brewster, and then she was deflected by the name. Euphemia! It had never occurred to her to speculate on Miss Brewster's Christian name, but Euphemia!

'The very dubious company I have the pleasure of just now,' Euphemia retorted, 'or I wouldn't have sent a cab for you.'

'Why, what do you mean, Miss Brewster?' Sally glanced up, all innocence. 'There's nothing dubious about me!'

Miss Brewster gave a wry smile. 'Not on the surface there isn't, and that's what makes you the most dubious of us all. And your wits and your good-girl reputation are the only things between you and Newcastle gaol; never forget it. There's a saying my father was very fond of: *He who first a good name gets . . .*' she hesitated, and left the saying suspended in mid air. 'But his favourite maxims were never fit for delicate ears. So for you, Sally, another one will do: *still waters run deep.*'

'That's funny, somebody else said that to me, a while ago,' Sally said, watching Will's mother carefully lifting a teacup to her lips.

'And whoever said it, said right!' Ginny exclaimed. 'Ee, I would never have believed it would enter our Sal's mind to do some of the things she's done. Her mother doesn't even know she's left nursing yet, let alone that she's had the police after her.'

'Her's had the police after her because her's a good lass, not a bad 'un,' Will's grandfather insisted, 'the best. The sort that won't leave a friend in the lurch. And you'm not a bad 'un yourself, either,' Grandfather said, daring to compliment his formidable hostess.

The cup shook a little in Mrs Burdett's hand. Sally reached up to steady it, and saw that she was near to tears. 'You think it's healing all right?' she slurred, directing her gaze towards the filthy plaster cast on Will's arm.

'The signs are good,' said Sally. 'He doesn't complain, he's got no temperature and there's no smell from it. His fingers are warm, and he's using them all right.'

'I can use it now,' Will assured her. 'It doesn't hurt, and it doesn't feel as if it's coming apart. It's going on champion, Mam.'

Miss Brewster stood up. 'Well, if we've all finished, we'll retire to the drawing room. I want your opinion on some of my liqueurs.'

'Before we do, I've got something for Will. From his uncle,' Will's grandfather said, handing him the bulky brown paper parcel that had rested beside his chair throughout tea.

Will took it by its string loop, and gave him a wry

smile. 'I think we can guess what this is. Open it for us, will you, Sally?'

She picked at the string to loosen the knots, and then carefully removed the brown paper.

'A box camera,' she said. 'And a book about photography.'

'I remember the camera very well,' Will grimaced. 'Thanks, Granddad.'

'It was your uncle's first one,' Will's grandfather said, 'and now it's yours. Get some practice in.'

'Might struggle, with the pot on,' Mrs Burdett slurred. 'He's left-handed.'

'I might do all right, an' all,' said Will. 'I can write with the other one now – just about, so I should be able to manage a simple box camera.'

Miss Brewster was in her element. 'This is one of my favourite potions,' she told them. 'It's a "brandy" I've steeped mandarin oranges in since last year. Try it.'

Sally accepted – she wouldn't have dared do otherwise. 'That's lovely, Miss Brewster,' she said, licking the sweet, sticky, orange taste off her lips. Ginny agreed, and so did Mrs Burdett.

'Why, it's all right, like,' said Will, 'for women.'

Grandfather wouldn't even try it.

'There's beer in the cellar,' Miss Brewster said, 'for the Philistines among us.'

'That'll be me, then,' said Will, getting up to fetch it, 'and me grandad.'

The tasting went on, with Miss Brewster offering one concoction after another, trying them herself and then pressing them onto her guests. Sally's head began to spin as she sipped and Miss Brewster became flushed, louder and more talkative. She began to regale them with the story of Will's escape from the clutches of the law, delighting in the ruse so much that even Will and Sally were agog. Then out came the sloe gin.

'This is my *piece de résistance*,' she announced.

Watching her pour it into lead crystal glasses put Sally dizzily in mind of the Sunday afternoon. 'Why, Miss Brewster, I'd left the three glasses in the kitchen sink when I went to hide Will. It was a dead give-away, but when I took the policemen through the kitchen, one of them had vanished!'

Miss Brewster displayed all her yellow teeth and her braying laughter filled the room. 'I know! I spotted them when I went through to open the garden door, and I pushed it in the pig bin, under the swill!' she exclaimed. But her grin became a grimace of disgust when she added, 'And I had to fish it out again when the coast was clear, while you were rescuing your beloved!'

'Like I had to rescue Will's things from underneath our . . . you know,' Sally said.

'Yes! They knew better than to disturb our "you

know!"' Miss Brewster roared again and Mrs Burdett joined her with a bit of the lustre back in her eyes, and a lopsided giggle that so infected Sally that she was as helpless with laughter as the pair of them.

'You're tipsy,' Will accused her, laughing himself.

'Yes, you are,' said Miss Brewster. 'Disgraceful!'

'I am,' said Sally, raising her glass. 'And this is the last. I'll have to be at work tomorrow, while you're all sleeping it off.'

When the noise had subsided, Miss Brewster looked directly at Mrs Burdett. 'Don't you worry your head. As soon as he's fit I'll send your Will to Stafford without fail. They won't rob you of the one you've got left. It'll be over my dead body, if they try.'

Seeing Miss Brewster slightly the worse for drink, Ginny suddenly asked, 'Why, how does that saying of your father's go, Effie? *He who first a good name gets . . .?*'

Miss Brewster hesitated, then took another sip of sloe gin and threw discretion to the winds. '*May piss the bed, and say he sweats!*' she declared, and covered her mouth to suppress a loud hiccup.

Solemn faced, Ginny said, 'Why, there you are then, Sal, that's what you can do.'

'Miss Brewster!' Sally protested, 'I haven't done that since I was three year old!'

★

For King and Country

'I'll teach you everything I know about distilling, and you can teach me all you know about photography. That's a fair exchange,' Miss Brewster had bargained after their little Christmas gathering, and nothing more had been done or said about it. Now, on New Year's Day 1919, they were trooping outside to use the last bit of film taking photographs of the dogs.

'That's what photography means, drawing with light,' Will announced, as Sally closed the back door behind them.

'Oh, really?' said Miss Brewster. 'I may be a woman, but that doesn't mean I'm a complete imbecile.'

'I never thought it did.'

'Well then, don't state the obvious.'

'I was only repeating what my uncle told me,' said Will.

She rounded on him ferociously. 'And how old were you at the time?' she demanded. 'Five?'

'Aye, about that,' he said, and looked at her with a straight face for a moment or two. Then to Sally's amazement, the corners of his mouth began to twitch and he burst into laughter, the first real laugh she'd heard from him since he got back from France, and so welcome to her ears.

It was answered by a broad grin from Miss Brewster.

'All right, then,' he said, still smiling. 'This is the simplest kind of camera there is. All you have to do is put a roll of film in, and press the shutter release. You can't change the distance between the film and the lens, or the aperture of the lens, or the time of exposure. So as long as you've got a good light, there's not a lot can go wrong – if that's not too obvious for you. You'll get a good, clear picture on a day like this.'

'All right, let's get on with it. Scutum! Gladius!' she called, and the dogs came bounding out of the outhouse.

'You can pose them if you want to,' said Will, with a wary eye on the bulldog, 'but you'll get a more natural photo if you wait for what my uncle calls "the unguarded moment". Why, then, that's with people. I'm not so sure about dogs.'

'My dogs *are* human, almost. More human than some people,' Miss Brewster said, stepping back and pointing the camera at Scutum.

The mastiff's big, soulful eyes gave some credence to her claim, but that bulldog! Sally wouldn't trust him as far as she could spit, and she could see that Will had no more faith in him, either.

'You want the sun behind you,' said Will. Miss Brewster moved round.

'You'll get a better photo if you get down on one knee,' he said, 'right down to their level, like.' Miss

Brewster did so, and Will crouched behind her, his scarred face nearly touching hers while the dogs sat watching them, alert and perplexed. 'Now look through the viewfinder, and move the camera till you get the picture you want. Keep it steady. That's it. Now, just a gentle squeeze . . .'

Miss Brewster squeezed the shutter. 'I'm going into Newcastle tomorrow to get some more film,' she said, 'and I'll get some developer, and some photographic paper. I want to learn to develop them.'

'You've got no dark room,' said Will.

Miss Brewster nodded towards the bell pit.

'There's no running water down there,' said Will, 'and you need a lot of it.'

'Hm . . .' said Miss Brewster.

'Our Ginny told us you might be here. I've come all the way from France so I can be Miss Brewster's first foot, and I've brought a pal,' Arthur announced, that afternoon. 'He's nearly as tall, dark and handsome as me, so that means she'll get twice the good luck, eh, Sal? He's stopping with me and Kath for a week or two until he's been to see a few of his mother's relations. Then we're off!'

'Off where?'

'On the boat to Australia, of course.'

'S'right,' said Arthur's companion, a burly, light-haired young fellow who towered over both her and

Arthur. She stretched out a hand. 'How do you do . . .?'

'Frank,' said Arthur. 'Frank Pickering.'

'S'right,' Frank drawled.

'Hello, Frank,' said Sally. 'It's nice to meet you.'

Frank nodded, and gave her hand a bone-crushing squeeze and a shake. Sally withdrew her mangled hand, politely masking all manifestation of pain.

'Why, are you going to let us in, hinny?'

'I daren't let you in until I ask her, but she's already had the first-foot. Just a minute,' she said, closing the door on them. Miss Brewster had insisted that Will do the honours of first-footing, surprising both him and Sally in view of his obvious lack of the third qualification.

Within a couple of minutes she was back at the door, to lead Arthur and Frank into the drawing room where they sat, polite and uncomfortable, on the sofa.

'She won't be long,' Sally said, and had scarcely perched herself on the leather pouffe when Miss Brewster made her appearance.

Sally jumped up. 'This is my brother Arthur, Miss Brewster.'

Arthur got to his feet and tossed a lump of coal onto the fire. 'Aye, why, first foot or not, there's not much point carting that back,' he said, wiping his hand briefly on his trousers before thrusting it out to Miss Brewster. 'Happy New Year, and many of

452

'em,' he said, pumping her hand. '"Lang may your lum reek, wi' somebody else's coal", like them tartan buggers say.'

'Excuse his language, Miss Brewster. He'll have had a bit to drink last night, and he's probably still under the influence,' Sally said, none too happy at the impression he might be making.

Arthur gave her a withering look, and held out a canvas bag to Miss Brewster. 'Our Ginny sent you a cake, an' all.'

Miss Brewster put the bag on the mahogany chiffonier and opened the cake tin it contained. 'That smells divine. Well, Mr Wilde, first foot or not, you and your friend had better have a het pint, or a glass of whisky. Which would you prefer?'

'I'll have a whisky, thanks,' said Arthur.

'And your friend?'

'What's a het pint?' Frank sounded dubious.

'Pale ale, sweet and hot, with whisky and nutmeg.'

'He'll have the same as me,' said Arthur.

Frank perked up considerably. 'S'right,' he grinned.

More comfortable and merry again after a couple of glasses of whisky and a slice of cake, Arthur gave Sally the news from home. 'Our Ginny's got our Lizzie and her new husband staying at the Cock,' he said. 'A captain. We might have known nothing less than a captain would do for our Lizzie.'

'He's not that new,' said Sally. 'They'll have been married two years this Easter.'

'He's new enough,' said Arthur, 'seeing he's spent most of his time in France and then in German prisoner of war camps since they got married. They'll be at our Ginny's for another week or two, and then he's taking her to Paris for a "honeymoon". It's all right for some.'

'He seems all right, though, or he did when I met him at their wedding,' said Sally, reminding herself to go to the Cock and pump the captain for all she was worth about those prisoner of war camps, while she still had the chance.

'Next holiday I get,' said Arthur, ''ll be the six-week boat trip to Australia. Frank says there's plenty of work in the mines round Woolangong, and it's a sight better paid than here, an' all.'

'S'right,' said Frank, then sotto voce to Arthur, 'Dunny out the back?'

'He means the lav,' Arthur interpreted. Miss Brewster gave directions, and Frank departed.

As soon as he'd disappeared, Arthur leaned towards Sally. 'Why then, what do you think to him?' he whispered.

'He seems very nice,' she said.

Arthur looked as pleased as punch. 'He's not a bad looking lad, is he? And he's a good worker. He'd be all right for you. If you fancied taking him on, you wouldn't have to wait for your nursing ticket, either. You could come to Australia with us, start a new life before the month's out.'

Sally looked at him, speechless herself for a moment or two, then, 'He hasn't got much conversation, has he?' she said.

She waved them off at the door, and then returned to the drawing room, where stood Miss Brewster, watching the retreating figures of her would-be first foot and his friend through the bay window.

Sally joined her. Their eyes met.

'He's not a bad looking lad though, is he?' Miss Brewster said, with an expression that was hard to fathom. 'And he's a good worker. He'd be all right for you, if you fancied taking him on.'

'S'right,' Sally agreed, and was almost deafened by braying laughter.

When she got back from work the following day, Sally found Will and Miss Brewster with their heads together in the dining room, examining a new camera.

'I saw it in Newcastle this morning, and insisted they deliver it today,' Miss Brewster told her. 'Magnificent, isn't it?'

'You could get some beautiful photos with this. A Newman and Guardia reflex, it's one of the best on the market, man,' Will said.

'*The* best, according to the salesman,' Miss Brewster corrected him.

'Not cheap either. You don't do things by halves. But it'll be a lot more complicated to use than a box camera,' he warned her.

'The photography bug's bitten me pretty deeply,' Miss Brewster said. 'And where there's an interest, learning's not too difficult, as a rule. And the salesman said it was perfectly possible to use a bathroom as a dark room, as long as you make it light tight. And that's precisely what I intend to do.'

Will looked up. 'I hope you're not expecting me to know everything that goes on in a dark room,' he said. 'The last time I was in a one was when I was about twelve year old. Even then, I did more watching than developing.'

'With what you remember, and what we can glean from the book, we'll soon master it,' Miss Brewster said, airily.

'You might waste a lot of money in the process,' said Will.

'I can afford it.'

He gave her a wry smile. 'Aye, I suppose you can,' he said, 'what with that perpetual money machine you've got going underground.'

'Quite – three hundred feet too deep. I need a more gentle occupation; I'm getting too old to chase up and down ladders. When I've learned everything there is to know about photography, perhaps I'll give that little enterprise up and become a respectable lady photographer,' she said.

'And keep respectable hours, like any other decent clockwork person,' Sally said. 'I think you should, before your luck runs out. At least you can't get gaoled for taking photographs.'

'There was a letter for you this morning. It's on the mantelpiece,' said Miss Brewster, when Sally returned from work with an agar plate in her coat pocket a couple of weeks later. She put the plate carefully on the hallstand, hung up her coat and went into the drawing room to rip open the letter and begin to read.

'Who's it from?' Will demanded.

'Our Ginny.'

'Why, what does she say?'

'Never bother, it's not about your mother. She doesn't say a lot, except her husband's back from France, so she's giving a party to welcome him, and for a farewell to our Arthur and Kath. They're off to Australia next month.'

'So soon!' Will said. 'I wish we had half a chance. I'd be off like a shot.'

But Sally had more immediate concerns than Australia. She pushed the letter back in its envelope and replaced it on the mantelpiece, then with a deep apprehension about what might be lurking under-neath, she looked at the filthy, crumbling plaster of Paris encasing his right arm.

'I suppose it's time we were thinking about taking that pot off, Will. It must have been on six weeks.'

'Aye, it's been on all of that,' he said.

'I just wonder whether it's healed properly.'

'There's only one way to find out, hinny.'

She grimaced, suddenly panic-stricken. And what are we going to do if the bones haven't united, or if it's gone the wrong way, she thought, and although she left the thought unspoken they must both have read her mind.

'We get a doctor in if you discover anything you can't deal with' Miss Brewster said. 'Dr Campbell might be a good bet.'

'He wouldn't. He didn't mind turning a blind eye as long as he could pretend he knew nothing, but he won't let us involve him,' she said. 'I know he won't.'

'In that case, I'll call the man who attended my father, if necessary.'

'Don't bother your heads about a surgeon,' said Will, ominously. 'You won't need a one. But this thing's going soft anyway. It'll crumble to bits before long, so it might as well come off.'

'We've got no plaster cutters,' said Sally, grasping for any excuse for delay.

But Will was evidently keen to know the worst.

'I've no doubt it'll come off the same way it went on. Let's get on with it. I'll go and stand at the kitchen sink, and soak it in plenty of water.'

'Put some vinegar in it,' said Sally, 'it kills some germs, and it might help get it off quicker.'

The soaking took longer than anticipated, and it was over an hour later that Will stood unwinding the last of the plaster impregnated bandage over the draining board, while Sally stood at the sink with her sleeves rolled up, scrubbing her fingernails again, after scrubbing her hands almost to the elbows, steeling herself to do battle with an enemy none the less deadly for being unseen. She thought of those colonies of micro-organisms and shuddered. With everything prepared and ready she picked up a towel still hot from the iron and dried her hands while Will removed the last of the bandage and the cotton wool padding.

'Push that clean tea towel under your arm and use it as a sling till we get you to the table,' she said, still fearful that the bone might not have united.

'Let me,' said Miss Brewster.

Will lifted his arm. 'It feels all right,' he said, striding to the table without the sling and taking a chair, leaving Miss Brewster holding the tea towel.

'You can take it off now, Will, but be careful not to touch the wound,'

He nodded and took hold of a corner of the dressing, stained rust and yellow and green with discharge, and peeled it back, gingerly at first, and then with more confidence. Thanks to the soaking it came away easily and he dropped it onto the newspaper lying open on the floor.

With her hands raised in front of her to avoid contamination, Sally leaned over the wound. Her heart gave a quick throb of relief at the sight of it: not a shred of decaying matter, not a streak of pus, not a whiff of sepsis. There was a livid scar, certainly, but the flesh was beautifully clean, and healed. The muscle was somewhat wasted and the skin needing a thorough wash, but that was all.

'It's healed. I can hardly believe it,' she said, raising her eyes to his face.

Tears stood on his eyelashes, and his nose was reddening. 'That's it, then,' he said. 'A reprieve.' He made a noise something between a sob and a snuffle, and Miss Brewster passed him a handkerchief.

Some of the items laid out in readiness on the table, thank God, would not be needed, nor would the padded splints, the lint, the bandage or the BIPP. Just the tweezers and scissors, to get the stitches out. 'And if you knew the sacrifice I nearly had to make to get that paste,' she murmured, thinking aloud just as Will blew his nose.

'What?' he asked, folding the handkerchief with his two hands.

'Nothing. Hold still, while I take a swab, just in

case.' She ran the swab along the wound, collecting nothing, and then rubbed it on the agar plate.

'Will you go to the party at the Cock, then?' Will asked.

'Of course. She's asked Euphemia an' all,' Sally grinned.

'I wish I was going,' said Will. 'I wish I was going to Australia, an' all.'

'I know you do, you've told us before,' said Sally, 'but I'm glad you're not going to the party. You're not invited, anyway.'

'We haven't put ourselves to all this trouble to let you get caught when we're nearly home and dry,' said Miss Brewster. 'You'll stay here. The dogs will keep you company.'

'Thank you very much, I'm sure.' Will looked disgruntled, and then he brightened. 'Why, now that thing's off, at least I'll be able to get a proper bath,' he said.

Miss Brewster shook her head. 'Not tonight. There's a line of photographs drying in there, remember?'

The concert room at the Cock Inn was bursting at the seams, with guests spilling out into the best room. Sally pushed her way in to see her sister Emma's husband sitting at the piano bashing out ragtime tunes, competing with the buzz of conversation from hordes of Arthur and Kath's relatives, and friends from school, pit and army.

'Sally!'

'Heavens, Elinor! I never expected to see you here.'

'Never expected to see me! Why, man, the party's about us, as much as your Arthur and Kath.'

'Us?'

A young man approached and put a possessive arm round Elinor, who smiled up at him.

Much taken aback, Sally said, 'Hello Frank!'

'You know each other, then?' Elinor looked as surprised as Sally.

'S'right,' said Frank, looking Sally in the face and drawing Elinor closer to him.

'Have you known each other long?'

'Long enough to fall head over heels in love, haven't we, Frank?'

'S'right,' said Frank, with a meaningful look at Sally.

'Frank's been stopping with his aunt and uncle since the year turned. They live next door to us.'

'You've known each other nearly a month then.' Sally said.

'A month's long enough, when you're in love,' Elinor said. 'Frank's taking me to Australia with him to meet his mam and dad. Then we're getting married.'

'S'right,' said Frank, with a nod in Sally's direction.

'Good heavens, that's fast work,' Sally said. Then recollecting herself added, 'Congratulations!'

'Thank you. We're all off together: us, and your Arthur and Kath. I'll be glad to get out of that laundry. Have you seen Mrs Burdett? She's leaving Annsdale an' all. Going to Stafford, so Ginny asked her to the party, an' all. She's in the best room with her father and your mother and another old woman that your Ginny knows.'

'Miss Brewster,' Frank chipped in.

'No, I haven't seen her, but I'll go and have a word before I go.'

'And have you not got a man yet, Sally?'

'No, I haven't,' Sally admitted.

'What a shame,' said Elinor. 'You'll end up an old maid if you don't look sharp!'

Sally spread her hands and shrugged, half expecting Frank to say, 'S'right!' He didn't, but was that a look of scorn she saw on his face as he led Elinor away? It was. Her lips twitched.

It was evident a woman only got one chance with Frank.

'Mrs Burdett's getting tired, Arthur,' Sally said, an hour later, 'and Ginny says they're staying here tonight, her and her dad. Will you give us a bit hand to get her upstairs, like?'

'Will I carry her up, you mean? Aye, I will. Have you seen Frank?'

'I had a few words with him earlier.'

'By, but you're too slow to catch a cold, our Sal,' Arthur frowned. 'It should have been you coming to Australia with us, not her.'

Sally shook her head. 'No. It would have been a bit too sudden for me, Arthur. Engaged and off to the other side of the world before you've known somebody a month!'

He jerked his head in Elinor's direction. 'Not for her though; she's quick enough off the mark.'

'She's starting to look a bit merry, an' all. I don't envy her, though. When it comes to marriage, look before you leap's my motto.'

He put his pint down to follow her to Mrs Burdett. 'He's all right, I tell you. You didn't need to look, I'd looked for you, and now you might never get the chance to leap. You've missed the boat, Sally man, in more ways than one.'

'And I took the plate into the laboratory, to grow what they call a culture, you know, but it didn't grow a thing,' Sally told Mrs Burdett after Arthur had gone, and she was helping her to wash in Ginny's bathroom. 'All the infection's gone, and the bone's well knit. He'll be as good as new. He'll be able to use his arm as well as ever he could.'

'Tell Dad,' she said. 'He'll make a good photographer.'

Her speech sounded better, Sally thought, and she
seemed to be gaining more control over her affected
limbs. Bed was now the furthest thing from her
mind, the good news had roused her, and she wanted
to hear Sally repeat it to her father. Miss Brewster
was sitting in Ginny's drawing room with him
and had already told him, but when Sally helped
Mrs Burdett in to join them she repeated the story
again to please her, and then left them all, chatting
amicably about Will's prospects in the photography
shop.

Her mother spotted her as soon as she landed
downstairs. 'They've no clean glasses,' she called. 'Go
and fetch all the empty ones in, and let's get them
washed, will you, Sally?'

Sally took a tray and went into the concert room,
quieter now and with its lighting romantically subdued. Jimmy sat at the piano playing the 'Destiny
Waltz', and a few couples were shuffling round the
floor, Arthur and Kath and Elinor and Frank among
them. The non-dancers sat in little groups at the few
tables around the edge of the room.

'Why, what do you think to our Elinor? Leaving
us all, and going all that way, on her own?' Elinor's
mother asked her as she picked up the empty glasses.

'She's a brave girl,' said Sally.

'She is, but I wish she wasn't going,' Elinor's mother said.

'Why, she's under age, isn't she? You could refuse to let her, if you wanted,' Sally said.

'Aye, but her dad says if Frank's willing to marry her, let her get off.'

'Aye,' said Elinor's father with some satisfaction. 'Let's get her off our hands, while we've got the chance.'

'Don't be so nasty,' his wife said.

'Am I hell nasty. She's nineteen year old! She's a grown woman.'

At that moment Elinor separated herself from Frank and proclaimed, 'I don't know a soul in Australia! I must have been barmy, to think about going all that way with somebody I hardly know!'

Her father's face fell. Sally looked towards Frank, anticipating, 'S'right!' but what he said was: 'What about the ticket?'

'Why, what about it?' Elinor demanded. 'I'm not going all the way across the world just because of a bloody ticket. To hell with the ticket!'

All the couples on the floor turned to look, the dancing came to a halt, and Jimmy stopped playing.

Arthur's wife broke the silence. 'And I'm not going either, come to think,' she burst out. 'I never wanted to go in the first place.'

'You'd better,' Arthur threatened. 'Because I'm

going, and you can do what the bloody hell you like about it.'

Kath's mother jumped to her feet, arm raised. 'Don't you speak to my daughter like that,' she warned, wagging her forefinger in his face. A couple of her brothers came to stand threateningly beside their mother, but Kath's father got up to restrain his wife.

'You keep your nose out. Don't interfere.'

Kath put her hands on her hips, and glared at Arthur. 'Go, then!'

'I fully intend,' he assured her, and despite Kath's brothers he thrust his face right into Mrs Leigh's and added, 'and I'll speak how I like to my own wife, you old witch. I'll be bloody glad to get to Australia. I'd go a lot bloody further to be out of your road.'

Kath's mother recoiled. 'Did you hear that? Are you going to stand there and let him talk to me like that?' she turned on her husband and sons.

Sally didn't wait for the reply, but sidled out of the concert room with her tray, before the fight started. She put the glasses down behind the bar, where Ginny was filling a clean one for Martin, and her mother was washing a few more.

Sally picked up the glass cloth to start drying them. 'Fancy going to Australia, Mam?' she murmured. 'Sounds as if there might be two tickets going begging. Elinor and our Kath reckon they're stopping here.'

Her mother looked up in consternation. 'What?

Not going? After Arthur's got the tickets? There'll be hell to pay if she won't.'

Ginny handed a customer his change. 'I heard the rumpus,' she said. 'I was just going to see what was up, but it's gone quiet again.'

'I'd keep well out of the way, Ginny, man. Like Kath's dad said, don't interfere. Elinor's dad looks about as mad as our Arthur, though. He thought he'd got her married off,' Sally said, vigorously polishing the glasses. 'I'm going upstairs to have a look at Mrs Burdett when I get these done. Make sure she's all right, like.'

When Sally returned to the concert room Elinor and Frank were among the few couples shuffling round the floor, as were her parents. Kath was nowhere to be seen, and Arthur was sitting with his beer, glowering across two tables at Kath's mother. Jimmy was playing a soothing waltz, soft and slow.

She took a seat by the piano. 'Where's Kath?'

'Gone off in a huff to get the bairns,' Jimmy said. 'She could have left them at our house with Em, but she's that way out. Arthur's told her he's going to Australia come hell or high water, so she can please herself what she does, and he's told her mam and dad that if she doesn't go, they'd better be prepared to keep her and the bairns, because that'll be the end of it as far as he's concerned.'

'He cannot do that,' Sally said. 'He cannot just leave them.'

Jimmy shrugged. 'It looks as if he will.'

'There's going to be two wasted tickets then, as well as the bairns'.'

'Maybes only one. Frank's doing his best to talk Elinor round.'

Sally grimaced. 'I've no doubt her dad's hoping he'll succeed,' she said, hoping against hope that he wouldn't, hoping that Christopher Maxfield's passport was still valid, and that all could be accomplished soon, before she lost the nerve and the will.

Jimmy nodded. 'You haven't even had a dance, have you, Sal?' he said. 'Pity there's no partner for you, hinny. What a waste.' He came to the end of the waltz and closed the piano lid, then got to his feet and stretched, flexing his fingers before addressing the company. 'That's all for a quarter of an hour, folks, unless somebody else wants to play. I'm off for half a pint.'

'I'll come with you,' Sally said, 'our Ginny might want a hand.'

Frank and Elinor followed them to the bar, along with half the company from the concert room. Sally lifted the hatch and went behind it to help Ginny to serve them all.

'I don't see why we can't stop in Newcastle,' Elinor was insisting, 'I don't see why two tickets should stop us from getting married here.'

'For the umpteenth time! Because it's too late to get my money back,' Frank howled, the longest sentence Sally had ever heard from him.

She was telling herself that she couldn't let the prof down, couldn't think of abandoning the pathology department, when her mind was suddenly flooded with the image of that tiny finch she'd once freed and sent soaring skyward.

Casting away doubts like outworn rags, she looked up and raised her voice above the hubbub. 'Why, we cannot let that stand in your way, Frank. I know somebody who might be willing to buy 'em, if you'll knock something off the price, like. You'd get some of your money back,' she said, and glancing at her mother who stood hardly a yard away, she felt an awful pang.

Chapter Twenty-One

Surrounded by luggage and people on the quayside on a frosty February morning, Sally put an arm round her mother's shoulder. 'Don't cry, Mam, you told us we had to go.'

'I know I did,' she sniffed, and dabbing her eyes turned towards Will, whose face was hidden behind both moustache and a full beard, with a cap obscuring most of his disfigurement. 'Look after her – Max.'

'Dry up,' Miss Brewster commanded, standing with her camera sideways on to them. 'I don't want to waste any film on people blubbering. And squeeze together a bit.'

Sally's mother gave a weak laugh, and Arthur, who was standing behind them with Frank, stretched his arms wide and pulled the three of them hard together. Will turned his scars away from the camera and as Miss Brewster squeezed the shutter a cab drew up beside them.

Mr Hibbs got out, and touched his grandson on the

471

shoulder. 'She can't let you go without saying a last goodbye. Nobody'll see, if you get in and sit beside her.'

Watching Will slide into the taxi, and knowing Elinor of old, Sally thanked her stars she wasn't there to witness the scene. That girl had a genius for opening her mouth and putting both feet in it.

Mr Hibbs nudged Miss Brewster. 'You go over there and stand with them, and I'll take your picture.'

She gave him the camera without protest, and placed herself between Sally and her mother, with Frank and Arthur behind them. After that it was Miss Brewster's turn again, to take the group with Will's grandfather. No sooner was that photograph taken than the cab door opened and Will emerged. Oh, dear, Sally had an awful sense of foreboding when she saw him go round the other side of the vehicle and open the door.

He caught her look. 'She insisted,' he said, helping his mother onto her feet. 'She's desperate to get a last photograph taken with us. It'll not take long, and we'll get her back in the taxi. It'll be all right.'

'Something to treasure,' Mrs Burdett said, now upright and supported by Will. She'd dressed carefully for this leave-taking from her only living son, and was wearing a fashionable new hat of fine beige wool to complement her best brown coat, but her stooped shoulders and unsteady gait marred the elegant impression she'd tried to make.

'Stay there. Don't come any further. I'll take you as you are; you needn't move another step,' said Miss Brewster. 'I've got the picture.'

'One with the ship in first, and then I'll go back,' Mrs Burdett said, leaning heavily on Will, but showing such determination that none of them dared gainsay her. Seeing that the sooner they humoured her the sooner they could get her safely back in the taxi, Sally took her other hand to help her to the spot she'd chosen. Miss Brewster moved a few yards away, to get some of the ship in the background, and then had to wait for people to pass in between them before she could take the photograph. After the first one, Sally stepped away, to let Mrs Burdett have a last photograph with her son alone, and then stood rooted to the spot.

Like witches in the grimmest fairytale, Dr and Mrs Lowery had appeared from nowhere, and drifted in between Miss Brewster and her subjects. Sally held her breath as Mrs Lowery started, and touched her husband's arm.

'We meet again, Nurse Wilde,' the doctor hailed her.

She nodded. 'It looks as if we do, Dr Lowery.'

Mrs Lowery nudged her husband, and nodded towards Will.

'And you're reunited with your sweetheart, I see. This is the young man who came to our house, looking for you, I think.'

'You're mistaken, Dr Lowery,' said Sally, and catching his glance she felt the full force of his aversion. She'd seen through him, and he'd never forgiven her. Despite her care of Kitten, he still hated her for it.

He gave an incredulous little laugh, and raising his voice demanded, 'Beatrice! Is this, or is it not the man who came looking for Sally?'

Beatrice sounded decided. 'Yes, it is.'

'You're sure?'

She opened her mouth to confirm it, and Mrs Burdett's knees gave way.

'Mother!' Will caught her, and clutching her tightly to him, managed to prevent her from falling, while she raised her eyes to Mrs Lowery's. Sally felt like someone standing on the edge of a precipice as the two women stared at each other, and then Mrs Lowery's eyes moistened as her gaze drifted from the face of the widow to that of her son.

'No,' she said, slowly, her eyes still on him. 'No . . . There's a superficial likeness, but I've never seen this man in my life before.'

'You damned well have, though,' Dr Lowery insisted. 'You know it's him, and you know him for a deserter. I detest the fellows. I say, you there!'

he turned to Arthur and, taking a very high tone, demanded, 'Fetch a policeman!'

Arthur stepped right up to him, closely followed by Frank. 'What are you bloody talking about – deserter? He's our Australian pal – Frank's old mate from Woolangong.'

'S'right,' Frank drawled over his shoulder, right on cue. 'He's my old mate from Woolangong.'

Sally was stunned to see the doctor's wife round sharply on her husband. 'You see? You're mistaken, Dr Lowery. I'd swear on oath it's not the same man. Not the same man at all. Don't make a fool of yourself in front of all these people.' Mrs Lowery walked rapidly on, past the taxi and away. After a final contemptuous glance at Sally, Dr Lowery followed.

'Come on, come on!' Arthur urged, 'they'll have shifted the bloody gangway if we don't get a move on!'

Their mother turned to him, and with disapproval written all over her face gave him a brief embrace. 'You shouldn't be going at all. You shouldn't be leaving Kath and the bairns. She's expecting you to go back,' she said.

'She's going to be disappointed, then. I'll send some money when I get settled, and then maybe she'll see sense, and come to join me. Or maybe I'll send nothing, and that'll make her see sense a bit sooner, her and her bloody mother an' all.'

'You get no better, Arthur,' she said, and turned to Frank. 'And I thought you were going to marry Elinor.'

'He would have done, if Kath had come with me – but she didn't, and he didn't want to see the ticket go to waste. So, he's got a free passage home in that nice big cabin I got for us and the bairns.'

'S'right. It's a bonzer,' Frank grinned, and picking up his luggage he started for the gangway.

'So long, Mam,' said Arthur, giving her an awkward final squeeze before following suit.

Sally held her mother tight. 'So long, Mam. Say so long to our Ginny and Emma, and the rest of them for me.'

Will gave his mother a last kiss and a squeeze, shook his grandfather's hand, and ushered Sally onto the gangway. She hurried along, but realizing after a few steps that he wasn't following she turned back and saw Miss Brewster on the gangway, preventing the men from removing it while she carefully took the film out of her camera. But it was the camera, and not the film that she tried to thrust into Will's free hand when the job was finished.

'A wedding gift, from a friend, though I won't be at the wedding.'

'I cannot take it,' he said. 'It must have cost a fortune.'

She hung it round his neck. 'You'd better, or I shall

be very offended. And hurry along, before the ship leaves without you.'

'I don't know what to say.'

'Start with thanks,' Sally suggested.

'Thanks, Miss Brewster. Thanks for everything you've done,' he said, and impulsively planted a kiss on her cheek.

She flushed slightly and her hand flew to the spot his lips had touched. 'Get off with you,' she ordered, 'and make sure you look after her – not that she's not capable of looking after herself!'

They obeyed, Will struggling after Sally with luggage and camera. 'And I'll never say another wrong word about spinsters as long as I live,' he said.

Sally found her cabin among those of the other women who were travelling alone, in that secluded part of the ship designated for their use only and which was forbidden territory to all male passengers. She dumped her luggage on her bunk, and then made her way back to the deck, to the exact spot where they'd separated. Will was leaning on the rail, watching the receding coastline.

'We're lucky to be here,' she commented. 'Your mother was mad, to come chasing after us like that, and you were even madder to let her get out of the taxi.'

'I was terrified she'd have another stroke if I didn't

477

let her have her own way, and who'd have thought that pair would have happened by? Anyway,' he grinned, 'I could have shown 'em my passport.'

'With your lovely photo on it.'

'You're jesting. But it's a good job I knew a decent photographer, and somebody with a neat forging hand.'

'I'm not jesting. And changing 1915 to 1918's not very complicated forgery.'

'And the date of birth – you've shaved a few years off that, an' all. But there's another reason my mother came to see us off,' he said, holding up a bright Belgian gold franc. 'She said she'd have hung on to them if we'd been going to Stafford, but as we're not, she wanted to give me them with her own hands. She had a dozen, and she's given us six. Our Henry left them with her after his last leave; told her he'd found them under a hearthstone that had been turned up by a shell.'

'Poor people,' Sally said, resting her elbows on the rail, and gazing misty-eyed towards the shore. 'Lost everything, a lot of them.'

'Aye. If there'd been any chance of getting them back to the rightful owners he might have handed them in, but there'd be none. Somebody would have pocketed them, so I suppose he reckoned it might as well be him.'

Sally shivered. 'I can't imagine what those people

must have suffered, seeing their whole villages destroyed, and everything gone. I loved Annsdale, just loved it, heart and soul. But I would have had to leave it anyway, to go to Stafford.'

He turned away from the rail and spun the coin in the air. 'It's an ill wind that blows nobody any good though, bonny lass,' he said, catching it and replacing it safely in his pocket.

She nodded at the camera. 'It looks as if you're doomed to photography.'

'As long as it's not in the back of a shop in Stafford, taking bonny faces.'

'What will it be then?'

'Interesting faces. Working faces, starting with the sailors on this ship. Maybe I'll do a portrait of you, and your Arthur and Frank. Then maybe the miners and their families in Woolangong. And maybe ex-servicemen's faces, and sheep farmers' faces, all sorts. Faces with a story to tell, all through Australia. And if I come across any landlords who aren't too talkative, maybe I'll sometimes have a few bottles of whisky to sell. I know what I'm going to do next, though.'

'What?'

'Why, your cabin's a lot too far away from mine, and I can't go there. I don't think you're supposed to be here, either, standing beside me.'

'Why, nobody stopped me.'

'I'm going to see the captain, find out if there's anybody on board can marry us.'

'There is,' she beamed. 'There's a Methodist minister. I heard him talking to some of the crew as I was coming back.'

'We'll soon be Mr and Mrs Maxfield, then,' he said, 'and that's who we'll have to be for the rest of our lives.'

The morning sun was scarcely three yards above the sea, and the heat was already oppressive. As the minister pronounced them man and wife a shoal of winged fish arose from the ocean like sparrows from a cornfield, and all heads turned to watch them.

'They're unbelievable!' one of the Donoghue sisters, who'd had the cabin next to Sally's, exclaimed, as the whole party moved to the side of the ship the better to see them.

'Good heavens, good heavens, I'd never . . .'

'Absolutely incredible . . .'

'They don't know whether they want to be fish or birds!' Arthur said, squinting against the sun.

'Flying fish! I never believed they existed,' Will laughed; clean-shaven now they were certain there was no one aboard who might recognize him. Beads of perspiration stood on his brow as he looked into Sally's eyes and, not sparing the miraculous fish another glance, he lifted the hand he'd placed the ring on to his lips.

Despite the sailcloth stretched above them to provide some shade, despite the cold bath Sally had taken before being played onto the quarterdeck with fiddles and squeezeboxes, and despite the lightness of her white muslin dress, a film of moisture covered the face she lifted to kiss the bridegroom's cheek. Then, drawing him to the rail to watch the strange creatures, she said, 'I'd never even heard of them, and I can hardly believe it now, even seeing them with my own eyes! Their wings are just like fairies' wings in story-books. But aren't they beautiful? They're going to bring us good luck, Will.'

He smiled down at her. 'They're not half as beautiful as you.'

The captain looked intrigued. 'Why do you call him Will,' he asked, 'when his name's Christopher?'

'She does it to annoy her mother-in-law,' Arthur chipped in.

'A gipsy once told me I'd marry a Will,' Sally said, with a bright glance at her husband, 'and I thought it might be bad luck to contradict her, so I had to re-christen him. It's just a silly pet name.'

'Not as silly as some I've heard,' the captain said, 'and you'll see some more christenings this afternoon, when we cross the equator. All the first-timers in the crew get a ducking when King Neptune comes on board, so we shall have some fun with that, and he might decide he wants to shave some of the youngsters as well. What with the concert and the dancing this evening, we shall have had quite an eventful day before we close our eyes tonight.'

'That's if they close theirs at all,' Arthur sniggered.

Frank grinned, and the captain barely acknowledged them. 'Ah, here comes the cook with the cake, and the waiters with the wine and glasses,' he smiled. 'I'll drink your health, and then I must away. Duty calls.'

'I'd never have believed,' Sally said, 'that people would go to so much trouble, just for us.'

'I can't get over how many people have befriended us,' said Will.

'You can always get friends, if you'll *be* a friend,' one of the Miss Donoghues turned from the rail to tell him.

'Come on, then,' Arthur urged the bridal pair, 'if we stand you with your backs to the rail, we might get some of these funny fish in the photos. It's the only way our Kath'll ever believe there are such things.'

He must be missing her, Sally thought. 'Thanks for letting us have your cabin,' she said.

'We hadn't much option, two single blokes among the married people. Somebody was going to give the game away sooner or later, and he would have shifted us anyway,' he said, nodding in the captain's direction. 'We've given it a good scouring, though.'

'Good,' the captain nodded. 'It behoves us all to be very particular about hygiene while in the tropics, or we shall have ship's fever. I've seen people die of it like rotten cattle.'

Will, Arthur and Frank fell silent, along with some of the other men. Doubtless they'd seen rather too much of people dying like rotten cattle, and not very long ago at that, Sally thought. 'Away then, Arthur,' she said, quick to dispel the gloom, 'let's get our photos taken, before we lose the fish.'

But by the time the newlyweds had manoeuvred themselves into position, and Arthur was ready to take the photograph, the flying fish were gone, and a score of porpoises were sporting in the waves, like leaping hares.

The sun hung in the west like a great orb of fire, staining both sky and sea. 'Have you ever seen anything so beautiful in your life?' Will said.

The sunset was mirrored in his eye, making it glow like a ruby. 'No, I never have,' Sally said. A warm breeze caressed her face and arms, wafting the light, white summer dress she wore, and the air was filled with the scent of the sea. She inhaled deeply. 'You're different, Will.'

'I feel different. I began to feel it as soon as we boarded this ship, and a couple of weeks at sea have convinced me. We're out of it, Sally. Out of the night. Out of the nightmare.'

She didn't point out that it was very nearly dark and night was swiftly falling, but looked at the reflection of the sun in the water, and understood. 'Leave it all behind, Will, what happened in France.'

'Funny thing is,' he said, 'it wasn't all bad. Everything you felt, you felt tenfold, or more, at times. Everything was larger than life: boredom, excitement, terror, love, bloodlust, hatred even. But you'd never felt more alive . . .' he paused, and Sally waited for him to go on.

'Really, though,' he said, 'it was murder. Sheer bloody murder.'

'It was what you were forced to do, and it's finished now. Leave it behind, Will.'

'You know, a sight like that makes me feel as if I have to see it for my brothers, see it and love it and feel the wonder of it for every one of them as much as for me. See it and feel it and love it fourfold,' he said, and that glow in his eye seemed to deepen.

She watched him, listening to the sighing and lapping of the ocean while absorbing his words. 'Fivefold,' she said at last. 'You should see it for Christopher Maxfield, as well.'

'Aye,' he agreed. And after some thought added,

'But I am Maxfield, now, in a sense. It was his money that paid for the wedding ring, even.'

'Yes, but you'll always be Will to your wife.'

He clasped her hand. 'Let's go to bed,' he said.

'Zero hour,' he whispered, throwing the covers on the floor and lying down beside her. 'Are you scared?'

'A bit,' she whispered. 'My stomach's a knot of nerves, but there's a sort of calmness at the same time, with my heart going boom, boom, boom, but quite steady.'

'And mine,' he said, putting his hand gently on her breast, and her hand on his. 'I'm the same. Can you feel it?'

'Scared?' she said. 'I didn't think men were scared . . .'

'Scared, and excited. Everything alive. I've never felt so alive. And scared, because there's not one virgin here, Sally, there's two. I never told you that, did I? And scared because I don't want to hurt you.'

She giggled, from sheer nerves. 'After all the lasses Will Burdett went out with? I can hardly believe it.'

'It's true, though. There's not one of them . . . So here we are, a virgin woman and a virgin man, both with a lot to learn.'

'Better make a start, then,' she laughed, furling her

fingers round his neck, and drawing his face down to hers.

'It's true, what they say. The best times between husbands and wives are in the dark,' Sally said, during the wondrous depths of that night. 'And in the dark it doesn't matter if the husband's face is wounded or if the wife's got a big nose.'

He laughed. 'You soft ha'porth! In the dark, looks matter about as much as they do to a blind man, I suppose.'

'Don't laugh at me. Looks shouldn't matter all that much. Love *should* be blind. But what I mean is, in the dark, looks don't distract you from knowing the man underneath, knowing him heart and soul. In the dark, there's only the *real* you.'

'And the real you.'

'Yes,' she breathed.